With the glow of streetlights behind him, the figure was indistinct. All Ben was sure of was that it was a man. Before he could react, the figure, instead of walking past him, lunged at him. Strong hands reached out of the darkness and grabbed him by the shoulders. Ben grunted with surprise as he was spun around. Drunk as he was, the motion felt like it kept going even after he had stopped.

"What the fuck—?" Ben said, his voice slurred. A bubble of gas rose from his stomach into his throat, leaving behind a terrible taste.

The person didn't say a word. He shoved Ben face-first against one of the pilings. His nose banged against the wood hard enough to stagger him, and tiny white stars splashed across his vision. Pain shot through his head like a sudden jolt of electricity.

"Leave her the fuck alone," the man said, his voice a low, animal-like growl. "You understand?"

Too dazed to react, Ben locked his knees, hoping they wouldn't buckle underneath him. He had the sense that—whoever this was—he was purposely disguising his voice so he wouldn't recognize it. All Ben saw was a silhouette, cut out sharply against the night sky.

Cover illustration by David Dodd
Design by Aaron Rosenberg
ISBN 978-1-941408-07-0 — ISBN 978-1-941408-08-7 (pbk.)
 For information address Crossroad Press at 141 Brayden Dr., Hertford, NC 27944
www.crossroadpress.com

First edition

THE COVE

RICK HAUTALA

With love and respect to our five sons…
Aaron, Andrew, Colin, Jesse, and Matti.
And a special "Thank you" to Holly . . . for everything.

"Rough winds do shake the darling buds of May,
And summer's lease hath all too short a date."

—William Shakespeare

"This is life's sorrow:
That one can be happy only where two are;
And that our hearts are drawn to stars
Which want us not."

—Edgar Lee Masters
Spoon River Anthology

ACKNOWLEDGMENTS

I grew up in Rockport, Massachusetts, a small coastal New England town. In fact, until I went off to college at the University of Maine in Orono, I lived in the "rural" part of Rockport, a little place called "Pigeon Cove." I was—and will always remain—a "Cove-ah" at heart even though I now live in Maine and have since the mid-Sixties.

I suppose I should state right off that none of the characters or incidents in this book are based on anyone I knew while growing up or know now. Any resemblance to anyone living or dead is entirely coincidental. While my story may not always show coastal people in the best light, I have written this book with love and sincere admiration for all Mainers (*"Maine-ahs"*), the most "real" people I have ever met.

That being said, however, I have obviously used memories of my own childhood and suggestions from other friends as inspiration. Two very close friends—Glenn Chadbourne and Teresa Osgood—provided me with plenty of stories about living in fishing villages along the coast and on the islands of Maine. I can't thank them enough for helping me "create" some of the "characters" in this book. I know it's a cliché to say that truth is "stranger than fiction," but my genuine concern here is that I've diluted the truly unique stories and personalities I knew growing up and which Glenn and Teresa shared with me. If I screwed it up, it's certainly not their fault.

I also want to thank the numerous friends who read early drafts and talked out this book with me at various stages in the long process of writing it. *Mi amigos* Christopher Fahy, Mike Feeney, Chris Golden, Dana Ellis, Matt Costello, Adrian Alexander, Bill Thorne, Mark Steensland, and—of course—Teresa and Glenn all gave valuable feedback and much-needed encouragement.

Most of all, I want to thank Holly Newstein for running a finer than fine-toothed comb through several drafts of the manuscript. I couldn't have done it without you, Holly. And if there are still any bruises or soft spots, they're all mine, not Holly's.

Last but certainly not least, I want to thank my three sons—Aaron, Jesse, and Matti—who provide on a daily basis love and inspiration to me simply because of the wonderful people they have grown to become.

My only regret is that my parents are not alive to read this book. I know they would have found some parts of it amusing just as I'm sure my mother would have objected to some of the "strong language." Sorry, Mum...most people really do talk that way sometimes. Of course, I never do.

People often say "If it was easy, everyone would do it." This is especially true about writing a novel. This was never easy to write, but it was also a pure joy to see what was happening down at the wharf. I hope you—the readers—enjoy this little jaunt to "The Cove." I know I did.

Enjoy!

—Rick Hautala

ONE

Welcome Home

Gotta face 'em all, sooner or later, Ben Brown thought as he stood by the kitchen sink, clutching his coffee cup and staring out the window. His gaze was drawn to the launch ramp on the south side of Catawamkeag Cove—known to everyone, locals and summer tourists alike, simply as "The Cove."

Already, cars and trucks were pulling into the rutted, unpaved parking lot, and people were arriving from all directions—some on foot, a few on bicycles and motorcycles. Even at this distance, Ben could hear the heavy rumble of Harleys.

"This is definitely *not* what I need today," he muttered as he took a gulp of coffee. It was bitter and burnt-tasting. A sheen of sweat sprinkled his forehead. It wasn't just from the early morning sun pouring in through the window. He was nervous about having to face so many townsfolk so soon after returning from Iraq.

He'd been home on leave before, but today felt totally different. His enlistment had finally ended after he'd been caught twice in old Donny Rumsfeld's stop-loss orders, and he had no desire to go back into the Army. It used to be that coming home to stay for a while—even for a few weeks or months at a time—had always been comfortable…relaxing.

Now, so much had changed it felt…weird.

For starters, his sister, Louise, had gotten married and moved out. So for the first time in this house, he had his own room. Pete, his younger brother who was still living at home, didn't have to share the same bedroom they'd had growing up.

But there were other, more complicated things facing him.

Right now, though, he had more immediate concerns. His father had suggested—quite strongly—that he wear his uniform to the launch, but Ben most definitely was not going to do *that.*

Looking out to sea, he could tell there wasn't much wind. The ocean, especially further out, was a ruffled, deep blue. Sunlight glittered on the water like an explosion of diamond chips. Down by the launch, yellow dust raised by vehicles pulling over to park by the side of the road or in the parking lot rose like sulfurous smoke and hung heavily in the air.

Sand and dust, Ben thought with a grim shake of the head. Not a goddamned one of them knows what real sand and dust are all about!

His throat went suddenly dry, and even another gulp of bad coffee didn't help. A taste—more like the memory of a taste—clung to the back of his throat like thick mucus. It was a dry, pungent taste—a curious mix of diesel and sun-baked clay and dusty palm trees whose dead fronds clacked like old bones in the hot wind, but it was mixed with something else…something indefinable. Whatever it was, Ben knew that no amount of coffee or beer or whiskey would wash it away completely.

He heaved a sigh and dumped what was left of his coffee into the sink and continued to stare down the hill. When he was a kid, boat launches had been so much fun. He had fond memories of his friends and family and neighbors gathering to celebrate each launch of a new lobster boat.

It was always an event.

The promise and hope the launch of a new boat brought to the entire town was like the birth of a child. Just as any new baby could grow up to be the one to cure cancer or become president, a new boat could be the one to revive lobstering in Catawamkeag Cove and bring the fortunes of everyone up along with it.

Anyone who was born and lived here was a "Cover"—pronounced *"Cove-ah"*—and no matter what you did, no matter how hard you struggled to free yourself from those invisible chains that bound you here, if you were born a "Cover," you would live and die a "Cover." And if you weren't born a "Cover," you would never be one, no matter what.

It had taken four years of duty in Iraq for Ben to recognize that. As much as he hated the Army, he was beginning to think reenlistment might be preferable to this. Maybe dying in Iraq or Afghanistan was the only thing that would get him out of The Cove permanently.

What an option.

Today, though, his father, Walter Brown—"Capt'n Wally" to everyone in town—was launching the *Abby-Rose*, named after his dead brother's granddaughter. If—

No. Not *if*...there was no way out of it...*when*...

—he showed up, he would have to make nice with everyone—relatives, neighbors, friends, and people he didn't like but had to pretend he did.

Ben was so lost in his reveries he jumped when the telephone suddenly rang. The old-fashioned bell-ring made him smile as he placed his empty coffee cup down carefully on the counter and walked over to the wall phone. As always, the spiral cord was a tangled mess that stretched to the floor. Ben added another few kinks to it when, after two more rings, he picked up the receiver and pressed it to his ear.

"When you getting your sorry ass down here?" his father said before Ben could even say *hello*.

"Yeah—umm, sorry 'bout that," Ben replied. "I was heading out the door when you called. You're slowing me down, Old Man."

"Don't you 'Old Man' me," Wally said with a snarl. Then, after taking a quick breath, he added, "So, you wearin' your uniform?"

"No, Pops," Ben said, trying to keep the irritation out of his voice.

At twenty-six years old, Ben didn't like being bullied or bossed around by his father like he was still a kid. When was he going to start treating him like an adult? The answer was *never*, but then again, Wally treated pretty much everyone in town the same way. As far as Wally was concerned, he was the "Capt'n," and everyone in town—local or vacationer—was obliged to treat him as such.

"You know your mother would want you to wear your uniform," Wally said. "You don't want to disappoint her, now, do yah?"

"Yeah, well, she's not gonna be there, now, is she? And even if she was, she'd have no clue what was going on, would sh-"

"Don't you be talking 'bout your mother like that," Wally said, cutting Ben off before he could finish. "We're all praying for her, and—besides, she'll be there in spirit."

Ben sniffed at the tone of righteous indignation in his father's voice. He couldn't remember the last time his father had gone to church. Maybe last year, when Ben was still in Iraq…. Wally would have gone to church when Louise married Tom Marshall, a "townie" cop. The truth was, his father probably wouldn't go to church again until six friends were carrying him in a polished wooden box.

"I asked your sister to take some pictures so's we can show 'em to Ma later."

"You think she'll even know what they're of?"

"I said don't be talking 'bout your mother like that. And you get the fuck down here so's we can get the festivities rollin'."

"I'm on my way," Ben said. He hung up the phone without even trying to untangle the cord. This house wouldn't be home if the cord wasn't all knotted up.

Ben considered brewing a fresh cup of coffee and taking his sweet old time walking down the hill, if only to grind his father a little more, but he decided against that. Besides, his younger brother, Pete, would already be down at the launch, getting things started. Pete, the homebody son, had no options other than to stay home and follow in his father's footsteps in the family lobstering business. Someone had to keep the family home in the family.

Might as well go face them all. Gotta do it sometime.

He already knew what they would say. They would declare how proud they were of his service to his country, even if they thought the war was a colossal cluster fuck. Several people would ask what he planned to do with his life now, implying that, if he was a "good son," he would take up lobstering full-time so the eldest son could take over for Capt'n Wally, who wasn't getting any younger. Many people would ask about his mother, Lilly, and how she and the family were doing now that, for the last month or so, she had been in Harbor's Edge, the local nursing home.

The twisting apprehension in Ben's gut was almost as bad as the wound-up, nervous feelings he got every goddamned time he and his platoon were out patrolling in Anbar. Maybe it was worse…

Yeah…

Except for that one time, this was much worse.

"Jesus! Will you stop your goddamned bawling?"

Tom Marshall stood in the bathroom doorway, leaning with one arm against the jamb as he stared at his wife. He was wearing his police uniform. His eyes were wide, and his face was flushed with barely repressed fury. His skin looked like it was on too tight. "You sound like a friggin' baby. Here. Use this."

Before Louise could react, he threw something at her. It felt like a bee sting when it bounced off the back of her head and landed on the bathroom floor between the sink and the toilet. She looked down and saw a bottle of Visine. She would have bent down to pick it up, but she was afraid of what he might do when she had her back to him and was even more vulnerable.

Wincing with pain, Louise rubbed the back of her head and stared at Tom's reflection over her shoulder in the bathroom mirror. It wasn't the first time she wondered why she didn't work up the nerve to grab his service revolver and use it on him. He *so* fucking deserved it. But she stuffed such thoughts down deep as she raised her hand and gingerly touched the swollen bruise under her left eye. It was bright red, fading to purple on the edges.

"What the hell am I supposed to do about *this?*" she asked in a broken voice. Tears filled her eyes, blurring her vision, but she blinked them back. She wasn't going to let him see her cry.

"What the fuck do I care?" Tom snapped. "Put some goddamned makeup on it. Anyone who knows you expects you to look like a friggin' whore, anyways." He pronounced the word as two syllables—*who-ah.*

He shifted his stance and clamped his arms over his chest like he was trying to contain an explosion. His leather gun belt made a loud creaking sound, like an old saddle. The light hit his blue eyes just right, making them glow with a near-insane gleam.

Up yours, Louise thought but didn't say. She knew what would happen if she did. When Tom was "in a mood," it didn't matter what she said or did. All she had to do was open her mouth or even look like she was going to say something—it didn't matter what—and he'd backhand her another good one…or worse.

Her eyes started stinging, and she couldn't stop the tears that rolled down her cheeks. Fear twisted her guts as she stared at her reflection in the mirror. Her light, brown hair hung in loose waves down past her shoulders, covering the sides of her face, but there was no way she could wear her hair to hide the bruise under her eye without people noticing.

They would see.

They would know.

How many times could she get away with the excuse that she had walked into a door or bumped into an opened kitchen cabinet door?

Beneath her misery and pain, though, she could see how pretty she still was. No amount of insult or abuse or injury from Tom could extinguish the glow in her hazel eyes. Still, it amazed her how, after less than a year of being married, so much life and energy had drained out of her. She felt a lot older than her twenty-four years. What was it her father always said? *"It ain't the years, it's the mileage."* It took some effort to see the happy young girl she had once been, and not all that long ago.

I deserve someone better than him…someone who will appreciate me, she thought.

She cringed, thinking Tom might be able to read her mind. He'd be a fool not to see the hatred burning like a banked fire in her eyes.

"Hurry up, will yah? And call your old man while you're at it. I need to know if he's gonna launch on time. It's supposed to be at nine o'clock, right?"

"Far as I know. Yes." She spoke precisely, trying to mask her emotions.

She glanced again at his reflection in the mirror. She pushed back on the regret that filled her. She wasn't about to let regret ruin her life the way it had ruined her mother's life. She wasn't going to put up with this much longer, that was for sure.

She had married Tom because he wasn't at all like her father. He was kind and caring. They had been sweethearts ever since high school, and she knew that he loved her. Something had changed drastically over the last couple of months, since sometime in the winter.

Maybe he was upset because she had miscarried last December after slipping on some ice in front of their house. Maybe he was worried that he was shooting blanks.

Of course, they'd have better luck if they made love more often… or at all, lately.

He must be getting some on the side. She knew Tom was man

enough, so if he wasn't getting it at home, he'd be off getting it *somewhere.*

But maybe it wasn't another woman.

Maybe it was his job.

Once things straightened out down at the police station with Bob Harlan, the new police chief…maybe after Tom got that promotion he deserved for over a year now, maybe then he'd start treating her nicer…the way he had before they married.

Until then…

Louise opened the medicine cabinet and took out her bottle of foundation. She winced, and tears sprang to her eyes as she daubed some onto each cheek.

"See you at the wharf," Tom said, and then he pushed away from the doorjamb and, without another word or even a hug or kiss goodbye, walked down the hall and down the stairs.

Louise froze where she was as she listened to him go out the side door. She jumped when he slammed the door shut behind him. It sounded like a gunshot, and she hated herself for instantly thinking—hoping he had shot himself. But then she heard him get into his cruiser—slamming the car door, too—and start it up. She didn't relax until the sound of his car had faded away. Finally, she felt safe enough to kneel down and scoop up the bottle of Visine. By then, she was crying so hard that no amount of Visine was going to get the red out.

Ben walked down the hill to the launch wearing tattered blue jeans and a faded green polo shirt that was so old the collar and cuffs were frayed. Sunlight streaming through the oak leaves sparkled like little flames on the sidewalk and street around him.

The swirl of activity reminded Ben of all the Memorial Days and Fourths of July he had enjoyed when he was growing up here, when he and his younger brother, Pete, and their friends had terrorized the town. If they had been kids now, they'd be lighting firecrackers and generally goofing off. Only later, once they were in high school, did they start sneaking pot and beer and bottles of booze from their parents' liquor cabinets, and fooling around with girls, seeing how far they could get. Second base was rare, and third base was rarer still. He wished he had known then that the girls were as interested in sex as the boys were.

"Hello there, Benjamin!" a woman called out. Her voice sounded as fragile as glass.

Ben turned to see Judith Harris, his former third grade teacher, smiling at him from the passenger's side of a big, blue Buick that was moving slowly down the hill alongside him. Even back in his school days, the kids had called her "Old Lady Harris," but never to her face. Ben had heard that Lester, Mrs. Harris' husband of over fifty years, had died last January of the flu. Speeding up a little to keep pace with the car, Ben leaned forward to see who was driving. He gave a little nod to Mark, Old Lady Harris' eldest son, who was hunched over the wheel. Mark, The Cove's high school basketball legend from years ago, was so tall he looked squeezed, even in the big Buick. He stared straight ahead at the road as though embarrassed to be seen driving his mother around. The rumor was Mark was living back at home again after getting divorced by his second wife, Daisy Delisle, who had moved to Florida with their three kids.

"Hey there, Mark."

"Gunner," Mark said, using Ben's nickname from high school. He made a point of keeping his eyes focused straight ahead. There were too many people milling about, and some of them crossed the road without looking, walking right in front of cars as if their attitude was "Come on. Hit me. I need the money."

"How you doing today, Mrs. H.?" Ben asked.

The old woman's face was as yellowed and wrinkled as old parchment. Tracings of thin blue veins throbbed beneath her almost translucent skin. When she smiled, she exposed large, yellowed dentures that had dark brown stains between the teeth. Ben wondered if she was a smoker.

"I can't complain…I can't complain," Mrs. Harris said. "How's your mother liking it over there to Grave's Edge?"

With typical gallows humor, many of the locals referred to Harbor's Edge as Grave's Edge. It had been going on so long that no true "Cove-ah" took offense. Ben started to explain to Mrs. Harris that he'd only gotten home last night and hadn't had a chance to go over for a visit yet. Instead, he stopped himself, smiled and said simply, "She's doing fine, Mrs. H.…just fine."

"Good to hear…good to hear."

Ben returned the smile, realizing both he and Mrs. Harris were saying everything twice. He remembered that had been a trait of hers when she was teaching, but it had gotten worse, now that she was so elderly. She had to be pushing eighty or even ninety.

"I'll be sure to tell her you said hello."

"You do that. You do that. She must be so happy to have your brother back home safe and sound."

Confused for a moment, Ben turned his head and looked at her.

"Beg pardon, Ma'am?"

"From Iraq. Your brother. You must be so proud of him. I hear he was wounded over there. Was he really wounded?"

She was obviously confusing him with Pete, but he didn't want to make matters worse, so he smiled and said, "He's—uhh, he's doing fine, but—No.... He wasn't wounded."

"Good to hear. Good to hear."

"Yes, we sure are happy to have him home safely."

Mark took his eyes off the road long enough to shoot an apologetic look at Ben. Traffic was starting to back up behind them, and before either one of them could say anything more, he stepped down on the accelerator and pulled ahead. A thin blue cloud of exhaust trailed in their wake.

Ben continued down the road until he was in the midst of the crowd. People he hadn't seen in a long time—some of whom he cared about and some of whom he didn't—greeted him and shook his hand and clapped him on the back and thanked him for his service to the country. He hated being the center of attention. Today was all about Capt'n Wally and his boat that was about to be launched. He was glad he hadn't worn his uniform. It would have only made things worse.

For the next half hour or so, Ben mingled with friends, neighbors, and relatives, shaking hands with some...hugging and kissing others, all the while exchanging small talk and platitudes. He answered their questions about his time in Iraq as briefly as possible, usually with a simple, "Yeah, sure is good to be out of there" and "Nope. No end in sight s'far as I can see."

Before long, he realized he had been keeping an eye out for one person in particular. He knew she would be here. She would *have* to be here. He hoped he was ready for the heartache he would experience when he first saw her.

After another fifteen minutes or so, someone in the crowd shouted, *"Here he comes!"* and everyone went silent except for scattered applause and a few boisterous cheers as Capt'n Wally's rusted red Ford pickup truck, towing his spanking new lobster boat, rattled down the street. Pete sat in the back bed of the truck, beer bottle in hand as he smiled and waved to the people as they passed. He already looked a sheet or two to the wind as he clung to the side panel for support. Ben sighed to see that—in this particular way, anyway, his brother was following in their father's footsteps.

Wally's left arm was draped out the driver's window, the skin looking like old leather as he negotiated a precise three-point turn with one hand and then started backing up. The crowd parted like the Red Sea to make way for him. Wally angled the boat trailer down toward the launch.

The boat was a nice one, a diesel-powered forty-footer with a bright white hull and green cabin rigged with more electronic gear than a spacecraft, including a digital depth finder and GPS navigational system. On the port side of the boat was a gas-powered winch that would take some—but not all—of the backbreaking labor out of the job of hauling lobster pots. Ben knew it was inevitable that his father would ask—no, *demand*—that he help him haul before he found other work.

Seeing the new boat, though, Ben wondered how his father could afford something like this...especially if money was as tight as he'd been complaining last night. Ben's first night home and all he got was an earful about how lobstermen were suffering this season and how the government was only making things worse. What with new regulations about what kind of rope the lobstermen could use on their traps and the rising cost of diesel fuel, no one could make ends meet without raising the price of lobster. With the economy in the tank the way it was, people weren't buying lobster the way they used to. The regulars down at the wharf were saying if something wasn't done to fix things and soon, they were either going to have to give up for good or this would be their last year lobstering.

Seated in the passenger's seat of the truck was the boat's namesake, Capt'n Wally's grandniece, Abby Rose. Ben was surprised to see how much she had grown. He remembered her as a skinny preschooler, but now she was almost a teenager. She was wearing a pretty white dress and couldn't have looked happier, like a girl going to her first communion. Her mother, Sally Rider, the daughter of Wally's younger brother, Ed, who had died of booze before he turned forty-five, was standing off to one side, watching silently with her hands clasped over her chest like she was at prayer. It looked like a weak current of electricity was tingling through her body, making her vibrate. Her sister, Nancy, was snapping pictures with a digital camera.

Ben smiled wryly at the irony of it all, relieved that the attention was no longer focused on him. Everyone was acting like this was the most wonderful thing in the world when, in fact, within a few days, the deck would be sloshing with bilge water and bait, and Wally would no doubt be piloting his prize through the narrows out to sea with a "skinful" of rum. And if things hadn't changed in the time Ben had been in Iraq, lobsters wouldn't be the only cargo Capt'n Wally would be hauling. Occasional bales of weed from offshore trawlers would be the most likely first cargo to make him any real money. After all, Wally may own the family home free and clear, since it had been in the family for over a hundred years, but he would have huge payments to make on this dandy new boat.

The crowd shifted down toward the water's edge, surrounding the truck and boat trailer. Many of them were taking pictures with cameras and cell phones. Matt "Animal" Costello had a hand-held video camera the size of his fist. Ben realized he hadn't seen his sister Louise anywhere. A wave of concern washed through him because of a few comments his father and brother had made last night about how Louise's marriage wasn't going so well. He scanned the crowd, hoping to catch a glimpse of her, but she was nowhere in sight.

"Fuck it all," he muttered as he patted his pants pocket, feeling for his cell phone. He was considering giving her a call when someone tapped him on the shoulder.

"Hey there, bro," a pleasant, light-sounding voice said. "Good to see yah."

"Lou-Lou Belle," he said.

He was smiling as he turned to her, but his heart sank when he saw her. Her eyes were bloodshot, and in the direct sunlight, the heavy makeup that covered her cheeks didn't quite hide the purple bruise under her left eye. She angled her head to the left as though shielding it from him as she hugged him and kissed him on the cheek.

"Don't call me that," she said with a resignation in her voice that indicated she knew he wouldn't stop.

"What? Lou-Lou Belle? What else am I gonna call my little sis?"

"My real name. I've always hated Lou-Lou Belle."

Ben was about to tell her that's why he called her that, to tease her, but instead asked, "So…how's things?" He tried to inject a note of happiness into his voice and hoped Louise hadn't seen his reaction to her face.

"I'm hanging in there," she said with a wan smile.

"Thanks so much for coming by last night to see me," Ben said sarcastically.

"Well thank *you* for not showing up until almost midnight. Some people sleep, you know. Any call after ten o'clock, and all anyone's gonna think is someone died."

"Sorry…I wasn't thinking. I've crossed so many time zones, I'm all screwed up."

Before he could say more, Louise reached into her purse and pulled out a compact digital camera. She raised it and aimed it at the truck and boat, snapping a few pictures in quick succession. The lens made soft whirring sounds as she adjusted the telephoto in and out.

"I'll catch up wit'cha later," Louise said as she moved away, heading toward the truck. "If I don't get some good shots, Pops'll be pissed."

Screw him, Ben wanted to say but didn't. They both knew how angry their father could get, and Louise was being careful not to do anything to set Wally off…not on his special day.

"Later," Ben said, but she was already too far away to hear. She headed down to the water's edge so she could get some close-ups when the boat went in.

Ben remained where he was, letting the crowd stream around him as if he were a rock in the middle of a river. He considered leaving now before anyone else spoke to him. Louise had it covered with the camera, and Pete was holding his own. The family was well represented. After the launch, there were plans for a party at

Huckins Wharf, on the other side of the harbor, but Ben was thinking he might skip that.

So far, he'd been lucky.

He hadn't seen Kathy Brackett yet, and the more he thought about it, as much as he wanted to see her and knew he couldn't avoid seeing her eventually, it might be a good idea to put it off for now.

He turned to leave but then drew to a halt.

Kathy was standing across the street under one of the tall maple trees in front of Lester Michael's house. Sunlight and shadow dappled her face and the large, white bundle she cradled in her arms. A baby stroller was parked next to her.

Now it was impossible to avoid her.

Gotta get it over with, he thought.

She was looking straight at him as if all the activity down by the launch ramp wasn't even happening. She looked like an illusion… one of those mirages he'd experienced while on patrol at high noon in the desert sun. She moved dreamily as she hitched her burden from one side to the other and raised a hand to wave. Ben looked left and right, making sure she was waving at him and then waved back. He forced a wide smile that felt frozen on his face as he started across the street toward her.

"I heard you were back in town," Kathy said. Her voice was as light and airy as always. The mere sound of it sent a dull ache through Ben's chest.

"So, apparently, has the whole town."

"Hey. Come on. You're the war hero, right?"

"Yeah. Right."

Kathy smiled and tilted her head to one side, then looked down at the bundle in her arms. Even at a distance, Ben caught a whiff of baby powder or shampoo.

"Well…aren't you?" Kathy asked.

"Hardly."

The bundle in Kathy's arms was squirming. She smiled softly as she looked down at the baby and chucked it under the chin while making soft cooing sounds.

"So how's—ahh, how's married life treating you?" Ben asked. A choking sensation grabbed his throat and started squeezing, blocking off his air supply. The sunlight and shadow gave Kathy's hair a sense of motion, even though there was no breeze. A cool dampness spread under his armpits.

"It's good," Kathy said with the hint of an edge in her voice that gave Ben pause.

"And…your baby…how's she—ahh, doing?"

"Amanda? She's doing great."

Kathy shifted to one side, cocking her hip to expose the tiny face wrapped inside the blanket. The baby was asleep, and Ben thought she looked impossibly small and fragile. He never could see family resemblances in babies, but politeness impelled him to smile foolishly and say, "She has your mouth."

Kathy smiled tenderly at her daughter.

"She's fine…she's great."

"And your husband? How's Hor—" He almost used Dwight Brackett's nickname, "Horse Lips," but stopped himself at the last second. No need to be insulting. "How's Dwight doing?"

"He's fine," Kathy said. "Still working at Ames Hardware and—you know, lobstering or digging bloodworms whenever he can."

"No clams?"

"Come on. He'll never dig clams. Not enough money in it after all those red tide scares. 'S'tough enough making ends meet these days. 'Specially now that we have a kid."

Ben grimaced at her use of the word *we* and nodded.

"Times sure are tough. He's—ahh…" He wasn't sure he dared say what he intended to say. He was hoping to let it drop, but Kathy caught him up on it.

"He's what?"

"No. Nothing. I was gonna say I thought he might…you know, be a little old for you."

Kathy gave him a sly smile that was impossible to read and said, "There's only seven years between us. We're doing fine."

"Good. Great," Ben said. He wanted desperately to change the subject, so he said, "So did that big box store finally get approval to build on the lot out by Five Corners?"

"Not yet. They're still pushing the town council something wicked for clearances, but Brian Hatcher's been fighting them hard."

"Brian Hatcher? Who the fuck is Brian Hatcher?"

"New guy in town. Moved here a year or two ago from West Virginia. He's getting all involved with town politics and is on the town council. But there's a lot more support for the store than you'd think."

"Umm.... Pete was telling me last night how things had gotten pretty heated last fall."

"Ahh." Kathy waved a hand in front of her face like she was shooing a mosquito. She gazed at her sleeping baby's face again as she spoke, lowering her voice. "It's mostly Ray and Jerry Hanson making all the fuss. They stand to make a killing selling the family property to the company that wants to build the store."

"They never worked an honest day in their lives," Ben said, his lip curling with disgust. When he was in high school, he had worked with Jerry Hanson as dishwashers at *Augie's,* a local seafood restaurant. Ben had never seen a worse slacker. "Neither one of them. And now they're hoping to cash in so they never have to."

"Yeah—and meanwhile, people 'from away' are fighting to keep the town the quaint little fishing village it's always been even though that new store would mean more jobs."

Kathy smiled at him, but the truth was Ben was barely engaged in this small talk with her. What he *really* wanted to talk about seemed impossible to bring up. Mercifully, above the murmur of the crowd, someone was calling his name. The bellowing voice echoed from the granite walls that lined the harbor.

Ben looked down toward the water. His brother was perched on the new boat, both hands gripping the gunwales for balance. Wally had backed the trailer down the cement launch ramp until the wheels were in the water.

"I think your brother wants you," Kathy said with a quick nod in Pete's direction.

All too anxious to leave her while at the same time not wanting to walk away, Ben started to turn. Before he left, though, he stopped and looked back at her. He had to ask one thing...so he could settle his mind.

"Does he know?" he said.

At first, Kathy looked perplexed by his question, but then her face went white and her eyes narrowed.

"You mean does Dwight know...about the baby?"

Ben swallowed hard. He couldn't speak as he looked away and nodded. His heart felt too large for his chest, and he found it impossible to catch his breath.

"Of course he doesn't," Kathy said. Her voice lost all of its lightness and was suddenly as hard as steel. Without missing a beat, she added, "And as far as I'm concerned, he never will."

TWO

Launch

Ben made his way slowly down to the water's edge, wending his way through the crowd, smiling and nodding to everyone who greeted him. He took up a position on the rocks, close to where Louise was darting back and forth, trying to find the best angle for taking pictures. Collars of dark brown seaweed floated like wet leather in the water, rising and falling on the gentle swells.

With the boat already all but floating, Wally got out of the truck and walked over to the passenger's door, where he made a great show of helping the flesh and blood Abby Rose down to the ground. The cement launch ramp was pitched at a steep angle, and she was a little unsteady on her feet. Ben attributed it to nerves, what with her mother hovering at the shoreline, saying over and over at high volume how "goddamned proud" she was of her daughter.

Wally folded his arms across his chest and waited until conversation died to a murmur. He was used to commanding attention.

"I wanna thank you all for coming by today," he said, his voice loud and confident.

Wally smiled as he surveyed the crowd like they were adoring subjects, come to honor the king. Sunlight washed over his tanned and weather-beaten face, giving him a glow of health. A sparkle lit his eyes. Ben thought the sparkle might be as much from however many shots of rum his father had already downed this morning as anything else.

"It ain't often we get to launch a boat like this, and never have we launched one named after such a beautiful little girl as my grand-niece here."

He patted Abby Rose on the shoulder as her mother squealed.

A scattering of applause made Abby Rose blush and look down at her feet.

"I ain't a man of many words—"

"'Cept when you got a skinful!" someone shouted.

"Like now," someone else yelled.

Wally shaded his eyes to identify whoever was wising off, but he was careful not to lose the moment.

"We're launching this here boat in the hopes that we'll all have a good season this year. That the price of fuel will finally start to come down so's honest, hard-working men can—"

"And women!" Carol Stone, who also lobstered, shouted.

"Yes…yes." Wally said as he rubbed his cheek with the tips of his fingers. "Hard-working *women* can make an honest living, too."

The crowd cheered and clapped, but Ben lowered his gaze. More like hard-drinking and doing anything legal or illegal to make a buck, he thought.

"So today," Wally continued, "we christen this boat the *Abby-Rose*."

A loud cheer went up from the crowd and echoed from the granite walls of the harbor as Wally reached into the truck and withdrew a bottle of champagne. He wrapped a white towel around it and then gave it to Abby Rose.

With one hand resting on Abby Rose's thin shoulder, he directed her to the bow of the boat, still helping her keep her balance. He leaned down and whispered something into her ear, and then, holding her hand in his so her tiny fist looked like a ball trapped inside a baseball glove, he brought her arm back and counted.

"One…"

He swung her arm so the bottle clinked lightly against the bow.

"Two…"

Another swing, and a louder *clink*.

"And *three!*"

On the third swing, Abby Rose smacked the bottle against the bow. The towel did a good job of catching most of the shattered green glass, which clicked like tumbling dice on the trailer frame and concrete ramp. A bubbling wave of white foam spewed into the air and splashed across the bow of the boat. It fizzed as it ran in thin, bubbly streams down the ramp and into the water.

Another, even louder cheer went up from the crowd. Close to the water, Louise was kneeling on one knee, rapidly firing her camera, as were several other people.

"You done good, Ab. Real good," Wally said, clapping her on the shoulder like she was one of his drinking buddies.

She smiled up at him, but, if anything, she looked like she wanted to run away from here as fast and as far as she could so people would stop gawking at her. She shied away when her mother rushed forward and gave her a big hug and kiss on the cheek.

"I'm so proud of you," Sally said, loud enough for everyone to hear.

Hanging back, Ben watched it all with an amused sense of detachment. He felt like an invisible observer.

Wally climbed up onto the boat and then, leaning down, hoisted Abby Rose up onto the deck to stand beside him. Pete got down from the boat, a little unsteadily, and slid into the cab of the truck behind the steering wheel. Leaning out the driver's window, he waited for the word from his father.

"You comin', Benny?" his father yelled.

Ben tensed, suddenly aware that numerous pairs of eyes had turned on him. No one had called him "Benny" in years—not since high school. He was sure his father had done it now simply to embarrass him. Payback for not wearing his uniform.

"I'm all set," Ben said with a quick wave of his hand. He knew, from the look his father shot back at him that he'd hear about it later, that he should have joined the family on the boat if only to show family unity.

"Come on, Ben," Louise said as she started for the boat. "You gotta."

But Ben shook his head and didn't move. To cover the awkward moment, Louise climbed up into the boat and then waved to the crowd with a wide smile on her face. She looked like Queen of the Rose Bowl Parade, but even at this distance, Ben could see the bruise beneath her makeup.

Once it was obvious Ben was going to be stubborn about it, Pete shifted the truck into reverse and backed the trailer deeper into the water until the truck's rear tires were submerged. When the boat started to lift free of the frame, Wally started up the engine. The deep-throated growl echoed from the harbor walls, and a thin haze of blue exhaust rose into the sky as the *Abby-Rose* backed up and then swung around, heading out toward sea.

Before he gassed it, Wally took a bullhorn from the side of the cabin and raised it to his mouth.

"Thank you all for coming! I hope to see you over at Huckins'! Free food and drink!" he shouted, his amplified voice echoing inside the stone harbor. He put the bullhorn down and raised a helium horn, giving it a long, steady blast. Several people in the crowd flinched and covered their ears.

Folks were still cheering and waving as the boat headed out to sea for a little trial run. Then, *en masse,* people started back toward the street.

Ben moved with the crowd, but he kept off to one side, staying on the thin strip of grass next to the parking lot. He overheard a few scattered comments about how everything had gone so well and what a beautiful day it was for a party and how everyone was looking forward to the festivities. If past launchings were any guide, the party would last all day for many of them and long into the night for some. The remaining hardcore celebrants—which would no doubt include Wally—would finish up the celebration at Dewey's Pub, known by everyone simply as "The Local."

As he worked his way through the crowd, Ben considered heading home so he could be alone with his thoughts. He didn't belong to this town any more. All too easily, he identified with Abby Rose's nervousness at being the center of attention, even if it was only for a few seconds. Everyone he bumped into was obligated to say something to him about how good it must feel to be back home. Ben smiled and shook hands and thanked everyone, but a cold pit slowly opened up in his stomach whenever he thought how if only they knew what had happened in Iraq…what he had done—and not done. Then, probably not a damned one of them would bother to look, much less speak to him again.

For sure…. That's gotta be him, Julia Meadows thought as she hunched behind the steering wheel of her Audi. She was parked on the side of the street, about halfway down the hill leading to the boat launch. She watched the dark-haired young man making his way slowly up the slope from the boat launch and head for the street. The crowd surged around him, and several people stopped and spoke with him briefly before getting into their cars and trucks, and pulling out of the parking lot. A curtain of dust rose into the air, choking people like a cloud of noxious smoke. Everyone was vying to be first to get over to Huckins Wharf so they could start eating and drinking. But Julia noticed how, even in a crowd, Ben moved as if he were walking all alone…or in another dimension.

She had to admit he was better looking than she had expected from what she'd heard folks around town say about him. The returning native son—the high school star athlete and now war hero—was taller and thinner than she had imagined. He walked with an almost cat-like grace that she found immediately intriguing. Earlier, before the boat launch, she had been sitting in her car, watching the festivities when she noticed him cross the street and talk to Kathy Brackett. Julia told herself she had come down here to watch the event so maybe she would feel like she was at least a little part of the town, but the truth was, she was here today solely to see Ben Brown and meet him, if she got a chance.

He walked past her car without noticing her. When he was about fifty feet past her, she started up the car and edged into the flow of traffic. People around here were courteous, at least. A battered, rusted-out Chevy pickup stopped to let her in. Julia smiled and waved at the driver, a huge man who, when he grinned at her, showed a remarkable lack of front teeth.

But as she drove along in the procession, never going more than ten miles per hour, she began to fear that Ben, on foot, might outpace her. She watched the way he walked and was fascinated by his long strides and the subtle confidence in the way he carried himself. His butt was trim and his legs well-muscled.

When she had caught up with him and was about to lower the window on the passenger's side and say something to him, he paused, glanced at her car, raised his hand as if to halt her, and stepped out into the street, cutting away from the flow of the pedestrians.

"Dammit," Julia muttered, and she quickly pressed the button to lower the window on her side and stuck her head out.

"Hey, there. Wanna lift?" she called out, surprising herself with her boldness.

Ben stopped in the middle of the street and looked at her, confusion crinkling his tanned brow as he raised his right hand and touched his chest in a "you mean me?" gesture.

"Yeah," Julia said, as a flush of warmth spread through her stomach. Up close, he was even better looking than she had thought.

"I'm heading down to the wharf and thought you might like a lift."

Ben was taken aback as he looked up and down the street. The rusted Chevy behind her was idling with a loud rumble as dark exhaust spewed from the tailpipe in a billowing cloud. After a second or two, the toothless driver tapped on his horn. Only two short honks, but enough to set Julia's nerves on edge.

"Hold yer ass, Dime's Worth," Ben shouted, and then he scooted across the street to the passenger's side of the car. Julia hit the automatic door lock button to unlock the door, and he opened the door and dropped down into the seat. The perplexed look on his face made Julia smile as she took her foot off the brake and moved ahead to cut the distance between her and the car in front of her.

"Who's Dime's Worth?" she asked casually.

"Him?" Ben turned and glanced out the rear window at the truck following them. "That's Henry Martin. 'Dime's Worth.'"

"How'd he get a name like that?"

"Long story," Ben said. He looked at her, frowning. "Do I know you?"

"No." Julia flashed him a quick grin. "But you should."

Maybe it's a good thing I came down here after all, Ben was thinking as he studied the driver in silence for a moment. Her thin face was tanned, and she had long, curly dark hair with amber highlights that cascaded down her shoulders. When she had turned to him and smiled, he caught a mischievous gleam in her brown eyes. His first thought was: This woman is interesting.

"So," he said, after clearing his throat and scratching his cheek. "Why should I get to know you?"

"You're Ben Brown, right?"

Ben nodded.

"I thought so. I've heard about you…around town."

"And you are—?"

"Julia Meadows," she replied. She held out her right hand for him to shake. Although her hand was small, he noticed how long her fingers were. She had a nice, firm grip that was cool and dry.

"Meadows…Meadows…" Ben frowned and shook his head. "Doesn't ring a bell. You're not from around here."

Julia said, "I am now. I moved to town last fall."

Ben let out a burst of braying laughter as he stared at her.

"Now why would you go 'n do a damned fool thing like that?"

Julia was silent long enough so Ben was afraid he'd said something wrong, but then the smile returned to her face.

"Yeah. Catawamkeag Cove…. How would the old-timers put it? 'It ain't much.'"

"You got that right. So how'd you end up in a godforsaken place like this…especially for the winter?"

"My dad's…his name's Capozza…Frank Capozza," Julia said simply. This was followed by a silence, and Ben debated whether or not to press her on this. It appeared to be an uncomfortable topic, but then it hit him.

"Capozza…. Yeah, okay. The big white house down by the river's edge…out on Steeple Road, right?"

Julia bit down on her lower lip, turning it pale.

"Uh-huh."

"I thought a retired couple was living there."

"That's my mum and dad," Julia said. "Only, my mum died last year. I moved up from Connecticut to help my dad out."

"He not doing well?"

"Parkinson's."

Ben nodded and couldn't help but glance at her left ring finger to see if she was wearing a wedding ring. She wasn't, and for some reason, that made him feel a whole lot better about getting a ride with her.

"I already knew life isn't fair," Julia said. "I didn't need to have my mum die to learn it."

"I hear yah," he said with a solemn nod, although he was a bit surprised by the sudden bitterness in her voice. He'd just met her, and although she had made a damned good first impression, there was no way he was going to unburden how he felt about coming back to The Cove after being overseas. He sensed that Julia's reasons, although not the same as his, might parallel his in many ways.

She was silent as she drove, being careful of the people on the street and a group of young boys on bikes who were whooping it up as they weaved in and out of traffic.

Not so long ago, Ben thought, that would have been me and my friends.

He took his time studying her, and the more he looked, the more he liked what he saw. She had a long neck, and his eyes kept drifting down to the roundness of her breasts beneath her purple t-shirt.

"So," he said, wanting to break the silence before it got awkward, "Why'd you pick me up?"

When she smiled, thin lines creased her face, bracketing her mouth. An angle of sunlight hit her face just right, making her brown eyes gleam.

"Like I said—I heard about you around town, and I wanted to meet you."

"Really?"

"Really."

Her directness took Ben aback. For a moment, he gazed straight ahead, letting what she'd said sink in.

"So what did you hear?" he asked.

Julia let out a low chuckle and said, "A *lot.*"

Ben froze, wondering if Julia was aware of the rumors about who really was the father of Kathy Brackett's child. Sweat broke out on his brow, and he wiped it away with the flat of his hand.

"You mean all the war hero bullshit?" he said and quickly added, "Pardon my French."

"I believe the French word is *'merde.'*"

They both laughed at that, and Ben found himself liking her all the more. Her casual openness was refreshing.

"So you must have heard the stories about Capt'n Wally, too, huh?"

"Some," Julia said. "Sounds like quite the character."

Ben snorted and said, "You don't know the half of it."

"You'll have to tell me."

Ben shook his head.

"My old man's got an image around town he's got to maintain.

My advice is, in a town like this? It's a good idea to take everything you hear with a few pounds of salt."

Julia nodded but said nothing. They drove a while in silence, each of them casting surreptitious glances at the other when they thought they weren't looking. Usually, it took less than ten minutes to circle around The Cove and get to Huckins Wharf, but with all the traffic and pedestrians, it was going to take the better part of half an hour. Ben decided to break the awkward silence.

"So, are you married or seeing someone?"

"'Seeing someone.' That's a quaint way to put it."

"I didn't mean it like that. I mean are you—you know, involved in a relationship. Married? Kids?"

Julia laughed and, shaking her head, said, "Not exactly."

Ben wasn't sure how to take that, but he noticed how she gripped the steering wheel so tightly her knuckles turned into white half-moons. He was confused by her reaction.

"'Not exactly' leaves quite a bit of wiggle room for interpretation."

"I'm sure it does," Julia said, still not answering his question.

Ben couldn't explain the sudden feeling of what could only be called jealousy that swept through him. Here he had been with this woman less than ten minutes, and already he felt possessive about her. The only thing to do was change the subject to something a little less edgy.

"So tell me—what are some of your impressions of The Cove so far? Moving here before winter starts doesn't strike me as something any sane person would do."

Again, Julia gave a short laugh that Ben found impossible to decipher.

Was she genuinely amused by the discussion, or was there some underlying bitterness that irritated or pained her?

"People are friendly enough, but they've never seen me as anything more than a summer person. Even though I live here now, I don't feel like I'm really home."

"And never will be," Ben said, smiling sympathetically. "Your family has to go back at least two or three generations for that."

By now, they had reached the top of Martin's Hill, which overlooked the harbor. Ben glanced down the slope at the boats anchored there. He couldn't see Huckins Wharf, so he didn't know if Wally had already tied up at the dock or was still out on a test run. He didn't see the *Abby-Rose,* out beyond the headlands.

Before Julia turned to start down Main Street, Ben reached over and tapped her on the shoulder. When she glanced at him, he pointed to a small white building on their right. A sign over the twin garage doors read: *Catawamkeag Cove Volunteer Fire Department.*

"Pull in there."

She shot him a questioning look.

"We can walk down to the wharf from here. That way, if you want to bug out early, you won't have to deal with much traffic."

"Good call," Julia said. She drove to the back of the parking lot, where it turned from asphalt to dirt, and parked at the edge of a small bluff looking out over the town. Dust swirled around the car as she killed the engine.

"Nice view," she said, narrowing her eyes as she took it in.

The bluff looked out over the rooftops of a few homes and some fishing shacks lining several stone wharves in The Cove. To the left was Main Street, lined with shops and restaurants. Beyond, lay the ocean. Sunlight glittered and flashed on the water where, off in the distance, the *Abby-Rose* had cut a wide circular arc and was heading back to the dock.

Ben smiled at a private memory and said, "Back when I was in high school, before the town put the new fire station here, this was where couples would come to go parking."

"Parking.... How quaint," Julia said.

Ben couldn't tell if she was mocking him or not. Her laugh certainly sounded a bit sarcastic, but a sad wistfulness in her eyes softened her expression.

"So...you wanna go down and mingle with the locals?"

For several seconds, Julia was silent, looking like she was debating what to do next. The corners of her mouth twisted down, and he thought her eyes had a wild look, like an animal that had been cornered.

"We don't have to," he added. "If you don't want to."

He tensed, wondering if she was going to ask him what else he might have in mind, but then she pulled the keys from the ignition and opened her door.

"Don't you *have* to show up? After all, it's your dad's big day."

Ben shook his head as he started to get out of the car.

"Every day is my old man's big day."

The party on Huckins Wharf was already in full swing by the time Ben and Julia started working their way through the crowd. He stopped now and then to talk with someone he hadn't seen since before he left for Iraq, making sure he introduced Julia to everyone he spoke with. It surprised him how he felt as though they were already on a first date and reminded himself not to presume anything.

There was plenty of free food and drink. Ben got a beer for himself and a rum punch for Julia. She made a joke about how it was only natural to drink rum while hanging out with a gaggle of pirates. Ben smiled at that and wondered if she realized how true that was, but he didn't say anything.

"You must have the magic touch," Julia said, leaning close and whispering into his ear. The warmth of her breath against his skin excited him.

"How's that?"

"Everyone's being a lot nicer to me today than they usually are."

Ben shook his head, not wanting to unload on her about how petty the locals could be.

"It's all a show. The minute our backs are turned, I can guarantee they'll—" He caught himself before he said what he had been about to say and finished lamely, "I'm sure they're already wondering about us."

Julia smiled as if at a private joke, but her smile suddenly froze and then melted when a voice boomed behind them.

"Well, well, well—lookie here. If it isn't the war hero."

Ben recognized the voice immediately and winced. He turned to face his brother-in-law, Tom Marshall, who was striding toward him. When he was close enough, Tom leaned forward and gave Ben a hearty clap on the shoulder that was hard enough to knock him off balance.

"How's it hanging there, Gunner? Low and loose and full of juice?"

"High and dry and waiting to die," Ben replied, falling instantly into an old high school routine. Tom had been a year behind Ben in school, but they hadn't really been friends, even when they were on the basketball team Ben's senior year, when the team made it to the state semi-finals. Of course, now that Tom was married to Ben's sister, their relationship had changed. He had to be nice.

"You here to party, or are you working?" Ben asked, indicating Tom's uniform.

"Pulled a day shift this week, so I thought I'd swing by 'n make sure you folks kept things under control. No open alcohol containers and all."

"We'll have none of that," Ben said, smiling as he raised his bottle of beer and took a drink.

"Glad to see you'd never do something like that," Tom said. He grabbed Ben's bottle, took a swig, then handed it back to him. Ben quickly wiped the mouth of the bottle with his palm. Tom looked at Julia as if seeing her for the first time. His eyebrows closed together as he frowned and said, "So…who's this?"

"Friend of mine," Ben said. "Tom. Meet Julia. Julia. This here's my brother-in-law, Tom Marshall. He's married to my sister. Speaking of Louise—" Ben looked around, scanning the crowd. "Have you seen her?"

"Not since back at the house," Tom said. Shadows filled his eyes, and he looked away.

People laughing and talking were gathered around the tables spread with food—hot dogs, hamburgers, every kind of salad imaginable, and chips and salsa. Others milled around by the dock. The loud rumble of the *Abby-Rose*'s engine drew everyone's attention down to the floating dock as Wally, smiling broadly, pulled up and cast a line ashore. A young boy on the dock caught the line and quickly tied it off.

"Well, I 'spoze I ought to mingle," Tom said. "Catch yah later." He hesitated, then looked at Julia and said, "Pleasure to meet you."

"Likewise," Julia said, but Ben caught the frosty tone in her voice. It would be hard not to.

"You'll have to fill me in on what's going on over there in Iraq," Tom said, slapping Ben on the shoulder again. "You gonna be down to The Local later tonight?"

"Probably."

"I'll be there. I get off at six. A lot of people will wanna see you.

Valerie Foster was asking for you."

"Really?" Ben cast a quick glance at Julia. He certainly didn't want her to think he might be hoping to have something better to do tonight than be with her. "We'll see."

"Hope to see you around, Miss Meadows," Tom said, nodding stiffly.

He walked away, his arms and shoulders swinging back and forth with an arrogant swagger he seemed to adopt only when he was wearing his uniform. Watching him leave, Ben couldn't help but think about a line in a Kurt Vonnegut book he'd read overseas about how you knew you were getting old when you realized you're being ruled by people you went to high school with.

It was only when they were walking down the gangplank to the dock to get onto the *Abby-Rose* for a little cruise around the harbor that Ben wondered if he had ever told Tom Julia's last name was Meadows. The more he thought about it, the more he was convinced he had introduced her simply as Julia.

THREE

The Local

Wally was certainly in his element, laughing and cursing in equal measure as he headed the boat out with a load of people for a little cruise around the harbor. The ride was much more pleasant than Ben had anticipated, but it was easy to see why. He thoroughly enjoyed being in Julia's presence, and he found himself drawn to her all the more.

She certainly was attractive enough. Beautiful, in fact. Her long, dark hair blowing in wild tangles in the wind mesmerized him. And he loved the way she smiled all the time, exposing wide, gleaming white teeth. Her lips were full with a hint of lip-gloss. He kept finding himself imagining what it would be like to kiss her. He couldn't understand why she wasn't already involved with someone else, but he was glad of that. Maybe she had avoided his questions because she was on the tail end of divorce or a bad relationship. It certainly was easy enough to pretend they already were a couple, and he was sure that's exactly what anyone who saw them together would think. That made him feel good.

Julia had a natural grace and an engaging personality. But she also was a bit reserved, and she seemed reluctant to insert herself into the conversation whenever Ben reconnected with someone he knew. That suited him just fine. He sensed her feelings of isolation from the townspeople, and he shared them, maybe more than he cared to admit. He winced whenever someone called him by his nickname, "Gunner."

As the boat rounded the headlands and headed down along the coastline, he found himself thinking how natural he and Julia were together, like they had known each other long before today. He stood as close to her as he could get, his hands braced on the railing, allowing the jostling of the boat on the water to let his shoulder brush against hers from time to time.

She didn't seem to mind.

If anything, she moved a little closer so their arms were touching. He was impatient for the boat ride to end so he could get her alone.

Jesus, stop it, he cautioned himself. *You just met the woman,* but he was already making plans for once they got back on land and she told him she had to leave, he was going to ask when he could see her again. He certainly got the vibe that she would be open to that. She actively engaged him in conversation whenever he wasn't talking to old friends, and she seemed genuine when she laughed at his witty remarks and observations.

Ben had to admit that it felt good to be back out on the water, too…especially after breathing the hot, choking dust and fumes in Iraq for the last few years. When Wally took a hard turn, the people at the back of the boat got hit with a cool, salty spray. Everyone laughed, but Ben was thinking how after being in the desert for so long, the open ocean was a true miracle of nature.

He and Julia stood together at the stern of the boat as it skipped across the water, leaving behind a smooth wake that folded back into the shimmering surface. Leaning close so she could hear him above the throaty rumble of the engine, he pointed out various landmarks—small islands where he and his high school friends used to go to hang out, or coves and points on the mainland where he or someone else—usually a drunk fisherman—had done something so foolish it was amusing.

Capt'n Wally slowed the boat as he came around to pass another lobster boat on the port side. Gulls swirled around the boat like a white tornado, looking for any chum that might fall into the water. A large golden retriever was standing on its hind legs, its front paws up on the gunwales as it watched the passing boat. The lobsterman—a grizzled, white-haired old coot—wearing a black rubber apron, barely looked up from his work baiting a lobster trap as he raised one hand and pointed in their general direction.

"That's as much of a wave as you'll ever get from old Peggy."

"Peggy?" Julia said, raising an eyebrow. They had to bring their heads close together in order to hear each other. Ben had to resist the almost overpowering impulse to kiss her right then and there.

"Short for 'Peg-Leg,'" he said with a wide smile as they left the old man behind, his boat rocking in their wake.

Julia laughed and said, "Do I need to point out to you that both words have two syllables? So 'Peggy's' not really *short* for 'Peg-Leg.'"

"'Course it is," Ben said, smiling broadly. "It's one word instead of two."

Julia almost laughed.

"So how'd he earn his name?"

"Lost his leg in a boating accident. It was dense fog one day, and he was out lobstering, drunk as a skunk, and he ran aground. His leg got cut so bad the doctor had to take it off to save his life."

"My God," Julia muttered.

"And his dog? What's his name?"

"Fred," Ben said.

Julia eyed him as if she thought he was making another joke, but Ben nodded and said, "Seriously."

"A guy named Peg-Leg…Peggy…in a town filled with people who have colorful names, and his dog is named Fred?"

"Ole' Fred's got better sea legs than half the town, too," Ben said. "Funny story about Peg-Leg. When ole Peggy's sober—which isn't very often—he's the nicest fellow you could meet, but once he gets a skin-full, he can be a real 'bastid,' as they say. One night he got to drinking, but he ran out of booze. He was going to drive to the liquor store out on Route One, but his wife wouldn't hear of it. Turned into quite a ruckus, I guess, and she ended up taking his artificial leg and hiding it along with his truck keys."

"No way."

"She told him when he was sober enough to find his damned leg and keys, he was sober enough to go get more booze. Supposedly, he even tried to get Fred to fetch it for him, but Fred was having nothing to do with it."

"You've got to be making that up," Julia said, looking at him with a twisted half-smile

"Absolute truth." Ben raised his right hand as if swearing in a court of law. "There's lots more stories even worse…or funnier, depending on your point of view."

Julia was silent as she watched Peggy's lobster boat recede in the distance.

"Stick with me, kid," Ben said, "and I'll tell you stuff you wouldn't believe in a million years."

"So let me guess," Julia said. "Your nickname is 'Gunner,' right?"

Ben paused, avoiding eye contact with her for a second or two, and then nodded slowly.

"Uh-huh."

"Your friends have been calling you that all day, so it wasn't hard to figure out. Is it because of Iraq?"

"Not really," he said, still terribly uncomfortable with this topic.

"So what's it mean?" Julia asked, still looking at him with wide eyes. She either didn't get or was ignoring his discomfort. "Did you always go hunting or was it because you—well, you always wanted to be a soldier or something?"

Ben said nothing.

"You must like to shoot things, then," she said. "Do you hunt?"

Biting his lower lip, Ben shook his head, wishing to God she would let it drop.

"So tell me. Why 'Gunner?'"

"It's slang for—for..." He shrugged and let it drop, hoping she wouldn't pick it up.

Julia started to say something but then caught herself and started smiling broadly. Then she laughed out loud.

"Oh, I get it...Gunner," she said.

In spite of his embarrassment, Ben was charmed by the mischievous light in her eyes.

"I guess I'll have to keep an eye on you," she said.

Ben had no idea what to say to that, but before he could say anything, Wally took a hard turn to port and came around so they were heading back to the harbor. The boat bounced hard over its own wake, and Ben used the rocking motion to shift even closer to Julia. His body tensed, and he was waiting for rejection as he slid his arm around behind her. His smile widened when she leaned hard against him, not rejecting him at all.

For the first time, he thought about how good it was to be back home.

The sounds of festivities still going on down on the wharf receded as Ben and Julia made their way up the slope back to the parking lot behind the fire station. They walked slowly, and Ben found himself struggling to think of some clever way to draw out their time together.

"You sure you have to get back?" he asked. He kicked at a tuft of weeds and sent a spray of dandelion seeds flying.

Julia nodded. She had her hands clasped behind her back and walked with a swing in her step that was charmingly little girlish. Ben found it incredibly attractive, and he was desperate not to let her leave him. Not yet. They were silent until they got to her car. Then she turned around and, leaning her back against the car, took a deep breath. She smiled as she looked up at the perfectly cloudless sky. High overhead, a seagull wheeled in a wide circle.

"Thanks for a fun morning," Julia said.

"And afternoon," Ben added as he glanced out over the town to the clock on the Congregation Church steeple. It showed that it was a little after one o'clock.

Where did the time go? he wondered.

Ben wanted to reach out and touch her but knew it wouldn't be right to hug and kiss her even though that's exactly what he wanted to do. Shaking hands certainly wasn't going to cut it, was it?

"I was thinking—" he began, but he stopped when she lowered her gaze and looked straight into his eyes. Her brown eyes sparkled like chocolate melting in the sun. The coy smile she gave him was almost too much to bear.

"Thinking what?" she said.

Ben cleared his throat and shifted his weight from one foot to the other. He didn't like how nervous he felt standing next to her without taking her into his arms.

Ease off, dude, a voice in his mind whispered.

"I was thinking maybe we should hang out sometime."

Julia's smile widened, exposing her teeth.

"'Hang out.' That sounds so quaint."

This was at least the third time she had called something he said "quaint." Ben couldn't tell if she was making fun of him or not.

"Yeah…I suspect things at The Local will be howling until all hours tonight. You want to see a slice of what life is *really* like in The

Cove, you ought to come down later."

"Sorry. Not tonight."

"Why not?"

"I...can't."

There was a finality in her voice that told Ben not to push any harder.

"Some other time, maybe" she said. "That'd be great."

"Cool," Ben said and immediately cursed himself for sounding like a nervous high school kid who was trying to ask the head cheerleader to the prom. Would Julia think saying *cool* was "quaint," too?

"Well..." she said. "I should get back and make lunch for my dad. He'll be wondering where I am."

Saying that, though, she didn't make a move to get into her car.

Is she waiting for something? Ben wondered.

He started leaning forward to give her a quick hug—nothing sexual...a friendly hug...nothing more—but she sensed what was coming and twisted away. She appeared to be laughing to herself as she opened the car door and sat down on the seat. Her hands gripped the steering wheel.

Ben held the door open for her and, once she was settled, nodded to her and swung it shut. He looked at her through the window, surprised by the intensity of his longing to hold her in his arms and kiss her.

What the hell is happening here? he wondered.

But it didn't matter.

He'd been without a woman—without any women—in his life for too long. It was good to feel this kind of attraction again, even if it never went anywhere.

Julia rolled her window down and smiled up at him, her teeth gleaming in the sunlight.

"Give me a call, then. We'll do something sometime," she said.

"Absolutely."

Ben raised his hand and gave her a little wave as she started up her car. The engine ran with a smooth purr.

"Your number's in the phone book?"

"The only 'Capozzas' on Steeple Road."

Ben was still smiling as she shifted the car into reverse and backed around. Her tires raised a thin cloud of dust that drifted into his face as she drove away. She tooted the horn once and stuck her hand out the window to wave goodbye. Ben waved after her and watched the dust slowly settle onto his sneakers. It filled his nostrils with a dryness that instantly reminded him of Iraq, but he pushed such thoughts aside as he watched her car disappear around the corner.

Even after it was gone, he didn't move.

He was listening to the quickly receding sound of her engine and the tires on pavement. Once she crested the hill, the sounds were gone. Only then did he turn around and start down the hill toward the wharf where the party was still going full steam.

"There you go, Dad."

Julia smiled as she placed the paper plate with an egg salad sandwich, neatly cut into quarters, onto the placemat in front of her father. She walked over to the counter and got her own lunch—a bowl of freshly hulled strawberries topped with whipped cream—and sat down at the table opposite her father.

She watched, not eating yet as he reached for his sandwich. His hand was shaking out of control, and it was painfully obvious that his Parkinson's was getting worse. As he gripped the wedge of bread and raised it to his mouth, globs of egg salad squeezed out and dropped onto the table and landed in his lap. Julia started to get up and come to him to clean up the mess, but she checked herself. He'd make an even worse mess before the meal was over, she was sure.

Frank Capozza, her father, was losing his battle with Parkinson's disease. It had come on him slowly, at first registering as a slight tremor in his hands and sometimes as an almost imperceptible nodding of his head as if he had started to drift off to sleep and then caught himself. He had fought it bravely for many years, staying rock solid throughout his wife's illness and death. After that, as if on cue, the debilitating disease had surged along his nerves like wildfire, reducing his muscles to useless, dead tissue.

Most days, his hands shook so badly he could no longer hold a newspaper or book. His head bobbed up and down like it was attached to a too-loose hinge. His voice, once so strong and commanding—especially when he was on a job site, overseeing the crew laying floor tiles or grouting a bathroom wall—rattled now like dice being shaken in a cup. Getting around the house these days was more shuffling than walking. He wore out a pair of bedroom slippers—which is all he ever wore—about every month. Frank's mind was still sharp, though, and he took every increased failing of his body personally and with simmering resentment.

Meals were the worst. They had become a battleground because Frank was determined to feed himself, to exert enough control over his muscles to propel his hand to his mouth, no matter how long it took. But his nerves were no longer receiving coherent messages from his brain, and they were as likely to bring his hand down to his lap or—worse—lock his arm in a spasm that would fling food across the room. He fiercely declined any offer of help from Julia, and she was growing increasingly worried about how feeble he was and how much weight her once robust father had lost. Since midwinter, he looked nearly skeletal.

Today's meal was going well, at least so far. Within minutes, two triangles of the sandwich were gone, and other than that first mess, there was only a light yellow smear of egg yolk across his left cheek. It looked like he had tried to paint his face with mustard.

"How 'bout a strawberry?" she asked.

Before he answered, she bit into a big one and closed her eyes for a moment, savoring the explosion of sweetness and the crunch of the tiny seeds.

Frank shook his head as though an insect was buzzing around him, and he was trying to shoo it away.

"You look happy today, Jewel," he said after a moment. "Did something happen I don't know about?"

"I dunno. Maybe," Julia said. "I'm not sure." She smiled distantly, wishing she knew the answer to that herself. Realizing she was drifting away, thinking about Ben, she blinked her eyes and focused on her dad. "But never mind me. You eat. Strawberry?"

He nodded, and she held out a plump berry to him before realizing he couldn't possibly reach across the table to get it. Standing up, she went to his side and knelt down beside him, positioned to pop the strawberry into his mouth when he gained enough control to open it. After what looked like a great effort—an effort that ignited his rage—he managed to drop his bottom jaw open. When he closed his lips and bit down on the strawberry, a thin stream of pink juice trickled from the corner of his mouth. Julia took his napkin and quickly wiped it away, then went back to her chair.

She watched intently as he focused on his hand, willing it to rise and pick up another triangle of sandwich and bring it to his mouth. She studied the back of his hand, remembering the thick tangle of black hairs that had once covered his hands, wrists, and forearms. Now, the hair was sparse and as white as tiny threads of cotton. The skin beneath was almost translucent, lined with blue veins and sprinkled with coffee-stain age spots.

How could this be the same man who, when she was a little girl, had greeted her so cheerfully when he came home from working at the tile company by swinging her up over his head time and again, tossing her into the air where she experienced a thrilling moment of freefall, and then catching her, safe and secure in big, strong hands?

Her eyes misted as she recalled the stories he'd told her about his youth as a street kid who was tough enough to run with the Rockets, one of the Italian gangs who ruled the streets of Waterbury, Connecticut, back in the early fifties. But he also had been tender-hearted and gallant enough to win the heart and, eventually, the hand of Patricia Corsetti, the prettiest girl at Holy Cross High School.

Now he looked so feeble…so helpless.

It wasn't fair.

"Yikes. Watch it there, Dad," she said when his fingers suddenly clenched and squeezed another glob of egg salad onto his lap. It landed with a dull plopping sound. Julia started to get up again, but he glared at her.

"I don't need your damned help," he said. His voice was tight with command, but it was so shaky the effect wasn't quite what he'd obviously intended. After a moment, his expression collapsed, and he looked at her with a pitiful look that couldn't hide his repressed frustration.

Julia leaned back in her chair and popped a strawberry into her mouth, trying to make it look as though his outburst hadn't affected her in the least as she chewed and swallowed. But how could it not when her frustration with her own circumstances was probably as intense as his?

Her father finally managed to get another mouthful of sandwich without mishap. He chewed noisily, his features relaxing slightly. As soon as he swallowed, he looked at Julia again and said, "You're just like your mother, you know that?"

"How so?"

"I mean, you wear your heart on your sleeve."

"What do you mean by that?"

"I mean, I ask you if something happened to you today, and you don't say a word, but it's clear as day something happened. I can tell by the look in your eyes."

"I'm that transparent?"

Julia wasn't sure if he nodded in agreement or if his head started shaking up and down because of his condition.

"To me, you are.... So tell me. What happened?"

"Nothing *happened.* I went to the boat launch down at Huckins Wharf this morning."

"A boat launch? Are you sure that's all?"

They were both silent for several seconds as Frank tried to take another bite of sandwich. Julia was breathing heavily. Again, she had to fight the urge to get up and help him. She couldn't stand to watch him struggle so much, but she knew that his pride wouldn't allow him to give in. He took any assistance only grudgingly.

"Yeah..." she finally said. "They were launching a new lobster boat, and I went to check it out. I wanted to see what the big to-do was all about." She paused and took a breath as she thought about her too-short time with Ben. "You want another strawberry?"

"Eat, eat, eat.... All the time with you, it's eat."

"You have to keep your strength up, Dad."

Frank looked at her and then lowered his gaze, his scowl deepening. Julia knew that his unasked question was: *Keep my strength up for what?*

"So who is he?" her father said after another long silence. He rested his hands on the edge of the table, where they twitched, his fingernails clicking like insects on the wood next to his placemat.

"Who's who?" Julia asked with an innocent shrug, but she fidgeted because she knew that he knew.

"It's obvious you met someone, and from the glow on your face, I'd say it was a man. So tell me. Who is he?"

Julia smiled thinly and shook her head, finally yielding. It was so like her dad to see through her like this. Growing up, she had never been able to get away with any mischief…not much, anyway…not when her dad was around. It was only once she was in high school, and he was spending eighty hours and more a week at his tile business that she had started acting out.

"Ben…his name's Ben Brown.

Frank lowered his gaze, his eyes crinkling at the corners. His head kept jerking up and down like it was tied to a string someone standing behind him was yanking.

"So who's this Ben Brown character?"

"He lives in town," she said, ignoring the slight jab. "He's a soldier…just got back from Iraq." She could feel herself warming up just being able to speak about Ben to someone. "His family's lived here, like, forever, fishing…lobstering. His father was the one launching the new boat."

"That would be Walter Brown, correct?"

Julia nodded, wondering but not asking how her father knew about Capt'n Wally.

"It was kinda interesting," she said, hoping to evade any more direct questions about Ben. "Practically the whole town turned out for it. I was surprised by what a big deal it was."

"It's a big deal, I guess, in a town like this."

"I think most of the people turned out for the free food and booze," Julia said with a tight smile. She cringed at the memory of bumping into Tom at the celebrations.

"That, too," her father said, "but if they were good, decent Catholics, they would have had a priest come down and bless the boat."

"I didn't see a priest around."

"Not surprised," Frank said, his head shaking. He started to reach for his last piece of sandwich, but suddenly his arm locked in another spasm. With a guttural curse, he brought his fist down on the table hard enough to make the silverware and plates jump.

Julia got up and hurried over to him. Her chest was tight with tension as she wrapped her arms around him and held him close.

"Hug me," she said, her voice muffled against him as she fought back tears. "Don't say a word…Just hug me."

It would do no good to cry in front of her father. Tears were for later...once she was alone...

Her father raised his right arm and draped it over her shoulder. Muscle tremors vibrated through his body as he tried to pull her close, but there was so little strength in his embrace it felt like a wind-blown tree branch was grazing her back.

And as she clung tightly to him she thought, *Is that what Ben Brown is? A chance to—finally—beat the odds?*

It was getting late, but for the die-hards, the party was just getting started. Throughout the afternoon, as food and drink ran out, people migrated up the hill to The Local. Once the sun started to set, the place was packed. Music, mostly indistinguishable heavy metal mixed occasionally with some twangy country songs, was buried beneath the cacophony of voices in shouted conversations and laughter. It was impossible to tell if there were any genuine arguments going on or if people were simply shouting to be heard. If the state hadn't banned smoking in bars, there would have been a multi-layered haze of cigarette and other types of smoke hovering overhead. Instead, people went outside, lit up and smoked, and then came back in, picking up right where they had left off.

By eight o'clock, Ben was buzzed. Not as bad as some people in the bar, but he certainly had had more to drink than he was used to. The problem was, friend after friend and even a few people he wasn't all that fond of came up and congratulated him for making it back home alive, unlike those poor kids from South Portland and a bunch of other towns in Maine who didn't make it. They bought him round after round, making Ben wonder how long these good feelings would last.

Probably not the night.

It would have been impolite to refuse, so by nine o'clock, he was well on his way to being looped.

Most of the questions and comments he heard were exactly what he'd expected. He went on automatic until his responses pretty much became a mantra: He hadn't done anything special over there; he was damned proud of the job his fellow soldiers had done—and were still doing; yes, the people really live like that. Almost everyone he talked to agreed (now, anyway, not back when the war first started) that the war had been a huge mistake and would only be worth it when and if—*big if!*—the Iraqis took charge and went after the militias so they could get their government up and running.

As time passed, the conversations devolved. People started telling stories that Ben had heard a hundred times before. Some of the stories were still damned funny while others were downright pathetic, but all of them made him keenly aware how much he was a part of this place, no matter how much he might want to get the hell out of The Cove.

It wasn't just "home."

The Cove was a living, breathing community filled with saints and sinners who shared all of their secrets…perhaps a bit too openly. And he was as much a part of the town as the rockbound coast.

"…so then Rockfish…he starts…he's flicking his porch light on and off, on and off, trying to warn the numbnuts on the boat that the feds were on to 'em and waitin' down on the beach," Danny "Preacher" Clayborn was saying. He had gotten the nickname because of the time years ago in high school when he took a hit of acid for the first and only time and started spouting Bible verses non-stop. The name—like most coastal nicknames—didn't make sense out of context, but it had stuck nonetheless.

"Right…right…" Ben said, nodding drunkenly. He already knew the punch line…as did everyone else gathered around the table. But it was going to be delivered as if it was brand new, and they'd all laugh as if they were hearing it for the first time. Ben gripped his beer glass, his shoulders jerking with laughter as if he had a bout of hiccups.

"So then…so then…" Preacher said, but he was laughing so hard he could hardly catch his breath. A bloodshot, half-crazed look filled his eyes as he leaned back and gasped for air. Tears were streaming down both sides of his face. "Then…then once them feds come up to his place, they ask him what the fuck he's doing, 'n he says—he says he's…" Preacher struggled to get the words out. "He says he's hailing his cats for 'em to come in for the night…*hailing* his goddamned cats!"

The people gathered around the table erupted with laughter that momentarily drowned out the jukebox and everything else. Ben laughed right along with them, but not for long. Leaning back, he pressed his shoulders against the wall as a sudden, inexplicable feeling of emptiness…of utter weariness and of not belonging filled him. The sudden sense of sadness cut deep as he looked around at the smiling, laughing faces surrounding him. He tensed, wondering why he felt so suddenly disconnected from them and everything else. He thought it might be because he hadn't been able to stop thinking about Julia Meadows, but he sensed that it was more than that.

It was odd, though, how Julia was never far from his thoughts.

Remembering her smile…and the way her face crinkled when she smiled…and how her bright, brown eyes lit up…and her long, dark hair floating in the wind when they were out on the water… and her body—

Jesus…sweet Lord have mercy…her body!

Everything about her filled him with an urgency that surprised him.

The sudden feeling of dissociation soon passed, and—thankfully—no one noticed, but Ben wanted—he *needed* to talk to someone about what he was thinking and feeling. He'd been hoping he and Pete could have a few words, but his brother was never all that talkative, and since Ben had come home, Pete had been acting downright resentful. Ben had no idea why.

He looked around the bar until he saw Pete. He was sitting in a darkened corner with Rachel "Bunny" Dawkins. His shaggy hair was hanging down over his eyes, and they were almost touching heads as they leaned close and talked. Locked in their private conversation, they were isolated…like there was no one else around.

There was no mystery how Bunny got her nickname. Back in high school—she was a few years behind Ben—she'd earned another nickname: "The Organ Grinder" or sometimes simply "Grinder." Pete had mentioned to Ben last night that he'd hit a bit of a rough patch with his steady girlfriend, Mona Jenkins. He didn't go into details. He seldom did about his personal life, but apparently he was dead set on getting even with Mona by shacking up with Bunny tonight…like it would be a problem getting Bunny into the sack.

"'Nother one for yah, there?" Phil "Cunna" Lippincott asked as he drained the last of a pitcher into his glass and smacked it onto the table hard enough to dent the wood.

"I dunno," Ben said, shaking his head. "'S getting kinda late."

"You can't refuse a drink with me," Cunna said. Ben didn't want to point out that Cunna had already had...he couldn't remember how many beers with him.

"Lemme drain the dragon first," Ben said as he heaved himself up from the table.

When he stood up, he noticed that either something was wrong with his left leg, or else the floor had a serious pitch to one side. When he steadied himself by leaning on someone else's table, his knee banged against the table leg hard enough to hurt. There was a loud *clink* as a glass fell over and broke, spilling beer across the table.

"What the fuck?" someone said in a tone that usually meant trouble in The Local. But then Ben saw that it was Jerry Hansen, and when they made eye contact, Jerry's scowl instantly transformed into a grin. He clapped Ben on the back and said, "Yo, Gunna, my man. Make sure you lemme buy you a drink 'fore the night's over."

Ben nodded, telling himself he wouldn't mind drinking at Wal-Mart's expense, and then forged his way to the restroom. When he got to Pete's table, he noticed that his brother was sitting alone. Ben looked around in time to see Bunny, leaving by the front door. She had her purse slung over her shoulder, and her hair bobbed with every step she took.

"Fuck it, man." Ben stifled a belch behind his fist. "'S pretty bad when you get shut down by Bunny Dawkins."

Pete glared up at his brother but said nothing.

"You sure you even got a dick, little bro'?"

"Up yours," Pete said.

At least that's what Ben thought he said. He couldn't hear him over the constant din. The knuckles of Pete's hand gripping his nearly empty beer glass went white. Shaking his head, his mouth so tight it looked like a stitched wound, he pushed back, got up from the table, fished his wallet out and dropped a twenty next to his empty glass. He bumped against Ben's shoulder, knocking him back as he walked past him.

"Hey!" Ben called after him. "I didn't mean nothin' by that."

But Pete was out the door without a backward glance.

His mood somewhat deflated, Ben continued on to the restroom, passing his father who was holding forth at the bar. When he entered the restroom, his nose wrinkled at the all too familiar stench of urine and pine disinfectant. One of the surest signs he was home was the smell of the restroom at The Local. Chuckling to himself, he relieved himself at the yellow-stained urinal and then zipped up. Somehow, he navigated back to his table where there was a freshly poured beer waiting for him.

For the next hour or two, he nursed that single beer until his head gradually began to clear...at least a little. After several more stories—none of them, thankfully, at his expense—Ben looked at his wristwatch and declared that he had to leave.

Everyone at the table disagreed, insisting that he stay a little while longer. To them, that meant until last call at one o'clock. But Ben begged off, claiming that he was still jet-lagged from the flight from Germany on his last leg home from Iraq.

"Hell, yeah," Preacher said. He rolled his eyes ceiling-ward and did a bit of rough mental calculation. "It's gotta be mornin' over there in I-rack, wouldn't'cha say? You'd 'bout be waking up right now."

"Good *morning,* Baghdad!" Stan "Diesel" Payne shouted, doing a piss-poor imitation of Robin Williams. "Time to get up 'n go out inta the desert 'n kick some sand-nigger ass, mutha-fuckas!"

A few people at the table laughed, but most of them stared into their beers. Diesel could be such an asshole sometimes. Earlier this evening, though, some people had been talking about how with all the Somalis living in Lewiston, the city was turning into "Little Mogadishu." Ben had heard more than enough of that *Hadji* crap from other soldiers in Iraq, but he realized he'd been foolish to think people back home wouldn't be just as prejudiced. People like Preacher and Diesel—hell, some if not half of the people in The Local right now—probably shared racial and religious stereotypes that were so ingrained in them nothing was ever going to change them.

Especially when they were drunk.

And as drunk as he was, he knew enough to let it slide...at least on his first night home.

"Fuck it," he said. "I'm beat to shit."

He ran the flats of his hands across his face as if he had splashed himself with cold water. It took some effort to focus, but at least he wasn't as buzzed as he had been earlier.

He glanced over to the bar where Capt'n Wally was still holding court, regaling people with his stories, probably bragging about his new boat. His face was flushed bright red, and his shining eyes twitched back and forth. By the look of things, the Capt'n was just getting started tying one on. He was knocking back shots of dark rum. Ben was sure that—like so many times while he was growing up—sometime later that night, probably not until two or three in the morning, he'd hear his old man stumbling into the house, muttering curses as he tried to negotiate the stairs. And more than likely, he'd be passed out on the couch in the living room when Ben got up in the morning.

Ben drained what was left of his beer and placed the pint glass down carefully on the table.

"That's it for me."

"C'mon, Gunna," Mike "The Veg" Tomlinson said with a pleading look in his eyes. He leaned close to Ben and blew near-toxic alcohol and halitosis fumes into Ben's face. "I ain't bought you a drink yet."

His eyes were so rimmed with red there was no white showing. The unlit cigarette dangling from his mouth bobbed up and down when he talked.

Don't you dare light that up now, Ben thought, or we'll all go up in flames.

"Sorry, man. I gots to get me some sleep," Ben said in a slur. Before anyone else interfered, he pushed away from the table and stood up. The floor tilted like the deck of a wave-tossed boat, and he placed one hand on Preacher's shoulder to steady himself.

"You aw'right there, bud?" The Veg asked with a hint of concern in his expression. Ben knew that not a damned one of them was in any better condition.

"Yeah…sure. No worries," Ben said. He smiled and nodded, then took a deep breath, hitched up his jeans, and started toward the back door. He nodded a few goodnights to people as he passed, but it was with immense relief that he stepped out onto the landing. The screen door slammed shut behind him, sounding like a gunshot in the night. He jumped, ready to hit the dirt, but then realized where he was and, leaning his head back, took a deep breath of fresh ocean air. The air was cool enough to make him shiver, and he caught the fresh smell of rain in the air. Off to the west, clouds were gathering on the horizon, blotting out the stars.

Sliding his right hand lightly along the weathered railing, he made his way down the steps to the narrow alley that ran between The Local and a small restaurant that changed owners and names about every year or two. The alley was dark, the buildings cutting out the night sky like stencils. It took a while for Ben's eyes to adjust, and for a while, the darkness flickered as if fireworks were going off in the distance. At the foot of the stairs were three or four overflowing trash cans. The stench of rotting garbage was thick enough to make him gag.

He started up the alley, heading toward Main Street. He was drunk enough not to trust his eyesight and coordination on a winding path in the dark. Much safer to walk home under the streetlights. But staying on the street was the long way home. An extra mile, at least. After a brief mental debate, he opted to take the shortcut home like he usually did when coming home drunk from The Local.

The path skirted the edge of the harbor and wound over Miller's Hill and through some neighbors' backyards. Ben was drunker than he cared to admit, so he took a moment or two to look around and get his bearings. The gentle slapping of the waves against the dock pilings and wharf was soothing, and once he was past the garbage cans, he paused and looked around, savoring the night.

No dry, desert heat.

No wind-blown grit that got into everything—your nose, your eyes, your mouth, even the crack of your ass.

No smell of unwashed men and gasoline…of burning rubber and gun oil.

Just clean, fresh ocean air.

Even with the tide out and the smell of rotting seaweed and clam-flats wafting over him, he felt an inexpressible measure of peace and contentment. The moon, looking like a curved sliver of old bone on the horizon, sparkled faintly on the ocean. Overhead, a dusting of stars sprinkled the sky like sugar on black velvet. The party was still going on in The Local at full-bore.

Damn, it's good to be alive, Ben thought, and once again—as they had all night—thoughts of Julia Meadows popped into his head.

"God *damn*," he whispered.

She was the reason he was feeling so good. He squared his shoulders and scanned the narrow strip of trail leading down to and then around the harbor. Out of the shadows, the dirt path glowed dull silver in the faint wash of moonlight. If he wasn't quite so drunk, he thought, when he got home, he should get his car and drive over to Julia's place to see if she was still awake and if she felt like doing something.

"Doing something…" Ben said, chuckling as he shook his head. There was no doubt what he meant by "*doing* something."

He walked a little further down the alley, but before he stepped out of its shadows, a sudden urgency in his bladder made him stop. Stepping off the path onto some rough ground, he unzipped his pants and started to piss against one of the barnacle-encrusted wooden pilings that supported the harbor-side end of The Local. His urine steamed in the cool night air as it splattered against the wood and ran in a foamy current onto the ground. By the time he realized he was pissing uphill, it was too late. Urine ran down the slope and onto his sneakers. He tried to sidestep the stream but lost his balance and almost fell.

When he was finished, he shook himself off and zipped his pants up. As he was turning around, he sensed more than saw a blur of motion in the shadows behind him.

"Hey, wha'zup—" he said once he realized a person was coming down the alleyway toward him.

With the glow of streetlights behind him, the figure was indistinct. All Ben was sure of was that it was a man. Before he could react, the figure, instead of walking past him, lunged at him. Strong hands reached out of the darkness and grabbed him by the shoulders. Ben grunted with surprise as he was spun around. Drunk as he was, the motion felt like it kept going even after he had stopped.

"What the fuck—?" Ben said, his voice slurred. A bubble of gas rose from his stomach into his throat, leaving behind a terrible taste.

The person didn't say a word. He shoved Ben face-first against one of the pilings. His nose banged against the wood hard enough to stagger him, and tiny white stars splashed across his vision. Pain shot through his head like a sudden jolt of electricity.

"Leave her the fuck alone," the man said, his voice a low, animal-like growl. "You understand?"

Too dazed to react, Ben locked his knees, hoping they wouldn't buckle underneath him. He had the sense that—whoever this was—he was purposely disguising his voice so he wouldn't recognize it. All Ben saw was a silhouette, cut out sharply against the night sky.

Ben clenched his hands into fists and was preparing to wheel around and take a swing at his assailant, but before he could do that, something hard—a fist or something even harder, maybe a baseball bat—slammed into the back of his head.

Darkness spread across Ben's vision like a black wave crashing against the shore and shooting high into the sky. His knees went rubbery, and he would have dropped if he hadn't grabbed onto one of the pilings in front of him. When he started to slide down, his legs giving out, barnacles sliced into the palms of his hands, making him yowl.

He sucked in a breath and tried to speak, but the only sound he made sounded like he had thrown up into his mouth and was gargling with it.

"Julia Meadows!" the voice said, rolling like a rumble of thunder in the darkness. "You stay the fuck away from her, or next time—I'll...I'll fucking kill you!"

Ben was still too dazed to react. A high-pitched ringing sound filled his head. When he started to turn around again, something hard rocketed out of the darkness and caught him on the left cheek, snapping his head back. The vertebrae in his neck crackled and snapped like a string of exploding firecrackers. Swirling flashes of white light filled his vision like a flurry of fireflies. Then the sky and earth were swallowed up by darkness. A loud *whooshing* sound filled his ears. He didn't recognize his own heartbeat.

"You *got* it?" the voice said from somewhere far, far away.

Ben tried to nod, but his neck was too stiff to move.

"Yeah...yeah," he said. "I got it."

His voice was little more than a croak. He sagged forward and spread his hands out to clasp the cool, rough surface of the wood, hugging the piling like a lover. He was grateful for its support. It was the only thing keeping him on his feet.

"You fuckin'-A better get it," the voice snarled, and then something sledgehammer hard slammed into his back above his left kidney.

Ben's breath gushed out in an explosive gasp that ended with a high wheezing sound as the night collapsed around him. His knees stiffened, and he took a few jolting sideways steps, but finally his legs gave out, and he crumpled to the ground in a slow *pirouette.*

He never even noticed the pain when the back of his head hit the sandy patch of gravel and crushed seashells.

FOUR

The Crowbar

"Oh, my God! You look terrible. What happened?"

"Would you believe me if I said I walked into a tree last night? Never even saw it coming."

Julia didn't laugh at his attempted humor. Standing in her doorway, she looked at Ben with the most amazing sympathy in her dark eyes. It pained him to see his pain reflected in her face.

"No," she said. "I wouldn't. Are you going to tell me about it?"

Ben winced when he raised a hand and touched the swelling under his left eye.

"I had a little too much to drink last night, is all," he said.

"It looks to me as though you were in a fight."

"Maybe." Ben chuckled. "A little one." He and Julia exchanged glances, and he added, "But you should see the other guy."

He hoped that would end the discussion, and it did...at least for now. Besides the bruise on his cheek, the bump on the back of his head and—especially—the pain in his lower back above the kidney hurt like hell. The tiny cuts on his hands from the barnacles stung as if he'd dipped the open wounds in lime juice.

But it was a gorgeous morning, and Ben wasn't going to let what had happened last night ruin the day. He had been awake long before dawn with another one of the dreams.

The dust swirled in burning, red-brown clouds around him. 30mm bursts from the Apache helicopter overhead fired into the group of insurgents running down the street in front of him. Ben led his platoon in pursuit, making their way through the dust. They passed men with their heads blown to pulp, men with their torsos opened from neck to groin. Suddenly a little Iraqi girl, no more than six years old, walked out of the cloud of dust into a shaft of light. She was crying, and her intestines were spilling onto the ground from her shot-up belly.

Ben bent down to pick her up and take her to a hospital, but her guts coiled tightly around his chest, like an octopus, making it impossible to breathe. She looked at him, staring deeply into his eyes, and then she sank her teeth into his neck. His blood started spurting everywhere, but he had no breath to scream…

Ben had awakened with a roaring shout and leaped out of bed in a cold, sweaty panic. After that, sleep was impossible.

As expected, his father had stumbled home sometime in the early morning hours. Ben wasn't positive, but he thought he'd heard a woman's voice, too. He had no idea if his father or Pete had brought a woman home. He hoped Pete had lucked out after all and caught up with Bunny Dawkins, but Ben didn't bother to check.

In spite of the warning he'd gotten last night, right after he finished with breakfast, he called Julia and asked her out for lunch. To be on the safe side, he decided to pick her up at her house and drive down to Brunswick. There was a little German restaurant on Chamberlain Street—the *Wursthause*—that was one of Ben's favorites.

"Don't you think you should go to the hospital and get checked over?" Julia asked as they walked across the lawn to Ben's old, green Toyota, which was parked in the driveway.

Ben shook his head and said, "Not really," as he opened the door for her and closed it gently after she sat down. Then he got in. When he started up the car, the radio came on. It was tuned to a rock station from Portland, but he lowered the volume so they could talk.

"Your father'll be all right if you're gone for a couple of hours?"

"We have a day nurse come in and stay with him. And—" Julia patted her purse. "I have my cell."

Ben nodded and then backed the car out of the driveway onto the street. Julia and her father lived in a nice house, but it was new and modern with lots of glass for the views, the kind of house most locals—Ben included—always bitched about because so many had been built around town in the last few decades. The old-fashioned term for summer people—especially ones who moved to town permanently—was "rusticators," but these days they were called "flatlanders"...and worse. Everyone around town grumbled about how the flatlanders were ruining the town.

On the drive down Route One to Brunswick, they mostly made small talk about politics and music and movies. Whenever talk came around to his time in Iraq, Ben changed the subject. He noticed that, when he asked about her life and how she had come to live in Maine, other than saying she had been born and raised in Waterbury, Connecticut, she was as elusive about her previous life as he was about his.

One thing he was happy to find was that his initial impression of her had been right. Besides being beautiful, Julia was bright and engaging and funny. She came back with several one-liners that had him laughing. But he also felt a sensuousness lurking below the surface that, given the chance, he was sure would come out. He hoped he would be able to explore this side of her sooner rather than later. In more ways than one, it had been a long, dry spell in Iraq.

"So," she said, "Everyone in The Cove has a nickname. You're Gunner."

"That's *Gunna,*" Ben said with a smile as he exaggerated his Down East accent. "Say it right. Like 'lobstah' and 'chowdah.'"

Julia stared straight ahead. She appeared to be considering something, but then her face suddenly brightened. Turning to him, she said, "So if you were to give me a nickname, what would it be?"

"Oh, I don't know." Ben said after a long pause. "I mean—it's hard to say. I'd have to know you a lot better." He took a breath. "To be honest, most of the nicknames we use are pretty mean-spirited."

"How so?"

"They're meant to...you know, razz people...make fun of them. Like the fat kid in school who's called 'Piggy,' and—"

He stopped himself before he gave Bunny's Dawkin's nickname, "The Organ Grinder," as another example.

"They get started as a way to remind the person about some flaw in their personality or something embarrassing that happened to them. After a while, they stick. Some nicknames...most people can't even remember how people got them."

"So you're saying you can't think of one for me?" Julia asked. Her expression had gone flat, and she stared straight ahead at the road. He noticed the knuckles of her hand clutching her purse were white.

"No…no…I'm just saying…. It's usually not a complimentary thing, is all. I wouldn't want to insult you."

"Or you don't know me well enough…to know what my flaws are."

"I haven't seen any yet," Ben said with a smile. "Then again, we just met yesterday."

Julia returned his smile, making the lines around her mouth deepen. He was filled with a sudden urge to pull over to the side of the road and kiss her.

"So you're saying I'll never get a nickname in town, right?" she said.

Biting his lower lip, Ben shook his head. He didn't want to tell her, but the truth was, he knew she never would get a nickname—at least not one anyone would use to her face. Already, last night at The Local, he had heard her referred to two or three times as "that flatlander pussy" or the "out of state cunt."

"You pretty much have to be born and raised here to get one, I guess," he finally said.

Julia nodded her understanding, but her smile quickly vanished. "So no matter *how long* I live here…even if I were to marry someone from town…"

Ben shifted uneasily at that.

"…I'd never really be accepted?"

"It's not that, exactly," Ben said, but then they made eye contact, and he shrugged and said, "Yeah. You're probably right." He took a breath and exhaled to release the tension. "What can I say? It's the way it is."

They soon brushed past the topic of nicknames, but Ben sensed that she was genuinely hurt thinking the people would never really accept her as part of the town. For the rest of the drive, they talked about other things, and the mood had lightened by the time they got to Brunswick.

They found a parking space on Chamberlain Street right in front of the restaurant. Julia commented that it might be a bad sign for a restaurant, since it was lunchtime. If the place was any good, shouldn't it be hard to find parking close to it? Ben insisted he led a charmed life, and they were lucky not to have to hassle with parking. Besides, the Bowdoin students had all gone home for the summer. The restaurant was so popular during the school year, you needed to make reservations well in advance.

The small bell on a spring above the door tinkled when they entered. The sign at the front of the restaurant read: *SEAT YOURSELF*, so they chose a table in the corner, by the front window looking out on the street. Their waitress, a young woman with her blonde hair done up in Princess Leia buns, came over to their table. Ben ordered a beer, and Julia asked for some red wine. After their drinks arrived, they ordered some appetizers and were settling back to talk some more when a voice called out, "Yo, Benny. Benny Brown. Back from Iraq all in one piece, I see."

Ben turned around, his eyes widening when he saw Richie "The Crowbar" Sullivan coming toward them. As always, Richie was dressed like a GQ model…if GQ models had faces that looked like a hundred miles of bad road. Today, he was wearing pressed beige Dockers and a brand new pair of white New Balance sneakers. His turquoise golf shirt fit his muscular frame tight enough to show that he didn't have an ounce of fat on his belly. He was tanned and wore his thinning gray hair swept straight back so it touched the back collar of his shirt. His biceps rippled beneath his tanned skin like lengths of knotted rope, the veins bulging as he held his hand out for Richie to shake.

"How's it feel to be home?"

Ben smiled and nodded. "Fine…just fine."

Richie raised an eyebrow. "You sure about that? Looks like someone mopped the floor with your face."

Ben forced a laugh. "Nothing like good times with old friends."

"Fuckin' war," Richie said. Grimacing, he shook his head and looked like he was about to spit onto the floor. "Never should'a gone there in the first place. Saddam wasn't much. We should'a cleaned out that numb fuck bin Laden in Afghanistan, first." As if noticing Julia for the first time, Richie glanced at her and said, "Pardon my French, ma'am." He lowered his eyes and bowed.

Ben smiled to himself when Julia didn't offer the French word for *fuck*.

"So how's your old man doing? How'd the launch go yesterday?"

"Fine...It was a good time. You should've come."

"I was gonna be there, but..." Richie held both hands palms up. "Stuff came up. You know how it is."

Ben nodded even though he could only guess at what "stuff" Richie was involved with. When it came to The Crowbar, it was best to be polite and not pry too deeply. Richie was a nice guy...generous to a fault, but the less Ben had to do with him, the better.

"It's a nice boat," Ben said, simply to make conversation.

"Ought'a be," Richie said. "I paid enough for the fucker." He glanced again at Julia and said, "*Pardonay moi* again."

"No problem," Julia said smiling at Richie. Ben shook his head. You had to hand it to Richie; he had a way with the ladies. But he was genuinely taken aback by what Richie had said. He had paid for the *Abby-Rose*? No. He financed it, more likely.

Ben was wondering if maybe Richie shouldn't have let that slip, but he knew Richie well enough to know he never let anything slip without intending to.

Ben knew his father would have had a problem getting a bank loan for his new boat after losing the *Sheila B.* last fall. The first night Ben was home, Wally had gone on and on about his looming financial problems. The sad truth was, most fishermen—no matter how good their credit, prospects, or reputation around town—found it pretty much impossible to get a bank loan for a new boat after they'd lost one at sea. He was considered an "unlucky" captain. With insurance sky-high and the price of fuel going up just about daily, the lobster industry was all but dying.

At the time, Ben hadn't given it much thought, but now he was sure his father had been forced—if "forced" was the right word—into dealing with Richie.

And Ben knew what *that* meant.

It meant a few more trips, preferably on foggy days or at night out into international waters to pick up bales of weed and maybe a few packages of cocaine and heroin that he would offload in a sheltered cove later that night. His stomach twisted at the thought of his father being obligated in any way to a man like Richie. Not that Richie was a bad guy. He just had certain expectations if you dealt with him, and the consequences of not paying him back had serious repercussions.

"So who's the young lady?" Richie asked after looking at Julia again and studying her more carefully.

It was a rare day—like today—that Richie didn't have his wife or another gorgeous woman hanging on his arm. The last thing Ben wanted to do was make it easy for Richie to turn the charm on Julia.

"Friend of mine. Julia Meadows. Julia. This is Richie Sullivan."

"Pleased to meet you," Julia said in an uncharacteristic sweet voice as she extended her hand. Their eyes met and held for longer than Ben liked as they shook hands.

"Likewise," Richie said. "So you live in The Cove?"

"I moved to town recently…to help out my father."

Richie smacked his lips and shook his head.

"Yeah. Gettin' old. Ain't it a bitch? Like they say—now it takes me all night to do what I used to do all night, if you catch my drift."

"I certainly do," Julia said with a wry smile.

Ben couldn't decide if she was actually intrigued by Richie or if she was mocking him, but he admired the way she gave it right back to him. She had spunk and clearly was confident that she could hold her own with Richie.

It occurred to him that the way he got jumped last night had all the hallmarks of a gentle Crowbar warning. He watched and listened as Julie and Richie bantered back and forth for a bit. His eyes narrowed as he wondered if they knew each other much better than either of them was letting on.

"Well," Richie said. He raised his arms and stretched them back and rotated his head from side to side until something in his neck popped. "I don't wanna interrupt youse any more than I already have."

He stuck his hand into his trousers' pocket and came up with a roll of bills in a money clip. After licking his thumb, he peeled off a fresh hundred-dollar bill and smacked it onto the table in front of Ben.

"Lunch is on me," he said, smiling as he looked back and forth between Ben and Julia. Ben noticed that his gaze lingered a little longer than necessary on Julia.

"I appreciate it, Richie. Seriously. But I can't take your money."

"'Course you can. It's the least I can do for you after what you done, putting your ass on the line over there." He hooked his thumb over his shoulder as though indicating the general direction of Iraq.

Ben was about to refuse again, but he knew Richie wouldn't back down. It wasn't his style. Even if Ben stuffed the bill back into Richie's pocket, Richie would drop it on the restaurant host and tell him to cover Ben's tab and keep the change. They didn't call him The Crowbar for nothing.

"Thanks…thank you," Ben said as he slid the bill off the table, folded it in half, and put it in his pants pocket. "You really don't have to."

"But I just did."

With that, Richie gave them each a quick nod and turned around. He strode out of the place, nodding to the host and waitress standing off to one side like he was the boss and owner. Knowing Richie, the *Wursthause* very well could be one of the "interests" he had that brought him up from Rhode Island from time to time, especially in the summer.

Neither Ben nor Julia mentioned Richie again until after their main course arrived, and Ben had ordered another mug of German beer. Julia was still sipping on her glass of red wine. Then, while she was trying to figure out how to get a grip on the huge bratwurst sandwich in front of her, Julia said, "He's quite the character, isn't he?"

"Who's that?"

"Richie."

"You mean 'The Crowbar?'"

"Is that his nickname?…Crowbar?"

Ben nodded, then forked a slice of spicy German sausage and raised it to his mouth. He took a small bite and chewed thoughtfully, savoring the explosion of flavors.

"How'd he come by that name?" she asked, but before Ben could tell her, she waved her hand in front of him. "No…. Maybe I don't want to know."

"It's not what you think," Ben said, still chewing sausage.

"You mean the people he has disagreements with don't end up getting beaten to death with a crowbar?"

"Now that you mention it…" Ben let it hang there for a second or two, then smiled. "No. He got that nickname because he's so smooth and hard as iron he can pry anything out of anyone."

"He does look like he's in good shape."

"He takes pride in how he looks. For sure. And—yeah, he's been known to resort to violence...allegedly...from time to time to settle certain...issues."

Ben got a chill, thinking that now his father was in serious debt to Richie, it didn't bode well.

"Allegedly."

Ben nodded and swallowed, closing his eyes as the flavors from the meat filled his mouth.

"You figured it out, right?" Ben asked before taking a long sip of beer.

For a moment or two, Julia looked at him, confused; then she slowly nodded.

"He's mobbed up," Ben said. "He's got his fingers in a lot of things around The Cove—drugs, real estate, a fish company, a laundry service. You name it."

"A laundry service?"

"There's a lot of money in that. Take a guess who all of the local motels go to for laundry service if they want to stay in business."

"Sheesh. He's that powerful?"

Ben nodded and took another sip of beer, letting it linger in his mouth so the carbonation tickled his tongue before he swallowed.

"And then some. Richie Sullivan is not someone you want to mess with or ever say no to if you can help it."

"I got the feeling that was the case by the way he forced that money on you."

Ben waved a hand at her. Then, pointing his fork at the sausage on his plate, said, "This is really good. You want a bite?"

Julia considered and then nodded, so Ben speared a piece of sausage with his fork and held it out across the table. She leaned forward, her hands braced on the edge of the table, so he could feed her. He was enamored of the way her eyes narrowed when she opened her mouth to take the food.

"Ummm..." she said, chewing slowly. "That is *good.*" She sat back and blotted her mouth with her napkin.

They ate for a while in silence until Ben said, "The thing about Richie is, he'll get hundreds more in interest from my old man every month."

"Because of the boat loan?"

Julia had apparently decided not even to try to lift her sandwich. She picked up her fork and knife, and started carving a small piece off the side.

"Yeah," Ben said, feeling a deep-bone chill inside, and—for the first time in his life—he realized that he was genuinely worried about his father. "Because of the boat loan."

It was the last week of May, so school wasn't out, and vacationers hadn't started moving to town in great numbers yet, so traffic was relatively sparse on the drive up Route One back to Catawamkeag Cove. Ben knew some back roads that would avoid the worst of the backups, but today, even the bottleneck at the bridge in Wiscasset wasn't bad. They sailed right through town.

"Red's Eats," she said when she noticed a small shack on the side of the road before the bridge.

"A classic," Ben said.

"You ever eat there?"

"Can't say as I have. Us locals avoid the tourist traps."

As they drove, they chatted about a variety of other things, laughing at each other's jokes and getting downright serious when Julia expressed how worried she was about how poorly her father was doing. In the back of his mind, Ben couldn't get rid of the nagging worry that his father was in deep trouble, too. Maybe even more than he realized. No matter how bad things were, owing The Crowbar any amount of money was going to make things worse.

But no matter how much he told himself not to let that encounter ruin the time he had with Julia, it was as though a dark cloud had shifted in front of the sun even though the afternoon outside the car was warm and bright.

"So," he said. The steering wheel played loosely in his hands as he navigated the road. "You probably have to get back home and check in on your dad, huh?"

Julia slipped her tongue out and licked her upper lip as she nodded, but Ben caught a look in her eyes—at least he *thought* he did—that said she would much rather spend the rest of the day with him.

That's what he hoped, anyway.

His throat constricted and his heart felt too large for his chest when he turned the corner onto her street, and her house came into view.

"I had a good time," Ben said as he slowed for the turn into the driveway. He stopped about halfway to the garage and slipped the car into *park*.

"Me, too," Julia said. She kept her eyes downcast.

Ben wished he could know what she was thinking.

"We'll have to do it again soon, but…what about Kathy?"

"Who?"

"Kathy Brackett. I heard you and she were an item before she married Dwight."

"'An item?' That's so…quaint."

He smiled and gave her a little jab on the arm.

"You know what I mean," Julia said. Her tone of voice was odd—low and serious and maybe tinged with jealousy.

"You were talking with her before the launch, and it looked like—" She heaved a sigh and kept staring downward. "Let's just say it looked like you were still more than friends."

"She's married, you know. And has a kid."

Ben almost choked on that and wondered if Julia had also heard that he was the father.

"And no matter what you might have heard around town, I'm not what they call a…a 'sport fucker,' if you'll pardon the expression."

"So you're *not* a *Gunna*?"

Ben fought back a rising surge of frustration. He wished he could find the words to say exactly what he was trying to say, but he was so confused…. *She* confused him. His mind was blank.

"That was back in high school, 'kay?" he said. "Truth is, I'd much rather spend time with you."

Julia raised her head and looked at him, blinking her eyes rapidly as though holding back tears. He was being drawn into the warm, brown depths of her eyes like a drowning man.

"Maybe we can go to a movie or something," Ben said. He wished everything he said didn't sound so damned stupid.

"Yeah…I'd like that," Julia replied.

Ben twisted in his seat so he was facing her squarely. His heart was racing as he looked at her. It was all he could do not to lean over…hug her…and kiss her; but he held back, telling himself it wouldn't be right.

Not yet.

Maybe with time.

"Thanks again for lunch," Julia said, reaching for the door handle, "I really liked the restaurant…and meeting The Crowbar."

"Word to the wise." Ben raised his hand and pointed a cautionary finger at her. "If I was you, I wouldn't use that name around town."

"What, you think he'd have me whacked or something?"

"Stranger things have happened."

The surprised expression on her face let him know that she got it.

Acting purely on impulse, Ben reached out and stroked her hair. A spark of…something jumped between them. She turned and looked at him, her expression softening as their eyes locked. A strand of hair shifted forward and hung down over one eye. All Ben could think about was how amazing it would be to wake up some morning, roll over in bed, and see her lying there next to him, her dark hair fanned out across the pillow.

"I don't usually kiss on the first date," Ben said, grinning crookedly.

"This was a date?"

Julia laughed, and Ben felt the tension break, but then—without warning—she leaned toward him. Narrowing her eyes, she placed her right hand on the side of his head, touching him lightly behind the jaw. Without saying a word, she applied enough pressure to draw his face close to hers. Her mouth opened, and then their lips met in a long, moist kiss. Her tongue flicked teasingly between his lips.

Surprised by the intense passion in her kiss, Ben almost drew back, but then he shifted and wrapped his left arm around her, inhaling sharply as he drew her close and crushed her against his chest. Her breasts flattened against him, and the heat of her body was intoxicating. He felt himself stiffening as her right hand shifted down to his leg and gently rubbed the meat of his upper thigh.

Ben had no idea how long the kiss lasted. Later on, while driving home, he remembered something Mr. Perry had said in science class when he was trying to explain Einstein's theory of relativity.

Placing your hand on a hot stove for even a few seconds, he said, can seem like an hour, while kissing a beautiful woman for an hour can seem like mere seconds. For now, Ben was lost in the embrace as the kiss lengthened, their passion growing. Her breathing came hard as she gasped for breath. When they finally broke the kiss, and Julia pulled back, she gazed at him with a dark, smoldering look.

Ben realized he was smiling at her and must look like an idiot.

"Wow," he said, his voice husky and constricted in his throat. It was difficult to breathe. The air didn't go deep enough into his chest.

Julia's smile widened, but then—without another word—she twisted around, snapped the car door open, and stepped out onto the grass. She hesitated with the car door open and leaned down, staring at him without saying a word. Their eyes met and locked. Ben licked his upper lip, tasting the salt that lingered there. His body was flushed, pulsing with excitement.

"See yah," Julia finally said. With that, she swung the door shut, turned on one foot, and all but ran up the walkway to the front door of the house.

"I sure hope so," Ben called after her, but the passenger's window was up, and he wasn't sure she heard him.

He watched as she ducked inside with one last quick glance and a wave over her shoulder, and then the screen door *whooshed* shut behind her. He sat there for a long time, wishing…hoping she would come back out, but the door remained closed. There was no sign of activity inside the house.

He reached up and rubbed his mouth, still amazed that they had kissed. He shook his head, started up the car, and backed out of the driveway to the street.

He didn't see Julia in any of the windows, but he was sure—he hoped—she was looking out, watching him drive away. He convinced himself that he could feel her gaze on the back of his neck, making his skin prickle.

As he drove home, he kept thinking, Umm, yeah…I want me some more of that!

The smell of disinfectant and human waste assailed Ben's nostrils the instant he and Louise stepped through the front door of

"Grave's Edge." He blew his breath out quickly like he'd taken a sip of hot soup.

Holding the door open, he watched as a young woman wearing a hospital smock with a bright floral pattern pushed an elderly woman in a wheelchair down the hall. The old woman, who couldn't have weighed more than eighty pounds, looked up at Ben. Her eyes had a milky white film and were sinking into her head like marbles in bread dough. Her mouth drooped open on one side, and a string of drool hung from her lower lip to her emaciated chest. Ben assumed she was smiling at him, and he tried to smile back. He waited until they had wheeled past him before turning to Louise.

"Jesus, this place is depressing," he whispered.

Louise nodded but kept staring straight ahead. He thought maybe this was her way of dealing with it—to shut it all out.

A dozen or so other residents perched in wheelchairs or scuffing along with walkers were gathered in the front foyer. Most of them were staring off at some distant horizon only they could see. One old man shot Ben a toothless grin and said, "Ahh. Comin' in for your meds again, huh, Johnny?"

Ben looked at him, trying to place a name with the withered face. The man looked vaguely familiar, but Ben drew a blank.

"Well, well, well, if it isn't Benjamin Brown in the flesh."

Ben immediately recognized the voice. Agnes Appleby, an old friend of his mother's, was seated on a stool behind the counter, reading some pages in a file folder. She closed the file, marking her place with her forefinger as she stood up.

"Mrs. A," Ben said. "How are you?"

"I can't complain," Mrs. Appleby said. Her smile exposed a top row of tiny, yellowed teeth, not much more than stubs. Her hazel eyes sparkled behind the lenses of her too-thick glasses. "Howdy, Louise. Here to see your ma, are yah?"

Ben shrugged and said, "How's she doing?"

The smile melted away from Mrs. Appleby's face, and her shoulders slumped. Her sun-tanned face went a few shades paler as she looked away for a moment.

"As well as can be expected, I guess. But truth to tell—she's declined quite a bit since you've been gone."

Ben glanced at Louise as if to ask if she thought the staff should talk so candidly to family members, especially with other patients close by. Wouldn't it depress them all the more to hear such negative talk? Or did they know and accept their fate? Or maybe they were so far gone it didn't matter what anyone said. On some level, they must all know this is the end and none of them would get out of here alive.

Ben and Louise's mother and Mrs. Appleby had been best friends since grade school. The stories his mother used to tell them about things she and "Aggie" had done together, growing up in the late forties and early fifties, could have filled a book. It struck Ben as patently unfair that his mother, who was still in her early sixties, would be stricken with early onset Alzheimer's while someone the same age looked perfectly healthy and full of life.

Yeah, Ben thought, *and who told you life is fair?* His father's words echoed in his mind as he looked around and saw the stark reality of these people at the end of their lives. He thought of how life ended in Iraq—sudden and bloody, while here it was by decay...and by inches.

"Let me walk you down to her room," Mrs. Appleby said. She placed the file folder she had been reading onto the desk and came around the edge of the counter. Then she turned and strode purposefully down the corridor to the left of the desk, leading the way. Wending their way between more residents in wheelchairs and walkers, Ben and Louise followed a step or two behind. She moved fast.

"She should be in her room," Mrs. Appleby said. "But—well, as you know, Louise, she's quite the wanderer."

Ben shot a questioning look at his sister, but Louise shifted her eyes sideways. Either she didn't catch it or else she was ignoring him.

"I want you to be prepared, Ben," Mrs. Appleby said. "You haven't seen her in a while and—well...I don't want you to be too surprised, is all."

Ben was about to say that he was confident he could handle pretty much anything after what he'd seen in Iraq, but suddenly he wasn't so sure. He didn't say anything until they arrived at the door. He was surprised to see a photograph taped to the door, one of his mother that had been taken when she was much younger, probably not long after she graduated from high school. She was standing outside her family home on Main Street wearing a sleeveless shirt and laughing at the camera. Her long hair fell in waves to her shoulders. Ben had never realized how pretty his mother had been back then.

"Why the old picture?" he asked, tapping it lightly.

Mrs. Appleby hooked her forefinger and scraped back and forth beneath her nose.

"People with Alzheimer's often don't recognize recent photos of themselves, but they do recognize themselves when they were much younger. Their memories get stuck at certain ages, usually in the late teens or early twenties."

"Really?" Ben said. He had never heard that before, but he guessed anything was possible.

Without knocking, Mrs. Appleby pushed the door open and walked in ahead of them. They followed behind. The medicinal smell in the room was like a solid wall. The shades were drawn, and the room was cast in gloom. It took Ben a moment to realize the bed was empty.

"See?" Mrs. Appleby said as she walked to the window and drew the shades. The sudden blast of light hurt Ben's eyes. "She's off somewhere."

She shook her head as though gravely disappointed and walked past Ben and Louise and out the door. Once in the corridor, she cast a glance up and down the hallway, and then started back toward the front desk.

"Does this happen a lot?" Ben asked Louise as they followed along behind. Mrs. Appleby was moving fast, and they had to hustle to keep up.

"It's been kind of a problem," Louise said keeping her voice low, like she was in a library.

"Kind of? And they don't keep tabs on her?"

Louise shook her head.

"She can't go very far. There's always someone at the front desk, and the other doors are locked. You'd set off an alarm if you opened them."

"I'm not worried about me. I'm worried about Mom. It's not safe for her to wander around like this."

By this time, they were back in the front foyer. They followed Mrs. Appleby down another short hallway to another door. She shouldered it open and entered. Even before he went inside, Ben could hear the blare of a TV show. It sounded like a soap opera. When he entered the room, his eyes darted from side to side, and for an instant, he felt like he was on patrol and had busted into the home of an Iraqi family.

In the flickering blue wash of light from the TV, Ben saw only four people in the room. Two women were sitting side by side in wheelchairs, their faces enraptured as they stared up at the TV screen. An old man was seated on a couch. He was watching something on the ceiling with as much intensity as the two ladies were watching TV. The fourth person was in the far corner, her back partially turned to the door as if she was trying to hide in the corner but had nowhere to go.

"There you are, Lil," Mrs. Appleby said in a quiet but cheerful tone. "You have visitors."

The woman in the corner turned away so she was facing the wall. Her shoulders shivered like she was standing outside in the cold.

"Hey, Ma," Ben said, taking a few cautious steps toward her. She reminded him of a frightened animal, and he didn't want to spook her. He looked first at his sister and then at Mrs. Appleby as if asking for instructions. Neither one of them said or did anything, so he turned back to his mother.

Her hair was shorter than he remembered. It glowed silvery blue in the light of the TV. Short, thin wisps fanned out like windblown spider webs. She was hunched over, but it was obvious she had lost at least twenty pounds if not more since he'd last seen her. She raised her left arm, which was no thicker than the handle of a baseball bat, and covered her face with her hand, trying to hide behind it.

I can't see you, so you can't see me.

"How you doing there, Ma?" Ben asked.

He took a few steps closer, but he had a strong impulse to turn and leave. He couldn't believe what he was seeing. How could this be his mother? It wasn't just the physical change. If his mother had been herself, if she had been mentally there, her face would have lit up, seeing him.

"Lou and I brought some pictures from the boat launch to show yah," Ben said. He turned to Louise, but she made no move to take her digital camera from her purse.

"Do I know you?" Lilly asked, her eyes widening as she turned around and stared at Ben. The whites were glazed with distance.

"Ma. It's me. Benjamin."

"Benjamin?"

She looked as though the name simply didn't register. When she cocked her head to one side, she reminded him of a bird, looking for a worm or bug in the grass.

"Hey! You wanna keep it down?" one of the women watching TV said, glaring at them.

"Sorry," Ben said, but just as quickly, Mrs. Appleby said, "Now Susan. You mind your manners." Then she moved over to Lilly and placed a hand on her shoulder.

"Benny's come to visit you, Lilly," she said. "What do you say we all go down to your room so we can talk?"

Ben's heart was breaking as he watched his mother's reaction. She looked at Mrs. Appleby, the distant glaze filming her eyes over like a skim of ice as she struggled to put this all together.

"Benny's here?" she said, and then she looked all around the room as if she didn't see him standing a few feet in front of her. Without a word, Ben moved closer and made as if to hug her, but she shied away from him.

"Let's go see Benny," she said. "Is he waiting in my room?"

"I'm right—" Ben started to say, but Mrs. Appleby hooked her arm and led her gently away. Lilly's feet, in pink fur-lined slippers, scuffed on the carpeted floor.

"That's right. He came here to show you some pictures."

"Pictures," Lilly said. "I like pictures."

They managed to get Lilly to leave the TV room, but she was reluctant to walk down the corridor back to her room. Her eyes kept shifting from side to side like a trapped animal looking for an escape route that wasn't there. Finally, with some gentle coaxing from Mrs. Appleby and Louise, they got her past the front desk and heading down the hall to her room.

In the hallway, staying a few steps behind her, Ben took the time to study his mother. It staggered him to see how much she had changed in so short a time. He remembered her as tanned and fit-looking from working out in the yard all her life, but now her skin was almost translucent, like there was a layer of clear jelly below the surface. Thin blue veins lined her arms and the backs of her hands like twisted strands of faded yarn. Her fingernails had no nail polish, and the cuticles had grown halfway up the nail, making them look like talons.

Once they were back in her room, Mrs. Appleby directed Lilly to the easy chair next to the window. She sat down and looked at each of them as though she had no idea who any of them were. Then she focused on the wall across the room, her eyes on some middle distance like her memory was a book, and she was flipping through the pages, trying to read. Her eyelids made faint clicking sounds when she blinked.

She smacked her lips as though preparing to say something, but then she stopped. Her lips were cracked, and a thin line of bubbly drool ran down her chin from one corner of her mouth. Mrs. Appleby snapped a tissue from the dispenser on the table next to the bed and wiped it away.

"I thought I'd drop by and see how you were doing," Ben said. "I just got back from the war."

"The war," Lilly said, nodding but looking as though she had absolutely no understanding. She inhaled slowly through her nose, the air making a watery wheezing sound in her chest.

Ben cast a worried glance at Mrs. Appleby, who regarded him with an expression of deep sympathy. She shrugged and said softly, "We do the best we can, but..." She let her voice drift away like a wind-blown leaf.

Ben nodded, finding it almost impossible to look at his mother.

How could this be the woman who had raised him—the tough fisherman's wife who took no guff and gave as good as she got? The avid gardener who could all but make roses grow in beach sand? The woman who was in constant motion from the time she got up until the time she went to bed, usually well past midnight. Her life had been filled with raising three kids...cooking and cleaning and sewing and PTA and church suppers and, at least once a week, dragging Wally home from The Local dead drunk. Most of all, how could this woman, whose bones looked as fragile as a bird's, be the same person who walloped him but good whenever he wised off... and then tenderly stroked his hair from his forehead and kissed him when he woke up from a bad dream?

"I just got back from...from Iraq," Ben said, resigned, now, to the fact that she simply wasn't registering anything that was going on around her.

He shifted nervously from one foot to the other. He wanted so much to reach out and hug her, but he was genuinely afraid that even the lightest touch would bruise her.

"We have some pictures...from the boat launch yesterday," Louise said. She started digging in her purse for her camera.

"A boat launch.... What boat launch?"

"Yesterday. Remember I told you about it?" Louise spoke with patient understanding, and Ben realized that she was much more used to this. "Dad's new boat, the *Abby-Rose*."

"Abby Rose...I used to know a girl named Abby Rose."

"This is the boat. Dad named it after Uncle Ed's granddaughter," Louise said.

"You remember Uncle Ed, don't you?" Ben offered.

"You have an Uncle Ed, too?" Lilly said, looking intently at Ben. "What a coincidence."

"It's the same Uncle Ed...Pops' brother," Ben said, but he knew, even as he said it, that it was futile to try to get through. All he could think of was the line about how the lights were on in the house, but nobody was home. His mother was gone.

"Good God, you'd think—" his mother said, her voice was as faint as a gust of wind, but that was all. She took a breath, deeper than before, and slowly rotated her head from side to side.

"What's that, Ma?" Ben said, coming a step closer.

"You'd think...that son-of-a-bitch would come and visit more often." She took another thin breath. "He should visit from time to time."

"Who's that, Ma?" Louise asked. "You mean Pops?"

"No. Ed!" Lilly snapped. She pursed her lips so tightly they looked like a bloodless wound. Ben glanced at Mrs. Appleby as if she could provide some assistance, but all she did was smile grimly and shake her head.

"Lousy son-of-a-bitch," Lilly said, and then she leaned her head back and closed her eyes, keeping them shut for so long Ben was suddenly afraid she had died right there in front of him. He jumped, genuinely shocked when his mother opened her eyes again and stared at him. Then she leaned so far forward in the chair Ben was afraid she was going to pitch on the floor.

"Come on, Ma," Louise said. "You know Uncle Ed's been dead for years."

"You have an Uncle Ed, too?" Lilly said, then she shifted her gaze to Ben and, in a low, conspiratorial voice, said, "You know they're all lesbians working here?" Her eyes twitched back and forth as though she couldn't quite control them. "You know that, don't you?"

Ben was at a loss. He had never heard his mother talk like this before.

"I hear 'em," Lilly said. Leaning forward, she placed her elbows on her knees and folded her hands as if in prayer. "You think I don't? You bet'cha ass I do. I hear 'em talking late at night…talking to each other and doing…doing *lesbian* things."

"I—umm, I don't think that's quite what's going on here, Ma," Ben said, thinking Louise or Mrs. Appleby could jump in any time now to take the pressure off him. It was tearing his heart apart to see his mother like this, and it was damned frustrating that there wasn't a thing he or anyone else could say or do to help.

Her mind was already gone. Now it was simply a matter of time, waiting for her body to catch up…and die.

As tears filmed his eyes, his view of the room wavered. The air was suddenly too hot…as stifling as the desert.

He looked behind him at the door and was overcome with the urge to get out.

"Well, I—ah…" Ben shifted his weight from one foot to the other. "I ought to get going. I just dropped by to say a quick hi."

Louise shot him a look of irritation as he began backing up toward the door, barely looking where he was going.

"I thought you'd want to see the pictures before we go?" Louise said.

"Pictures? Of what?"

"The boat launch," Louise said.

"Maybe we should come back later, Lou," Ben said, "when she's feeling better."

"That might be a good idea," Mrs. Appleby said, her voice low and mild as she looked at Louise. Then, to Ben, she said, "She has much better days than this sometimes."

"Does she even know who I am?" he asked, incredulous.

Mrs. Appleby's eyebrows shot up like two inverted commas.

"You can never tell," she said as if that would end the discussion instead of begin it.

Ben realized he was talking about his mother as if she wasn't even in the same room, but—in some important ways—she wasn't.

A sense of unreality swept through him as he moved closer, reached out, and patted his mother gently on the shoulder. Just once. It was like touching a plastic bag filled with dry bones.

"I'll stop by tomorrow and see how you're doing, Ma, okay?"

Lilly had no response. She looked at him vacantly, as if she had no idea what he'd just said. Once again, her gaze was fixed on the opposite wall as if she was expecting something to happen. It was impossible to know what.

Ben turned his back to his mother and strode to the door. Louise and Mrs. Appleby followed behind him, joining him in the corridor. Mrs. Appleby closed the door quietly behind her and lowered her gaze as she slowly shook her head from side to side.

"Sweet Mother of God," Ben said.

"It's difficult, I know," Mrs. Appleby said, obviously pained as the three of them walked back down the corridor to the front desk. "Alzheimer's is a terrible, terrible disease."

The day was almost psychedelically sharp as he and Louise walked outside into the clear, bright sunlight. They were both silent until Ben shouted at her, "Why didn't you or someone tell me how bad off she was?"

"I didn't want you to worry," Louise said. "I figured you had enough shit to deal with over there."

He knew what she meant by "over there," but that didn't stop the rush of anger. He crossed the parking lot to his car. When he got to it, he let out a low, strangled moan that came from the bottom of his gut. He clenched his fist and slammed it against the roof of the car hard enough to dent the metal.

"Jesus, Lou!" He looked at her, feeling helpless. "Promise you'll shoot me if I ever get that bad, okay? Just fucking shoot me!"

Louise looked at him, her eyes full of tears, and said nothing.

When he got into the car and sat down behind the steering wheel, inexpressible sadness filled him like a flood of water. He was shaking and had to wait before trying to get the key into the ignition. He was wondering if Louise or anyone else on the planet loved him enough to do that if he ever needed it.

FIVE

Night Trip

"Yah think you're making enough noise there, Chucklenuts?"

Capt'n Wally stood at the helm, glaring at his son, Pete, who was about to cast off. Pete froze with the rope in his hand and looked up at the granite wharf. It was late at night. A string of streetlights cast a powdery blue haze along the rutted dirt road that led past the dock to the fishing sheds with their bait barrels and teetering stacks of lobster pots. The smell of rotting bait was thick in the air. The sounds were the gentle whisper of waves running underneath the floating dock and slapping against the hull of the *Abby-Rose,* and the distant whine of traffic on Route One.

"You don't think you'll wake up half the town when you start up the engine?" Pete asked.

Without seeing his face, Pete knew that his father was still scowling. He dropped the mooring line onto the deck while holding onto the gunwales with one hand.

"That can't be helped," Wally said, and with that, he hit the starter. The diesel engine rumbled softly as water churned out from underneath the stern in a boiling froth.

"Get a move on," Capt'n Wally snapped, and Pete vaulted into the boat. A second later, Capt'n Wally revved the engine, almost knocking him to the deck as he pulled away from the dock.

"Gotta blow off the fumes," Wally said. Pete wondered if by "fumes" he meant the boat's engine or himself as Wally fetched a full fifth of rum from a compartment. With one hand, he spun the cap off and tossed his head back, gulping down several mouthfuls. Smacking his lips, he wiped his mouth with the back of his wrist.

"There.... That'll take off the edge."

"You gonna turn on your running lights?" Pete asked.

Wally didn't dignify the question with an answer.

Pete never liked being on board a boat at night. It was bad enough heading out on foggy days, but in the darkness—even in a boat equipped with up-to-date electronics—his orientation always got fouled up. He wished he had inherited his father's ability to dead reckon. At times, Wally's abilities seemed almost supernatural, but Pete still wondered if it wasn't just that his father was damned lucky.

After maneuvering carefully between some boats, with the running lights still off, Wally gunned the engine. The boat was moving well above the harbor speed limit, and before long they were in the channel, heading out to sea. Pete cast an anxious glance back at the shore, wondering if a Coast Guard patrol had seen them leave. If they had, they would immediately be suspicious of a boat heading out without running lights. Pete feared the night might end badly.

"Where we headed?" Pete asked, shouting to be heard above the steady growl of the engine. Salt spray flew from the bow of the boat as it cut into the chop. It peppered the windshield until the boat leveled off.

Capt'n Wally said nothing as he stared straight ahead, his jaw tensed, his teeth set after he took another swig of rum. Pete thought he hadn't heard him but, more likely, he was ignoring him.

Fuck you, Pete thought but didn't say.

He was thinking how nice it would be to have a slug or two of rum himself to bolster his courage. He'd already told his father that he wasn't too keen about going on this run tonight, but Capt'n Wally had made it clear that he was going. He needed him. Even after Pete told his father about the talk he'd heard that there was a new DEA agent in the area who was squeezing everyone's balls, his father wasn't deterred. They'd make this run and dozens more like it all through the summer and into the fall. If Capt'n Wally had a new boat to pay off, the quickest way to do that was to bring in as many kilos of weed and other drugs as he could. Too bad for the Capt'n, but Pete bitterly resented that his father was dragging his ass out on another one of these miserable night runs.

Why did he always have to do all the grunt work?

Why not Ben?

Now that he was out of the Army, Ben was going to have to start pulling his weight. Sooner or later, G.I. Fucking Joe would have to put away his glory and get a goddamned job and stop freeloading. If he thought he was welcome to stay at the house and not contribute, then he had another think coming.

And Ben's snot-ass behavior yesterday gave Pete another reason to want to bring the hero down a couple of pegs.

Scowling, Pete hunched down and fished a pack of cigarettes from his jacket pocket. He shook one out and, cupping his hand to protect the lighter from the wind, lit up. As he straightened up, he exhaled hard and watched the puff of blue smoke dissolve into the darkness. A feeling of loneliness welled up inside him, and he thought about his girl. Except she wasn't his girl…not yet.

He turned to look at Capt'n Wally's back as the old man navigated a steady course out to sea.

It bothered Pete that his old man never talked to him unless he needed him to help out without something…usually a thankless, miserable task like this. And Pete knew he would do whatever his father asked of him because while Ben might be the hero, Pete was the dutiful son…the one who didn't leave home…the one who stayed behind in The Cove and kept the family business going. Not that anyone appreciated it.

"Screw it," Pete muttered as he took another drag and then snapped the cigarette away. It corkscrewed into the darkness and then was gone.

"What you say?" Wally asked, barely glancing over his shoulder.

"Nothing," Pete replied.

The two men said little else as they passed the bell buoy to starboard and took a southeast bearing. Pete came closer and watched when his father turned on the GPS and other navigational systems. His father's face glowed a ghastly green in the light from the screen, but the lights kept flickering and, before long, Wally was cursing.

"What's the problem, Pops?" Pete asked, craning his head forward and looking the equipment over.

"Fuckin' thing keeps fuckin' the fuck up," Wally said. His voice was tight with repressed fury, and no sooner were the words out of his mouth than the screen winked off, plunging them into darkness. It took a moment or two for Pete's eyes to adjust.

"You check the connections and stuff?" Pete asked.

Wally turned his head slowly and looked at him like he'd asked the most ridiculous question imaginable.

"How 'bout trying the lights?" Pete asked.

Wally flipped a switch, and the running lights came on, but they didn't need them. The night was clear, and they were out on the open water. In the faint moonlight, they could see a fair distance in all directions.

"Fuckin' electronics.... Don't even need 'em half the time, anyways" he grumbled and then drank some more rum. "Why do I fuckin' bother?"

Pete had nothing to say to that. He appreciated the modern equipment. It sure took a lot of the guesswork out of the job.

"So where we headed?" Pete was sure he already knew, but he was trying to engage his father in conversation.

"The Nephews," Wally said holding a steady course as he headed further out to sea. The moon, small and waning, was low on the western horizon. Reflected light and shadow rippled in the water like jagged, black teeth. Far out to sea, Pete could make out the dark shapes of several islands. He wasn't sure which—if any—was The Nephews.

The Nephews was a small group of islands more than twenty miles out from The Cove. Wally hadn't told Pete what time they were to meet the trawler, but he had the impression they were running late. Maybe that's why Wally was in such a pissy mood.

It was a beautiful night, but out on the water, it was cold. Once Wally had the boat up to speed, the ride was smooth, if bracing.

"You wanna knock?" Wally called out, holding the bottle of rum out to Pete.

Finally, Pete thought as he took the bottle from his father, tilted his head back, and gulped down a mouthful of rum. It burned in his chest like he'd swallowed a smoldering coal. He snorted and shook his head.

"Good for what ails yah," Wally said with a short laugh.

"So where we dropping off?" Pete asked, trying to make conversation.

"Usual place. Pulpit Rocks," Wally replied. He snatched the bottle of rum from Pete and tossed down another hefty belt. How he could navigate and drink like that was a conundrum to Pete, and he shuddered to think that, if his father kept it up, he might have to navigate back for him. He'd be able to find The Cove easily enough, but finding Pulpit Rocks in the dark was another matter. If the navigational system was useless, so was he.

Wally notched the speed up a bit and scanned the immediate area. To starboard, the coast was a dark slash against the night, broken only by distant streetlights and the lights in homes. Once or twice, they tracked the headlights of a car moving along the shore road. Pete knew what his father was looking for, but as far as he could tell, there were no other boats in the area. Satisfied, Wally killed the running lights and then goosed the engine. The boat cut across the waves smoothly.

They rode for a long time in silence. Pete was tempted to ask for the rum back, but he decided that one of them had to keep a clear head. Even liquored up, Wally's reputation was that he could navigate through pea soup fog blindfolded, but Pete didn't want to put that to the test. He settled back at the stern and watched the shoreline slowly shift perspective. His stomach went suddenly cold when he saw a light moving against the darkness of the distant shore.

"Shit."

Wally was staring straight ahead, apparently lost in his own thoughts. Pete watched the shore, wishing—praying it had been an optical illusion. He tried to look to one side of what he was trying to see, a trick he'd learned that helped him see better in the dark. At first, there was nothing, but then a boat appeared, heading toward them.

"I think we got company," he called out, pointing to starboard.

It was all but impossible to see if there really was a boat out there, angling to cut them off, but Pete was certain of it. Something like this would fit in perfectly with the kind of week he'd been having.

"You best put your running lights on," Pete said.

Wally looked back, his eyes narrowed with concentration, and then he shook his head and said, "Fuck it," and left the lights off.

Friggin' Pops never listens to me.... Nobody ever listens to me, Pete thought bitterly. His jaw muscles clenched as tightly as a bear trap when he clearly made out the boat speeding toward them. Minutes stretched out like hours as tension churned inside his gut.

"Definitely a boat," Pete called out and then muttered, "Fuckin' Coasties" under his breath as he watched the dark silhouette slide silently across the lighter gray of the ocean. The red port light glowed in the darkness like the baleful eye of a demon. Then, while the boat was still quite a distance away, a powerful searchlight winked on. The beam swept across the water, turning the waves into quicksilver flashes until it landed on them and stopped.

Pete listened to the rising drone of the boat's engine as the boat approached. One thing he was sure of—this wasn't the trawler they'd come out to meet.

"This is the United States Coast Guard," a voice bellowed over an electronic megaphone. The words sent a spike of cold up Pete's spine.

"We are armed. Please heave-to, Skipper."

"God-fuckin'-damn it," Wally said as he cut the engine and let the boat drift to a stop. The backwash of his wake rocked the *Abby-Rose.* The rolling motion didn't help Pete's stomach, but Wally took another swig of rum as he stood there, waiting as the Coast Guard vessel closed with them. At least it wasn't any DEA assholes.

Pete shielded his eyes with his hand. He felt naked in the harsh glare of the searchlight and didn't know what else to do but stand there. It took too long for the Coast Guard boat to come alongside. Pete could hear voices, squawking over their radio. The spotlight played across the deck and into the wheelhouse, where Wally stood, squinting, but not bothering to shade his eyes.

"What're you fellas doing out at night without your running lights on?" the voice over the bullhorn asked. The man's silhouette stood out starkly against the night sky, like a cutout made with black paper.

Someone else on the Coast Guard vessel threw down a line. Pete knew the drill. This wasn't the first time—or last, he assumed—the Coast Guard had stopped him. He picked up the rope from the deck and tied it to one of the cleats.

"Just launched 'er this week," Capt'n Wally said, smiling into the searchlight, squinting like he was facing the sun. "We was takin' 'er out for a little spin…a little shakedown."

"You didn't have your running lights on," the man with the bullhorn said.

"Yeah, the boat's new, 'n the Christless electronics are fucked from here to Sunday. They keep switchin' off and on. Same with the Christless nav systems."

As if to demonstrate, Wally flipped a switch, but the lights came on.

"There.... See? Now the fuckin' thing works. I oughta—"

"Prepare to be boarded," the voice from the boat said, and seconds later, two dark figures clambered down a rope ladder to the deck of the *Abby-Rose.* Pete backed up, wanting to be as far away from them as possible while Wally stood his ground in the wheelhouse, one hand resting on the wheel.

"You the skipper?" a young man said, addressing Wally. He had a flashlight in his hand, but he didn't need it. The spotlight aimed at them from the deck of the Coast Guard boat lit up the deck as if it were daytime. Their shadows stretched across the deck.

Wally nodded but said nothing. Pete was surprised that his father didn't have a snappy comeback, but he noticed how his father regarded the young man with an expression of utter contempt. Pete wondered if the Coastie noticed when Wally glanced at his wristwatch as if he was running late for an important date.

"What have we got here?" the other Coastie said as he approached the three bags of salt stacked up in the stern.

The words "ROCK SALT" were printed in bright red on the top bag. The ones below it were identical, but without waiting for an answer, the Coastie took out a utility knife and stuck the blade into the top bag. He grunted softly as he ripped up, making a gash about six inches long. The bag split open from the weight of its contents, and rock salt spilled onto the deck in a rattling rush.

"Like it says." Wally said with a shrug. "Rock salt."

Pete groaned, knowing he'd be doing cleanup once they got back into port.

The two Coasties set about searching the boat. When they removed a hatch cover to look down into the hold and engine room, Wally stepped forward.

"Careful you don't put that cover upside down," he said.

One of the Coasties looked up at him, his eyebrows raised in silent question.

"'S bad luck to put the hatch covers upside down on deck," Wally said.

Pete smiled to himself. He had heard that from his father before, but he wasn't sure if his father actually believed it or if he was messing around with the Coasties. Either way, they appeared unimpressed, and they continued with their search. When they were done, without a word of thanks for their cooperation or apology for making such a mess on the deck, they climbed back up the rope ladder to their boat.

"We'll escort you back to the harbor," the voice over the bullhorn said. "Please start up your engine and come back to port with us."

"Fucking Goddamn," Wally muttered under his breath, but he smiled and waved at the silhouettes that lined the rail. Then, to make his contempt obvious, he straightened his shoulders and snapped a salute while Pete untied the rope from the cleat.

"How much does this suck?" he said as he joined his father in the wheelhouse. He wanted to throw out an *I told you so* but decided he liked his teeth just fine where they were.

"Tell me about it," Wally said as he started the engine, revving it more than necessary. Then, without a glance at the Coast Guard vessel, he took off, heading back to The Cove.

Once or twice, for show, he reached down to the running lights switch and flicked them off and on a few times at random, hoping to convince the men on the patrol boat that he really was having trouble with his electronics.

Pete didn't need to be told how pissed his father was. They'd clear things up with the Coast Guard, no problem. It was a good thing they hadn't met the trawler because they'd be in a world of hurt if they had a few bales on-board. Still, they were going to have to wait while the Guardsmen went through the *Abby-Rose* with a fine-toothed comb. No doubt The Crowbar was going to bitch about the turn of events.

Pete glanced at his father's face, underlit by the flickering glow of the GPS screen and couldn't help but chuckle.

"You think this is funny?" Wally said, glaring at him and looking ready to take a swing.

Pete raised his hands defensively and shook his head. He stopped laughing and said, "No, I was thinking.... When we get back to port and these guys tear through the boat.... Maybe they'll find out what's wrong with the electronics."

Wally's mouth twitched into a half-smile, then his scowl deepened again, and he snorted and spat over the side of the boat.

"These guys? Useless as tits on a bull."

Someone's outside, Julia thought.

It was late.

Past midnight.

She was sitting in a chair in her bedroom with the window open as she read. She'd gotten a history of Maine islands from the library, but the book wasn't holding her attention. A soft, warm wind shifted the curtains back and forth like lacy bellows. The sound of spring peepers in the swampy area behind the house filled the night, ringing like jingle bells.

She put the book down and went to the window. Leaning with both fists on the windowsill, she looked out, but the light on in her bedroom made it impossible to see anything. She considered turning the light off but decided not to. That would only alert the person outside that she knew he was there.

That was the *last* thing she wanted.

She knew he was there, and she knew who he was. It irked her that for the last several weeks, he had made a habit of creeping around the house like this, like he was a common criminal.

She didn't find the irony of that idea the least bit amusing.

Her father was in his bedroom down the hall, asleep. Leaving the window, she tip-toed down the hall to his door. She pressed her ear against the cool wood and listened for the faint sawing sound of his breathing. When she heard it, she tried to suppress the feeling of agitation that filled her. She had to be honest with herself and acknowledge the resentment she felt about her situation.

She hadn't signed on for this.

She hadn't asked or wanted to move to Maine to take care of him after his first heart attack, but here she was. She had given up everything she knew and loved back in Waterbury, Connecticut, to move to Catawamkeag Cove so she could tend to her father.

In the privacy of her own thoughts, she had begun to hope that her father, as much as she loved him, wouldn't live much longer.

It was a cruel, unforgivable thought, but she had to be honest—at least with herself—and admit that she was deeply unhappy with the turn her life had taken.

She had moved to Maine with an open mind and the best of intentions. At first, the beauty of Catawamkeag Cove had enchanted her. The small town values—the close-knit sense of community and family—had come straight out of a Norman Rockwell painting. She had wanted to live here and experience it. She had been eager to make friends and be accepted, but so far, that hadn't happened. The people in town, while friendly enough in public, were closed off to the point of clannishness. She never got past meaningless pleasantries. At first she was puzzled; then hurt; and finally she had come to despise this lovely, unforgiving place.

And that was no way to live.

Over the last few months, once spring came, she had become almost desperate to get out of town. But now Ben Brown had certainly put quite a monkey wrench in the works. Still, she was confident that eventually she would find a way out. She felt in him the same desire to leave that burned so brightly in her.

And then there was the poor fool she was sure was still following her around like a sick puppy.

Her father was the last thing keeping her here. Once he was gone, as sad…as terrible as that would be, the life insurance money and what she could get from selling the house and whatever of the furniture she didn't want to keep would be more than enough for her to move back home to Waterbury and resume the life that had been wrenched away from her.

Saddened by these thoughts, she made her way slowly back to her bedroom, trying her best not to think about who was waiting for her outside. She stood close to the window and, after making a show of undressing for bed, turned off the light. She hoped her late-night visitor would get the hint and leave, but she feared she was going to have go outside and talk to him face to face and tell him that she didn't want to see him…not tonight…not tomorrow night…not *any* night.

Never again.

As far as she was concerned, they were done with. It had been fun…an amusing diversion, perhaps, if not the desperate groping for acceptance and love she feared their relationship might have been. One thing she knew for certain was there wasn't the slightest possibility he would be in her future.

Not anymore.

Not after meeting and spending time with Ben Brown.

Ben was everything she had ever looked for. A tough guy with a soft heart. Warm, funny, charming. And sexy.

She smiled into the darkness.

And she knew beyond question the feeling was mutual.

With the light out, she moved over to the window again and knelt down to the floor like someone about to pray. Leaning her elbows on the windowsill, she stared out at the night, inhaled deeply, and listened to the night sounds—the spring peepers and the hushed sigh of the wind.

It filled her with peace and contentment, something she hadn't experienced since…

She couldn't remember when.

She didn't see him, but that didn't mean he wasn't still out there. She could feel his desire, crackling like a charge of static electricity in the night air. He was waiting for her to come out to be with him.

Suddenly angry with herself for the mess she was in and the darkness of her own thoughts, she stood up, turned on the lights, and walked downstairs, and went to the front door.

I can do at least one right thing tonight, she thought.

She threw the door open.

Agnes Appleby got out of work at midnight after pulling a double shift at Harbor's Edge because Jenny Delfonso had called in sick.

Again.

She had never liked driving late at night…especially alone. The older she got, the more fearful she became. She had to wonder if the town really had gotten more dangerous over the years with the steady influx of people "from away," or if she was getting cranky and paranoid in her old age.

Either way, things weren't the way they used to be, and Agnes didn't like it.

She also wasn't thrilled at the prospect of going home to Amos, her husband. No doubt the "old skunk," as she called him—even to his face—would be drunk on his ass as usual and waiting up for her so he could complain about something.

The thought made her stomach ache.

That wasn't at all what she needed after working a sixteen-hour shift. At least the old bastard never raised a hand to her; but after all these years together, she wondered if perhaps physical abuse might be easier to take than the constant harangues. It certainly would be clearer and more direct. The older Agnes got, the more she found that she preferred clear and direct.

Her sense that something was wrong spiked when she turned the corner onto Steeple Road and a policeman stepped out onto the street from behind the bushes that lined the road near the Capozzas' house. It took her a moment to recognize Tom Marshall. Like everyone else in town, she had known Tommy since he was a kid, and she had never gotten over the feeling that he was playing cop, not a real one. How could she respect the authority of someone she had seen being pushed around town in a stroller or toddling around with saggy, leaky diapers hanging down the backs of his legs?

As soon as her headlight beams hit him, he froze like a rabbit caught in the sudden light. Shielding his eyes with one hand, he looked like he was winding up to duck back out of sight, but then he squared his shoulders and stood his ground on the side of the road as Agnes slowed to a stop and rolled down the automatic window on the passenger's side.

"'Evenin', Mrs. A," he said, touching his forehead as if he wore a hat and was saluting.

"Good evening, Tommy." Mrs. Appleby's eyes widened as she turned her head, gazing up and down the length of road. "Is something the matter?"

For a second, he looked at her; then he glanced over his shoulder as if looking for someone who should have been standing there behind him.

"The matter? Ahh—No...no. Everything's fine, Mrs. A."

There was an odd thinness in his voice that she didn't like. It told her otherwise. Her mind instantly filled with anxiety about teenagers drugged-up on crack cocaine or oxys, pillaging the neighborhood, looting houses, and raping and killing innocent people.

"Whatever are you doing out here?" she asked. "I don't see your cruiser."

She wasn't at all reassured by what he'd said.

"I'm parked down the road a bit. You didn't see it?"

"Never did."

"Hmm…well, I—uh, we had a report of a coyote in the area. I thought I saw something and chased after it."

"A coyote? Really?" Agnes wasn't convinced. Something in his posture and attitude signaled that he was not being entirely truthful here. "I hope you're not just saying that, and there's a bunch of hoodlums out causing trouble."

"Oh, no…no. Nothing like that."

Tommy looked at her with a smile that looked like it was screwed on too tightly.

Mrs. Appleby leaned across the seat and looked past him at the Capozza's house. It occurred to her that something might have happened to the old man who lived there with his daughter.

Mrs. Appleby decided not to push it. Police work was police work, and Tommy—whether he was "playing" cops or not—wouldn't tell her what was going on if he thought she didn't need to know.

But she knew Tommy Marshall all too well. She had never really trusted him. How he ever became a policeman was beyond her. More likely, he was one of the people the police should be looking for.

Mrs. Appleby was about to shift back into gear and drive away when the front porch light on the Capozza's house winked on. A warm, yellow glow spread like a burst of sunlight across the lawn. Tommy Marshall tensed visibly as he turned again and glanced over his shoulder at the house. The front door opened, and a wedge of darkness inside the doorway widened.

"Damn," he muttered under his breath.

Mrs. Appleby almost said something to him about how it wasn't proper for a police officer to swear, not in front of an elderly lady, but she let that pass.

"I—ah, I have to talk to someone at that house," Tom said. "They—umm, they're the ones who called in about the fox."

"I thought you said it was a coyote."

Tom appeared momentarily flustered, but then he said, "Coyote—fox—whatever," and turned to make his way up the walkway to the front door.

For several seconds, Mrs. Appleby sat there in her car, watching him; but when he turned and looked at her as if to say *"I've got it under control.... You can go now,"* she shifted into gear and drove away. It only took a quick glance into her rearview mirror to see all she needed to see.

The door opened wider, and the Meadows girl stepped out onto the small porch. With the light on in the house behind her, her figure had a luminous glow. Tom mounted the front stairs and reached out to her. Obviously, they were about to embrace, but she lost sight of them when she rounded the corner, and the scene was lost behind some shrubbery.

Mrs. Appleby was so filled with disgust she shivered. Shaking her head and clicking her tongue, making a *tisk-tisking* sound, she complimented herself for figuring out why Tommy Marshall was sneaking around the neighborhood so late at night.

She knew people did things like that all the time, but what galled her most was knowing that Tommy Marshall was married to Louise Brown, the only daughter of her best friend—and now patient—Lilly Brown. She never thought she'd ever feel this way, but she had to admit that she was glad Lilly was already so far gone with Alzheimer's she would never have to grapple with what was going on.

"It would rip her heart out if she knew," Mrs. Appleby muttered as she pulled into her driveway and stopped the car. For the longest time, she sat there, her hands hooked over the steering wheel like a hawk's claws, her eyes wide as she stared at her reflection in the rearview. After a few minutes, Amos—who must have been watching from the kitchen window—came to the door and called out, "You aw'right out there?"

Mrs. Appleby sighed as she pulled her keys from the ignition and squeezed them in her hand. A hard edge dug into the palm of her hand, making her wince. She fought back tears. Feeling as though an invisible weight was strapped to her shoulders, she got out of the car and walked up the brick-lined walkway to the front door.

When all's said and done, she thought, *I could have done a lot worse than marry Amos.* He certainly had his faults. What man doesn't? Many years ago, before they got married, her father's only comment about Amos had been "He ain't much."

And he hadn't been…but through the years, he had been a loyal husband, a good provider, and—at least as far as she knew—he had never slept around on her. Of course, if he had messed around and if she'd ever found out, he'd be singing soprano.

"You can't…. Why are you doing this to me?"

Standing on the doorstep, Tom stared into Julia's dark eyes. They were wide and moist. Reflected bits of light looked like tiny flames, but the flatness in her eyes made it clear that nothing he was saying was getting through to her.

"I don't mean to hurt you. I really don't," she said and for the first time since they'd been talking, she placed her hand lightly on his arm at the bend in the elbow. The touch was reassuring, but there was nothing behind it—no passion…no affection.

"So why can't we…I don't see why we—you know, can't keep on doing what we're doing."

Julia inhaled sharply through her nose and held her breath while looking past him, like there was something more interesting happening behind him.

"Because we can't…. It's over…. I…I don't feel anything for you, Tom."

"You never did. Did you? Admit it."

Julia's focus shifted closer, but she lowered her head and looked down at the doorstep. He wondered why she wouldn't look him directly in the eyes.

The silence lengthened, but after a while she said simply, "It was fun while it lasted, but it's over."

"What if I don't *want* it to be over?"

Now—finally, she looked at him, but he could tell by her expression that she had already checked out. He meant nothing to her.

"You're married," Julia said.

"I was married when we first got together."

"Yeah?" Julia narrowed her eyes as though something internal pained her. "And it was a mistake. I…I don't know what I was thinking, but I…I should have known better. I shouldn't have let you—"

"Let me?"

A sudden rush of anger made the light behind her shift to dark pink. The night sounds suddenly collapsed on him, and the air was too thick to breathe.

"You never *let* me *anything!*" Tom yelled. "*You're* the one who came on to *me,* remember? That night I stopped you for speeding...? You came onto me faster than that friggin' Saab you were driving."

"It's an Audi," Julia said.

"Whatever!" Tom shouted, clenching his fists so tightly the blood pounded in his hands.

After a moment, she shifted her gaze down and said, "And I was wrong. I was—" Her body stiffened, and she raised her head, spearing him with her steady stare. "Okay, you want the truth? I was never interested in you...not the way you wanted, anyway."

"Don't say that," Tom said, stung by her words.

"I mean it. You were.... Look, I knew it was wrong at the time, and I never meant to hurt you, but it's got to stop. Now."

"You didn't answer my question," Tom said. He took a single step closer to her so he was towering over her.

"What question?" she asked.

"What if I don't want it to end?"

Julia considered, but only for a moment. Then she stepped back inside the house. The knuckles of her hand gripping the door edge were as white as chalk.

"You don't have a choice," she said. Her voice was cold. "You're married. You could lose your wife and your reputation in town will suffer. Me? What do I have? As far as I can see, I'm just the outsider who will *never* be accepted in this town."

"But we talked about.... You said how you wanted to go away with me."

Julia shook her head and started easing the door closed. He could tell she was bracing herself so she could slam the door shut and lock it when...if he lost his patience. A heavy pounding sound filled his head, and he told himself that's exactly what he should do.

Who would blame him if he lost his shit on her?

She deserved it for stringing him along the way she had.

"So's that all I was to you? Just a fuck buddy?"

When Julia didn't answer him, he clenched his fists, doing all he could to choke back his rage, telling himself he couldn't do it.... Not here.... Not now.... An off-duty cop can't just stop by someone's house and wail the living shit out of them.

"You know what?" He twisted his head to the side, hawked deeply in his throat, and spit into the darkness. "Up yours. I don't need you."

"Au revoir."

Snorting loudly, he turned and walked away. His neck flushed, and his fists were tingling. A part of him wanted her to say something…to call him back and tell him it was all a misunderstanding. The skin behind his ears prickled like he was standing with his back to a roaring campfire as he waited to hear her voice, but she still hadn't said a word as he left the yard and stepped out into the street.

The darkness sucked in around him, clinging to him like a wet shirt. Sweat ran down his sides from his armpits, tickling like a trail of ants.

Fuck her! he thought as he braced himself and stopped. He began to turn around and look back at her.

The sound of the door closing and the faint click of the bolt turning in the lock finally convinced him that she had nothing more to say to him, but he was determined to change that.

She'd talk to him, all right.

SIX

Suitcase

Ben was sitting at the kitchen table, his elbows resting on the table and his head in his hands when his brother sauntered downstairs and into the kitchen. Pete was wearing a wrinkled t-shirt and plaid boxers that drooped down the back of his legs.

"What're you doing up so early, Cracker?" Ben asked.

"Don't call me that," Pete said as he reached inside his boxer shorts and scratched his ass. He blinked and looked around like a mole that had just burst out into the sunlight. "No one calls me that anymore."

"Li'l Crackah…? I like it."

"Well I don't."

"I heard you and Pops come in wicked late last night. Must've been close to dawn."

"Maybe," Pete said.

Without another word, he wandered over to the counter, fetched a cup down from the cupboard. He sighed as he poured a steaming cup of coffee from the pot Ben had brewed earlier. He took a tentative sip, wincing at the heat or the taste—or both.

"You wash the pot before you brewed this?"

Ben nodded.

"No wonder it tastes like shit."

"You didn't answer my question. Why'd you get home so late?" Ben asked. "You finally get lucky with Bunny?"

Pete scowled but didn't say a word.

"Fuck, man," Ben went on, "the other day down at The Local? She was all over me…all but had her hand in my pants right there at the bar."

Pete's expression was flat, unreadable as he leaned back against the counter and sipped his coffee. The slurping sounds were starting to get on Ben's nerves, but before he said anything, Pete turned his back to his brother and stared out the window. From where he sat, Ben could see the tops of the trees swaying in the wind and a long stretch of blue ocean.

"'S not really any of your goddamned business what I do, now, is it?" Pete shifted around and stared at Ben for a long, uncomfortable moment. Then he placed his coffee cup down on the counter, poured some sugar into it without benefit of a spoon, and swirled it around before taking another sip. All the while, Ben looked at him with a steady stare. Pete had always kept to himself when he was a kid, but as an adult, he was a total dick.

"You really wanna know where I was? Pops and me took the boat out 'n got stopped by the fucking Junior Navy."

"The Coast Guard? No shit."

"Yes, shit."

A tingle of tension ran through Ben's body. It took some effort not to say: *I knew it! I knew this was coming!*

"You taking it out for a late-night spin?"

"What the hell you think?" Pete snorted and spat into the sink.

"Wash that down," Ben said, and Pete did as he was told.

Ben closed his eyes and pinched the bridge of his nose, telling himself not to say what he wanted to say.

But he couldn't help himself.

"Pops is up to his balls in debt to Richie Sullivan, isn't he?"

He opened his eyes and stared at Pete, who looked back at him with a perfectly neutral expression. Then he sipped some more coffee and shrugged.

"I don't tell Pops how to run his business, and maybe you shouldn't be sticking your nose into ours."

"Why are you being so pissy?"

"I'm not pissy."

"The fuck you aren't." Ben sat back and took a breath, wanting to clear the tension in the air. "You pissed Mona dumped you?"

"Fuck, no."

"It's okay if you are—"

"Screw her. She's fuckin' history."

"What is it, then? You aren't pissed because you had to go out with Pops and try to pick up those bales, are yah?"

Pete bit down on his lower lip, pressing the blood out of it as he looked at Ben.

"He needed help," Pete said, "and—what the fuck? I got bills to pay, too, you know? I just don't see why—" He cut himself off, leaving Ben hanging.

"See why *what?*" Ben asked.

"Nothing...nothing."

Pete turned away, as if that ended the discussion. The kitchen grew so silent Ben could hear the wall clock ticking in the entryway.

"So is Pops going out to haul today?"

"You'd have to ask him."

"Yeah," Ben said, "he's probably gonna try 'n make the pick-up you guys missed."

Pete didn't say anything, but they both knew the answer. All Ben could do was shake his head. It wasn't worth the breath to tell his brother how "The Crowbar" was going to pry everything he could and then some out of Capt'n Wally. He'd end up paying for two or three boats by the time Richie Sullivan was done with him... if Wally didn't end up getting busted and doing jail time...or worse.

"What you up to today?" Pete asked. "You gonna start looking for a job?"

Ben didn't like the way his brother had shifted the topic, but what could he do? Trying to reason with Pete was like trying to reason with a tree stump. You'd probably get further with the tree stump.

"I'm in no hurry," Ben said, easing back in the chair and folding his hands across his belly. "I got some savings I can live on so as long as Pops is good with having me here for a while. I'm not gonna jump into anything just yet."

"'Cept maybe into bed with that Meadows chick," Pete said, looking at Ben with a twisted smile.

"How did you—? Who told you about that?"

Pete took a sip of coffee, eyeing him over the rim of his cup. Then he swallowed and said, "Word gets around."

"I guess the fuck it does."

"So how is she? She nice and tight?"

"Up yours."

"She looks like she'd be nice and tight."

Pete's smirk widened into a goofy, gap-toothed grin. He put his cup down on the counter and scratched the side of his nose.

"It's not like you don't wanna bang her, though. Right? I mean—if you haven't already. Am I right? Come on. I mean, the tits on her…?" He cupped his hands and bounced them in front of his chest like he was hefting two grapefruits. "Whoa."

"You know what? Seriously…fuck you," Ben said.

He got up slowly from the table, his fists clenched. He was ready to fight, but then he caught himself. He wasn't going to revert to the old days when he and Pete squabbled over everything and fought pretty much on a daily basis.

Pete's face froze, his eyes glaring at Ben from beneath his shaggy fringe of bangs. Crossing his arms over his chest, he rolled his head from side to side like he was working out a kink. He inhaled loudly through his nostrils and then let his breath out in a sigh.

Ben knew his little brother all too well. He could tell that Pete had something else to say but was holding back, getting ready for a fight. Only now, they were adults, and they could really hurt each other. Ben was confident he could still beat up Pete, but Pete wasn't the wimp he used to be.

"Come on," Ben said, using as mild a tone of voice as he could muster. "Out with it. What have you got up your ass?"

"Nothing…. Not a goddamned thing," Pete said. He paused, the air in the room suddenly dense and hushed. "It's just…I hear you ain't the only one who's trying to get into her pants."

"What?"

"From what I hear, she's been spreading her legs for a couple a' people in town."

"You're shitting me."

"Would I shit you?"

Ben was stunned, and he remembered thinking how it didn't make sense that a woman as attractive as Julia wasn't with somebody.

"You know who it is?"

Pete shrugged, now looking all innocence.

"No clue, but…you know how things are around here. You hear things."

"Like what?"

"Things."

"Fuck you, man. Tell me. Who else is she fucking?"

But Pete only smiled and shook his head. Ben felt a sudden urge to jump him and start wailing away on him to force him to tell him what he knew, but he stayed seated. He wanted to forget all about what Pete had said, but he was convinced that Pete was talking about the person—it *had* to be the same person—who had sandbagged him out behind The Local.

Remembering that Julia had not been exactly straightforward with him when he asked if she was seeing someone, he stood up, kicking his chair back so it clattered on the floor. Pete cowered as though expecting him to attack.

Ben stood there a moment, trembling inside, but then, without another word, he strode to the door and grabbed the keys to his car from the hook on the wall next to the phone. Clenching his teeth to keep from yelling, he swung the kitchen door open. He wished he could tear it off its hinges. The sudden blast of warmth from the sun hit him, making sweat pop out on his face and arms. Before he left the house, he turned and locked eyes with Pete, who was leaning against the counter and watching him with a faint, satisfied smile.

"It's tough when you don't get everything you want, ain't it?" Pete said.

"Tell Pops to call me on my cell if he wants some help hauling today, 'kay?" Ben said, ignoring the taunt.

"Sure thing," Pete said, raising his empty coffee cup as though toasting his brother.

Ben slammed the door shut behind him as he walked out. His ears were burning as he went down the driveway to his car and got in. As he sat behind the steering wheel, he realized he was breathing so hard and fast his body was shaking. Forcing himself to move slowly, and feeling every muscle and nerve in his body twitch with tension, he slid the key into the ignition and started up the car.

He had no idea where he was going or what he was going to do. All he knew for sure was that he had to get out of that damned house and away from his brother.

He needed some time alone so he could think things through. He needed to figure out why he had reacted like that, as if he was jealous of Julia Meadows…like he had any kind of claim on her in the first place.

He didn't like feeling as though he had fallen for her so hard and so fast a simple comment like Pete's would set him off. It might be a good idea to take the advice of whoever had jumped him out behind the bar and forget all about her.

The only problem was, it was already too late for that.

"You want to explain this?" Louise Marshall said.

She was standing barefoot on the front steps, wearing a tattered pink bathrobe as she greeted Tom, who was striding up the walkway to the house. She held up a battered brown leather suitcase in one hand.

"What the fuck?" Tom said, drawing to a stop.

"I was doing laundry, 'n I dropped a sock behind the washing machine. When I went to fish it out, I found *this*."

"Yeah?"

"What do you mean, 'yeah?' Would you care to explain why there's a suitcase filled with what sure as shit looks like cocaine in our basement?"

"What's to explain?"

"What the—?" Her voice choked off, and something pulsed painfully behind her eyes. "You brought *how* many bags of cocaine into *my* house?"

"Oh, so now it's *your* house?"

Tom mounted the steps and stood beside her, towering over her.

"I live here, don't I?" she said. The pain behind her eyes blossomed, and pinpricks of light swam across her vision. She coiled back, expecting to be hit, but she somehow found the strength to say, "You don't think you owe me an explanation?"

"I don't owe you doodley-squat."

He grabbed the suitcase from her, then pushed past her and entered the house. He walked down the short hallway to the kitchen and let out a long groan when he dropped the suitcase to the floor and sat down heavily in one of the chairs at the kitchen table. Louise followed a few steps behind, clutching the neck of her bathrobe closed at her throat.

"Gimme some coffee, will yah?" Tom said.

Louise considered for a moment, then said, "Get your own damned coffee."

"Jesus H. bald-headed *Christ!* I come home frigging exhausted after pulling a double shift, and you can't even get me a goddamned cup of coffee? You should have a whole fucking breakfast waiting for me."

Louise clenched her fists, wishing she had the courage or strength to go at him. She stared at the suitcase on the floor, her mind churning with things she could say.

Over the last few months…ever since she miscarried…something fundamental had changed in their marriage. She was positive he must be seeing another woman, but she hadn't found any real evidence.

No lipstick stains on his shirt collar…no strands of hair that weren't hers…no late night, muffled phone calls…

But that's the only way she could explain the nastiness, the violence, the way he treated her like he hated her now.

She was convinced he was having an affair.

The only question was: *How serious is it?*

When she found the suitcase stashed away where he obviously thought she wouldn't find it, her first thought had been that he was packed and getting ready to leave her. She almost passed out when she opened the suitcase and saw so much cocaine.

More than twenty big bags.

She had no idea what its street value might be, but it had to be thousands, maybe hundreds of thousands of dollars worth…maybe even a million.

"I want to know why you have this in *my* house!"

"You're forgetting that *I'm* the one who pays the fuckin' bills."

She stepped forward and kicked the suitcase, hearing the heavy bags shift inside as it fell over.

Tom's eyes fluttered as he looked up at the ceiling for a moment and ran both hands down the sides of his face.

"Truth is, it's none of your goddamned business, all right?"

Louise felt heat rush to her head.

"It sure as fuck is. If we get busted, I could end up in jail, too, with this much coke in my house."

"We won't get busted. I'm a goddamned cop."

Tom took a deep breath and clenched his hands in his lap. She could see that he was struggling to maintain his self-control, and she knew all too well from past experience that she should drop it—*now*—before she got hurt.

"It's not the first time," he said.

"What?"

"The first time I had—uh, evidence in the house."

"What do you mean, 'evidence?'"

One side of Tom's mouth twitched into a smile as he looked her straight in the eye.

"We've been having some problems with stuff going missing from the evidence locker, so the chief asked me to stash this at my house to make sure it's safe."

"Bull," Louise said.

"Go ahead. Call Harlan if you want. Ask him, if you think I'm lying."

Louise glanced from Tom to the wall phone and then back at her husband. She was actually considering calling his bluff, but she knew he had her. If he was telling the truth, the worst that would happen would be that Tom might get reamed out at work for letting his wife know about what he was doing. If he was lying to her, she'd be putting herself as well as him in jeopardy so when Tom got busted, she'd get busted, too. She stared at the suitcase on the floor, blinking her eyes rapidly to stop the tears that were gathering there.

"You're a rotten son-of-a-bitch, you know that?" she finally said.

Tom looked at her, his expression all but saying: *Got'cha, bitch!*

"So," he said. "You gonna make me some breakfast or what?"

He looked at her with an insipid smile she wanted to wipe off his face with a frying pan if she had to. She told herself to let it go. In a sense, Tom was right. It wasn't any of her business. *She* obviously wasn't any of his business. He pretended not to notice her at all as he eased back in his chair and loosened his belt. He unbuttoned the top three buttons of his work shirt, reached inside, and scratched his chest.

Louise started to turn to the counter to make him breakfast, but then she stopped. Moving quickly, she snatched her car keys and purse from the counter and was out the door and in her car before Tom could so much as get out of his chair.

As she started up the car and backed out of the driveway, she had no idea if she was relieved or hurt that he wasn't standing in the doorway or running down the driveway to beg her not to leave him.

She had all the proof she needed to know that while he might not be packing to leave her—not yet, anyway—he was up to something he didn't want her to know about.

And as she sped down the road, not even thinking about where she was going, Louise decided that she didn't want Tom Marshall in her life anymore.

From here on out, it was simply a question of how she could get away from her husband without getting hurt any more than she already had been.

So much for "'til death do you part," she thought.

After his encounter with Pete, Ben drove down to Lucy's Cove and watched the ocean's restless, eternal beat until his mind cleared and his blood pressure went back to somewhere around normal. He drove back home, showered, and considered going back out to "Grave's Edge" to see his mother again, but honestly, he didn't think he could handle it alone.

Maybe if he and Louise went over together again, it would be easier to face what was happening to his mother. He had been so disturbed by her condition they had to leave before showing her the photos of the boat launch.

"For all the good that would do," Ben muttered. His neck and scalp felt cold and tight, as if the blood had drained out of his head.

No matter what they did, their mom wouldn't have any idea what was going on and never would.

Ever.

What he really wanted to do was call Julia and see if they could spend some time together. He had no idea what her days were like. She hadn't talked much about her routine and what it entailed, helping her father. It certainly must be a lot harder, more demanding that simply trundling him off to a nursing home and waiting for him to die. Then again, he hadn't asked. He had no idea what her father's medical condition was, but it certainly couldn't be as bad as what was happening to his mother.

So why not call her up and see what she was up to?

Why couldn't they get together, hang out, have some laughs, maybe sleep together, and leave it at that? He didn't see anything wrong with a little casual sport fucking. He sure as hell wasn't looking for a serious relationship, much less in the market to get married.

But Julia was different, somehow.

The old Gunner confidence that came so easily to him with every other woman he'd ever known disappeared when he was with her. The jealousy Pete had aroused in him was something he'd never felt before. He decided it might be good to take a day off, let things settle down, maybe try to find out who her other guy was…if he, in fact, existed. Pete may have been saying that because he could see how much it galled him.

So if he didn't call Julia, what did that leave him for the day?

His options were limited. He could go down to The Local and see who was there. Like the saying goes—"It's five o'clock somewhere."

Another option was to start looking around for work. After being through what he'd been through, he had promised himself he would take as much time off as he needed to get his head together after some of the shit he'd seen…and done.

He could always go down to the wharf and see if his father needed help, but he wasn't about to volunteer. He'd never enjoyed being out on the water, and he was content to wait for his dad to ask him. He certainly didn't need the money. He had enough in savings, and if he pitched in and helped with expenses living at home, he could get by for quite a while.

He knew he should check in at the VA hospital in Augusta. Back in Iraq, you were supposed to suck it all up and deal. If you asked for help, there went any chance for promotion. You were a pussy or a fag. So you drank too much, or drugged, or had dreams. Or offed yourself.

But he wasn't in Iraq anymore. And the dreams were getting worse. Back home, nobody would give him shit if he admitted he had a little PTSD.

Shit, he thought. What is a "little" PTSD? Denial is what it was. Fuck that!

He knew he needed to get his shit together, but that would take time.

What had happened in Iraq had happened. It was over and done with. He could accept all of it—good, bad, and indifferent. He had seen what he had seen, and he had done what he had done, and that was the end of it.

As bad as Iraq was, being back home had its own parcel of problems. He knew that as soon as he saw a car hauling ass up the driveway. A plume of dust rose in its wake as it squealed to a stop. He didn't realize it was his sister until the car door opened, and Louise got out. He went to the side door and met her on the side steps.

"We gotta talk," she asked without preamble. Her hair was a mess, and her face was pale and slick with sweat. She was breathing like she'd just run a marathon. And she was barefoot and wearing nothing but a tatty pink bathrobe.

"Yeah.... Sure."

Ben stepped back so she could enter the house before him.

Even before she spoke, he knew what was coming, and an unaccountable fury filled him, wrapping around his heart like burning hands.

"So...will you talk to him?" Louise said after she'd told Ben everything that had happened this morning. She had calmed down some, but her eyes were filmed with a frantic light. They kept darting from side to side, and she couldn't look him straight in the eyes for very long.

Ben didn't like what he had heard, but he wasn't sure it was his place to have a little "heart-to-heart" with his brother-in-law. Tom had been a year behind Ben in school, so they'd run with different crowds. Frankly, they had never really liked each other.

Ben wished now he had told Louise what he thought of Tom before they got married. Then again, Tom had gotten her pregnant, and maybe he had done the right thing, marrying her. Still, what he was doing was no way to treat his wife...especially after losing a baby. He couldn't very well tell Louise it was *her* crap and *she'd* have to deal with it. Their parents had taught them that family stuck together, no matter what. Cop or no cop, Ben absolutely wasn't going to stand by idle while someone was abusing his little sister.

"What do you think's really going on? You're positive he wasn't telling the truth about the evidence locker?"

"Jesus, Ben! Get real. You actually think Harlan's going to ask a friggin' patrolman to keep that much coke at his house?"

"There's a lot?"

"Um-hmm. A lot."

Ben grunted and stroked his chin, gazing out the window at a patch of cloudless blue sky.

"It doesn't add up," he said, "that's for sure. You think maybe he's gonna try 'n sell it on the side and make a few extra bucks?"

"A few? For Christ's sake, you should *see* how much of that shit there is! It's gotta be worth thousands—maybe millions. I dunno. But you know, sure as shit, eventually the cops are going to notice those bags have gone missing."

Ben started to say something but thought better of it. The pieces were starting to fall into place.

Tom wasn't planning to sell the coke he'd stolen and surprise her with a vacation or a brand new house, that was for sure. He was going to sell it and use the money to take off. Since what he'd done constituted a felony, he damned well better have a ticket to someplace out of the country. But it was clear that Tom had no intention of taking his wife with him. This wasn't something you'd spring on a spouse. It took planning. He couldn't imagine even someone as stump-stupid as Tom Marshall saying something like, *"Hey, Honey…I scored a couple a' hundred large…. What say we pack up and move to Jamaica"?*

And as soon as this occurred to Ben, something else snapped into place.

That night out behind The Local…. He hadn't recognized the voice of the guy who had blindsided him. He'd done a good job of disguising it, and the alley had been too dark for him to see his assailant's face.

Now, Ben was convinced it *had* to have been Tom.

He's the "other guy."

The son-of-a-bitch has his eye on Julia and is planning—maybe foolishly hoping—she'll run away with him.

"So leave him," Ben said simply, hoping what he'd been thinking didn't register on his face. "Leave the son-of-a-bitch. Pops'll always let you move back in."

She stared at Ben, her eyes glassy, her face as pale as marble. She swallowed once, hard enough to make a loud gulping sound that, under other circumstances, would have made them both crack up. But the fear and pain…the look of absolute helplessness in her eyes touched Ben.

"Look, I…I know I gotta do that eventually," she said, her voice barely audible. Then she let out a deep sigh. "People around town are gonna talk."

"They'll talk anyway," Ben said. "They're already talking about that bruise on your face, and from what I hear, it ain't the first." Louise blanched at that. "I don't mean to be cruel or anything, but if he's the loser I always thought he was, I'd say get out now while the getting's good…before you get seriously hurt…or worse…"

Her hand went to the cheek where Tom had smacked her the other day. The swollen bruise had turned dull purple with irregular yellow edges. Tears filmed her eyes, and when she sniffled, her throat made a choking sob.

"I'm telling yah," Ben said. "You gotta leave him. And the sooner the better."

"But Tommy's—"

"Tommy's a douche bag. Anyone who beats his wife deserves whatever shit comes down on his head. I don't give a flying fuck about Tommy Marshall, Lou-Lou. I care about *you*."

Ben slid his hands across the table, took hold of her folded hands, and squeezed them tightly. He was surprised how fragile they felt, and he had the unnerving thought that someday his sister was going to be as frail as their mother was now. Hopefully that wouldn't be for a long time, but it would happen eventually.

He smiled wanly, remembering what a little toughie she had been when she was young. She'd pitch right in with Wally and the boys, loading lobster traps onto their father's truck to take down to the wharf, hefting bait barrels, and hand-hauling traps when the winch on the *Sheila B.* wasn't working right.

Now, seeing her so wounded and afraid, his heart went out to her.

Ben smiled reassuringly and took a breath, holding it for a count of five before letting it out.

He didn't like what he was thinking about Tom Marshall.

If he went over to talk to him, he was afraid he would lose his shit right there on the spot, and they'd end up at each other's throats. Still, his little sister needed help.

"Okay," he said. "You want me to talk to him, I will, but I guarantee it won't do any good."

"All you can do is try. Please. I want this worked out so I don't have to be afraid of him. I want to get out of this at least with my dignity intact."

And your jaw intact, Ben thought but didn't say. He was sure Tom wasn't about to grant Louise anything, especially not her dignity. That son-of-a-bitch had hurt—was still hurting—his sister. If he weren't a cop, Ben would hunt him down today—within the hour—and pound the piss out of him.

As it was, he knew he was going to have to have words with Tom. If it came to blows, which was likely, given how he was standing up for his little sister, he wanted to make sure he confronted Tom in a public place where there would be plenty of witnesses so it would be clear to everyone that he was defending himself. The last thing he needed was to be charged with assaulting a police officer.

"So when do you want me to talk to him?"

"Well..." Louise narrowed her eyes and looked up at the ceiling as though reading something there. "I have to be at work at the grocery in an hour, and he's home sleeping now. You think maybe this evening?"

Ben shrugged and said, "I'll probably drop by The Local tonight. He still hang out there off hours?"

Louise said, "I don't know what he does off hours. He's gone a lot of evenings, I never see him, that's for sure."

"I was hoping I could see—"

Ben didn't finish the sentence, but a devilish grin spread across Louise's face. Her eyes twinkled like chipped ice, and it was good to see her smile again when she said, "You're thinking about seeing Kathy, aren't you?"

Ben hadn't been expecting that. Julia had been on his mind so much lately that honestly he'd forgotten all about Kathy Brackett. A twinge of guilt hit him when he thought about how he hadn't even made an effort to go see his daughter.

"No...no way," he said. "Christ, Lou. She's married and has a kid. I don't mess around with married women."

"Don't bullshit me, Ben. You can tell me." Louise's grin spread a little wider. "If you're trying to—you know, get back with her…"

"I'm not. Honest. I have zero interest in her."

"Well…some people down at the store said they saw you and Kathy talking the other day."

"At the boat launch. Yeah. So what? We were talking. I talked with a lot of people that day. There's nothing between me and Kathy."

Still smirking, Louise shook her head. Ben could tell there was no way she believed him.

"Nothing? Not even a baby?" she said.

SEVEN

Proposition

"You have *got* to be *shitting* me."

That was Ben's only possible response.

It was early afternoon. After talking with Louise, he had mowed the lawn, which had taken the better part of two hours because he had a tough time getting the lawn mower started. The blade was as dull as a butter knife and probably did nothing more than stun the grass. Once he was done, he called Julia, but she said her father wasn't having a good day, and she wanted to keep an eye on him. After taking a shower, he had walked downtown, figuring he'd head downtown to The Local for a few cold ones.

He was walking along Main Street when Tom Marshall accosted him.

Grabbing him by the arm, Tom had guided Ben into the alleyway between Ken's Bait Shop and the Shell station.

For a tense moment or two, Ben had been sure Tom was going to have another "up-close and personal" with him, like they'd had behind The Local the other night. His fists were clenched, and he was ready to fight, but he wasn't about to start anything now…not under these circumstances…not when there weren't any witnesses.

He was surprised when Tom, speaking low and shifting his eyes back and forth like a trapped animal, asked him a favor. He wasn't at all ready for what Tom said, and he had to ask him a second time before it finally sank in.

"You want me to *what?*"

"How many fucking times do I have to repeat it?"

Ben shook his head in disbelief.

"There's no way…. No way in hell!"

"You saying you won't help out your own brother-in-law?"

"Not by doing something like that, I won't. No fuckin' way." When Tom looked at him in earnest silence, he added, "Jesus, even if I wanted to, I've been away long enough so I have no idea where to start. I don't know who's running what any more."

"Same people as before. You know that. You're friends with Richie Sullivan, ain't yah?"

Ben snorted. "Nobody's really *friends* with Richie. You know that."

"Yeah, ole Richie's a force unto himself."

"I'm not saying I don't know him," Ben said.

"And you deal with him."

"I've never *dealt* with him. Not really."

"What the hell does *that* mean?"

"It means I don't work for him, and I don't borrow money from him, and I don't owe him a fuckin' dime, and that's the way I like it."

"Your old man does, though."

Ben stiffened when he thought about how much his father must owe The Crowbar for the *Abby-Rose*. He struggled to contain his temper as he stared down the alleyway toward the harbor, fighting back a sudden rush of anger that threatened to consume him and Tom. Through the gap between the buildings, he could see several lobster boats and sailboats, bobbing on the water. The sky was clotted with puffs of white clouds that moved slowly eastward. The dark shadows they cast on the water looked like billows of spreading ink.

It was all so peaceful, but it also looked distant...absolutely foreign.

"I've never dealt with Richie Sullivan...for *anything*."

Tom shot Ben a lopsided grin. His eyes danced with excitement, but there was a hint of urgent desperation behind his smile.

"Your father has," he said. "He's been hauling in bales of weed for Sullivan for years. That's a known fact...even down at the station."

Rage boiled inside Ben, and it was all he could do not to haul back and slug Tom Marshall right there on the spot. Witnesses or no witnesses, it'd be good to take this cock knocker down a few pegs. It felt like someone had laid a hot iron bar across the back of his neck, but instead of lashing out, he shook his head like he was tired of dealing with a retarded person. When Ben tried to push past him to get back out onto the street, Tom shifted his stance and positioned himself to block.

Ben was trapped. His muscles tensed like coiled springs.

Fight or flight, baby, he thought, and I never run.

Tom must have realized if he put any pressure on Ben, he would push back. Hard, if he had to. He had a reputation.

For his part, Ben couldn't believe Tom had confided in him like this. Since Ben couldn't pound the piss out of the moron, he should at least tell him to find someone else to sell these drugs he supposedly had "found."

Was he high or something? Maybe he had sampled the merchandise.

"I'm not gonna do it, and I'm not gonna stand for you threatening my father."

"Did I threaten Capt'n Wally?" Tom raised his hands, palms up as though testing for rain. "He's my fuckin' father-in-law, for Chrissakes. I'm just saying what everyone knows. He owes Richie big-time."

"From what I can tell, he's busting his ass from dawn 'til dusk lobsterin' so he can pay off that damned boat" Ben was taking short, shallow sips of breath to control his pulse, but it wasn't working very well.

"Just remember...you do something to hurt him or put him in jeopardy, you also hurt your wife, too."

Tom's expression darkened as if a cloud had passed across his face. Especially after his talk with Louise, Ben could read the simmering guilt in his eyes.

"You think I don't know that," Tom said without much force in his voice. "Still, that don't change a goddamned thing. I'm a cop, too. And I have to enforce the law. Let's just say I heard some things."

"Like what?" Ben shuffled forward, keeping his body at an angle to Tom to make a smaller target. "What've you heard?"

Ben's eyes narrowed as if taking aim at Tom. He'd kill him if he had to. He knew he could. He'd done much worse in Iraq. In the end, no matter what happened to him, his sister would be a lot better off without this jerk messing up her life.

Tom stroked the corner of his mouth with his forefinger as if wiping away a line of drool.

"Things...like that there's a new DEA agent in the area who's gonna be bustin' balls. Word is, he's a real hard one, and he's beefing up patrols so he can put a dent in the drug traffic."

"A dent is all he'll make, and a little one at that," Ben said. "I'm telling you, Tom. You better be goddamned careful about who you talk to about that suitcase you say you've got. If you weren't married to my sister, I'd report you myself."

Tom's face flushed as if he had just this moment realized Ben now had something he could use against him. He took a step back, shifting his weight from one foot to the other, his eyes sliding from side to side as though he was looking for the quickest escape route.

"You wouldn't fuck over family now, would you, Ben?" Tom asked, his voice warbling with a nervous quaver.

Ben stared at him silently for a lengthening moment, letting him chew on that for a few seconds. Then he exhaled sharply and said, "Not if you don't. But speaking of family, I wonder what Chief Harlan would say if one of his men was charged with domestic violence. How'd that sit?"

Tom said nothing.

"I don't think that would sit too well. Would it?" Ben said, pressing the point home.

With that, he stepped forward and pushed past Tom, who backed up so quickly he stumbled on the uneven ground and almost fell. Without a backward glance, Ben strode up the alleyway to Main Street. He was convinced now more than ever that Tom had already hurt "family" and that he wouldn't hesitate to do it again.

Ben was also sure, now, that Tom didn't have that guilty "dog that just crapped on the rug" expression just because he was knocking Louise around at home. Tom knew that Ben knew who had jumped him out behind The Local.

Ben opened the door to The Local and stepped inside, taking a moment to let his eyes adjust as he looked around to see who was there. He smiled to himself, satisfied that he had put Tom Marshall in his place. And he assured himself that, if Tom didn't stop beating up on Louise, he would do whatever he had to do in order to keep his brother-in-law in line.

When it came right down to it, Tom Marshall was a pussy.

"Hey there, handsome," a woman seated at the far end of the bar said.

"Hey, Bunny," Ben said, touching his hand to his forehead and nodding.

"Lemme buy the war hero a drink."

Ben considered, but only for a moment. Then he strode over to the bar, pulled out a stool, and sat down. He could have a beer with her—maybe even a couple, but he would be damned careful where he put his pecker.

Ben stayed at The Local all afternoon, drinking with Bunny Dawkins. She was as flirty as ever, and the beer was doing its best to wear down his resolve. She almost convinced him to go back to her place, but then his cell phone rang. It was Julia, and she said she could get away for a few hours.

He had more of a buzz on than he would have liked, but he walked home, got his car, and drove over to pick her up. They decided to take a walk, so he drove out of town until they came to a secluded dirt road that Julia had never noticed before. At the end of the road, about half a mile down, was a small parking lot surrounded by oak and pine. They got out and followed a winding path down to a small stretch of beach.

The tide was ebbing, and small waves hissed like a nest of serpents across the sand. Glistening flat stretches of wet sand at the water's edge were littered with clumps of seaweed and stranded shells. A warm, offshore breeze was blowing against them. The sea was choppy, scattering the slanting sunlight like glitter. Overhead, seagulls wheeled in wide circles, their cries sounding faintly below the sound of the wind.

As they walked, Ben kept stealing glances at Julia, marveling at how beautiful she was. The sunlight played in the amber highlights of her hair as it floated and twisted in the wind. Whenever she looked at him, her brown eyes sparkled like melted chocolate. When she smiled, he had all he could do not to stop right there, engulf her in his arms, and kiss her.

Their conversation was as wandering and aimless as their walk.

"It's such a gorgeous day," Julia said, her eyes squinting with pleasure as she looked up and down the beach. "You'd think there'd be more people—at least someone else out here."

"There'll be enough of 'em in a couple of weeks when the summer assholes start showing up," Ben said.

"You townies really don't like the tourists, don't you?"

Ben shrugged.

"There's a certain level of resentment. Sure. They move up from out of state and buy up all the best land and build their Christless summer homes, blocking the view."

"They bring a lot of business to town, too," Julia said.

"Yeah—and our taxes go up. These Flatlanders think they know better than we do about how to run things, so they start telling us what we should and shouldn't do in our own damned town. Fuck them! They treat us like the hired winter caretakers for their fuckin' summer homes."

"You're talking about me, you know. Or my father, at least. My folks moved here after they retired."

Ben sighed and shook his head, smiling.

"Sorry...I shouldn't get so worked up about it. Maybe it's the beer talking."

He felt like a fool and read in her eyes that she was wondering: *Is that how people in town see me?*

"The other day, you said you had to go back several generations for you to be a true native. Does your family go back that far?"

"Further, from what my folks have told me. Supposedly someone in my family was one of the first to settle here back in the 1600s."

"Really..." Julia said, letting it sink in as they continued strolling along the beach.

When they rounded a rocky bluff, the breeze died down, and the air became actually hot. They stopped in unison and, leaning against a large, moss-covered stone outcropping, gazed out to sea. The rock was still warm from the day and radiated heat into their backs.

Out on the horizon, through the haze, Ben made out the dim silhouette of an oil tanker. Closer to land, the ocean was dotted with variously colored lobster buoys that bobbed and glistened in the waves. A lobster boat chugged by, but with the wind against it, the sound of its engine was a faint, insect-like hum. Ben recognized a friend of his—Ken "KY" Young, but he didn't wave. He didn't want to draw undue attention to himself and Julia.

"Don't you ever get sick of this town?" Julia asked after a lengthy silence.

"What do you mean?"

"I mean—do you ever feel like running away?"

Ben smiled as he considered her question. He shifted his stance so he was standing closer to her, their shoulders almost touching. He imagined the warmth he felt was more from her body than from the sun-heated rocks. Her hair was an amazing tangle of dark brown waves that framed her face, shading her eyes.

"I joined the Army, didn't I?" he said.

"That sounds like out of the frying pan and into the fire."

Ben didn't reply.

"It was pretty horrible over there, wasn't it?" Julia said, her eyes narrowing with sympathy. The look melted his heart, and once again—as was so often the case whenever he was with her—he had to hold himself back from hugging and kissing her.

"I don't really like to talk about it, but—yeah, some serious shit went down."

Thankfully, Julia didn't press him on it. He knew he was never going to forget what he had seen and done, but he didn't need a constant reminder. Just thinking about it stirred up things he didn't like.

"So have you decided this is it—you're going to stay to be a Cove-ah for the rest of your life?"

Ben noticed the strain in her voice. She sounded nervous… tense…like she was holding something back from him. He wondered what it was she wasn't saying. He kicked a divot in the sand with the heel of his sneaker as he stared out across the vast blue expanse of the ocean. KY's boat was long out of sight, no doubt in the harbor after a long day hauling pots.

"Once a Cove-ah, always a Cove-ah," he said.

"No matter where you go?"

Ben snorted and shook his head.

"I've always dreamed of getting out, no doubt, maybe moving to California or Texas or…wherever. Now, I haven't got a clue what I want to do," he said at last. "I guess I could always take over the lobstering business from my old man. I know that's what *he'd* like, even though he's never come right out and said it."

"What about Pete. I thought he was doing that," Julia said.

Ben wondered how she knew anything about his family situation. As far as he could recall, he hadn't mentioned anything about Pete or his father's lobstering business. Of course, she might have picked it up from around town, but she showed an interest and knowledge of his family situation that...well, he didn't want to think it meant a lot more than it appeared on the surface.

"I have no idea what's going on with Pete," Ben said. "I mean—he's twenty-four years old. Never been to college. Still living at home. No prospect of ever getting married."

"What's so bad about not being married?" Julia asked with a sudden vehemence that startled Ben.

"Nothing...nothing a'tall. It's just with Pete.... He's kind of a sad case. He hooked up with a girl in high school, never dated anyone else, and she dumped him recently."

Julia looked away and bit down on her lower lip as she nodded. "You ever go to college?" she asked.

The subtle shift in conversation surprised him, as if she knew as well as he did that they were dancing around a sensitive subject.

"I tried a semester at the community college in Auburn, but—" He shrugged. "It wasn't for me."

Julia nodded.

"How 'bout you?" he asked.

Julia's face went pale. Her eyes narrowed, and the lines around her mouth tightened as if she'd bitten into a lemon.

"Yeah. Upstate New York. Ithaca College."

"Never heard of it. What'd you study?"

"Guys. That's where I met my ex-husband. Charlie." Her eyes took on a glassy stare as she looked out over the water again. "It didn't last long. Four or five years. I don't even remember. I guess it was my trial run."

Ben wasn't sure why, but he felt a sudden twinge of jealousy, thinking that other men—maybe many other men—had been with her. He wondered if Julia meant what she had said about studying guys and might be the kind of woman who had trouble settling down and remaining loyal to one man.

Not that it matters, he told himself, flushing with guilt. Guys like me don't end up with women like her.

"You graduate?" he asked, hoping to keep the subject light.

Julia nodded and said, "I got a degree in early childhood education, but I never used it. Never got around to it."

Ben sensed there was more here than she wanted to get into right now, so he let her comment drop, and they were silent for a long time as they both looked at the sky and sea. Finally, after a long silence, Julia shifted her stance and turned halfway around toward him.

"Ben," she said with a deep-throated huskiness in her voice that made him respond instantly. He raised both hands and gripped her shoulders. After a beautiful moment of tension as they gazed into each other's eyes, he drew her close.

She didn't resist. She collapsed into his embrace.

Her arms snaked around his waist and pulled him close until their hips were pressing together…hard. Grinding. He lowered his face to hers, and she stretched up to meet him. Their mouths were open as if they each had something important to say but couldn't quite phrase it. And then, slowly, Ben moved his head forward until their lips met. As soon as they touched, a hot flood of passion swept through Ben, and he was kissing her desperately.

Within seconds, their hands were all over each other, feeling… rubbing…kneading…touching. Ben's hands cupped her breasts and felt their soft, warm roundness. She broke off the kiss and, moving closer, moaned as she blew softly into his ear. And then her hands slid down over his hips and around to the front. She started rubbing her hand up and down across the hardness of his groin, sending electric sparks sizzling through him.

Ben nuzzled his face against her neck, intoxicated as he inhaled her fragrance and licked the salt on her skin and nibbled the lobe of her ear. For a moment…a moment that crackled like lightning in the air…they pulled away from each other and smiled, their gazes locked. The liquid glow in Julia's brown eyes was all Ben could see as slowly…slowly…they knelt down together on the sand, and then she was in his arms again, kissing him and squeezing him while making soft, low moaning sounds.

Ben eased her down onto the warm sand, unmindful of the grit as they slowly, carefully undressed each other, caressing and exploring and reveling in each other's body as each new part was exposed. And then, with the sea hissing on the sand beside them, they made love for the first time.

"Chief says he wants to see you."

It was a few minutes before his shift, and Tom was seated in the canteen, his feet propped up on the table as he sipped a cup of coffee that had obviously been on the burner a few hours longer than it should have. It might taste like crap, but at least it was hot and had caffeine. In an instant, Charlie Evans' words instantly turned the warmth he'd been feeling into ice.

"Right now?" Tom asked. He dropped his feet to the floor and tried to control the tremor in his hand as he placed the Styrofoam coffee cup onto the table.

"No," Charlie said, rolling his eyes. "He was thinking sometime next week…or whenever you're in the mood." He paused, then added, "Of *course* right now."

"Any idea what this is about?" Tom asked as he got to his feet.

"Not a clue," Charlie replied, and then he ducked back out the door.

Tom stood beside the table for several seconds, feeling lightheaded. His knees were rubbery, and he was afraid they would fold up on him like a fifty-cent lawn chair if he took a single step. Steadying himself with one hand on the back of the chair he'd been sitting in, he stared at the closed door Charlie had exited.

What the fuck? he thought. They gotta be onto me.

He was convinced he was going to be busted…. He'd go to trial… maybe even do time in Warren. Just great. A town cop in the state pen. How many men had he arrested and helped put there? He'd never come out alive.

"Screw this," he muttered as he picked up his cup and dumped the contents down the sink. He tossed the cup in the general direction of the trash can and missed, but he didn't bother to pick it up.

He could always run.

He didn't have any ready cash. He would have, if Ben hadn't been such a dick about his proposition. Still, why not go home, pack a few things, get the suitcase with the drugs, and take off? Maybe go to Boston…or Providence to unload it. He knew people in Rhode

Island. Hell, if Ben hadn't been such a prick and hooked him up with Richie Sullivan, maybe Richie would have hooked him up with someone down there. He might not get the best price, certainly not what it was worth, but it'd be something. And right now, *anything* was looking better than what he was facing.

"Jesus Harold Christ on a rubber crutch," he whispered.

He was still wondering if he should bolt or not when the door opened, and Chief Harlan walked in.

"Hey. You coming up to my office?" he asked. It didn't matter what he said or who he was speaking to, whenever Harlan spoke, the flat, emotionless pitch in his voice always sounded threatening.

"Yeah...I'm on my way."

"Make it snappy," Harlan said, and then he left, the door whooshing shut behind him.

Tom turned to the sink, ran the water until it was good and cold, and splashed his face several times. The cold shock numbed him, but it felt good. It cleared his head...helped him focus. He had to face whatever was going to happen, no matter what kind of shit came down.

A minute later Tom knocked on the police chief's door, a few quick raps.

"I'm in. You're out," Harlan shouted.

The metal doorknob was slick in the palm of Tom's sweating hand as he turned it and pushed the door open. He saw a man wearing a dark blue suit in a chair next to Harlan's desk. They both rose to their feet when Tom entered the room.

"Shut the door."

Tom did as he was told and lingered by the door

"Come in...come in. Have a seat," Harlan said, indicating the empty chair next to the mystery man and his desk. Tom walked over to it and sat down.

"So," he said, his voice dry and flat. "What's this all about?" He was amazed that he could speak at all

After a short pause that seemed to stretch out forever, Harlan sat down behind his desk and said, "Tom. I'd like you to meet Jerry Lincoln. Jerry's with the DEA. Jerry. This here's Tom Marshall."

Even before the introductions were over, Tom felt his stomach clench. Sweat popped out on his forehead as he nodded to the man.

Jerry extended his hand for Tom to shake. Tom's arm felt as limp as a twisted dishtowel as he reached out to shake hands. Lincoln's grip was strong and firm enough to hurt as they shook.

"You see, Jerry's got a bit of a problem," Harlan went on, "and I think you're just the man who can help him out with it."

"I—Yeah. Sure. I'll do whatever I can," Tom said, confused and worried about the direction this conversation was taking.

Tom took a moment to ease back in the chair, trying to look perfectly relaxed and comfortable as he tried to gauge the man.

If anyone looked like a narc, it was Jerry Lincoln. He was thin as a rail, muscular, with blond hair cut in a severe crew cut that exposed his pink scalp beneath the short bristles. His face was thin and lined. There was a cold, flat gleam in his pale, blue eyes that Tom found genuinely unnerving.

"So what's the problem?"

"I need some information," Lincoln said, "about some people around town."

"Information?"

"It's common knowledge there's a network of people working with organized crime in this area."

"I wouldn't say it's all that organized," Tom said, trying to inject a bit of humor to smooth over his initial nervousness. Maybe things weren't as bad as he thought.

"We know some local fishermen bring drugs in from boats offshore," Lincoln said without the slightest trace of a smile.

"Yeah..." Tom shifted in his seat. "I've heard rumors to that effect..."

"We're trying to crack that ring, and I need someone—a local who's willing to give me information."

Tom sat up straight as if a jolt of electricity had passed through him. He raised his eyebrows and slowly smiled, relieved that he wasn't in the world of shit he'd been imagining. What he really wanted to do was throw his arms out wide and whoop for joy.

Lincoln was looking for a snitch.

It was almost too good to be true, but Tom cautioned himself not to overplay it in case this was a setup.

What if they were trying to lull him into a false sense of security?

"Since 9/11, we've gotten increased funding through Homeland

Security," Lincoln said, "so we're expanding our investigations into some of the off-shore activity here and up the coast all the way to Canada. I understand you have significant contacts with various local fishermen and lobstermen."

"Well...yeah. Sure. I know all the guys down at the wharf," Tom said with a shrug as much to relieve the tension inside him as acknowledge what Lincoln had said. "I know everyone 'round here."

"And you wouldn't find it a problem to inform on some of them if you were to, say, find out some of them were running drugs?"

"The law's the law," Tom said. "My job's enforcing it."

"What if it were even someone you know well like, say, your father-in-law, for instance?"

"Wally...Wally Brown?" Tom covered his mouth with the flat of his hand and rubbed his cheek as though it had been bee-stung. All the while, Lincoln sat there and stared at him with a cold, unblinking look.

"Your father-in-law is a known associate of Richard Sullivan, otherwise known as 'The Crowbar.' Sullivan's a member of an organized crime family based in Providence."

"I don't know anything about that, but—yeah.... Sure. I know Sullivan. He owns a bar down in Boothbay."

"Among other business interests," Lincoln said tonelessly.

Tom glanced at Harlan, who was leaning back in his chair and staring out the window as though he wasn't even a part of this conversation.

"I'm not so sure I'd want to be checking into what Richie Sullivan's doing," Tom said with a nervous laugh. "I—uh, I'd rather not end up going overboard with a cement block tied 'round my ankles."

"I'm not interested in you going after Richie Sullivan," Lincoln said. "The way I'm going to get to him is by breaking the system he and his criminal associates have going. Get one of the little guys in the ring and squeeze him until he gives up whoever's above him."

Tom leaned back and released the tension gathering in his shoulders.

"So that's my proposition to you," Lincoln continued. "Can I count on your help?"

"I don't see why not."

"I was hoping for a little more enthusiasm than that," Lincoln said, and Harlan shifted his eyes and looked at him.

"Absolutely. You can count on me."

"You can take some time to mull it over, if you'd like. Once things go to trial, you know, you might end up having to testify against people you've known all your life."

The sensible response, Tom knew, would be to agree to take some time before he decided. He knew it wouldn't look good if he jumped at this proposition too fast, not without at least appearing to give it due consideration. They certainly wouldn't expect him to decide right here on the spot, but Tom found himself smiling.

"Yes, sir," he said. "I'll do whatever you want me to do."

Lincoln and Harlan exchanged glances that, once again, gave Tom a spike of suspicion that this might not be what it appeared, but he realized he was in too deep to back out now.

Tom glanced at the wall clock and said, "I—ah, I have to get out on my patrol."

He stood up and, again, shook hands with Lincoln. The man's tight grip made his fingers tingle.

"Thank you for your cooperation," Lincoln said, his voice flat, his face nearly expressionless.

He turned to leave. Tom sensed both men's eyes boring into the back of his head as he opened the door and walked out of the office. As he closed the door behind him, he wished he could hear what the two men said next.

He made his way down the hallway, realizing he'd been holding his breath, so he let it out in a slow whistle. It felt like he had been holding it for the entire duration of the interview. Tiny white spots of light zigzagged across his vision. If Harlan had any idea he'd stolen those drugs, they would have busted him right there and then.

No way they'd let him walk.

He was sure of that.

So if he played his cards right, he stood a chance of looking a whole lot better in the department and still getting the money he needed—finally—to get the hell away from this goddamned town and his fucking wife and her family.

If he hurt his wife's family in the process, and Capt'n Wally did some time in jail…who the fuck cared?

EIGHT

Slashers

The sun was a soft, ruby-red ball near the horizon. Long shadows of pine trees and scrub brush stretched across the rocks and darkening sand that glistened like spilled oil. A crow sat in a dead tree nearby, cawing its ragged call. In the aftermath of their love-making, Ben and Julia cuddled on the sand, resting in each other's arms. Finally, Julia shivered.

"We ought to get going," she said, holding herself close against Ben. He ran his fingertips along the length of her arm as though reading the sprinkling of goose bumps and sand like they were Braille.

Moving languorously, they got up, brushed themselves off, and got dressed. The wind was blowing strong off the water now, chill-ing them and drying the sweat on their skin, but both of them were smiling, filled with contentment.

For Ben's part, he couldn't remember the last time he had felt so close, so damned *good* being with a woman. When a memory of Kathy Brackett crept into his mind, he pushed it aside. Any feelings he might still have for Kathy had been whisked away this afternoon by the sun and the sand, by the breeze off the ocean and the gentle touch of Julia's hands all over his body.

Before today, he had been convinced that the jagged pieces of his life would never fit together perfectly smoothly, but then again—whose did?

He had wondered hundreds if not thousands of times if he would ever feel genuine love again. Sexual attraction? Sure. But he had been convinced that any real connection with a woman was gone from his life for good. He'd been sure that some part of him—the part that would allow him to give himself unconditionally to a woman—had been dead. That had been the first casualty of seeing—and participating in—the depraved things human beings can do to each other in war.

After what just happened with Julia, he wanted desperately to believe some of the things he was feeling were real.

For Julia's part, she felt an amazing sense of satisfaction and triumph mixed with inexpressible joy. For weeks…for months, now, she had been hearing talk around town about Ben Brown coming home from Iraq almost as if he were some sort of mythical being, not a flesh-and-blood human. Although none of the townsfolk had ever spoken about him directly to her—she was, after all, an outsider—she had overheard enough so, even for her, Ben Brown had become something special…so special, in fact, that she wondered if *anyone* could live up to such high expectations.

But now on the beach, he had…and then some.

He had proven to be a sensitive and skilled lover who had done things to her—*with* her—that had amazing intensity. Maybe it was being outdoors instead of in one of their bedrooms…maybe a wild, savage spirit had energized their lovemaking…maybe she had been so pent up, so frustrated by Tom Marshall's inadequate lovemaking…maybe it was the element of danger, of being seen making love on the beach…

Whatever it was, *something* gave their lovemaking an extra edge that had been beyond anything she had ever experienced.

Or maybe…just maybe…Ben Brown really had lived up to the unrealistic expectations she had built up.

To her amazement, she had experienced a powerful connection with him.

After the disappointment of her first marriage, she had convinced herself that she was immune to love. Love was nothing but a foolish, immature infatuation. There was no way it could be some deep and lasting connection she had grown up thinking it might be.

Now…she wasn't so sure.

But what she did know was, she wasn't lonely anymore.

Neither one of them said much as they walked, hand in hand, up the winding dirt path to the top of the hill that overlooked the tiny cove. Julia leaned her head against his shoulder, smiling and breathing in the musky scent of sweat in his armpit. The wind cooled their skin and blew Julia's long, dark hair back over one shoulder like a fanned cape. Ben stopped and, brushing her hair back, leaned down and kissed the nape of her neck. His tongue lapped her salty flesh like he was a kitten, drinking fresh cream. He inhaled sharply, taking in the lingering scent of her perfume and her warm, salty flesh.

"Do you think anyone saw us?" Julia asked. She giggled, but her voice was edged with worry.

The thought had never crossed Ben's mind, but the suggestion gave him a jolt. If someone from town—anyone—had seen what was going on down there on the beach, word would spread through town fast. He'd definitely get teased about it tonight at The Local if he showed up.

Then again, someone already knew he was interested in Julia. That's why he'd been threatened the other night.

"If they did..." Ben smiled, remembering some of the things they had done to each other. "I guess we gave them quite a show."

"Tongues will wag," Julia said with a light laugh.

They stood for a long time, kissing and clinging to each other, their hands touching...rubbing...feeling...caressing...exploring soft and firm curves beneath clothes. Ben felt himself stirring again and was more than ready to drop down to the ground right there and go at it, but Julia broke off the embrace. Panting heavily, a mischievous gleam lighting her eyes, she said, "Don't get started now, lover boy. Save it for later."

Ben smiled and shook his head, thinking: *Good...there's gonna be a "later."*

"Oww, the things you do to me, woman."

They turned and, hand and hand, started along the path back to where they had left Ben's car.

"What's the name of this place—the beach, I mean?" Julia asked.

"Sand Beach."

"How original."

"Quaint, even," Ben said.

"Do many people know about it?"

"Just us locals. It's one of those places we don't like the summer people knowing about."

"What, you think they'd ruin it?" Julia glanced back down the trail, a wistful look flickering in her dark eyes.

"You haven't lived here long enough to see what's happened to this town. Hell, even in the short time I've been away, I can't believe how much it's changed."

"A lot can happen in four years."

"Yeah, but if tourists knew about this place, then where would we go to make love?"

Julia laughed.

"I'm sure we'd come up with something," she said, and then she leaned forward and kissed him on the mouth. Ben grabbed her and hugged her close, making the kiss more passionate as he pressed his hips against her until she began to breathe hard.

"It's *our* place now," Julia said once the kiss was over, and she was snuggling against him, reveling in his body heat. "Do you know who owns the land?"

Ben considered for a moment.

"I'm not really sure, now that you mention it. It might belong to one of the Nelsons."

"So what do you say we buy it and build a house out here?"

Ben knew from her reaction that she immediately regretted saying something so sappy, but he actually found it endearing.

"Couldn't afford the taxes," he said, and then they continued to walk, their fingers laced together like ivy. Through a break in the woods, Ben caught a glimpse of the roof of his car, parked at the end of the dead-end dirt road. At first, he didn't register the meaning of the faint cloud of dust being whisked slowly away by the breeze, but then they broke out of the woods, and he saw that his car was sagging heavily to one side as if the driver's side wheels were stuck in a rut.

"Goddamned son-of-a-*bitch!*"

"What is it?" Julia asked, but he didn't answer. He started running toward his car, all the while staring in amazement at the tires on the driver's side, front and back. Both of them were flat. The hubcaps were almost touching the dirt road.

"Whoever did this just did it."

Ben looked down the road. Seething with anger, he watched the swirling dust settle to the ground and drift into the woods like a cloud of yellow smoke. It was the last trace of the culprit's escape, but there was still a sense of a nearby presence.

"Fucking *son*-of-a-*bitch!*"

He kicked the dirt, and a spray of gravel and dirt peppered the side of the car like a scattering of buckshot.

"Is it safe to assume you don't have two spare tires in the trunk?" Julia said, trying to sound reasonable to counterbalance Ben's anger.

"They must have heard us coming and taken off." He looked back the way they had come and then at the road again. "I bet they would have done all four tires if they'd had time."

"You keep saying 'they.' Do you know it was more than one person?"

"No!" Ben shouted.

He turned to her, his eyes flashing like summer lightning. He tried to suppress his rage, but he clenched his fist and pounded the top of his car. The impact sounded like he'd hit the bottom of an empty oil barrel and was hard enough to dent the metal.

"Don't do that," Julia said, her voice wavering. "They've done enough damage as it is." It took effort to keep her voice calm. She knew she had to maintain calm here, but she was starting to panic because she was suddenly convinced this message was directed at her as much as Ben. After the conversation she'd had last night with Tom, she had a pretty good idea that he might have done this, but she didn't want to believe that he—a town cop—was capable of such a thing.

"Why the *hell* didn't we *hear* them?" Ben sputtered as he massaged his wrist. He started pacing back and forth beside the car, staring down the road as if he could somehow will the culprits back into view.

"I dunno. Maybe it was some punks, you know?" Julia said. She hung back, unnerved by the intensity of Ben's outburst and afraid he might turn it on her. "Maybe the…the trees blocked the sound. The wind was maybe blowing in the wrong direction or something."

"What if…" Ben swallowed hard, trying hard to control his anger. His hands were aching, the knuckles of his hand standing out as he clenched his fists, squeezing them like he was strangling a live snake. The muscles in his forearms swelled like pressurized hoses. "Damn.… What if one of them was watching us the whole time?"

"You mean standing guard?"

Ben nodded, and Julia's eyes widened as she hugged herself and looked back down the trail, still feeling as though the threat hadn't gone away. The skin on the back of her neck crawled with the sensation that—even now—unseen eyes were watching her from the margins of the woods. She moved closer to Ben and slid her arm around his waist, hugging him protectively. When he put his arm around her shoulder, the tension inside him vibrated like electricity in a high voltage wire, but she felt reassured as he held her tightly.

"I'll call for a tow truck to come out and help us."

"Damn," Julia said as she glanced at her wristwatch. "This really screws things up. My dad's expecting me back by now. It's suppertime."

"Fuck! Fuck! *Fuck!*" Ben kicked a divot into the dirt. "If only we'd come back thirty seconds sooner!"

"Getting angry won't solve the problem."

Ben looked at her, his expression as hard as a stone carving.

A thought suddenly hit her, and she rushed over to the car and looked inside. Relief washed over her when she saw her purse undisturbed where she had left it on the floor on the passenger's side.

At least she hadn't been robbed.

Ben fished the car keys from his pocket, unlocked the door on the passenger's side, and took his cell phone from the seat. He dialed his home number, not really expecting anyone to answer, and was surprised when Louise picked up.

"Hey, Lou-Lou Belle" he said with forced cheerfulness.

"Hey yourself. Where are you?"

"Out."

"Well, Pops was looking for you earlier."

"Really?"

"He wanted you to help him haul today."

Ben glanced at Julia and shot her a smile. He almost blew her a kiss but stopped himself before he did anything that "quaint."

"Why're you at the house?"

Louise hesitated for a moment, then said, "I stopped by to see if Pops was home."

That didn't ring at all true. Ben knew she was probably trying to get away from Tom again, but he decided to let it pass...let her be the one to mention it.

"Look—ahh, do you have the phone book handy?"

"Hold on a sec." After a short pause followed by the sound of things being shuffled around, Louise said, "Yeah. Got it right here."

"Can you look up the number for Skip's Garage and call him for me?"

"What's the problem?"

"Flat tire. I want him to pick up my car."

"What, you can't change a flat?"

"Give me the number. I'll call him," Ben said. He didn't for a moment consider telling her the truth. Word would get out eventually about him and Julia, but there was no sense starting it.

"No...no...I'll call. Where are you?"

"Parking lot for Sand Beach."

"What are you doing out there?"

"Taking a walk."

"All right...who is she?"

"No one."

"You're not with Kathy, are you?"

"Absolutely not."

"Come on...you can tell me," Louise said, adopting the pleading, pathetic voice that had always worked so well on him when they were young.

"There's nothing to tell. I'm not with anyone. Are you gonna call Skip's or not?"

Ben narrowed his eyes and shook his head as Julia came up close to him and, resting her hand on the crook of his elbow, leaned forward and kissed him on the cheek. He stared past her at the sky. The sun was setting, and darkness crept across the land. In the west, a low band of purple clouds streaked the sky like old scars.

"Yeah," Louise said. "I'll call. Anything else?"

"Just make sure there's plenty of cold beer in the fridge when I get home, 'kay?"

"Roger that," Louise said, and then she cut the call. Ben was grimacing as he closed the cell phone and turned back to Julia.

"You're not with anyone?" she said. There was as much hurt as anger in her eyes. "You didn't think it necessary—you didn't want to tell her you were with me?"

"It's not like that," Ben said. He had to look away for a moment to collect his thoughts.

"What *is* it like, then?"

"I didn't—It's none of her goddamned business what I do," Ben said. "I'm sorry, but…people will talk…"

"So what if they do?"

Ben wondered why he hadn't come right out and told Louise he was with Julia, and he couldn't come up with a good reason.

Besides, what did it matter?

It certainly wasn't like he'd be embarrassed to be seen with her. If anything, he was glad that a woman as attractive as Julia had even given him a second look. She sure seemed to be pursuing him as fast as he was pursuing her.

Julia wasn't convinced, but even though her feelings were hurt, she decided to play it all off as a joke. Hooking her arm around his, she pulled him toward her so fast he almost lost his balance.

"Oh, I can't *wait* to meet the rest of your family," she said, and then she blew softly into his ear, making him shiver. As angry as he still was, Ben finally relented and kissed her on the mouth. Julia slid her hands around him and held him as close as she possibly could. When they separated, both of them were smiling.

"Someone'll be out to get us…eventually," he said. He was considering trying to get her to go off into the woods with him for a quickie, but there was no telling when Skip would show up with the tow truck.

Julia pursed her lips and regarded him for a long time in silence. She could all but read his mind. It was as clear and open as any man's.

"What?" Ben finally said, suddenly uncomfortable under her steady gaze.

"I'm going to have to walk home," she said.

Ben frowned at her, then shook his head.

"No way. Skip'll be along soon enough."

"But my dad." She shrugged. "I should be there."

Worry gathered in her eyes like an approaching thunderstorm, and he felt another surge of fury because right now, there wasn't a damned thing he could do to help her.

"I'll go with you. I can leave the keys in the car. Skip will know what to do."

"Don't be stupid. If the jerk who did this is hanging around, he might do some serious damage to the car."

She had a point. Still, it would be dark soon. He didn't like the idea of her walking all the way to Steeple Road from here. It had to be four or five miles, at least.

"What if the jerk follows you home?"

Julia gave him a startled look, but that lasted only a second. She walked over to the car, got her purse, and slung it over her shoulder.

"I think I can take care of myself," she said, and by the gleam in her eye and the set of her jaw, he was convinced she was telling the truth.

"Are you sure?" he said. "I mean…it's not very gentlemanly to leave a lady stranded. Especially after…you know."

"Screwing her brains out?"

Ben nodded.

"Jesus, Ben. You're acting like I'm some kind of moron who can't take care of herself. I can walk and chew gum at the same time, you know?"

"No, it's just…I don't want this to…to…" He didn't know how to finish, so he let his voice fade away.

"You don't want this to *what?*" Julia said.

"I don't want what's happened to make things weird between us, is all."

"What the hell are you talking about?" Julia settled her purse strap on her shoulder and stared at him, looking genuinely astounded. Then she came up to him and hugged him so tightly he lost his breath for a moment. When she tilted her head back, and their lips met in a long, passionate kiss, it really did take his breath away. He clung to her, not wanting to let her go, but he knew—eventually—he would have to.

"All right, then," he said after the kiss ended. "I'll catch you later. You think we might hook up later tonight?"

Julia looked away, considered for a moment, then shook her head and said, "Not tonight. Tomorrow, maybe…"

"What do you mean, '*maybe*?'"

She let out a trilling laugh and then turned and started walking down the road. Her figure was indistinct in the fading light, and when she disappeared from sight into the gathering darkness, Ben was left with the unnerving impression she had never been there… that she was an illusion that had now faded, leaving behind a vacuum so cold and empty he found it astonishing.

He covered his mouth with his fist as if stifling a cough, unable to believe the things he was thinking about her, and he scolded himself for allowing himself to fall for her so hard and so fast.

He kept staring down the narrow dirt road long after she had disappeared, knowing that—no matter what kind of second thoughts he might be having—he wasn't going to back away from following this no matter where it led.

The harsh, white glare of headlights behind Julia washed the side of the road, stretching her shadow out thirty feet in front of her. The muscles in her neck and shoulders tightened like springs as she waited for the car to drive past her.

Please don't stop…. Don't even slow down…

But when the crunch of tires sounded on the roadside gravel, she knew the car had pulled over to the side of the road and was coming up right behind her.

And she had no doubt who it was.

A mixture of fear and anger filled her as she kept walking. She was convinced Tom was the one who had slashed Ben's tires.

Who else would have?

The car came closer, its tires crunching on the roadside gravel, the headlights getting brighter. She looked left and right, but saw no place to run. Out of the reach of the headlights, the road in front of her was swallowed by darkness. Suddenly, the headlights swung around her to the left as the car got back onto the road and pulled up beside her. In the corner of her eye, she saw that it was a police cruiser.

She kept walking, looking straight ahead, but the driver—she knew, without looking, that it was Tom Marshall—drove along next to her. She heard a faint whirring sound as the passenger's side automatic window slid down.

"Hold up a second?" he said.

Julia didn't even glance at him. She kept walking, her eyes fixed on the stretch of road illuminated by the headlights. After she had gone another fifty feet or so, the cruiser pulled ahead and skidded to a stop at an angle in front of her, cutting her off. The headlights slashed across the landscape, clouded by swirling dust that rose from its sudden stop.

Julia was filled with panic, but she told herself not to let it show. For a long time, she stood there wishing she knew which way to run. Then the flickering blue and red emergency lights came on, sweeping the darkness away. She waited for the *whoop-whoop* of a siren, but it never came.

Balling one hand into a fist and holding it at her side, she raised her other hand to shield her eyes from the flashes. She felt small and vulnerable as she stared at the cruiser, waiting to see what Tom would do next.

The night was warm, and her skin was still sticky with sweat and sand from the beach, but a chill slithered up her back. Her shirt clung to her back and shoulders like clammy hands. She tasted salt when she flicked her tongue over her upper lip and waited.

The driver's door of the cruiser opened, and Tom Marshall stepped out. He left the car running, and the plume of exhaust spewing from the tailpipe turned a ghastly red in the glow of his taillights and flashing lights. Knocking his police cap back on his head, he walked up to her.

"What's a pretty little thing like you doing all alone on a dark road like this?" he said.

He might have been trying to inject a bit of humor into the situation, but Julia was frozen. She regarded him with what she hoped was a perfectly flat expression. As frightened and nervous as she was, she also was angry at him and wanted to tell him…to *yell* at him to leave her and Ben the fuck alone.

But he was right.

She *was* vulnerable out here all alone. It would have been much safer to stay with Ben and wait for the tow truck to show up.

Her body fairly vibrated with tension, and she was ready to punch and kick him if she had to, for all the good it would do. Tom was at least six inches taller than she was, and he had a good seventy-five to a hundred pounds on her.

"I'm just out for a walk, if you don't mind," she said, trying hard to control her emotions. "That's not against the law, is it?"

Tom chuckled softly and said, "Not that I'm aware of, but I'd have to check the town ordinances to be sure. I could always take you down to the station for questioning."

He paused and for a long, tense moment they stared each other in the eyes. Tom had the advantage on her here, too because the lights were bright behind him, and she could barely make out his features while she was pinned to the night like a medical specimen on a lab table.

Julia took a quick glance behind her to see if there was a nearby house she could run to if she had to, but outside of the cone of light, all was darkness.

She was trapped by the one man she was determined never to see again.

If she'd had doubts before, what was happening right now confirmed her suspicions that Tom had slashed Ben's tires. He must have been hoping to create a situation exactly like this…to get her alone again.

"You heading home?" Tom asked, his voice loose and casual.

Julia grunted but said nothing.

What she wanted to say was, *It's none of your goddamned business what I'm doing or where I'm going,* but she kept her mouth shut.

Sarcasm wasn't going to help with a guy like Tom Marshall, and—obviously—being direct with him—like she had last night—apparently wouldn't work, either. She had always sensed that, just below his joking exterior, a ferocious temper lurked like a rat trap, ready to spring. Thankfully, he had never unleashed it on her, but she didn't want him to try it now.

"Can I give you a lift?"

"I'd prefer to walk, thank you."

"It might not be safe out here," he said. "I mean—this ain't New York City, but…you never know who you might bump into."

"I'll be fine," Julia said.

"You sure of that?" Tom's nostrils flared as he turned his head to one side as though sniffing for whatever danger lurked in the pressing darkness.

Julia clucked her tongue, but a chill slithered through her when she wondered if he really had slashed Ben's tires.

What level of violence might he be capable of?

What if he did this just so he could get me alone?

"Look—ahh, Tom…" She shielded her eyes against the flashing glare. Fear and anger vied within her for equal expression, but she didn't dare submit to either. "I…I really don't want any trouble here. I told you last night—We're done. It's over, and if you continue to harass me, I'll report you if I have to."

"Harass you? Is that what you think I'm doing here?"

He took a step forward, and Julia matched him with a quick shuffling step back.

"I am not *harassing* you," he continued, his voice taking on the pitch of a pleading little boy. "If anything, I'm doing the exact opposite." He took a breath. She heard it shudder in his chest. "I want you to like me. I want you to love me and for us to be together."

"It's not going to happen," Julia said, her voice cracking like a whip in the still air. The words were out of her mouth before she thought them through or gauged how he might react.

"You're not being fair, Julia. You're not giving me a chance."

When he took another step closer, Julia backed away again. Trickles of sweat ran down the inside of her shirt, chilling her, but she repressed a shiver.

"Look…Tom. I don't want any trouble, okay?" She spoke slowly, patiently, like she was explaining a difficult concept to a child. "And I certainly don't mean to hurt your feelings or…or insult you or anything, but how many times do I have to tell you? It's over. We're done."

For a long time—seconds that stretched into minutes—he stood there…motionless…staring at her. The flickering red and blue lights behind him haloed his body, giving him the strobe-like illusion of moving even when he was standing perfectly still. Julia had no idea what was going through his mind, but she was still afraid that he would suddenly snap and do her harm.

"I wish you'd give me another chance," he finally said.

"There was no chance to begin with," she said. "Don't you get it?"

"Never?"

"Never."

"You don't want to say that," Tom said, his voice pitched low and as hard as nails.

"Yes I do."

Julia was surprised that she had found the courage to confront him like this—especially alone on a deserted road at night; but after what had happened between her and Ben today, she had to end this…

Now.

"You always bitched about this town…how everyone shut you out, and how much you wanted to leave, right?" Tom said.

"Don't start in with that, Tom…. Please."

"But I've got *our* ticket out of here."

"How many ways do I have to say it? I am *not* interested."

She was tempted to throw in his face that she knew he had vandalized Ben's car in order to get to her, but she decided to hold back. It would only make matters worse.

"What if I told you I had two hundred thousand dollars?"

Julia shook her head sadly, her hair fanning both sides of her face like wind-blown curtains. During the time she and Tom had been together, they had talked about splitting for the Caribbean or Mexico, but that's all it had ever been. Something to talk about.

Two hundred thousand dollars might go a long way toward her dream of escape, but she knew, now, it had all been a fantasy.

And she certainly never meant to include Tom.

Even if the sex had been good—and it hadn't been—Tom had been a diversion, a break in the lonely isolation of her life in The Cove. In a matter of months if not weeks, she would have found living with him limited if not boring beyond belief.

Besides, she deserved better, and Ben Brown *was* better.

A line from Shakespeare drifted through her mind: *I have to be cruel to be kind.* She would have said it now, but it probably would have confused Tom.

"I don't want your money," she said. "I don't *need* it. I have to stay here with my father."

"That's not what you said before when you—"

"It's what I'm saying now." Julia said.

She was clenching her fists so tightly the heels of her hands were going numb. Her pulse whispered in her ears, blocking out any night sounds.

"It's over, Tom. Get used to it and get on with your life."

"What if I—"

"Go back to your wife," Julia said simply.

Tom let out an exasperated gasp as he stood there, trembling. Julia was afraid he would do something desperate. She had no doubt he was capable of violence. A man who would slash someone's tires out of sheer jealousy was desperate enough to do just about anything.

"I could make a lot of trouble for you, you know?" he finally said.

Julia lowered her gaze and shook her head even though she knew, given half a chance, he not only *could*—he *would* make good on his threat.

"You know what?" she said, forcing strength into her voice she didn't really feel. "You'll do whatever you gotta do. But I'm telling you right here and now—if you make trouble for me, I sure as hell will make trouble for you."

She was amazed by her words and had no idea where they came from.

"So now you're threatening me?" Tom snorted derisively and shook his head. He placed his hands on his hips, his shape swelling in the night.

"No," Julia said mildly. "*You're* threatening *me,* and I won't stand for it."

Tom sniffed and then, twisting to his right, made a raw grumbling sound deep in his throat before spitting into the darkness. "How could you—?" he said, but then he stopped.

That was all Julia needed.

She didn't have to tell him she would reveal their affair to his wife and his boss and the whole town.

He knew, and she knew.

Sighing and forcing her shoulders to relax, Julia walked around the cruiser and kept going down the road. The flashing emergency lights lit up the roadside with hallucinatory stabs of brightness that threatened to throw her off balance, but she kept going...hoping... praying this was the end of it.

You did it, she told herself, fighting down a heady rush of excitement so strong she was afraid she was about to pass out. *What a pathetic jerk he is...I can't believe I slept with him!*

The distance between her and the cruiser gradually lengthened.

The lights were still shining on her back, prickling her skin like a tanning lamp, but the heat gradually lessened with each step she took. Soon, the cool night air embraced her like she had been plunged into cold spring water. Goose bumps spread across her arms and legs.

As she walked, she strained to hear what Tom was doing behind her, but the night muffled everything around her. The air was dense, as if she were embedded in damp cotton. She hadn't heard him get back into his cruiser, and there was no indication that he was coming after her on foot.

Was he standing there, trying to accept his loss…or was he debating what to do to her?

As desperate as he was, Julia didn't think he was so far gone he would actually attack her. He was clearly capable of violence, but she was fairly certain he would have the sense not to turn it on her.

When she was more than a hundred yards away from the cruiser, the flashers suddenly winked off. Then the headlights swung around in a wide arc away from her, throwing crazy sweeping shadows across the road and then plunging everything into darkness so thick it vibrated with rippling afterimages.

Julia fought back the urge to turn and watch Tom drive away, but she knew if he saw her do that, he might take it as a faint sign of encouragement, and she didn't want that.

She had to keep on walking and not look back.

One thing made her almost giddy with joy, and that was knowing the path was now wide open for her to be with Ben Brown.

And as far as she was concerned, that was all she needed.

NINE

Killer Fog

Capt'n Wally was ripe, royally pissed.

Nobody…*nobody* told him what to do.

But he was smart enough to know when someone had him by the short 'n curlies and was more than capable of twisting his ball right the fuck off if they wanted to.

Mere minutes ago, Richie Sullivan had left the wharf, driving away in his fancy new yellow Lexus—a color Wally thought of as "baby shit gold." Leaning against one of the wharf pilings, his body tight with rage, Wally watched the dust settle at his feet.

Throughout their talk, Richie had never lost his temper, never once raised his voice. He didn't have to, but he made it perfectly clear how pissed he was at Wally for not making the pickup the other night. He also wanted reassurance from Wally that he would get out to The Nephews today to meet up with the trawler before it headed back to Gloucester.

While onboard, inspecting the boat he'd financed for Wally, Richie, the damned fool, had even whistled some stupid tune.

Didn't he know how unlucky it was to whistle on a boat before it headed out?

Hadn't he ever heard of "whistling down the wind?"

Jesus, Wally didn't need that!

It was a bad enough morning as it was. Fog had rolled in overnight and—so far, anyway—it didn't look like it was going to lift any time soon. It was going to be a bitch of a day, no matter how he sliced it, and he sure as hell could use some help. He had no idea where Pete was—probably sucking down beer at The Local. As for his deadbeat oldest son…Ben had let him down yesterday by not showing up like Pete said he would to help him haul. If only he could count on either one of his sons, he wouldn't have so goddamned many traps to pull today; but as far as he could see, they were both as useless.

Even worse, he need to check his northerly lines today and hadn't planned on heading south toward The Nephews, where the trawler would be waiting. One top of that, it was low tide, and if this Christless fog didn't lift, he'd run the risk of running aground, fancy electronics be damned.

"Goddamned *son*-of-a-fuckin'-*bitch!*"

He knew he wasn't cursing Richie or Pete or Ben so much as he was cursing himself for getting involved with Richie in the first place. He should never have gotten into a position where Richie had the upper hand and could bust his balls like this.

He should have known better.

He should have seen it...hell, he *had* seen it coming, but what choice did he have?

The bank in town—the place where he'd done business his entire adult life with people whose grandparents had grown up with his grandparents—had turned down his loan request, and all because he lost the *Sheila B.* last spring.

What kind of bullshit was that?

Did losing a boat mark him forever as a Jonah...someone who would lose every boat he captained?

Of course, the bankers told him there wasn't anything they could do. Loans went through the head office in Boston. Wally remembered a time, before banks were bought and sold like used cars, when a man's word was the only bond he needed. Losing a boat could happen to the best captain.

Not anymore.

Not when banks in Canada and freaking Bahrain owned the "local" banks.

So really, he'd had no choice but to ask Richie for a loan...even though Richie didn't have the sense not to whistle on board. He'd probably see nothing wrong with putting a hatch cover upside down on the deck or carrying a black bag onboard, either.

"And now he's cracking my balls like fuckin' walnuts," he muttered as he walked down the ramp to the dock and got on board. He was so tense something in his shoulder popped when he hefted his bait barrel and twisted around to set it in the boat. He grunted and rotated his arm as he walked to the wheelhouse.

"Goddamned gettin' old sucks, too," he muttered and then spat overboard.

The harbor was curiously silent, the fog muffling all sounds as he got ready to cast off. It'd be nice to have a dependable sternman, he thought, but that wasn't going to happen. He'd have to make do on his own.

When he started up the engine, the throaty rumble echoed dully from the granite walls of the harbor. A fish or maybe a seal splashed in the water close beside his boat, but all Wally saw were the ripples that spread out in dark, concentric rings across the smooth water.

He cast off and headed out of the harbor, relying much more on sight and sound than he did on his instruments. He never placed much trust in electronics, and these new ones were useless, as far as he was concerned. He was grimacing as he made his way between some moored boats, and he didn't start to feel relieved until he rounded the headlands and headed out to sea, toward The Nephews.

That morning, Ben woke up with a hangover that pounded inside his head like a drop forge.

After Julia left the beach parking lot, he'd had to wait over an hour for Skip to show up with the tow truck. Skip swapped the remaining good front tire with the flattened one in the back so he could tow it back to the garage. Once they got there, Ben had to wait another hour for Skip to replace both tires…to the tune of two hundred and fifty dollars. Then he'd gone straight to The Local for a few cold ones. From there, he had called Julia—a few times, as he remembered—and asked her to come down and join him. She had insisted that she couldn't get away. Her father hadn't had a very good day, and she was concerned it was because she hadn't been around as much as she used to be because she was with Ben. She felt obligated to stay with him for the night, and she promised to see Ben the next day for lunch.

The night at The Local had gone on longer and stronger than he'd anticipated. Scores of old friends showed up and kept buying him round after round until he was plastered. He had a vague memory of calling Julia one last time on his cell when he was taking the shortcut home, but he couldn't remember what either of them had said…maybe something about lunch today.

Now it felt like someone had wound a metal band around his head above his eyes and was twisting it slowly tighter and tighter until his eyes bulged from their sockets.

"Killer fog…" he muttered, a phrase he and his friends had used in high school to describe how drunk they got whenever they stole liquor from their parents or, in a few instances, got lucky enough to convince someone of legal age to buy them a six-pack or bottle of wine from Art's corner store.

He sighed as he sat on the edge of the bed and looked out the bedroom window. Even filtered through the dense fog that had settled over The Cove, the gray morning light stung his eyes. The sun looked like an incandescent bulb behind gauze as it struggled to burn off the fog.

He winced with every step as he walked down the hallway to the bathroom and relieved himself. Even the slightest motions made his bones and muscles ache. Pain rippled like shifting sheets of dry lightning behind his eyes.

"I gotta remember not to *do* that again," he whispered to himself as he ransacked the medicine cabinet for aspirin or Tylenol. He found some Advil, shook three tablets into his hand, and gulped them down with several mouthfuls of water.

At least there hadn't been any dreams last night.

His first and clearest thought was to give Julia a call and find out if the lunch plans were real or a drunken fantasy. He thought they might have plans to do lunch but wasn't sure. Now he was hoping she couldn't shake loose until later so his hangover would have time to lessen if not disappear.

What he needed was breakfast and maybe a little exercise. A jog around the block might help…if he could stand the pounding of his feet on the pavement. Or maybe the weights he'd used in high school were still down in the cellar. Now that he was out of the Army, the last thing he needed was to get soft.

He flushed the toilet, staring at the water as it swirled in the bowl. Then he went to the sink and splashed some cold water on his face. The water didn't penetrate. His eyes were crusty, and his skin felt like it was wrapped too tightly around his skull. When he looked at his reflection in the mirror, leaning forward to study his bloodshot eyes and pale face, he was shocked to see what a wreck he looked, but he smiled and told himself it was almost worth it. Last night at The Local had been a good time, at least the parts he could remember.

After a breakfast of orange juice, toast with peanut butter, and a bowl of stale Cheerios—Pete always left the bag open inside the box—he went back upstairs and took a long, hot shower. That brought him a few notches closer to human. As he got dressed, he started feeling guilty, thinking about how much Julia did for her father while Capt'n Wally pretended his wife didn't exist. In a real sense, she didn't exist. She had already checked out. He thought maybe another visit to the rest home might be in order if only to assuage his guilt.

He was resigned that he would never accept or get over what had happened…what was happening to his mother. Resentment and guilt stewed inside him with equal measures of anger. Facing rather than avoiding her situation might be exactly what he had to do…in a lot of areas of his life.

When Ben got to "Grave's Edge," he smiled at the man at the front desk—a balding middle-aged guy he didn't recognize—and, without waiting to say what he was doing there, walked down the hall to his mother's room. He hesitated outside the door for a moment, his gaze fastened on the old snapshot of his mother. He couldn't get over how young and full of life she looked, and it was hard to accept that, of all the possible outcomes to her life, this was what fate had handed her.

Did she deserve it?

Did any of us deserve what happened to us?

With the suddenness of a rifle flash, memories of Iraqi children and civilians—lifeless rag-heaps lying by the roadside—passed before his eyes. He blinked hard until they went away, and he was left staring at his clenched fist as he rapped on the door.

Then he waited.

When he got no response, he turned the doorknob, feeling its slickness in his moist hand, and wedged the door open. It took only a moment for his eyes to adjust to the dim light in the room. It was obvious his mother wasn't there.

Wondering what to do next, he closed the door and was turning around when he sensed motion behind him. He turned and saw Mrs. Appleby, striding toward him. He smiled and nodded a greeting.

"Benny," Mrs. Appleby said with a tight smile plastered on her face.

"Mrs. A," Ben said, trying to hide his agitation. He hooked his thumb toward the door like he was hitching a ride and said, "You know where my mom is?"

Mrs. Appleby looked up and down the hallway and then said, "She's around. She's quite the wanderer."

This was the second time Mrs. Appleby had characterized his mother like that, and he wondered if it might be a cause for concern.

"Let's try the TV room," she offered.

Together they started back up the hallway toward the front desk. The same elderly people—or perhaps different ones—lingered in the lobby by the front door. Some sat in wheelchairs while others leaned on walkers or sat on the Spartan furniture. Several had expressions that flashed with the desperate hope that *someone*—a loved one—was coming to pick them up and take them away from this place. The lingering smell of feces and disinfectant was enough to dishearten anyone.

"I don't know if I should tell you this or not," Agnes Appleby whispered to Ben, leaning close to him as they walked.

Ben tensed, expecting some bad news about his mother, but he wondered why Mrs. Appleby was being so circumspect. If his mother had died or had a stroke or something, she wouldn't be able to hide it. Maybe there was a problem with one of the staff or one of the doctors on call mistreating her.

Before Ben could say a word, she hooked him by the arm and led him away from the front desk to a corner of the lobby furthest away from any of the residents.

"What is it?" Ben asked.

Mrs. Appleby sucked her lips in, making them thin and pale as she shifted her eyes from side to side. She looked like a paranoid person about to reveal some secret about alien abductions or a plot to assassinate the President.

"It's...well, I know it's really none of my business, but sometimes...you know how sometimes you get a bad feeling about something, and you don't want to talk about it, but you're also afraid if you don't say something, and then something bad happens, it will...it's something you wouldn't be able to live with?"

"I'm not quite following you here," Ben said. "Does this have anything to do with my mother?"

Mrs. Appleby narrowed her eyes, her lips pursed as if she'd bitten into a lemon.

"No...no...not at all."

"What is it, then?"

Mrs. Appleby took a shallow sip of breath, held it for a moment. When she let it out, her nostrils whistled faintly.

"I don't mean to be prying into your personal life, Ben. I really don't. But I understand you've been seeing a certain lady."

Ben was stunned. He drew his head back and looked at Mrs. Appleby with wide eyes. It took him a few moments to shift gears from his mother to Julia. "What are you...? No. Ahh—yes. I mean... What does this have to—?"

Mrs. Appleby cut him off by placing her hand on his arm above the elbow and squeezing hard enough to hurt. Her face was earnest and intense as she drew closer.

"It's your sister—"

"Louise?"

Mrs. Appleby nodded tightly.

"Her husband, Tommy Marshall.... He's been cheatin' on her."

Ben scowled and shook his head.

"I don't see where this has anything to do with my—"

But he stopped before he finished the thought. In a flash, something clicked into place, and he thought he caught her drift.

"Are we talking about my sister or Julia Meadows?"

"That woman you've been seeing? Miss Meadows? She's a nice enough person, I suppose, but—well, I saw something out by her house the other night on my way home from work that got me to wondering."

"You think she—" He wanted to put this as delicately as possible for a woman of Mrs. Appleby's generation. "She's been having an affair...with Tom Marshall?"

"I don't think," Mrs. Appleby said. "I *know.*"

Ben's suspicions suddenly became reality. The idea of Julia doing the same things with Tom that she had done with him yesterday on the beach made his stomach churn. And the idea that Tom would have the balls to approach *him* to get a connection to sell the coke so he could take off with Julia and leave Louise ...

A vein began to throb in his temple.

"Are you positive, Mrs. Appleby?"

But Mrs. Appleby stared at him with wide eyes and shook her head firmly.

"He was creeping around outside her house the other night, 'n when I talked to him, he acted like a cat who ate the canary, all guilty and such." She took a wheezing breath as though winded from telling him all of this. "I'm telling you just so's you can...I don't know. Do what you have to do. I know if Tommy was cheating on your sister 'n your mother ever found out? T'would break her heart, t'would."

"You and I both know my mother's not really capable of understanding much of anything," Ben said, feeling a stab in his heart even as he spoke the words.

"Don't say that about your mother," Mrs. Appleby said, sounding like a Sunday school teacher scolding a child. Tears gathered in her eyes, and it was obvious Mrs. Appleby was sad as much for herself as she was for his mother.

He nodded, chastised, but he was already mentally shuffling through numerous possible scenarios. He wasn't sure what he should do with this information if it was true.

The first thing he had to do was find out if Julia had been messing around with Tom.

And if she still was...

After that—?

Well, he'd have to see.

But in an instant, his impression of Julia Meadows changed, and not for the better. He had surprised himself, the way he was falling for her so fast, but now he was conflicted about his feelings for her.

"I didn't mean to upset you," Mrs. Appleby said.

"You didn't upset me, Mrs. A," Ben said, knowing he was lying and hoping she wouldn't see it. He patted her reassuringly on the shoulder. "I'll have to see what's what."

Blinking back her tears, Mrs. Appleby gave him a sympathetic look as they locked eyes.

"I thought you should know before...you know, before something happens. That's all."

"Absolutely. I understand. Totally. Thank you for telling me."

"You know what good friends your mother and I were...*are*, and I...I don't want anything bad to happen to your family."

It's a little late for that, Ben thought, but he didn't say it as he and Mrs. Appleby started walking down the corridor side by side toward the TV room. Before they got there, Ben happened to glance out the large bay window that looked out over the backyard. His mother, wearing a floral bathrobe, was walking across the wide expanse of lawn out behind the nursing home. Not far away was a sloping hill, leading to a bluff that overlooked the ocean.

"What's she doing out there?" Ben asked. He watched her for a few seconds but then felt a jolt of panic when he realized his mother was unsupervised. As far as he could see, there was no attendant nearby.

Mrs. Appleby looked to where Ben was pointing. When she saw Lilly, her expression froze for a moment and then shifted into one of shock.

"Oh, gosh," she said, glancing quickly at Ben. Then she started walking briskly toward the nearest exit. "How the dickens did she get out there? The alarm on the door should have sounded the instant she opened it."

The mournful sound of the foghorn on Ram Island carried eerily through the dense fog. Between blasts, an eerie silence prevailed. The air was warm and heavy; the pewter gray sea was calm and flat, scored only by the expanding rings of black ripples the *Abby-Rose* made as she bobbed like a cork in the water.

Capt'n Wally's mood had not improved. He'd lost his favorite knife overboard—a knife he'd had for twenty years or more. He'd foolishly left it on the gunwales while he was trying to unsnarl a rope that was jammed in the winch. At least so far, anyway, the day's catch had been decent. The work sure would have gone better with a sternman to help out, but apparently his two sons had better things to do than help out their old man.

Telling himself to stop ruminating over things which he couldn't control, he started up the engine and headed in a south-easterly direction. He'd haul traps along the way, and if he saw a trawler out near The Nephews, then maybe he'd come aside and see what was up with them.

Wally much preferred being out on the open ocean rather than on land. Here, he didn't have to answer to anybody or put up with any bullshit. Here, he was master and commander. But it galled him no end to know that he wasn't really doing what he wanted to do. Being all but ordered out to The Nephews to do grunt work for Richie Sullivan wasn't his idea of not having to deal with other people's bullshit.

Finding the trawler in the pea soup fog was going to be a trick. He leaned forward over the wheel, staring at the dense wall of gray in front of him. Looking sternward, he could barely make out his wake in the water. If the rising price of fuel weren't cutting into his profits so deeply, he wouldn't be doing this. He wouldn't be Richie Sullivan's or anyone else's errand boy.

He spotted another of his buoys and pulled up alongside it. Cutting the engine, he timed it perfectly so he drifted up close to the buoy and hooked it with a gaff. After running the rope over the winch wheel, he started it up. Beads of water squeezed out of the rope like he was wringing out a sponge as he raised the lobster trap from the ocean floor. When it broke surface, he rested it on the gunwales, glad to see a dark mass flapping around inside the trap.

He had something.

After scraping off the kelp and seaweed that clung to the trap, he opened the door and dug out a solitary lobster. He scowled at the dark mass of eggs on the lobster's underside.

"Fuckin' berries," he muttered. It was standard to cut a "V" notch into the end of the lobster's tail to mark it as a fertile female so no one else would harvest it. As he reached down to his belt for his knife, though, he swore and spit over the side of the boat when he remembered losing it overboard.

Carrying the lobster into the wheelhouse, he fished around in his toolbox until he found a pair of tin snips, which he used to mark the lobster.

"Goddamned good fuckin' luck," he muttered as he casually tossed the lobster over his shoulder. Just then the Ram Island foghorn sounded, drowning out the splashing sound the lobster made when it hit the water.

Wally re-baited the trap and dropped it over the side, watching it sink slowly into the dark depths. Then he powered up to look for his next buoy. The further out he went, the heavier the seas became. The boat slapped the heaving waves, and every now and then a salty spray splattered against the wheelhouse window.

Wally was surprised when, without warning, the dark bulk of The Nephews came into view on his starboard side. In the heavy fog and the mainland long out of sight, he hadn't realized he'd already made it out this far. He heaved quickly to port to avoid the rocks on the southern point of the island that appeared in the water like shark's teeth at low tide. Many a boat had run aground on those rocks and gone under.

All thoughts of lobstering left his mind as he scanned the thick fog for any indication of the trawler. He might as well have had his eyes closed, for all he could see. The wall of fog was growing denser. The sound of the foghorn was muffled as though wrapped in cotton.

If the captain of the trawler had any sense, he wouldn't be out here in fog this thick, but then again, these fishermen were a tough bunch, and they were interested in profit a lot more than their personal safety. If Richie said they'd be here today, they'd be here.

Powering down and motoring slowly, Wally circled the island on the starboard side, giving the point of land and rocks a wide margin of safety. His eyes ached from staring so long into the fog, and he doubted the trawler was anywhere nearby.

Maybe they weren't coming…or had already come and gone.

Maybe Richie was busting his balls for not making the pickup the other night and sending him on a wild goose chase.

Maybe he should say *Fuck it!* and head back to the harbor.

And maybe he would tell Richie Sullivan to stuff it where the sun don't shine because he wasn't going to risk his life and another boat to pick up a fucking bale or two of weed.

But if he did that, his life wouldn't necessarily be in danger, but things could happen that might make his life and livelihood a lot harder.

Wally was fuming, and not just about his knife as he came around the tip of the island and headed south, keeping the island in sight on the starboard side. The lonely cry of seagulls, unseen on the rocks above the heaving water, drifted to him. Off to port, so close he almost could have reached out and touched them, was a raft of eider ducks, riding the heaving swells. They started squawking and swam out of the way as he motored past them, but they didn't fly off.

He was rounding the southern tip of the island when the huge, indistinct shape of a ship loomed out of the fog off his starboard bow. Wally eased up on the engine and approached the ship with caution, waiting until he was positive it was the trawler he was looking for, not a Coast Guard cutter, before he hailed it.

There was a flurry of activity on the deck, the indistinct shapes of men moving about. Then a man approached the port railing and called out, "Ahoy there, captain."

Wally recognized the man's voice immediately. It was Ernie Favaza, a grizzled old pirate out of Gloucester who ran his trawler to the Georges Bank and Flemish Cap only when there weren't more lucrative opportunities closer to home. Behind him, on the deck, members of his crew—it looked like four people—were moving about.

"Finest kind," Wally called out. "'S that you, Ernie?" He felt a measure of relief when he finally saw the name *Sally Girl* stenciled on the rusted side of the boat.

"Sure as shit is," Ernie called back. "You were expecting the Pope?"

He and Wally had done enough business over the years to be friendly with each other, but they had only encountered each other in circumstances like this. It was a good idea, as the seamen said, not to "shit where you eat." When you're running drugs from Mexico or Colombia, it's best not to know your contacts on a personal level. People in government would call it "plausible deniability." Fishermen called it common sense.

"I understand you have something you want me to deliver," Wally said.

"Got it for you right 'ere."

Even as he was speaking, two of the crew, young men wearing heavy-weather gear, shifted two bundles toward the railing. The bundles were wrapped in black plastic that glistened in the moist air. Another man threw a length of rope down to the deck of the *Abby-Rose,* and Wally quickly tied off. Both boats heaved up and down. This far out, the swells were heavier, but the men worked quickly and efficiently. They dropped the bales, each weighing about a hundred pounds, onto Wally's deck. They landed with a dull thud that sounded like cannons in the distance.

"That it?" Wally called up as he shifted the bales to the stern and placed a few bags of rock salt on top of them.

"'S'all for now," Ernie replied.

"Catch'ya later, then," Wally said.

He quickly cast off, revved his engine, and pulled away, staying clear of the trawler's bow. The boats had drifted with the current during the transfer, and he was now a considerable distance further south of The Nephews. Still, he didn't trust the electronic navigation equipment half as much as his own sense of direction as he made a heading for Horse Head Cove, an isolated cove about ten miles north of town where he was supposed to meet his contacts.

When he got closer to shore, he'd call the number Richie had given him on his cell phone. Chances were, he'd be dropping off the bales with Mark "French Fry" Payne and Silas "Chuckles" Weaver, a couple of local reprobates who hadn't worked an honest day in their lives.

If that's who he was meeting and those two numbnuts had already started drinking today, like they usually did, he'd be lucky if they found their way to the rendezvous point without bringing a parade of cops and DEA agents.

Tom Marshall was feeling good...better than good...*damned* good as he drove the narrow, winding back roads from The Cove to Boothbay Harbor. It was a little past noon. The dense fog that had blanketed the town all morning was finally lifting. The sun was peeking through, and the air was thick with humidity, more like

July than May. A warm breeze slipping through the open car windows blew his hair back. He had the radio tuned to WPOR, the country-western radio station from Portland, but the volume was down low so he could run through some of the various possible scenarios that might occur once he got to where he was going.

He had to be ready for anything.

It had taken only two phone calls and a quick meeting down at the wharf with Danny "Puppy" Lawrence, a local carpenter Tom knew from high school, to arrange to sell the cocaine he had stolen from the evidence locker.

Tom had insisted on no questions asked, but he had no doubt that Puppy, who fronted for Anthony Gillette, the biggest and best-known dealer in the area, knew perfectly well where the drugs had come from. When the bust happened last winter, it had been in the local news for weeks on end. That had been about six months ago, and what with backups at the courthouse and legal delays filed by the defense attorneys, it still hadn't gone to trial. Chances were the defendant—Randy "Cutter" Pitts, the only person actually charged—would walk. Even if he didn't, Gillette and his boss, Richie Sullivan, were so well insulated from the case they would never be tied to it. Of course, everyone in town had no doubt The Crowbar was running the operation.

Not that any of that mattered.

If Puppy or Gillette started any trouble, the police department had a file several inches thick on both of them. Tom was confident Gillette would pay him off to keep his mouth shut. Besides, Tom reminded himself, this was a once in a lifetime deal. It wasn't like he was going to make a habit of fencing evidence. Once he had the cash in hand, he was going to give Julia one last chance to come away with him, and then—with or without the bitch—he was going to get the hell out of Dodge.

"Fuck Louise and the horse she rode in on," he said, glancing at his reflection in the rearview mirror. The skin around his eyes crinkled like broken porcelain when he smiled.

Once upon a time, he might have loved his wife...maybe back in high school when she first started putting out for him under the high school stadium bleachers. But that had been years ago, and then she went and got herself pregnant. In the year since they'd been married, after she miscarried, she'd packed on at least ten pounds...maybe more, and in all the wrong places.

If only Julia had moved to town a year or so sooner...before he agreed to marry Louise.

But fuck Julia Meadows, too!

She couldn't treat him like he was some numbnuts fuck buddy she could use and dispose of on a whim just because Ben Brown was after her ass.

Who the fuck did she think she was?

He might have started out more interested in the money she would eventually inherit from her father once he kicked off than her pussy, but now that he had a shot at getting some righteous bucks on his own—as sweet as her pussy was, he didn't need her so much.

A tingle of expectation tightened his belly as his car zipped around curves, rising and falling over the gentle crests in the road. He remembered riding on this road as a kid, pretending it was a roller coaster. Realizing he was going a good fifteen to twenty miles per hour over the speed limit, he eased up on the gas. Not that it mattered. If a cop pulled him over for speeding, even someone who didn't know him, all he had to do was flash his badge and he'd be let off.

Being a cop had certain advantages. He was going to miss some of those advantages once he lit out, but he had a better, brighter future planned.

Especially if Julia came along...

"But even so...even so," he muttered as he stared for a second at his eyes in the rearview. They looked as hard as steel.

When he was honest with himself, he had to admit he knew all along that she was going to dump him. Guys like him didn't end up with women like her. It only made it worse, knowing she was dumping him for that jerkoff Ben Brown.

He tried to keep that particular thought in the back of his mind, but he was determined, before he blew town, to have a little up close and personal with 'ole Bennie.

Tom eased his speed down to the limit once he hit downtown Boothbay Harbor. He was still running through all the possible scenarios that might happen as he pulled into the parking lot of The

Galley Restaurant, like he'd arranged on the phone.

The parking lot was crowded. Sunlight gleamed like flames from an arc torch off mirrors and chrome, leaving squiggly afterimages across his retina, but it didn't take long for Tom to spot Gillette's car. It was parked at the far end of the lot under the shade of a large oak tree.

Gillette and another guy Tom didn't recognize immediately were leaning against the side of his car, smoking and casually surveying the parking lot. They were dressed like tourists, both of them wearing mirror sunglasses, brightly colored golf shirts, khaki shorts, and sneakers. Gillette looked like a doofus with his white socks pulled halfway up to his knobby knees. Shadows danced like little waving hands across their faces.

You ask me, he thought, *they look like a couple of fags.* His smile widening as he nodded a greeting, but his stomach tightened like the skin on a drum as he pulled to a stop beside the parked car and killed the engine.

"Afternoon," he said, groaning as if from the effort as he got out and walked around the back of his car and over to them.

"Howdy," Gillette said, raising his sunglasses and perching them on the top of his head. The other man nodded but didn't speak. He took a last drag on his cigarette and snapped it out across the parking lot. It hit the asphalt, sending up a tiny shower of sparks before it rolled under the tire of someone's car.

Tom took a good look around as if he half-expected to see someone else—like maybe a couple of town cops or undercover DEA agents—lurking in the shrubbery, waiting to take them all down.

"How's it hanging?" Tom said with a beaming smile.

He held his hand out for Gillette to shake. As they did, he nodded at the other man.

"Low 'n loose, and full of juice," Gillette said tonelessly. "You?"

"High and dry, and waitin' to die."

The man Tom didn't know smiled and grunted but said nothing. His smile was devoid of any humor, his thin lips as white as marble. His eyes were unreadable behind his reflective sunglasses.

"You got the shit?" Gillette asked without preamble.

He was a short man with dark hair clipped into a crew cut. His eyebrows met together over his nose in a uni-brow. The spiky bristles of his hair kept his sunglasses firmly in place. His eyes looked as cold as chips of gray ice.

"You got the money?" Tom asked.

"What'da yah think?" Gillette raised the left side of his eyebrow so it looked like a dark comma.

Tom kept eyeing the silent man. If anyone had the attitude of a stone-cold killer, it was this guy.

"Care to introduce me to your friend?"

"Not really," Gillette said as if that was the end of it.

Tom shot him a quick look; then he turned and started walking around his car to the driver's side.

"What the fuck?" Gillette said. He sounded upset, but he made no move to come after him.

Tom stopped at the back of his car, turned around, and then said, "I don't do shit with people I don't know. Have a nice fuckin' day."

They locked eyes for a long moment of silence. Then Gillette said, "Tom. This here's Marcus Zimmerman. A friend of mine from Providence."

Zimmerman smiled as if for the first time in his life. When Tom walked back to them, Zimmerman held out his hand. Tom leaned forward, and they shook hands. He noticed how dry and cold Zimmerman's grip was—and strong.

"Pleased to meet you, Mr. Zimmerman," Tom said, making a point of not repeating his name. "How's Bobby doing?"

Zimmerman either didn't get or chose to ignore the Bob Dylan reference. Maybe he'd heard it too many times. There was no way Tom could tell which way he was looking behind those mirrored shades, but he felt the man's gaze boring into him.

"So," Gillette said, rubbing his hands together. "You got the shit?"

"I can get it easy enough."

"Oww, man. Now you're twisting my *cojones*. You said you'd have it with you."

Realizing it was foolish to act like some big league dealer on some bullshit TV cop show, Tom nodded and then walked to the back of his car. When he started opening the trunk, Gillette pushed off his car and, glancing left and right, said, "For fuck's sake. Not in public."

"Where, then?"

"Get in your car. Follow me."

Gillette and Zimmerman turned to get into their car.

"Where to?" Tom asked.

"You'll see," Gillette said, and without another word, they opened the doors and got in. Gillette was driving. He started up the car, letting it idle as Tom got into his car and started it up. They both backed around and drove out of the parking lot. In their wake, they left a faint trail of blue exhaust that hung suspended in the still air.

Tom followed Gillette out onto Main Street. After going a short distance, he took two quick turns, first right and then left, heading out of town. They went a mile or two down the main road until they came to a turnoff leading onto an unmarked dirt road on their right. Tom recognized it but couldn't remember ever driving down it. Without using his turn signal and barely tapping his brake, Gillette took the turn going a little faster than was safe. Dust kicked up from his rear tires like the ass end of his car was on fire.

Tom followed them, keeping a few car lengths behind in case he wanted—or needed—to make a quick U-turn. He was on alert because although he didn't know Gillette all that well—he lived in nearby Lewiston—Tom knew his reputation for pulling crazy shit. He wouldn't put it past him to try something stupid—even with a cop...*especially* with a cop.

Going off to some place out of the public eye was one of the scenarios he'd tried to think through. If Gillette was leading him out there so he could take the coke, maybe at gunpoint, Tom wanted to be ready. Leaning across the seat, he reached into the glove compartment for the pistol he kept there for insurance. Leaning closer to the steering wheel, he rolled his hip to the left and slipped the gun under his belt into the small of his back.

Less than a mile down the rutted dirt road, Gillette pulled over into a narrow turnaround and stopped. Tom parked behind him, automatically angling his car behind Gillette's like he would his cruiser when he was pulling someone over for a routine traffic violation.

He remained in his car, taking the time to look around while waiting to see what they would do next. Trees lined both side of the road—scrub pine and second-growth maples. To his left, the ground sloped down, and there were ferns mixed in under the trees. To the right was a sloping hill covered with denser growth strewn with moss-covered granite boulders.

After a long moment, in which the two men appeared to be discussing or arguing about something, Zimmerman got out on the passenger's side and approached Tom's car. He was no longer wearing shades, and the sunlight washed the side of his face with a bronzed glow. When Zimmerman was standing next to the car, he motioned for Tom to get out.

As far as Tom could tell, the man wasn't packing. Both of his hands were in plain sight, and the pockets of his shorts weren't sagging as if he had a gun in one of them. He might have a small piece behind him, but Tom didn't think so. Maybe ole Zimmerman here was better at *looking* tough than really *being* tough.

Tom rolled his window down and stared up at the man, trying his best to give him back a blank, expressionless stare.

"So where's the shit?" Zimmerman said, his tone of voice echoing Gillette's.

"I know your name, but I still don't *know* you," Tom said. "I only do business with people I know."

Zimmerman looked momentarily flustered as he glanced from Tom to the waiting car and then back at Tom. After staring at each other in silence for several tense seconds, Zimmerman visibly relaxed his shoulders and then walked back to Gillette's car. He leaned down to the driver's window and had a brief conversation with Gillette that Tom couldn't hear. Then Zimmerman stepped back, and the driver's door opened. Gillette got out and came over to Tom's car with Zimmerman a few steps behind him.

"Why you bustin' our balls like this, huh?" Gillette asked, scowling at Tom above the rim of his shades. Tom looked at the double reflection of himself in the lenses and smiled as if for a camera.

"I ain't bustin' anyone's balls here. I told your buddy that I'll only make the deal with you."

"You got the shit wit'cha or not?"

"Yeah. I shoved it up my ass for safe keeping."

Zimmerman, a few steps behind Gillette, scowled at that and said, "See, Tony? That's what I call 'bustin' balls.'"

Tom relaxed. It was obvious Gillette didn't have a gun either, and they were acting worse than amateurs. Knowing he had the upper hand, Tom drew the keys from the ignition. They stepped back when he opened the car door and stepped out. He walked to the back of the car, inserted the key, and popped the trunk. He looked at the suitcase, lying next to the spare tire, and smiled.

Gillette and Zimmerman came up behind him.

"Lemme have a look-see," Gillette said.

When he spoke, his voice startled Tom, and he jumped. He automatically started to reach for the gun in the small of his back but checked himself. Without a word, he flipped the two latches on the case and raised the lid to display several large, clear plastic bags. All of them were packed with white powder.

Gillette reached into his pocket and pulled out a small pocketknife. He clicked open the blade and then took one of the bags from the bottom of the suitcase. He slit it open and dipped the tip of the blade into the white powder, then withdrew it and raised it to his left nostril. He snorted it in with a single, quick sniff. After a second or two, one side of his mouth curled up into a smile.

"That's pretty good shit," he said, nodding with satisfaction.

He replaced the bag and clicked the case shut, his hands lingering on the suitcase for a moment, as if he were caressing it. When he started to pick up the suitcase, Tom grabbed his arm with his left hand. At the same time, he pivoted to the right and reached around behind his back to brush the handle of his hidden revolver for reassurance. He wasn't going to take any crap—of any kind from *anyone*—especially not from a guy like Tony Gillette.

"Money first," Tom said, fighting the jolt of excitement that tightened his voice.

Gillette scowled at him and then, catching Zimmerman's eye, nodded. Without a word, Zimmerman walked over to their car and reached in through the open window on the passenger's side. When he pulled back, he was holding a thick manila envelope. He brought it to Gillette and handed it to him, and Gillette passed it to Tom. Then he shook his arm free of Tom's grasp and picked up the suitcase.

No one said a word as Gillette and Zimmerman walked back to their car, opened the trunk, placed the suitcase inside, and slammed the trunk lid shut. While all of this was going on, Tom opened the envelope and pulled out the wad of cash. He smiled as he started flipping through the bills, but when he was about halfway through the stack, he stopped. His satisfied smile melted into a frown. Then he glared at Gillette, who was getting into his car.

"Whoa! Hold on a second, *compadre*," Tom shouted as he ran over to the driver's side. He took a slow, calming breath, trying to tamp down the rush of anger inside him. The electric window slid down smoothly like a sheet of ice. Gillette looked up at him, both ends of his uni-brow raised.

"'S there a problem?" he said.

Tom gripped the manila envelope so tightly in one hand his veins popped out as he shook it in front of Gillette's face. The paper made a thick crinkling sound like a crackling fire.

"Looks to me like you're a little light here," Tom said.

"A little light?" Gillette turned to Zimmerman and said, "A little light, he says."

"By about half," Tom said, slapping the fat envelope against his open palm. It made a wet smacking sound like someone's face being slapped, and that's exactly what Tom was imagining doing to Gillette.

"You got a lot of money there," Gillette said.

"It's not what we agreed to."

"Really? And how much did we agree to?"

The disingenuous flatness in Gillette's voice made Tom's anger spike. Angling his body to one side, he was ready to pull his gun and waste the bastard and his friend right then and there.

"You said two hundred large."

As though genuinely surprised by the amount, Gillette threw his head back, bouncing it off the headrest.

"'Two large?' Get this guy." He turned, laughing, to Zimmerman, then looked back at Tom. "Are you fuckin' *kidding* me?"

"You said two hundred thousand dollars."

"No, no, no, my friend. That's what *you* said. That ain't what *I* said. I never agreed to no two 'large.'" He turned to Zimmerman again, snickering like they were both in on a private joke. "Zim? You were there when we was talking on the phone, right?"

Zimmerman nodded but said nothing.

"You ever hear me say anything about 'two large?'"

"I did not," Zimmerman said tonelessly.

"The fuck you think you're pulling here?" Tom said. He leaned on the side panel of the door, gripping it with both hands as if he was about to roll the car over if Gillette tried to drive away. He kept an eye on Zimmerman, too, making sure the dickweed didn't go for a hidden gun.

"I ain't pullin' nothin'," Gillette said. "Honest to fuck, I'm not. *You're* the one been twistin' *my* jimmies."

"You'll make three…four times that, once you step on it." Tom was struggling to control himself. He lowered his voice and spoke softly, trying hard not to sound like he was begging. "I don't want any trouble. All I want is what we agreed to."

Gillette gripped the steering wheel with both hands and stared straight ahead for a long time. His jaw worked back and forth as though he was chewing a tough piece of steak. The veins on the side of his head were throbbing. They looked like tangled strands of purple yarn under his skin.

"Way I see it? You're simply givin' me back what's rightfully mine in the first place."

"Richie Sullivan's, you mean."

"Yeah. Go on and think that if you want." Gillette was still staring straight ahead. "Sullivan ain't shit. But the way I see it? You been paid a decent finder's fee." He slowly rotated his head and, raising his shades with his right hand, stared at Tom. The distant gray light in his eyes chilled Tom.

"A finder's fee," Tom said, rolling the words off his tongue as if trying to get used to them.

"Yeah. To show how much I appreciate you returning my property to me."

Tom was speechless. He couldn't stop imagining pulling out his revolver and shooting both of them right here on the spot. Do to them what he had feared they might try to do to him. He was sure Gillette didn't have a gun. Both of his hands were wrapped around the steering wheel, so even if he had one, he'd be dead before he got it. There was no telling what Zimmerman had. His right hand was down by his side, out of sight between the car seat and the door. He might already have a gun in hand.

"'Sides, Tommy," Gillette said in a mild, placating voice. "Who you gonna complain to, the cops?"

He laughed, but Zimmerman didn't laugh. His hand was still down below seat level and he was leaning forward slightly, scowling as he looked over at Tom.

"My advice to you, my friend," Gillette said, "is be happy with what you got. The way the world is today? There's a lot of scumbags out there who'll fuck you over first chance they get. Another guy did this deal? You'd already have a bullet in your head. Wouldn't he, Zim?"

"It's likely."

Tom narrowed his eyes and shook his head.

"Who's to say I don't waste you right here and now and take the shit and keep the money?" Gillette said.

Zimmerman, meanwhile, shifted in his seat. Thinking he was going for a gun, Tom jumped back and dropped into a crouch. His right hand went to the small of his back for the gun, but his thumb caught the hem of his shirt. When he finally managed to get the gun, his hand was so slippery with sweat, it slipped out of his grasp and clattered onto the dirt.

Gillette watched all this with thinly veiled amusement as he turned the key in the ignition and shifted into gear. Zimmerman raised his hand. He wasn't holding a gun, but he had his thumb cocked back and his forefinger extended. He aimed it at Tom and mouthed the word *BANG* as Gillette pulled onto the road.

Gillette tromped down hard on the accelerator. The tires skidded in the dirt, kicking up a spray of gravel that pelted Tom. As he drove away, the car fishtailing slightly from side to side, he stuck his left hand out the driver's window and flipped Tom the bird. The tires squealed when they hit the road and gained purchase on the asphalt. As the car sped away, Tom was left choking on dust, exhaust fumes, and his own helpless rage.

It was late.

The night was hushed, the house dark. A swatch of moonlight the color of old ivory angled across the floor of Ben's bedroom, which had been Louise's when they were growing up. The windows were open, and the curtains made faint scratching sounds as they drifted back and forth on a light breeze.

Ben was asleep. Because the night was warm, he slept bare-chested, wearing only boxer shorts, but his sleep was thin and another dream came.

He was sitting in a small skiff with low sides in rough waters off Rocky Point. Waves sloshed over the sides, and briny water swirled like black ink around his ankles, making his feet disappear. Using his Kevlar helmet, he started bailing out the boat, but the water he scooped out turned into hot sand that hissed like a nest of snakes when it hit the ocean.

As he scanned the horizon where the dark sky and darker sea blended into an almost indistinguishable line, a sudden bright red flash lit up the night. He bent down to pick up the oars to start rowing back to shore, but when he looked up to settle the oars into the oar locks, he sensed a presence behind him. Turning, he stared at an Iraqi child sitting in the bow of the boat.

A girl—maybe thirteen years old—wearing a beautiful silk *hijab* that covered her head. It might have been red or blue, but it looked black, framing her pale face. She stared at him without blinking, smiling shyly. Her wide teeth glistened like pearls in the darkness.

"Hey, kid," Ben said. "Want some candy?"

He reached into the pocket of his fatigue jacket where he always kept packs of Skittles for the kids he met when he was out on patrol. "All part of winning the hearts and minds," his C.O., Brian Hadlock, had said.

Without answering, the girl stood up and moved forward, gliding toward him through the water in the bottom of the boat without taking any steps, until she was standing directly behind him. Her hands were so cold the chill penetrated his body when she placed them on his shoulders.

Without warning, a mortar exploded not fifty yards away, the impact rocking the boat wildly from side to side. Hot shrapnel sizzled when it hit the water. Ben twisted around and grabbed the girl, throwing her down to the floor of the skiff and covering her with his body. The girl began to scream a high-pitched wail that rose in the night like a siren. The salt water in the boat turned to sand.

"You're all right…. You're all right," he kept saying, trying to sound both reassuring and in control at the same time, and she stopped screaming for a moment.

When he shifted back and looked at her, another mortar explosion flickered on the horizon, illuminating the distant land like an angry wound. The boom came seconds later, hitting him like a punch in the small of the back.

Terrified, the girl looked at him, her eyelids rolling back like the hinged eyes of a doll. When she opened her mouth to scream again, a torrent of beetles and scorpions and spiders poured from between her teeth and fell onto her thin chest before scurrying up and over the sides of the boat. They made a rapid *plunk-plunking* sound as they fell into the water. The girl's body burst apart under him, and rivulets of blood flowed like dark streams onto the sand in the bottom of the skiff. Her hands thrummed madly on his shoulders.

He flailed crazily at the hordes of insects, swatting at them as they continued to pour forth. He wanted to push himself off the girl, but there was no place to go. He wanted to scream, but his breath was trapped in his chest. Another mortar exploded, right in front of the boat, lighting everything up with its white phosphorus light. Humming pieces of metal whizzed by his head but—amazingly—missed him.

He let out a wild, piercing wail that matched the little girl's.

The transition from dreaming to reality was too quick.

Kicking the bedcovers aside, Ben rolled onto the floor, hitting hard enough to send spikes of pain up his legs to his hips. He was still yelling incoherently, not even realizing he was the one making these sounds as he scrambled about on the floor, slapping the hardwood with both hands as he felt around for his rifle.

He knew it was here…somewhere…

He reached under the bed and skinned his knuckles on the underside of the bedsprings. His yelp of pain was shrill in his ears, and it hadn't stopped when a sudden blast of bright yellow light filled his vision.

"Get down…get down…. Incoming!" he shouted at the three indistinct figures standing before him, lost in a watery blur.

It was impossible to make out their features, but he lunged for the one closest to him, wrapped his arms around the person's legs, and twisted his weight around to try to bring him down.

"What the fuck—?" someone shouted.

Ben didn't recognize the voice. It sounded almost like Hadlock, but it couldn't be Hadlock. His CO had died when an IED took out his Hummer in Ramadi.

"Jesus H. Christ," another voice said. This was a woman's voice, and Ben was confused why a woman would be here in the barracks.

"Get down!" he shouted as he slapped the hardwood floor with the flats of both hands. His vision was swimming with swirls of bright light mixed with shadows so sharply defined they looked like razorblades.

Then one of the figures bent down and, reaching forward, grabbed Ben by the shoulders. Rough, calloused fingers dug into his skin hard enough to make him wince.

"Jesus, Ben! Snap out of it."

Somehow, he recognized his father's voice, and he shook his head, trying to imagine how in the world his father had made it to Iraq. But as his vision adjusted to the bright light, he gradually realized that he was down on the bedroom floor on his hands and knees. His breath roared in his lungs, and he was panting like he'd just finished running a marathon.

"What the fuck's wrong with you?" someone else asked, and now he recognized his brother's voice.

Ben flushed with embarrassment, his skin burning as he slowly rocked back onto his heels and crouched on his haunches, wrapping his arms around his legs. His throat was raw. It felt like he'd swallowed a gallon of seawater, but somehow, he managed to take a deep, steady breath and look around as the familiar surroundings of his sister's bedroom gradually came into focus.

"You were wailing like a goddamned banshee," his father said.

Ben looked up at him and Pete and only then realized that the third person standing there was Bunny Dawkins. She was wearing nothing but an old yellowed strap t-shirt that reached halfway down her thighs, which were white and dimpled with cellulite. The rounded sides of her breasts were hanging out the sides. The expression on her face was one of pure shock.

"Damn," Ben said as he cupped his hands over his face and rubbed hard.

"Sounds like one hell of a doozy," Wally said.

Ben nodded but said nothing as he took a few deep breaths through his fingers. He focused on the whistling sound the air made. Then, once he was ready, he looked up at the three night-time visitors.

"Sorry about that," he said. He knew he sounded lame, and he was embarrassed by what had happened.

"What the hell was it," Pete said, "a flashback or something?"

Still breathing through his cupped hands, Ben nodded and looked at him.

"Yeah…something like that," he said.

"You okay now?" Wally asked.

He regarded Ben with a long, steady stare. The earnest concern in his father's face was obvious, but there was something else. Not disgust, really. A certain amount of disappointment mixed with worry that there might be something seriously wrong with his son. It didn't matter that his son had seen and done things nobody should have to see and do. He shouldn't be letting his emotions show like this.

"Yeah…I…" He stood up slowly as cold aches throbbed deep inside his joints and muscles. His bruised hand ached. "I'm fine."

"You want me to get you a glass of water or something?" Wally asked.

Ben shook his head, embarrassed that Bunny Dawkins was seeing him vulnerable like this. It was one thing if it was among family members, but because Bunny had witnessed it, word would get around that he wasn't holding his shit together very well.

"I can get my own damned water, thanks," Ben said, scowling as he waved Wally away.

Pete snickered and regarded Ben with a long, sly look.

"What the fuck's the matter with you?" Ben said. He took a threatening step closer, ready to wipe that smirk clean off his little brother's face if he had to.

"Me? No…nothing," Pete said, raising his hands and taking several steps back.

Still, he was wound up, and the note of mockery in his brother's voice irritated him more than it would have ordinarily. He squeezed his fists so tight his wrists began to throb.

"Why don't you and your girlfriend go back to bed?" Ben said to him.

Wally chuckled and, moving up close to Bunny, slid his arm around her plump waist and said, "What makes you think she's with Pete?"

TEN

Honey Pot

"I've been looking for you," Julia said.

Shouting to be heard above the Alice Cooper song that was blasting from the sound system, she sidled up to the bar next to Ben. She smiled as she placed her hand on the crook of his elbow. His biceps were tight beneath his shirt sleeve, and the mere touch of his skin reminded her of their afternoon on the beach.

Ranged along the bar at The Local, clustered around both sides of Ben, were several men. Julia recognized a few of them from around town, but none of them had ever done more than nod a silent greeting to her whenever she passed on the street. She noticed the way their gaze lingered on her breasts now, and it made her skin crawl.

"Oh...hey...yeah, hi," Ben said. "Whatta surprise seeing you here."

It was obvious he'd already had more than a few beers. His eyes were glazed, and his voice was slurred.

"I thought you had to stay home and take care of your old ma—your father," Ben said.

One of the men at the bar—a skinny guy with thinning dark hair, white beard stubble, and a serious gap between his two upper front teeth—started to say something but then apparently thought better of it and took a sip of beer instead.

"He's doing better," Julia said. She leaned close enough so the warmth of his breath washed over her face. It reeked of sour beer, and she realized the folly of meeting up with him here tonight. She should have waited until morning. "I was.... Can we go outside and talk?"

A couple of the men at the bar perked up at that. One of them—a chubby guy who was wearing a stained wife-beater t-shirt—gave

Ben an "atta-boy" punch on the arm. It looked hard enough to hurt, but Ben didn't wince. He glanced at his beer, which was almost gone, tossed his head back, and drained what was left and then slammed the empty glass onto the bar. Kicking away the barstool, he hooked Julia by the arm and walked with her to the front door. He staggered, but only a little.

Even though the night air was tinged with the smell of mud flats at low tide, the fresh air was a relief from the sour smell of booze and men's body sweat. The moon was hiding behind a raft of high, fast-moving clouds. Far off in the distance, she could hear waves slapping gently against the wharf pilings.

Neither of them spoke as they walked down the side street, their feet scuffing the gravel as they passed a collection of dilapidated fishing shacks. At the end of the dirt road, they took a narrow, winding road leading out onto a point of land that overlooked the harbor. Lights in the houses across the bay rippled in the water, and the air was fresher, tangy with salt and moisture.

Julia was glad that Ben held her hand, lacing his fingers between hers and gripping her firmly but not too tightly. He was unsteady on his feet, and she told herself that it was a mistake to try to talk to him when he was like this.

"You're the center of attention down there," she said, indicating the path leading back to The Local with a quick flip of her head.

"Awhh…just talkin' a load of bullshit about what it's like over there."

She didn't need to be told where "over there" was. Since they met, she had wanted to broach the subject with him. Besides being curious about what he had experienced over there, she wanted to know how he felt about what he had seen and done…. Was it as bad as the news showed? She sensed he carried wounds from the war…that he had demons banging around inside his head…that he struggled to keep them under control and not let anyone see.

For now, anyway, she decided to leave it alone.

They walked past a few houses, most with the lights off except for the outside lights, until they came to a bluff overlooking the water. There, they stopped. The riotous sounds coming from The Local had long since faded away, and the night was filled with the rhythmic rush of waves against the shore. In the distance, a dog barked. Ben stumbled and almost fell as he leaned his head back, took a deep breath, and then belched.

"How romantic," Julia said, smiling.

"Sorry 'bout that."

Julia laughed, but her stomach was tight with tension. She knew she had to say what she had come here to say. It was going to be tough, but if she was going to have any kind of chance with Ben like she hoped, she had to get this out of the way.

"I…" She started, but her throat constricted. "There's…ummm… there's something I have to talk to you about…something I have to tell you."

For a moment or two, Ben was so silent she began to wonder if he had even heard her. The only sound was the waves washing against the rocks somewhere below them in the dark.

"Don't bother," Ben said. Suddenly, he didn't sound nearly as drunk as she thought he was. "I know what you're gonna say."

Julia was stunned.

"Really?"

"Yeah." Ben covered his mouth with his fist and belched again. "You think you know who slashed my tires yesterday."

"How do you—?"

"Is that what you were gonna say?"

"No. I mean—Yes, but I…"

Her voice faded away as a sudden rush of dread took hold of her. Even more than in the bar, she regretted her decision to try to talk to him tonight.

"'S Tom Marshall, right? That's who you think did it?"

As soon as he spoke that name, Julia froze.

"You don't have to tell me 'cause I know."

"Know what?"

"That you been screwing him."

Again, Julia couldn't speak. The directness of his statement stunned her. Her eyes stung as tears gathered, distorting her vision. The night swirled around her.

Ben turned and placed both of his hands on her bare arms above the elbows. His touch wasn't so reassuring any more. He squeezed her upper arms, and the tips of his fingers dug into her flesh hard enough to make her wince.

"Stop that," she said.

Ben eased up the pressure but didn't let go of her.

"I been wonderin' if you were gonna 'fess up," he said, "or if you weren't gonna tell me 'n just hope I'd never find out 'bout it."

"How did you…? Who told you?"

"Does it matter?"

Ben threw his head back and almost lost balance again. He had to let go of her as he wind-milled his arms to keep his balance. His eyes were glazed in the glow of the starlight overhead.

"A town like this? You have to remember there ain't many secrets. None, in fact. Everybody…*everybody* makes everyone else's business *their* business."

"You're all Cove-ah's, huh?" Her neck got heated as she flushed with embarrassment. A tiny voice in the back of her mind was telling her that no one—not even Ben—was ever going to accept her.

"You bet'chur sweet ass we're all Cove-ahs."

He grabbed her arms again, but it was more to help him maintain his balance than anything else.

"You can't get away with doin' shit like that." Ben said. "You were—Maybe you still *are* sleeping with my sister's husband. You know he's married, right? 'Least he was."

Julia winced at the accusation. For an instant, she considered denying it, saying Tom had never confessed that he was married; but then, ever so slowly, she nodded and said, "Yeah. I knew."

"And you—what? You didn't care? You didn't give a sweet shit how my sister feels when…not *if*…" He let go of her with one hand and poked her in the chest with the tip of his forefinger. "…*When* she found out about it…. You never even gave it a second thought, did you?"

Julia twisted to one side and broke his hold on her. In a sudden rush of anger, she almost slapped him across the face but checked herself.

Okay…that's it…I blew it…it's over even before it started.

Tears filled her eyes. Ben was standing so close to her she could see the harbor lights reflected in his eyes. His breath reeked of beer, and she wanted to convince herself he—like every other man in this godforsaken town—was a good-for-nothing drunk with PTSD to boot.

But Ben was different.

"I didn't know," she said, fighting back tears. "I mean, I knew he was married, but I never…I—" She paused and took a gulp of air through her mouth. It burned in her throat like she'd swallowed a flame. "I was so lonely, and I didn't know you then. You were still overseas."

"And that makes a difference, how?"

"I guess not, but if I had met you first, I would never have done it. I never meant to hurt anyone." She hoped her pleading would get through to him, but he seemed to be oblivious to what she was saying. He gazed at her with un-focused eyes and a thin, cruel smile on his lips.

"I'm sorry," he finally said, "but no one…*no one* hurts my family and gets away with it." He hawked up some mucous and spat into the dirt at his feet.

Julia fought the impulse to hug him, to hold him close and beg him to believe that she was sorry, that she loved him and wished with all her heart she could take it all back, but her pride was too strong. Leaning away from him, she crossed her arms over her breasts and regarded him with a cold, steady stare as she shook her head.

"I was an idiot," she said, her voice mixed equally with sadness and disgust. "A complete idiot even to think I could…could—"

But she let it drop, unable to finish.

What was the point?

It wouldn't have mattered anyway because Ben turned his back on her and started walking away. She stood there, rooted to the spot, watching him stagger down the path toward the road. The light from the row of streetlights alternately lit and shaded him until he rounded the corner and was out of sight.

Julia wiped the tears from her eyes with the flat of her hands. Her heart felt like a cold stone suspended in her chest. Once Ben was gone, and the only sound in the night was the waves on the shore, she started walking back to where she had left her car. Even the dog had stopped barking.

It was a little past midnight. Tom was upstairs, undressing for bed when heavy knocking sounded on the front door.

Louise had tucked in earlier, before Tom got home, but she had awakened when her husband trudged up the stairs, his boots clumping on every step hard enough to drive in any loose nails. She feigned sleep under the blankets, not wanting to give Tom any reason to pick a fight with her. She wasn't convinced that Ben's threat to charge Tom with domestic violence would be enough to stop him…not if he got into "a mood."

"What the fuck is that?" Tom shouted.

"Someone's at the door."

Louise's voice was thick with sleep and muffled by the blankets she had pulled up over her face to shield herself from the bedroom light.

"No shit, Sherlock."

Wearing his white-strap t-shirt and boxer shorts, Tom left the bedroom and went downstairs as more heavy knocking sounded on the front door. He flipped on the light in the foyer. Curious, Louise got out of bed and came to the head of the stairs and looked down to see what was going on.

Tom eased the curtain away from the sidelight next to the door and looked outside. When he saw who it was, he froze for a moment. Then he sighed and shook his head before he threw the switch for the porch light. A bright wash of yellow light flooded through the window.

"Jesus Christ," he muttered as he drew away from the door.

"Who is it?"

He turned and shot an angry glance up the stairs at her; then he rubbed his face with the flats of his hands as though splashing his face with water.

"It's your goddamned brother," Tom said, but the last word was lost beneath the rapid banging on the door.

"My *what?*"

"Your brother…Ben."

"What the hell is he…?"

Louise started down the stairs but stopped halfway, her hand gripping the rail as she watched Tom undo the lock and throw the door open wide. Ben was obviously drunk and, barely able to stand, was leaning against one of the porch support posts.

"Come outside, you fuckin' useless piece of shit," Ben said, slurring each word so he was barely intelligible.

"Ben, my man, you are trashed." Tom kept his voice low and mild, but Louise knew by his stance that he was ready for Ben to do something stupid.

"I want you out on the lawn…right now…'n face me like a man… one on one…*mano a mano.*"

Tom leaned casually against the edge of the open door, ready to slam the door shut in Ben's face if he had to. He shook his head and said, "It's late, Ben, 'n you obviously have had a bit too much to drink—"

"Don't think I dunno it was you." Ben belched and then spat against the side of the house, missing Tom in the doorway by a few inches.

"Go home, Ben. Sleep it off," Tom said.

"You comin' out or not? You gonna face me like a man, or are you gonna act like the little chicken shit pussy I know you are?"

Tom raised his hand and then pointed his forefinger at Ben.

"I don't want any trouble," he said mildly, as if he was lecturing a child. "*You* don't want any trouble, either."

Louise had the distinct impression he would have punched her brother square in the face if she hadn't been standing there.

"You're the one who's…" Ben leaned forward, craning his neck to look up the stairs A looping string of saliva hung from his lower lip, and he obviously was having trouble focusing. "'S that you, Lou-Lou?"

"Yeah, Ben. It's me."

She came down a few more steps but didn't go to the door to meet him. Tom blocked her, and she didn't want to do anything to piss him off.

"You aw'right in there?"

"Of course I'm all right," Louise said.

She frowned, thinking this wasn't at all like Ben. He could party with the best of them, but he rarely if ever got falling-down drunk and belligerent like this. She cast a fearful glance at Tom, wondering what he was going to do.

"I think the best thing for you right now would be if you went home," Louise said. "Do you need a ride?"

"I gotta score to settle with your husband, first," Ben said. He was about to say more, but he belched again, wrinkling his nose at the taste that flooded his mouth. Without warning, he spun around and vomited into the garden beside the steps. Tom didn't move to help him.

"We don't have a score to settle," Tom said once Ben was through being sick after several wrenching heaves. "You got something to say to me, wait until—"

"No! Fuck you, and fuck waiting! I want you…out here…on the lawn…right now so's we can't settle this once 'n for all. If you don't, I swear to Christ I'm comin' in."

"I'd like to see you try," Tom said, "'specially drunk on your ass."

"You think I'm scared a' you? You think I won't pound the living piss out of you for what you did?"

"What, exactly, do you think I did?"

"You know damned right well."

Tom leaned forward and lowered his voice so Louise was barely able to hear what he said.

"If this is about that deal I was talking to you about…. Forget it. Just keep your fucking mouth shut."

"What deal? I'm talkin' about my tires. Out at Sand Beach. Don't pretend you don't know what I'm talking about!"

"I have no clue what you're talking about," Tom said, sounding genuinely dismayed.

Louise had been at the family house when Ben called for road service, so she knew exactly what he was talking about. She wasn't sure what this had to do with her husband, but now was not the time to ask questions.

"You think I wouldn't find out? You think I wouldn't know?"

Tom sighed and shook his head as though deeply saddened to see Ben in such a condition.

"I haven't got the faintest clue what you're talking about, but if you don't get off my porch right now, I swear to God I'll fuckin'—"

"What? You'll fuckin' *what?*" Ben's voice echoed from the surrounding night. "You'll arrest me? Or beat the shit out of me?" He snorted. "Go ahead! Try!

When Tom didn't move or speak, Ben started to laugh, but the tone was so hollow and sinister it frightened Louise.

"That's what I thought," he said. "You're a fucking chicken shit pussy. You hide behind your badge because you can't act like a real man."

"And you do?"

"Fuckin'-A, I do."

Ben lurched to one side and had to struggle to stay on his feet.

"You mean like right now?" Tom said, his voice thick with disgust. "This is what you call being a man?"

"You ain't nothing but a coward…a cheating, lying piece of shit!"

Suddenly energized, Ben clenched his right hand into a fist, cocked back his arm, and threw a wild, arcing punch at Tom. Before it landed, Tom stepped back and half-closed the front door. Ben's knuckles raked across the wooden surface, leaving behind a long, thin streak of blood on the white wood.

"*Son* of a *bitch!*" he shouted as he bent over and shook his skinned knuckles. Beads of blood welled up like little rubies where the skin had peeled away.

Tom opened the door wide again and, without a word, surged out onto the porch. Without any warning, he landed a hard jab to Ben's stomach.

The air *whooshed* out of him like a broken accordion. Ben staggered backwards. He stepped down, jolting when he hit the ground as if he had miscounted the number of steps. He staggered like a marionette, his body jerking and twisting awkwardly in space. Then he went down hard, landing flat on his back on the grass with his arms splayed out on either side of him. His eyes looked dim as he stared up at the stars as though trying to figure out exactly what they were.

"Jesus Christ, Tom!" Louise rushed down the stairs and outside and knelt beside her brother. "You didn't have to sucker punch him like that."

"He threw the first one," Tom said, eyeing her with a cold, steady detachment that told her he knew he had never been in any real danger. "You heard him. He threatened me."

"What was he talking about—that deal? What deal?"

Tom bit down on his lower lip and shook his head but didn't answer her. Louise eyed him, her body trembling with repressed rage. She immediately suspected this had something to do with the suitcase of coke she'd found, but she wasn't going to push it now.

Ben needed help.

"He's drunk, for Christ's sake," she said, staring down at her brother. His eyes were closed now. He was out cold. His breath came in short, watery gasps that sounded like he was drowning. "I have to get him home." She glanced at Tom, who hadn't moved from the doorway. "Can you *please* give me a hand?"

Tom snorted and waved his hand at her as if he was shooing a bothersome fly.

"Leave him where he is. He won't even remember how he got here when he comes to."

"I can't leave him outside all night," Louise said.

"Probably not the first time…or last."

She stared at him for a moment, but when Tom made no move to assist her, she pushed past him and went into the kitchen where she grabbed her car keys and purse. She threw on a long overcoat over her pajamas and then, still barefoot, went back to Ben, who was still unconscious on the front lawn. Sliding her arm under his head, she raised him a little. His breathing altered, getting deeper and less raspy. His head lolled from side to side, and his eyes flickered open a little when she slapped him lightly on the cheeks.

Still standing in the doorway, Tom folded his arms across his chest and scowled at her.

"For God's sake, Tom. At least get me a cold washcloth or something."

"I'm telling yah, Lou. Leave him be. He'll sober up fast once the morning sun hits him."

Screw you, she thought but didn't dare say. If Tom got pissed now, she might end up unconscious on the lawn, too.

Her knees were damp from kneeling on the lawn, but she kept trying to bring Ben around. After a short while, Tom muttered something under his breath that she didn't hear and then went back into the house, closing the door firmly behind him.

Louise glared at the closed door, wanting to scream out loud how much she hated Tom, but she stuffed her emotions down and turned her attention to Ben.

After another five or ten minutes, he started coming around. Lying on his back and groaning, he kept rolling his head from side to side. The bones in his neck popped like someone cracking their knuckles. When he exhaled, his breath reeked of sour beer.

"Hey...hey there," Louise said as she ran her fingertips across his brow and down the sides of his face. Ben started groaning softly, but he didn't say anything that made much sense. Once his eyes opened to narrow slits, he looked at her and smiled tightly. When he tried to speak, the only sound he could make was a wet smacking of his lips.

"Come on, Big Ben," Louise whispered as she shifted around and slid her hand around his back and under his armpit. "You gotta get on your feet."

"What the—Where am I?" His voice sounded like his mouth was full of gravel.

"Let's see if we can get you down to my car. I'll take you home."

"I'm at your place?" Ben looked around, confusion clouding his eyes. Finally, with effort, he lunged forward and sat up. He looked befuddled as he brushed grass and dirt from his elbows. "What'm I doin' at your place?"

"Good question," Louise said.

Having grown up with Capt'n Wally for a dad, Louise was used to dealing with people in this condition, but it pained her to see her brother like this. Of everyone she knew, he was the least likely to tie one on and end up having a blackout. She wondered if he was doing crap like this because of his time in Iraq.

Without saying a word, Louise struggled to get him to his feet, cursing Tom under her breath for not helping, and then started walking him toward the driveway where her car was parked next to Tom's. He leaned heavily on her shoulder, like she was a crutch.

Ben was still unsteady on his feet. Even the slightest change in elevation made him stumble and cling to her for support. Once she got him into the car, draped like an old suit across the front seat, she got in, started it up, and drove away casting a quick backward glance at the house before it receded from sight.

They drove in silence, but long before she pulled into her father's driveway, she had decided that this was it.

She wasn't going back home to Tom.

Nobody treats my family like that and gets away with it, she thought... a Cove-ah through and through.

The pain behind Ben's eyes was much worse than the hangover he'd had the day before. This one radiated out like an exploding star, sending shockwaves through his head every time he moved. Lying in bed, squinting at the sun-lit window, he tried to piece together what had happened last night. Not much of it came to him, and the little that did was hazy and confused. The only thing he knew for sure was that he had been mean to Julia when they went for a walk by the harbor.

After that...he had no idea except that the knuckles on his right hand were skinned and swollen. He'd punched *something* hard enough to hurt himself. He wondered now if it had been a person and if so, then who?

Someone was stirring around downstairs, and the aroma of frying bacon and fresh-brewed coffee wafted up the stairwell.

His first thought was that his mother must be down in the kitchen, making breakfast for him. A second later, the memory that his mother was in the nursing home came back with a jolt.

It must be his father...or maybe Pete.

Maybe one of them had gotten up to make him breakfast, knowing how bad off he was after last night.

Judging by the splash of sunlight spilling across the windowsill and floor of the bedroom, he guessed it wasn't very early, but his dad and brother would have been up long before now and gone off to work.

Was Julia downstairs?

She might have let herself into the house to surprise him with breakfast in bed, but he doubted it.

He had said some pretty nasty things to her last night. And even if he hadn't killed their relationship, she had her father to tend to. She didn't have time to be messing around in his house.

His body ached as he tossed the covers aside and shifted around to place his feet squarely on the floor. He realized he had fallen asleep with his clothes on. When he raised his arm and sniffed his armpit, he quickly pulled away from the sour smell of sweat.

It took some effort, but he struggled to his feet and shuffled down the hall to the bathroom. After running the tap until the water was warm enough, he splashed his face a few times and then stared at his bloodshot eyes in the mirror.

I gotta stop doing this, he thought, and then it hit him that he'd said and thought the exact same thing yesterday morning. There was a pattern developing here that he wasn't sure he liked. He was going to have to get his act together.

After urinating and pulling on a fresh t-shirt, he decided he'd shower after breakfast. Feeling as creaky as an old man, he trudged downstairs. Every step jolted his body and sent waves of dull pain up the back of his head.

When he got to the kitchen, he was stunned to see his sister standing in front of the sink, washing a frying pan. A plate heaped with fried eggs, bacon, and two pieces of toast sat on the table next to a glass filled with orange juice and a steaming cup of coffee. With sunlight angling in through the window illuminating it, it looked like a dream.

"'S getting cold," Louise said, glancing over her shoulder at him. Her smile was thin and pale, and thin shadows cut across her face like old scars.

"Wow," Ben said, rubbing a spot in the center of his forehead. "I never…"

"You still take your coffee with milk and three sugars?"

"Uh-huh."

The flood of sunlight that lit up the kitchen dazzled Ben. Everything looked so homey, so picture-perfect normal, but darkness nibbled at the edge of his mind. A myriad of questions filled his head, but his stomach started to growl, so he pushed everything aside as he stared at the breakfast waiting for him. He smiled at his sister, but his smile turned into a grimace of pain from the mere motion of pulling a chair out and sitting down.

After leaning the frying pan in the dish rack, Louise poured a cup of coffee for herself, added milk and sugar, and sat down across from him. When she stirred it with a spoon that clinked on the side of the cup, the *tink-tinking* sound made him wince again.

"Quite a night you had last night," she said, eyeing him over the rim of the cup as she took a sip.

Ben grunted but resisted the impulse to nod. The slightest motion would hurt too much. He was angry with himself because he wasn't able to look her directly in the eyes. He might not remember everything he had said and done last night, but he certainly remembered what he suspected—*and knew*—about her husband. It was only a matter of time before he would have to confront her about it.

"Pete was at The Local when you were there. He said you were pretty wasted when you left."

"I guess to Christ I was..."

He picked up his fork, filled it with egg, and started eating. The tastes exploded in his mouth—especially the orange juice, which he gulped down.

"He says you left with that Meadows woman."

"Julia...yeah."

"You gonna tell me what happened?" she said.

After he'd swallowed a mouthful, he held up his hand with the bruised knuckles and shook it.

"I'm kinda wondering how I did this."

"That's easy. You punched my front door."

"Not Tom?"

Louise shook her head, her mouth pinched shut. Without makeup, her lips were thin and bloodless. Like him, she looked like there were things she had to say that she would just as soon not say. She made eye contact with him but couldn't hold it for long. Instead, she shifted her gaze to the window that looked out to sea, her eyes filmy and blank.

"Kinda wish I had," Ben said, smiling weakly.

"Hit Tom you mean?

"Yeah."

"This has something to do with that Meadows woman, doesn't it?" Louise said, blinking back tears.

"Julia.... Her name is Julia."

Ben felt compelled to try to comfort her, but he didn't. He couldn't. He didn't like the disdain in her voice when she talked about Julia. Instead, he picked up a strip of bacon and bit into it. The crunching sound filled his head like clacking rocks.

In the bright morning light, Louise looked so small, so vulnerable. All his life, he stuck up for his little sister, being a big brother, vetting all of her boyfriends; but for the first time in his life, he realized she had grown up. She looked like their mother, with her soft hazel eyes and careworn face.

And like their mother, Louise was going to have to put up with her husband's infidelities the same way their mother had put up with Wally's numerous indiscretions.

It pained him to see this fate for her, and he prayed that she had the brains and fortitude to get out of the marriage now before there was irreparable damage.

After a long silence, she said, "I know Tom's been screwing her… Julia." Her voice was low and shaky.

The expression on Ben's face froze as he tried to hide his reaction. He had to stop himself from banging his fist on the table and shouting at her that he knew Tom had jumped him out behind The Local and slashed his tires to scare him away from Julia. Fighting to suppress his anger, he said, "Yeah. He has."

"She told you that?"

Ben nodded.

"That lousy son-of-a-bitch," Louise whispered without turning away from the window and looking at him.

"Lou-Lou Belle. You know me. You know I'd never tell anyone what to do or how to live their life. For God's sake, my life's so messed up, who'd take my advice? But I think—"

He stopped when she raised her hand and flicked it at him like she was brushing lint from her shoulder.

"It doesn't matter. I saw all I needed to see last night," she said.

Tears leaked from her eyes, streaking her cheeks. Ben's heart went out to his sister, but he couldn't bring himself to go to her and give her a reassuring hug and kiss on the cheek. He'd had so much practice stuffing his own emotions deep inside that it felt like they'd never come out. That was one of the things he liked about Julia. She made him believe there might be a possibility he could actually *feel* again.

Was that the fate of all the women in his family?

Were they supposed to suffer their sorrows alone and in silence, and carry on as best they could, living with men who repeatedly deserted them emotionally?

"If I…in any way…had anything to do with—"

"Shut up, will you?"

The strength in Louise's voice startled him, making him sit back and stare at her. He forgot all about his breakfast and the throbbing pain in his head.

"Why do you think it's always about you, huh?" Louise said. "Can you answer me that?"

She wiped her face with her fingertips and slowly rotated her head to look at him. Her eyes were glassy, but the look of determination on her face amazed him.

"You're just like Dad. You think everything revolves around *you*. Why do you think you're responsible for everything?"

"No way," Ben said, raising his hands and pulling away from her. "I don't think it's always—"

"You don't know *anything*." Louise's face flushed. Rosy spots appeared on her cheeks. "You don't know diddlysquat about what's going on between me and Tom. Okay?"

"Uh-huh…sure…okay."

Ben wanted to tell her that, oh, yeah, he *did* know…more than she realized, but he leaned forward in his chair and rested his elbows on the table. He was prepared to let her rage. She obviously had a lot of pent-up emotion she needed to vent.

"Even before you got home from Iraq, I knew he was screwing her, okay? He never came right out and admitted it—even when I confronted him, the chicken shit. But he didn't have to. A woman knows when her man's not being faithful. And once you started seeing her, he…he changed even more. That's when he—"

Her voice choked off, and she raised her hand to her cheek and rubbed it as though soothing a fresh injury. After a long, silent moment, she turned and looked out the window again. Her body was wracked by tiny tremors as she twisted her clasped hands in her lap and took short, noisy sips of air through her mouth. Ben was afraid she was going to hyperventilate.

"I want to know what any of this has to do with what happened last night," Louise said after a while. "You came over to the house, drunk on your ass and spoiling for a fight with Tom."

"I did?"

"You did. And you made a complete ass of yourself."

Ben speared another clump of scrambled egg and was about to put it into his mouth, but his stomach suddenly lurched with a sick, sour flood. He didn't think he could eat another bite as he weighed whether or not to tell her that Tom had sandbagged him and then vandalized his car. He didn't want to add to her misery, and he certainly didn't want to add more confusion to an already messy situation.

"I…I'm not sure if there's a connection," he finally said. "I…I got fed up with seeing the way he was treating you, and I wanted to have it out with him."

Louise sniffed with thin laughter and shook her head.

"Really?" she asked.

Ben looked down at his hands in his lap.

"Really. I haven't got the faintest clue. I don't remember a goddamned thing after I left The Local. I don't even know how I got to your house."

"Apparently you walked. At least your car's in the driveway. And what—if anything—did this have to do with your car. You were railing to Tom about your tires."

Ben shook his head even though the slight motion sent splinters of pain through his neck.

"You're not the only one, you know," Louise said.

"What do you mean?"

"You and Tom…you're not the only ones who have been sniffing around that woman's door."

"What are you talking about?"

Louise started to say something but then stopped herself and pursed her lips like she had bitten into something sour.

"It's none of my business," she said, turning away from him and staring out the window again.

"Lou-Lou. Come on," Ben said.

He almost got up from the table and confronted her directly, but he knew he couldn't force her to talk. Like their mother, when she wanted to be stubborn, she excelled at it.

Still, it pained him to see how hurt she was under all the tough talk. But then she squared her shoulders and turned back to face him squarely.

"By the way. I'll be wanting my bedroom back. You'll have move in with Pete."

"No fucking shit," Ben said, smiling. "Good for you, Lou-Lou."

But he couldn't help shaking his head at the thought of sharing a bedroom with his brother. As if he didn't need further proof that he was sliding backwards, not going forward.

The sun was as hot as a blast furnace on Pete's back. He had his Red Sox cap on backwards so it shaded his neck as he and his friend Dwight "Horse Lips" Brackett worked their way along the clam-flats. Each of them was wearing thick rubber gloves and carrying clamming forks and two plastic buckets—a small one for blood-worms and a larger one for sandworms.

Digging for bloodworms was back-breaking work, but the prices local fishermen paid for bait—especially tourists who didn't know better—was one of the few things that kept Pete and several other locals financially solvent these days. Still, it was a hell of a way to earn a couple of hundred bucks, especially when he'd rather be out on the ocean on a hot day like this. But since Ben got home from Iraq, he wanted to be out of the house as much as possible. He had already hauled all of his lines over the last few days, so he and Horse Lips had decided to make some extra cash.

"Watch yourself over there," Horse Lips called out as Pete wandered over to a wide, flat area. "I ran into some wicked honey pots t'other day. Lost one a' my goddamned boots trying to get out of it."

Honey pots are sinkholes in the sand that don't look as dangerous as they are. Inches below what looks like smooth, wet sand flattened by the retreating tide are sinkholes that are a lot like quicksand. If you step into one, you might lose a lot more than a boot. Over the years, up and down the Maine coast, there have been stories about people being sucked in...even drowning, if the honey pot was deep enough.

"Honey pots, my ass," Pete muttered.

The expression had always carried gross sexual connotations that amused him, but hearing Horse Lips say the words made him think—*again*—about Julia Meadows.

Anger seethed inside him, making him grip the handle of his worm bucket so hard his palm and wrist began to ache.

Who the hell did she think she was? Why did she have to go and start screwing my brother? It isn't fair.

Growing up, Ben had always gotten the newest and best things while he had to settle for hand-me-downs and second best...

sometimes third best, if you counted Louise. But when it came to toys and clothes and, later, cars and women…it didn't matter. Ben was always favored. He got whatever he wanted, and Pete was always left in the dust.

Hell, Horse Lips should be pissed at Ben, too. After all, he had shacked up with his wife Kathy before he married her, and word around town was Ben had fathered her baby when he was home on leave two years ago.

"Fuckin'-A-tweety!" Horse Lips suddenly shouted.

Pete looked in his direction and saw him scooping up one of the biggest bloodworms he'd ever seen. The dark red worm had to be at least six inches long. Its stubby, centipede-like legs were thrashing wildly. It twisted like an angry rattlesnake in Horse Lips' gloved hand before he plunked it into his bucket.

Pete turned and walked further away, looking for a good spot to dig, but he wasn't really paying close attention to where he was going until he felt a sudden sinking sensation. Looking down, he realized that his left foot had sunk into the sand to the ankle. Before he could shift his weight back, his leg was sucked in deeper until it was halfway to his knee. When he pulled back, his boot came free with a loud wet, sucking sound.

"Tole yah to be careful," Horse Lips said. His weathered face looked as wrinkled as an old leather suitcase when he laughed at Pete.

Pete sneered and shook his head, not sure if he was disgusted more with himself for stepping into a honey pot or Horse Lips for laughing at him. He frowned when he looked into his bucket. It was less than half-full. He didn't have anywhere near as many worms as he hoped to have by this time.

"Bad diggin's today," he said. "You think shit like pollution or global warmin's killin' off the bloodworms?"

Horse Lips squinted one eye shut and then shook his head.

"Beats the hell outta me," he said. "It ain't none a' my concern."

"How 'bout all them jellyfish in the harbor lately. That ain't normal?"

Horse Lips dropped his bucket and then with a savage grunt jabbed his digging fork into the hard-packed sand.

"We always had shitloads of jellyfish in the harbor," he said as he leaned back and levered over a huge mound of wet sand. "Christ, you don't 'member getting covered with 'em when you was a kid, swimmin' off the docks? Gross little fuckers!"

"Yeah, but I read in the newspaper t'other day where some scientists say there's a lot more of 'em world-wide. Said global warming's fuckin' up the ocean, killin' off the bigger fish and octopuses and shit that eat 'em."

"Fucked if I know," Horse Lips said, still digging.

He took off a glove, reached into his shirt pocket, and pulled out a pack of cigarettes. He shook one out, wedged it between his lips, and then held the pack out to Pete, who put down his buckets and fork and moved closer. He took off his glove to take the offered cigarette. Horse Lips fished a Bic lighter from his pants pocket. He clicked it, cupping the flame in his hand, held it to Pete's cigarette before lighting his own.

Pete stepped back and inhaled deeply, then blew out a plume of smoke that wafted away on the gentle on-shore breeze. The nicotine felt good when it hit his bloodstream, making him lightheaded. Pete didn't smoke often, usually only when he was drinking, but he was never one to refuse a free cigarette, especially at today's prices.

"So," Horse Lips said, letting the smoke curl from his nostrils. "What's your brother been up to, now 'at he's back?"

Pete winced as though he'd been stung in the ass by a hornet and said, "Fucked if I know."

"I hear he's shaggin' that Meadows woman."

Pete tried to keep the sudden rush of anger from showing on his face as he shrugged and took another drag of the cigarette, trying to look casual. It was tempting to remind Horse Lips that Ben had also been screwing his wife not long before they got married—and maybe after, but he let it slide.

"I'm tellin' yah," Horse Lips went on, "that's one fine piece of ass. Wouldn't mind gettin' me some of that flatlander pussy. You?"

"She ain't much," Pete said, waving his hand as though clearing away the smoke. He took another deep drag of his cigarette and, turning away from Horse Lips, stared out to sea. The water glittered like it was sprinkled with thousands of flashing diamonds.

The scene was so peaceful, but inside, he was seething.

For a moment or two, he considered taking out all of his

frustrations on Horse Lips. They were alone on a deserted clam flat. What was to stop him from smacking the crazy asshole a couple of good ones with his clamming fork and then sinking his body in one of those honey pots?

By the time anyone found the old coot, he'd be so decomposed or crab-eaten his own mother wouldn't recognize him.

Pete chuckled at the thought as he took one last drag from his cigarette and then flicked it in the direction of the water. It hissed and sputtered with a thin ribbon of smoke when it landed on the wet sand, rolled over, and went out.

"What's so funny?" Horse Lips asked, frowning as he took another drag. He always smoked his butts down to the filter.

"Huh? Oh, nothin'...nothin' a'tall," Pete said as he pulled his rubber glove back on. "Just thinkin'."

"'Bout what? How tasty that Meadows woman's pussy'd be?" Horse Lips shot him a lascivious grin that only increased Pete's agitation. He tensed, clutching the handle of his clamming fork, but only for a second or two. Then he relaxed his shoulder muscles and bent over to pick up his bucket.

"We ain't gonna get any worms dug standin' around here waggin' our jaws," Pete said.

Without another word, he picked up his stuff and walked about fifty yards down the beach away from Horse Lips. He groaned as he bent over and started digging. The muscles in his arms and back were wire-tight as he savagely plunged the clamming fork into the wet sand several times, turning over wet clumps of sand until—finally—he saw a small, squiggling bloodworm in the wet grit. He picked it up and tossed it into his bucket, and kept on working, jabbing his fork over and over again into the damp sand, all the while thinking how it wasn't Horse Lips he wanted to wail on...

And if Ben *still* hadn't gotten the message that he should leave Julia Meadows alone so he might have a shot at her, then he'd have to make sure he got the message loud and clear the next time.

ELEVEN

Separation Anxiety

"Cluster fuck's more like it," Capt'n Wally said. "That pair of chucklenuts was so drunk they could barely row the god-damned boat. We was lucky we didn't get caught off-loadin' 'em. And then when they was loading up the truck—and whose brain-storm was it to use the Cove Lobster Company truck for moving the shit—they was making enough racket to wake the dead."

Richie Sullivan looked at Wally with a dull, neutral expression, making it clear this was Wally's problem, not his. They were both seated on the *Abby-Rose* as it bobbed on the water, tied to the dock. Each man had a bottle of Sam Adams beer in hand. Moisture beaded up on the sides of the bottles and dripped onto the deck.

"Whaddayah want me to do about it?" Richie asked with a shrug.

"Hire someone who knows what the Christ he's doing…some-one who don't have his head up his ass, not those two peckerheads."

Richie nodded thoughtfully and took a sip of beer, inhaling deeply as he leaned back against the gunwales and looked up at the sky. His body was taut and lean. The muscles in his arms bulged like packed sausage. A gentle breeze off the water ruffled his hair. He looked for all the world like some rich flatlander, enjoying his summer vacation.

"I'll check into it," he said after a moment. "But before then, I got another pickup for you."

Wally choked back the curse that almost escaped him. He knew—and Richie knew—he was in no position to complain. They wouldn't be sitting here on this boat if it weren't for Richie.

"I got my traps to tend, you know?" Wally said.

Richie shrugged and said, "I'm sure you can fit it in. They won't be here for a couple of days. Get your traps pulled before then."

"This more weed?"

"Does it matter?"

Wally considered, then shrugged and shook his head.

"Six of one, half a dozen of t'other," he said.

Richie nodded and then drained his beer. When he was through, he tossed the empty over his shoulder. It hit the water with a loud plunk, quickly filled up until the bottom dropped, and then bobbed there in the water, half-submerged. A school of tiny fish, flashing like silver blades in the water, rose and circled the object, inspecting it before disappearing again into the darker depths.

"You oughtta think about doing more harbor tours," Richie said. "I got some friends coming up in a few weeks who'd love to go for a cruise."

"Say the word," Wally said. "I'll see what I can do."

Even as he said this, he hated how compliant he sounded. He despised that Richie exerted so much control over him, but there wasn't a damned thing he could do about it…at least not until the boat was paid off.

"I was headed out," he said with a cheery note in his voice. "Wanna come out and be my sternman?"

A crooked smile lifted the corners of Richie's mouth as he shook his head, almost laughing out loud. Wally couldn't help wondering how Richie would handle it when he reached into the bait barrel with his clean, manicured hands. It'd be fun to have some kind… *any* kind of control over Richie. But Richie was too smart to put himself into that position.

"Not too friggin' likely," he said.

Wally tossed his empty overboard and then heaved himself up from the plank seat. He brushed his hands on his pants leg.

"Well, I gotta be heading out," he said. "You sure you don't wanna come along?

"Some other time maybe," Richie said as he stood, and they shook hands. Wally noticed how dry and soft Richie's hands were.

Never did an honest day's work in his life, he thought.

Richie looked a bit unsteady on his feet as he walked to the port side of the boat, but Wally couldn't tell if it was the morning beer or the gentle rocking of the boat. Maybe both. Richie stepped over the gunwales and onto the dock. Wally took mild satisfaction in knowing that The Crowbar probably would have gotten seasick if he'd agreed to come out to sea with him. He tried not to smile as he imagined Richie doubled over, hurling his guts out over the rails.

"Catch yah later, then," Wally said raising his hand to his forehead and giving Richie a salute.

"Later." Richie winked and pointed his forefinger at Wally like it was a gun.

Wally was steaming as he watched Richie walk up the gangplank, but his ire faded as he turned to the business of getting ready to cast off. Turning around quickly, he saw something that gave him pause.

Two men were walking on the narrow, rutted dirt road leading up the hill from the docks.

They might be a couple of early season tourists, out for a morning stroll around the harbor. But there was something about them... something in their gait that caught—and held—Wally's attention. A small voice in the back of his mind whispered that these guys were cops or federal agents.

Had they been watching him? Maybe photographing and recording his conversation with Richie?

"Shit-fuck-*balls!*" Wally muttered as he watched the men get into a dark-colored, nondescript car that was parked at the top of the hill. It was far enough away so he didn't hear it start up. As they drove away, a thin cloud of dust rose in its wake.

If anything said "Feds," it was that sleek, dark blue car...that and the fact that both men had been wearing dark suits. Wally knew not many tourists wore dark suits on a bright, warm late spring morning.

"What the hell do you think you're doing?"

Tom's voice, coming so suddenly from behind her, startled Louise. She jumped and spun around to face her husband. Dressed in his officer's uniform, he stood in the doorway, leaning with one elbow on the doorframe. His brow was furrowed, and his eyes gleamed with an unnaturally bright glow.

"Packing," Louise said, irritated by the high-pitched squeak in her voice.

Christ, she thought. I sound like goddamned Minnie Mouse.

"Packing? For what?" Tom lowered his arm and took three or four steps into the bedroom. The leather of his utility belt creaked like an old saddle. Consciously or not, he dropped his hand to his service revolver and rested it on the handle as if he were making an arrest and was prepared to draw if there was any trouble.

Louise glanced at the dresses, blouses, pairs of shorts, socks, and other things she had laid out on the bed. She had been heading into the bathroom to get her toiletries when he showed up.

"I…I'm leaving for a while."

"You don't say," Tom said, not a question but a statement.

Louise had thought she had plenty of time to pack up and move back to her father's house while Tom was at work today. He'd started on the morning shift and shouldn't have been home until five o'clock.

"What you mean to say is, you're leaving me?"

Louise bit down on her lower lip.

"I can't *take* it anymore," she said, enunciating each syllable.

"Take what?" Tom's voice snapped like a piece of dry wood.

"You," she said simply, surprised that she found the courage to say anything. But now, the mere fact that she had spoken the truth gave her courage, and she continued, "I don't think…. No, I *know* you don't love me anymore."

"Oh, so you know that?" Tom nodded his head up and down like a puppet with a loose hinge in its neck. "Tell me exactly how you know that?"

"I…It doesn't matter because I—" She sucked in a breath, not believing she had the courage to say what she was going to say. But she did.

"I don't love you anymore, Tom. I want out."

"'S that a fact?"

Tom took another step closer and folded his arms across his chest. He was smiling at her, but there wasn't a hint of kindness in his eyes. The cold light never left them.

Louise was struggling not to let her fears show, but she couldn't stop herself from backing up, keeping the same distance between them.

"So you're running back home to your father, is that it?"

"Yes. Yes, I am."

"And that's it? You want out, and you think you can just walk out on me like this?"

"What do *you* think, Tom? You treat me like crap, you…we never go out…and we don't make love anymore, and you…you hit me." As she said this, she raised her hand to the side of her face and touched the fading bruise.

Tom stared at her steadily until cold trickles of sweat ran down her sides from her armpits. Her chest ached. She wished she could take a deep enough breath, but the air in the room was too thin to breathe.

After a terribly long moment of staring at each other, Tom smiled a slow, thin smile. The tension left his body, and he was chuckling to himself as he took a step to one side, clearing a path to the door.

"Fine," he said. His voice was as empty as an echo in a steel drum. "Go ahead, then. Leave."

But before Louise could react, he lunged forward, his hand raised as though to deliver a quick backhand slap. Then he drew back and dropped his hand, apparently satisfied to see her flinch.

"Get the fuck out of here…. *Now!*"

Without a word, Louise started stuffing her clothes into the suitcase on the bed, but Tom stepped up and pushed the suitcase and most of the clothes onto the floor.

"You don't get to take a goddamned *thing!*" he shouted, his face flushing, his eyes bulging.

For a flashing instant, she considered fighting him. She imagined going for his throat and ripping it open with her fingernails or teeth.

Instead, she stared blankly at the heap of clothes on the floor and waited for the initial rush of anger to pass.

After that, all she felt was deep sorrow.

Don't push it, she thought. You need to get out of here alive.

"But I need—"

"You're not taking a goddamned thing with you!" he shouted. "You or your fuckin' father and your goddamned brothers can buy you whatever you need. You leave me, you're lucky to leave with the shirt on your back."

You are totally unfair, she wanted to say, but she didn't dare to.

But she knew what she had to do.

She had to leave now…walk out…and not look back.

Sucking in a deep breath, she squared her shoulders and started for the door. She was going to pass within arm's length of him, and she was coiled, ready for the punch when it came, but—surprisingly—she got to the door, and he hadn't moved a muscle other than shifting his eyes to track her.

Go! Get out! Run! her mind was screaming, but she told herself that she was going to leave him walking tall. With or without any of her belongings, her dignity was intact.

Her legs felt as thin and light as balsa wood as she walked down the stairs and down the hall to the front door. She paused only long enough to grab her purse and car keys from the small table by the front door.

She didn't look back. She didn't have to. She sensed Tom's presence at the top of the stairs, watching her. His gaze bored into her back like laser beams.

At least her car was undeniably hers. She had bought it before they were married, so let him try to stop her from driving away from what she was convinced was the biggest mistake of her life.

Screw you, she screamed in her head, but she told herself not to let his hatred and bitterness poison her life.

She opened the door and left.

It was a little after eleven o'clock in the morning. Ben was standing in the kitchen with the phone pressed to his ear. His vision kept going in and out of focus as he leaned over the sink and stared at the ocean view outside the kitchen window.

"I—ah, think I owe you an apology," Ben said into the phone.

"Only one?" Julia said.

Her voice was mild and sounded pleasant enough, but there was an edge to it that told him she might not be able to forgive him for what he had said and done last night no matter how many times he apologized. He winced when he touched the palm of his hand to his forehead, wishing his memory of the night was a little clearer. It still felt like a high school marching band was rehearsing inside his skull.

"How about a dozen apologies, then" he said, smiling feebly.

"A dozen times ten, maybe." She paused.

"I know…I know and…well, really, I *don't* know. I was out of it, and I—I know that's no excuse, but ever since I got—"

He'd been about to say something about how his drinking had only gotten bad since he came home from the war, but he knew she would see that as a copout.

How could he expect her to believe him?

What he had to do was make sure he didn't drink like that anymore…especially if he wanted to keep—or restore—his relationship with her. He feared it was broken for good.

"I know I was pretty stupid."

"Stupid and hurtful," Julia said. He was so used to avoidance in his family, he admired how direct she was being with him.

"So…can you forgive me? I really…"

I really miss you was on the tip of his tongue, but he didn't say it.

"I really would like to spend time with you."

"Spend time?" The edge in her voice was still there—harder now. "Is that all I am? A time-filler?"

A sudden stab of pain shot a flash of yellow light behind his eyes. He winced and closed his eyes.

"No…no…" he said. "It's not like that…not like that at all."

"What's it like, then?"

Ben paused. After opening his eyes and blinking rapidly for a second or two, he focused on the distant horizon. A sailboat whisked into sight from around the headlands, moving across the water as fast as a cloud. Its sail was a small white triangle against the vibrant blue of the ocean. Further out, he could make out the outline of a lobster boat.

She's hinting at something, he thought. She wants me to say that I love her.

"How 'bout I come over…maybe later today…and apologize to you in person?"

"I'm not so sure about that," Julia said. Ben caught a definite teasing inflection in her voice this time as though she were toying with him. "I'm pretty busy today."

Ben's eyes went out of focus again. The view out the window became a blue and green blur with erratic white streaks.

"Look," he said, after taking a breath and mustering up courage he wasn't sure he had. "If you want it to be over, say so. All right? We're both adults. I think we can handle it."

"Technically," Julia said, "yes. We're adults."

Ben wasn't sure if he should take that as a joke or a slam.

"I'm just saying—if you don't want to see me anymore, I can live with it."

"Can you? Really?"

For the first time, Ben caught a frightened pitch in her voice, like someone had their fingers around her throat and was squeezing ever so gently. He considered carefully before he spoke next, but after he cleared his throat and, surprising even himself, he said, "No…not really."

There was a long silence on the other end of the line—long enough for Ben to wonder if the call had dropped. But then she took a slow, deep breath that, at the very end, caught in her throat almost like a sob.

Jesus, is she crying?

"I might be able to get out later this evening," she finally said.

"Are you sure you want to?"

After another long pause, Julia said simply, "Of course I do. Don't be ridiculous."

"Fuck her," Tom muttered between clenched teeth.

As he pulled to a stop in his driveway and killed the engine, he realized the same thing applied to both of the women in his life—Julia *and* his wife.

When he turned off the car's headlights, the night collapsed around him like the inside of a coal mine. He stared straight ahead at the closed front door of his house. It looked impossibly far away, and with the car windows closed, the sudden hushed quality of the night was disorienting. He wondered if this was what death was like.

One moment you're here…and the next moment you're gone… gone so fast you never even realize it.

You're…just…

Gone.

He'd stopped off at the liquor store earlier today and bought a bottle of whiskey. He was feeling the need to knock back a few and think things through. As far as Julia was concerned, she could go fuck herself along with Ben Brown and anyone else she might have been boning. And Louise? Well, maybe he had loved her once upon a time...back in high school, maybe, when he was "young, dumb, and full of cum," as he and his buddies joked. If she wanted to move out on him, that was fine with him. Let her goddamned pirate of a father support her.

For the last hour or so, he had been parked out at Sand Beach, sipping from the whiskey bottle as he watched the sun set behind the pines. The wind blowing off the water had carried the smell of hot sand and seaweed at low tide. Then he drove home.

It hadn't taken long for the whiskey to go to his head, especially drinking on an empty stomach. Now that he thought about it, he realized he'd been so upset about the direction his life had taken that he hadn't eaten anything since breakfast. The last thing on his mind, though, was food. He was filled with rage...pure and simple rage.

He spun the cap off the bottle with the heel of his thumb. It fell to the car floor, but he left it when it landed as he tipped his head back and took a long pull. The whiskey burned his nose and throat as he swallowed slowly, savoring the taste. His mind clouded, and anger churned in his stomach like a cauldron filled with molten lava.

He sighed and smacked his lips, knowing that sooner or later, he was going to have to try to get into the house. The door looked impossibly far away.

He took a deep breath and held it. Once he felt ready, he pulled the key from the ignition and fumbled for the door handle. After a few awkward tries, he got the car door open and spilled out onto the driveway. He banged his knees hard on the asphalt but was too drunk to notice. A tiny, lucid part of his mind was grateful only that he didn't break the bottle or spill much as he heaved himself to his feet and started for the door, staggering and muttering to himself the whole way.

It took an inordinate amount of concentration to get the right key into the door lock and turn it, but—finally—he swung the door open and stepped into the kitchen.

His senses were alert as he looked around, trying to determine if his wife had been—*or still was*—in the house. When the thought struck him that she might have come back while he was out and taken the clothes she'd been packing, he stomped up the stairs and down the hall to their bedroom. The door was closed.

"You fuckin' better not be here..." he called out as he slammed his shoulder against the door without turning the doorknob. The wood around the latch plate splintered, and something in his neck or shoulder made a crackling sound. He was barely aware of what was going on around him as he pushed the door open and all but fell into the dark bedroom.

"Fuckin'-A," he muttered. He fumbled around for the light switch until he found it and turned the ceiling light on. The sudden brightness hurt his eyes, but he smiled when he saw Louise's clothes still piled up on the bed, exactly the way she had left them.

Tom belched, and the burning taste of whiskey and vomit filled his mouth. When he realized he was still clutching the whiskey bottle, he tossed back a mouthful, gasping with satisfaction as he wiped his mouth with the back of his hand.

"You're goddamned lucky...I'd fuckin' kill you if you wuz here."

Satisfied that Louise hadn't been back, he raised the bottle as if toasting her and took another huge gulp. The alcohol fumes exploded inside his head, and the room rocked like the deck of a boat tossed about by a storm.

Staggering and muttering obscenities, and punctuating his verbal stream with an occasional watery belch, Tom lurched over to the window between their two bureaus. He set the bottle down carefully on Louise's bureau, knocking over a photograph of her and her family in the process. His vision kept going out of focus as he unlocked the window and ran it up.

Then he wheeled around and lunged back to the bed. Scooping up an armful of clothes, he carried them to the window. A few things dropped along the way, but he barely noticed. Forgetting about the screen in the window, he twisted his body to one side, mentally counted to three, and then, swinging around to gather momentum, heaved the clothes out the window. The screen ripped from its frame as the clothes cascaded out into the darkness.

"Serves yah fuckin' right!" he bellowed as he shook his fists at the gaping window.

Snorting with laughter, Tom went back to the bed and grabbed another armful of clothes, which he also carried to the window and tossed outside. The room filled with his maniacal laughter. Once the bed was clear, he scooped up the few items that had fallen to the floor—a bra, some panties, a lime green t-shirt, and some mismatched socks. Sitting down heavily on the edge of the bed, he threw these out the window, one at a time, making a game of it and calling out "Bulls eye" every time something shot out into the darkness.

When he was finished, he grabbed the bottle off the bureau and took another drink. His knees were rubbery as he stumbled over to the window. Bracing both hands on the sill and crouching low to try to stop the room from spinning, he stuck his head outside. Inhaling sharply, he filled his lungs with the clear-smelling night air. The darkness spun crazily around him, zooming in and out of focus as he looked down at the clothes, strewn on the lawn and hanging from the shrubbery that bordered the house. They looked like a tangle of shredded ghosts.

"There yah go, you lousy cunt!" he shouted. His voice echoed in the night like a lost soul calling from the woods behind the house. "Come 'n get 'em if you want 'em!"

Gripping the windowsill with both hands, he stared into the night, no longer capable of clear, conscious thought. An unaccountable sadness suddenly welled up inside him, and tears filled his eyes. He let out a heart-rending sob that ended with a resonating belch, and then a hot gush of vomit spewed from his mouth. The sickly sour taste almost gagged him as his stomach convulsed until it was empty, and then he started dry-heaving, hacking like a cat trying to cough up a fur ball.

Finally, when he was done, his head dropped forward and banged hard against the windowsill. He slipped to the floor onto his knees and then collapsed over onto one side and sprawled, unconscious, on the floor.

TWELVE

Rampage

"Cop or no cop," Capt'n Wally said, "I say we go over there and have a little chat with the cocksucker."

In the living room, Wally was ensconced in his worn leather easy chair. The TV was on, but the sound was down. The remote dangled loosely in his hand. No one was paying much attention to the ballgame, even though the Red Sox were beating up on the Yankees for the second night in a row. What made it even sweeter was they were playing at Fenway.

Louise sat on one end of the couch with both of her feet tucked up beneath her butt, the way she had always sat to watch TV since she was little. Ben, beer in hand, was at the other end of the couch. He couldn't stop glancing at the digital clock on the cable box. He was already more than half-an-hour late picking up Julia.

"I don't want you to do anything, Pops," Louise said in a thin, quavering voice. "This is between me and my husband."

"Husband? Hah!" Wally snorted and made a hawking sound deep in his throat. If he'd been outside, he would have let fly a louie. "What kinda husband does shit like that to his wife?"

You did a lot worse to Ma over the years, but at least you never beat on her, Ben thought but didn't say. He suspected by her expression that it was Louise's immediate thought, too.

"I'll go back tomorrow," Louise said. "I'm sure he'll at least let me take some of my personal stuff."

Wally sighed and shook his head before taking a sip of beer. His gaze shifted to the TV for a moment in time to see Youk field a hot grounder at first—"a worm burner"—for an easy out.

"Fuckin' Yankees can't hit to save their lives tonight," he muttered and then shifted his attention back to his daughter. "Either Ben or Pete oughta go with yah…just in case."

"In case what?" Louise said, as if she didn't know. Without thinking, she raised her hand to her cheek and rubbed it.

"I'll go with you," Ben said, focusing for a moment on their conversation. "Maybe I should go alone."

"Yeah, that's a great idea." Louise scowled and shook her head. "So you and Tom can go at it? Get real."

"I can wait until he goes to work," Ben said.

Louise narrowed her lips and shook her head in adamant denial.

"No way. This is my shit to deal with, and I'll deal with it. I don't want either you or Pete getting involved. Got it?"

"You know I'll always stand up for you," Ben said.

Wally sat there, staring at her and not saying a word. She wasn't sure what was going on in his mind, but she knew she didn't like it. Ben knew exactly what their father was thinking…. He was thinking, if he had his druthers, he'd go over there with a baseball bat and beat the living shit out of that asshole…maybe even kill him.

"I can handle this," Louise said. "Seriously."

"Maybe, but I'm going with you," Ben said. He knew not to stand up to Louise once she had her back up, but he was thinking maybe she didn't realize how serious this was.

"No," she said. "You're not. I'm a big girl and I don't need you or anyone else standing up for me. I'm not a kid."

"You're still my little sister," Ben said.

"Well no one—and I mean *no one* treats my daughter like that and gets away with it," Wally said, as much to himself as them. A dull glow lit his eyes like hot coals smoldering inside his head.

"We're not gonna solve a damned thing, sitting here bitchin' about it," Ben said.

The instant he said that, the back door banged opened and then slammed shut. They all tensed and listened to the heavy clump of approaching footsteps. Ben noticed that his sister's face was lit up with expectation mixed with apprehension.

Is she really hoping Tom's come over to find her and apologize? he wondered.

With the kitchen light behind him, a shadow stretched down the hallway and seeped into the entryway. A second later, Pete walked into the room. He paused and looked around, obviously confused by the way everyone in the room was staring at him.

"What? Why's everyone looking so pissed?" he asked, and then his expression froze. "Oh, Jesus. Did Mom wander off again and—?" He stopped before he finished the thought.

"No. Mom's fine," Ben said. "It's Lou. She's been having some—ahh...some domestic issues."

"Domestic issues," Pete echoed. He tipped his head to one side and regarded his sister for a second or two, then shrugged as if to say there wasn't a darned thing he could do about it.

"Where the hell you been, anyways?" Wally said, a little snappishly. Before Pete answered, he drained the rest of his beer.

"Out," Pete said. "What's it to you?"

Ben noticed that, as he spoke, Pete lowered his gaze and, shifting his eyes to the side, looked slyly at him. He had that same stupid guilty look he always had whenever he did something wrong that usually involved Ben. Ben decided not to pursue it.

"Speaking of out," Ben said, glancing at his wristwatch. He burped as he leaned forward and placed his empty beer bottle on the coffee table in front of him. "I've gotta head on out. Got some plans of my own."

He stood up and, stretching his arms over his head, looked from his father to his sister to his brother.

"Kinda late to be going out, don't'cha think?" his father said. Now that the family issue was resolved—at least for the time being—he was focusing on the baseball game again. The Sox had increased their lead.

"You popping down to The Local for last call?" Pete asked, brightening. "I'll go with yah if you—"

"Nope," Ben said as he patted his jeans' pocket to feel for his car keys. "Got other plans."

He noticed that his brother's expression hardened.

"Oh, I get it. You're hooking up with that slut," Pete said.

It wasn't so much what he said as it was the way he said it. Or maybe it was the lingering smirk on Pete's face that set Ben off. Whatever it was, he clenched his fist at his side, took three quick steps across the living room floor and without a moment's hesitation punched his brother in the gut.

Pete's eyes opened wide as he grunted and doubled over. His mouth made a large *O*, and his face turned purple. His breath whooshed out of him as he dropped to his knees, clutching his stomach.

"Watch your goddamned mouth," Ben snarled. He didn't back down an inch as he stood above his brother, his fist still clenched and raised.

"Fuck...you," Pete gasped, his voice so broken it was barely audible. A thin string of drool hung from his lower lip and dangled over the floor.

Ben drew his arm back, preparing to swing again, but Wally shouted, "Jesus H. bald-headed Christ! Enough of this bullshit!"

Ben glanced over his shoulder at his father and then stepped back, relaxing his guard as he eyed Pete. He didn't offer to help him as he clutched the doorframe and hauled himself back onto his feet, moving hand over hand like he was hauling a lobster line. Broken blood vessels covered his cheeks like tiny red threads, and he was puffing like an overworked engine as he tried to catch his breath. A silvery gleam filled his eyes, and Ben knew—if their father hadn't been there—they would have gone at it again until one or both of them was sprawled on the floor, bleeding and breathless... or unconscious.

"What the *fuck* is wrong with you?" Ben said, glaring down at Pete. He clenched his fist and raised it, ready to strike if he had to.

"With *me?*" Pete was still laboring to take a deep enough breath, but impotent fury colored his face. "What the fuck is wrong with *you?* All I said was—"

"I know what you said." Ben took a single step forward, and Pete shied back, hunching his shoulders. "And if you *ever* say *anything* like that again about Julia, I swear to Christ I'll mop the goddamned floor with your ass."

All the while, Louise was staring openmouthed at her two brothers. While they were growing up, she had played the role of peacemaker between them, but they hadn't gone at each other like this since high school.

"Will you two *please* stop it? You're acting like a couple of bullshit macho shitheads."

She unfolded herself from the couch and walked over to Pete.

"You okay?" she asked, but when she reached out to touch him, he pulled away from her. Without a word, he walked over to the couch and sat down. When he put his feet up on the coffee table, he knocked Ben's empty beer bottle onto the floor, but he either didn't notice or care.

"Don't wait up," Ben said, and without another word, he walked out into the kitchen. As he was going out the backdoor, he heard his sister ask no one in particular, "What the fuck's up *his* ass?"

The curtains in Julia's bedroom windows billowed in and out like lacy wings. A warm breeze flowed across the floor and over their naked bodies like velvety water. A single candle on the bureau lit the room, but it had burned down so the orange flame wasn't much larger than a fingernail.

Ben had been lying on his back, but he rolled over onto his side and gently ran his hand along the soft, rounded curves of Julia's hips and waist. They had just finished making love, and her skin was slick with sweat. He paused to lick the salty taste from his upper lip.

"Wow," he said, smiling at her in the dimming light. Her face stood out in sharp relief against the whiteness of the pillowcase, her dark hair fanned out like a splash of black ink. She was smiling, her eyes narrowed and crinkling at the sides as she looked at him with a look of total contentment.

"Yeah," she said with a tiny exhalation followed by a light chuckle. "Wow."

"Sheets are so much better than sand."

They both laughed, and then she ran her fingertips lightly across his cheek. She shifted her hand down across his sweat-slick neck, chest, and waist until she held his manhood lightly but firmly. She gave it a gentle squeeze. Ben responded immediately. He remembered his last home leave and the time he'd spent with Kathy Brackett, but this was so much better he quickly pushed such thoughts from his mind.

"Let's give it a rest for a sec, huh?" he said, grinning like an idiot as he slid his hands between her legs and started rubbing her gently. She closed her eyes and moaned softly, thrusting her hips forward and pressing herself against his hand.

"Look who's talking 'give it a rest,'" she said in a husky whisper.

Ben responded immediately. Rolling her over onto her back, she needed little urging to spread her legs for him. Shifting onto his side and then getting up on to his knees, he leaned over her, kissing her full on the mouth. Their tongues darted playfully in and out, but then he broke the kiss off and started kissing a winding trail down her neck to her collarbone and then lower, to her breasts. He took his time licking each nipple in warm, wet circles before moving lower. His tongue flicked across her ribcage and stomach and then moved even lower, going down on her.

Julia clasped the sides of his head with both hands as though to guide him, but he didn't need any directions. Before long, he was kissing and lapping and applying pressure with the tip of his tongue to the soft, moist folds of her flesh. She twined her fingers in his hair, moaning softly as she twirled his sweat-dampened locks. The sounds of ecstasy gradually built in volume and intensity. Ben couldn't help but wonder briefly if the bedroom walls were thick enough or if Julia's father was sleeping soundly enough for him not to hear them.

But he didn't let that slow him down.

After bringing her to a climax so hard she clamped his head between her thighs as if to never let him go, he shifted up so he was leaning over her, resting on his elbows. He was as hard as an iron spike when he entered her with a long, slow thrust that was so intense he got dizzy. Pinpoints of white light spun like tiny comets across his vision. He began moving in and out slowly, trying to control his tempo, but it wasn't long before he found release impossible to resist. With a sudden shudder and groan, he reached orgasm and then collapsed onto the bed beside her.

He was totally spent.

Sweat ran in thin streams down his face and neck. For a long time, they lay beside each other, not saying a word…breathing heavily. Julia trailed her fingertips across his chest, ribcage, and hips, caressing…exploring…soothing. Ben wiped the sheen of sweat from his forehead with an edge of the pillowcase and then, rolling his head to the side, gazed at her. In the dim light of the candle, she looked gorgeous beyond belief. He decided right then and there that, at least as far as he was concerned, he wanted to go to bed with her every night and wake up every morning just so her face would be the first thing he saw every day.

"So," he finally said, his breath coming in fast hitches, his pulse still racing. "Do you forgive me?"

Julia regarded him in silence until she smiled, making her eyes narrow. They looked like two beads of hot tar.

"Yes," she said. "Of course I do."

Ben smiled and shifted around so he was lying flat on his back next to her, looking up at the ceiling.

The feeling of peace and contentment vanished in an instant, as if a switch had been thrown in his head. Cold, winding tension filled his belly. The sweat on his skin went icy, chilling him. Deep in his bones, he felt suddenly threatened…that some unknown or unseen enemy was closing in on him. The urge to leap out of the bed…to *go* somewhere…to *do* something got steadily stronger until it was almost too much to bear.

"Are you all right?" Julia asked. She sat up and leaned over him, her eyes widening with sudden concern.

Ben tried to speak, but his chest felt constricted as if being squeezed by iron bands. He was unable to take a deep breath, and his pulse was suddenly racing a mile a minute, thundering in his ears like distant bomb strikes. He pushed her away and twisted around so he was sitting on the edge of the bed, his feet planted on the floor. Julia touched him lightly on the back, but he flinched at her touch and pulled away. His legs felt brittle, and his knees were like un-oiled hinges as he stood up and began pacing back and forth, pausing at each pass by the window to peer outside as if expecting gunfire.

"There's something out there. I know there is. I *know* it," Ben said, his voice guttural with fear.

"Ben? What is it? You're scaring me." Julia pulled the bed sheets protectively up to her chest.

Each step Ben took jarred him, making his vision bounce. The candle shot shadows across the floor and walls at dangerous angles. The air in the room was dense, and it was only with effort that he inhaled deeply enough.

"Ben…tell me. What's wrong?"

Julia's voice had a cold echo effect as if it was coming from far away…from the throat of a deep, stone-lined well.

When he looked at her, her fear-widened eyes frightened him all the more. For a split second, he expected to see a swarm of insects flooding from her opened mouth. She looked like a jungle cat prepared to pounce.

"I…I…I don't know," he managed to say, but that was all before his throat closed off. The thin piping of his voice sounded strange to him, like someone else…someone he couldn't see in the shadows…had spoken.

Julia remained in bed, watching him as he paced back and forth at the foot of the bed. He kept clenching and unclenching his fists and gritting his teeth as he repeatedly punched his upper thighs while making soft, chuffing sounds in his throat.

"It's…I—I…Jesus, my heart's beating like crazy."

"Sit down and relax," she said. "You're stressing."

Her voice was mild and soothing, but there was an edge to it that cut through Ben's rush of panic. He stopped pacing and looked at her, trying to let the sight of her calm him down and anchor him. His hands were shaking with deep tremors that felt like mild electric shocks. His throat was as slick and dry as sheet metal.

"Come on, Ben. Please." Julia let the sheet slip away, exposing her breasts and stomach as she patted the edge of the bed. "Sit down. Get a grip."

"Get a grip? Get a grip?" Ben muttered, shaking his head. His skin was prickling with cold. What he really wanted to get a grip on was a gun. Then he'd certainly feel better. He took another breath and held it for a while before letting it out in a slow hissing whistle between his teeth.

Try to stay frosty, man, he thought, but he said, "Christ, what the fuck is wrong with me?"

Julia didn't say a word. She continued to stare at him, her dark eyes swelling in the orange glow of the candle.

"I…"

Ben started pacing again, but he moved more slowly now…more deliberately as the rush of adrenalin gradually subsided. He shivered from the cool night air on his skin, and when he looked at Julia again, he felt suddenly embarrassed.

"Jesus," he said, lowering his gaze.

He stopped pacing and stood at the foot of the bed, looking directly at her. The worry and concern reflected in her eyes touched him deeply.

"You're stressed, is all," she said.

"I guess to fuck I'm stressed."

"Is it…. Do you need to talk?"

Ben knew she had been about to ask him if this was in any way related to the war, but—thankfully—she didn't. He considered in silence for a moment, then shook his head.

"Not really," he finally said. "It's just…you know. It's some family shit."

"Come on," she said, patting the edge of the bed again. "Sit down."

This time, he did as he was told and sat down on the edge of the bed, but he kept his feet on the floor. She shifted close to him and wound her arms around his waist, clasping her hands like a low-slung belt in front of him below his navel. Sighing, she leaned her head against his sweat-slick back, holding him close, her lips brushing lightly against his back. The embrace was almost too tight, and another cold rush of panic filled him, but soon enough it, too, faded away. He took a few deep breaths and willed his rocketing pulse to slow down.

"If you wanna talk about it—about anything, you know you can," she said. "You're safe here."

Her breath made a warm spot on his back between his shoulder blades. He felt something wet trickle down his back and knew she was crying. The thought of her concern for him touched him deeply, but it also made him angry with himself.

What the hell just happened? he wondered as he sat there leaning forward, his elbows resting on his bare legs. The tingling sensation was subsiding, too, thank God.

He knew he had lied. This had nothing to do with Louise's situation. And it didn't have anything to do with what his mother was going through. As for his father—well, he would have to deal with whatever shit he was in with Richie Sullivan on his own. It was none of Ben's concern. And as far as Pete was concerned…. Screw him, too. They had drifted apart over the years, especially once they hit high school, but what did it matter? Like they say, "You can pick your friends and you can pick your nose, but you can't pick your family."

No.

Whatever was bothering him was much more than any family problems. And as much as he might want to avoid it...as much as he might pretend it wasn't happening to him between the dreams and now this panic attack, he had to face the cold, hard truth that he, Ben Brown, the invincible Gunner of Catawamkeag Cove, was being eaten alive from the inside by PTSD. Of course, he might excuse it by telling himself no one could be unaffected by the things going on in the war zone. But he couldn't admit to himself that he might be cracking under the strain. And, he told himself, there was no way he could let Julia see him weak like this...weak and vulnerable. He had to hold it together no matter how much it took.

"I'm here for you," Julia said. "You know that, I hope."

"I do," Ben said even though—right now—he had no idea what he knew or felt.

She spread her hands out and started rubbing his chest and stomach. Her touch was like magic, soothing and arousing him, but Ben was so drained he wasn't at all surprised that he didn't respond.

He pulled away and turned around to hug her, their arms wrapping around each other and pulling each other close. Their skin was sticky with sweat as he clung to her so tightly her pulse beat against him. When he pressed his lips to her neck, she was shaking. He was afraid she was crying and wanted to reassure her, but words failed him. All he could do was hold her close, no matter how far away from her he actually felt.

An hour or so later, after he had calmed down at least enough so he was breathing normally, he got up from the bed, picked his clothes up off the floor, and started dressing. Julia was still awake. She watched him, looking wounded.

"You're not going to stay the night?" she asked.

Ben grunted and shook his head. He didn't like that she had seen him with all defenses down, but he also sensed that it had further cemented the bond growing between them. Walking over to the bed, he leaned down and kissed her, long and passionately on the mouth. She moaned softly.

"I have to leave…for now," he said, "but don't worry, I—"

He had been about to tell how much he loved her, but he held back the words he knew, from the expression on her face, she wanted to hear.

"You'll come back, won't you?" she asked in a fragile voice that sent pain stabbing through his heart. He wanted desperately to throw down the rest of his defenses and tell her how he felt—tell her that he loved her and wanted to spend every day and night with her.

His arms and legs felt like they were filled with sand as he slowly finished dressing and then, with one last hug and kiss, walked out the door.

Tom woke up sprawled on the bedroom floor by the opened window. A cool breeze that smelled like fresh-cut pine was blowing in, chilling him. The left side of his face was pressed against the threadbare carpet. Drool had leaked from the corner of his mouth and dribbled onto the floor. It had dried, and his cheek was crusty now. He wiped it away quickly as he sat up and looked around, trying to figure out where he was and what had happened.

The room was dark.

Once he recognized his bedroom, he still had no idea what time it was or how he had come to be lying on the floor, asleep…passed out was more like it. A sour churning in his stomach was an all too clear reminder that he'd had too much to drink, but his memory didn't go much beyond that.

When he shifted to get to his feet, his hand knocked against the now-empty whiskey bottle. It spun around as it rolled across the floor until it clunked against the baseboard somewhere in the darkness.

"Goddamn," he whispered when he raised his hand to his forehead and rubbed it. The pain between his eyes was as sharp as a honed steel blade. He shivered wildly. He didn't remember opening the window, but what had happened was starting to come back to him as he heaved himself up off the floor and went to close the window. A pair of his wife's panties was caught on the edge of the windowsill. To confirm his dim memory of what he had done—Did I really throw all of her crap out onto the lawn?—he looked outside at the pile of clothes strewn about in the yard beside the house.

"Fuckin' goddamned..." he muttered as he straightened up. When the sourness in his stomach churned, he reeled away from the window and ran into the bathroom.

He winced when he turned on the light and stared at his reflection in the bathroom mirror. His cheeks were pasty white, splotched with thin lines of broken blood vessels. Above his left eyebrow was a purple bruise about the size of a half dollar rimmed with broken blood vessels. It looked like an exploding star. His bloodshot eyes stared back at him, watery and sticky.

After studying his reflection for a long time, he turned on the tap, letting the water run until it was lukewarm. Then he filled his cupped hands with water and splashed his face a half dozen times. The water felt as though it barely penetrated, and he was only marginally better when, sputtering, he wiped his face on a hand towel.

His upset stomach settled, and he was glad that at least he didn't puke.

Shuffling back into the bedroom, blinking his eyes in amazement, he turned on the bedside light and sat down on the edge of the bed. When he leaned forward, something popped in his shoulder. His chest ached something fierce, and he wondered if he might have cracked a rib or two either in a brawl he didn't remember or from tossing all of Louise's clothes out the window.

His eyes weren't adjusting well to the light, and he squinted as his gaze shifted around the room until it came to rest on the telephone. It took him another few seconds to register that's what he was looking at. When he finally did, he considered calling his wife's cell phone to find out where she was.

Would she even answer?

If she had half a brain—which, to tell the truth, he doubted—she would ignore his call because...well, because he deserved to be ignored.

"Man, you fucked up big time," he whispered to himself, sighing as he closed his eyes and shook his head.

He never reached for the phone.

As far as he was concerned, their marriage was over. Dead. He'd seen to that.

But that didn't dispel the bitterness and anger welling up inside him. It took a while to figure out that most, if not all, of his anger wasn't really directed at Louise or that bitch Julia Meadows. He wasn't even that pissed at Ben Brown for getting the girl Tom wanted.

No.

He was pissed at Tony Gillette.

That's who had *really* fucked him over.

"Women? Screw 'em..."

Women come and go, but Gillette...now, *that* cocksucker had screwed him out of a hundred thousand dollars. That was some serious cash. So what if he had done something illegal to get it? So what if he had a hundred thousand in hand? There still should be...

What was the expression?

"Honor...honor among thieves," he muttered.

Gillette had fucked him over, and there was no way Tom was going to let that slide. Stealing cocaine from the evidence locker was a felony. If he got nailed for taking it and then selling it, he'd end up in jail, for sure. He certainly couldn't stick around town after what he'd done, but he needed all the money he could get so he could get the hell out of The Cove and never come back.

So it was a given. He would get out of town. A hundred thousand was enough money to make a clean start somewhere, maybe down in the Caribbean or Central America. Still, he hadn't gotten what he was owed.

And *that* was something he simply wasn't going to let stand.

"What the Christ?" he muttered as he grabbed the bedside clock and stared at it. It was a little past midnight.

"The night's still young." He smiled as he placed the clock down and got up off the bed.

He knew he should leave well enough alone and take off tonight while he had the chance. A hundred thousand bucks could go a long way toward that new life he imagined...

"But two hundred thousand would go *twice* as far," he whispered as a wicked grin spread across his face.

He had a pretty good idea Gillette would be at some bar, probably the Sea Shell down in Boothbay Harbor. That was his usual hangout. He'd be drinking and partying with his hoodlum friends and maybe that creep Zimmerman.

A small part of Tom's mind warned him not to start thinking crazy thoughts.

Not now…

Not while he was still foggy from last night's binge.

But this crap between him and his wife would take time to figure out, and unless Gillette started yapping about what he'd done, Tom knew he was clear…at least for now.

And in that time, he would figure out how to deal with Gillette. If he wasn't going to get the rest of the money that son-of-a-bitch owed him, then maybe…just maybe before he split town he would make the cocksucker pay.

That might even be more satisfying than getting the other hundred thousand he was owed.

"Are you crazy? You'll wake up Amanda."

Ben stood on the doorstep, trying to focus on Kathy Brackett's face, but his vision kept twitching from side to side. After leaving Julia's, he had intended to drive straight home; but for some reason—he liked to think it wasn't on purpose, that it just happened that way—he ended up heading down Mill Stream Road, toward Kathy's house.

After sitting outside in front of the house for fifteen or twenty minutes, listening to the night sounds, he was confident Horse Lips wasn't home, so he had gone up to the door and knocked on it.

"Sorry…sorry," he said, raising a forefinger to his mouth and shushing himself.

"What the hell are you doing here?"

Kathy eyed him with obvious suspicion.

Ben thought guiltily that if he was a real man, he would have stepped up and claimed the child as his own instead of letting Kathy and Horse Lips raise her.

And—honestly—who wanted to grow up with a father named "Horse Lips?"

He leaned forward and cast a quick glance left and right inside the house. "Is your—ah, husband home?"

Kathy hesitated to answer, and that was all Ben needed to know that he wasn't.

"Probably down at The Local, you think? Drinking with my old man."

"Might be," Kathy said. "How would I know?"

She stepped out onto the front stairs, forcing him to take a step back. After listening for a moment to make sure all was quiet, she eased the door almost all the way shut. Ben noticed that she kept one foot on the doorsill and was positioned so she could hear if Amanda started to cry.

"I really don't think it's a good idea for you to come around like this," she said in a harsh whisper.

"Probably not, but I…I feel…"

Ben's voice drifted away as his gaze shifted out across the lawn. Shadows cast by the nearby streetlight cut across the dew-covered grass, looking like thick, black velvet.

"You feel what?" Kathy spoke softly, but there was an edge in her voice. "You feel guilty about what you did? What you didn't do? What is it?"

Ben turned to her. With the lights on inside the house shining behind her, it was difficult to see her features. Strands of her hair glowed like silver spider webs in the halo of light surrounding her head.

"I know you have every reason to be angry, but I—"

"I'm not angry with you," Kathy said, her voice modulating. "I'm really not. I'm married now, and I love my daughter, and I'm—"

"*Our* daughter," Ben said.

"Yes, our daughter. Her name's Amanda."

"Amanda," Ben echoed.

"And as far as I'm concerned, there's nothing between us, Ben." She heaved a heavy sigh and looked distracted, but her voice was strong when she continued. "I don't mean to be cruel or anything, Ben, but all you were was the…the sperm donor."

Her matter of fact tone took Ben aback. Here he had been wracked with guilt for essentially stranding her with a child. Even if, at first, she had felt pain and resented him, she had obviously moved on, making the best of what life had given her.

"And are you happy?" he asked, his voice low, serious.

Kathy hesitated for a moment. He thought she was holding back something, but then he realized she was straining to hear inside the house if the baby had awakened and was crying.

"I don't think 'happy' has anything to do with it," she finally said. "This is my life. This is the hand I've been dealt, and I'm making the best of it I can."

"Kathy..." he began, but he had no idea how to express what he was thinking without making an ass of himself. Maybe there was too much to say, and not enough words to say it in, but whatever it was, it was obviously too late.

After an awkward moment of silence, Kathy glanced at her wristwatch and said, "It's after midnight. Dwight'll be home soon, and I don't want him to see—"

"Can I ask you one favor?"

Kathy hesitated again, then nodded and said, "What?"

He sucked in a lungful of air and tilted his head back to look at the star-sprinkled sky as he struggled to focus his thoughts.

"My mom's over to Grave's Edge."

"Harbor's Edge." Kathy nodded. "Yeah...I heard."

"She's not doing so well, and I was wondering if you'd...you know, go over to visit her sometime and maybe bring the baby—bring Amanda along so she can see her."

Kathy didn't reply immediately, and Ben thought he might be asking too much of her, but he wasn't going to back down now.

"You don't have to—She doesn't have to know Amanda's her granddaughter or anything." He laughed a tight laugh even as it felt as though someone was reaching down inside his chest and squeezing his heart. "Hell, even if you told her, she'd forget it three seconds later, but I—Even if she doesn't know it, I'd like her to see her granddaughter...just once."

Kathy was silent for a long time. When the headlights of a car coming down the street illuminated the yard, he was certain it was Horse Lips, and he'd be busted; but the car passed by and didn't stop.

"Will you?" He was ashamed of the note of desperation in his voice.

"Yeah," Kathy said. "Okay...I'll do that."

"Thanks," Ben replied. He moved forward as if to hug or kiss her. "You have no idea—"

"Would you please leave now?" Kathy said, peering down the

road as if expecting to see her husband's headlights approaching.

Ben stepped back and exhaled, feeling some kind of weight lift off his shoulders. He slid his hand into his jeans pocket and grabbed his car keys. Then, without another word, he walked to his car, got in, and drove away.

THIRTEEN

Storm Warnings

The Local was almost deserted an hour before last call. After trying—without much success—to deal with all of the bullshit back home, Wally had decided to drop by for a few. The weather forecast was for rain tomorrow, heavy at times, so Wally knew it would be all right to tie one on tonight if he wanted to. He would nurse the demons by sleeping late tomorrow morning.

He hadn't intended to talk business, but then Tony Gillette came in and sat down at a corner table with his *goon du jour,* a guy from New Jersey named Marcus Zimmerman, who—Wally had heard—was "spending the summer" in The Cove...no doubt because there was some heat on him in New Jersey.

"What's up, Capt'n?" Gillette called out with a wave of the hand when he saw Wally sitting at his usual perch at the bar. His face was flushed, and he had a wider than usual grin plastered on it.

Wally looked over at him and nodded a silent greeting, raising his forefinger to his nose as if flicking something away.

"C'mon over and lemme buy you a drink," Gillette said. "Whadda yah drinkin'?"

Wally had already had his quota of bullshit for the day and didn't need any more...not after that shit storm back at the house between his sons. Gillette was pretty near the last person in the world he wanted to see.

Still, a free beer was a free beer.

"Shipyard," Wally said as he got up from his stool and sauntered over to the table. He hooked the bottoms rungs of a chair with his foot and pulled it out, then sat down with an exasperated sigh.

Shantelle came over with the glass of beer and placed it in front of Wally. She made a point of letting her hip brush up against Wally's shoulder, and he looked up at her with a devilish grin. He'd banged her a couple of times after hours, but it was nothing serious—just a chance to get some young trim. Tonight, though, she was coming on stronger than usual, flirting like she wanted him. After banging Bunny for a few nights, he was thinking he might oblige Shantelle for a change of pace.

Once Shantelle had sashayed back to the bar, Wally clasped the beer glass in his beefy hand, raised it to his lips, and drained close to half of it in several loud gulps.

"Ahh," he said, smacking his lips and wiping a collar of foam from his mouth with the back of his hand. "Like Ben Franklin said. 'Beer's proof God loves us and wants us to be happy.'"

"Franklin said that?" Gillette said, raising his single eyebrow.

"Indeed he did." Wally belched as he hooked a thumb into his belt loop and eased back in his chair.

Zimmerman was sitting to Gillette's right, absolutely silent and unmoving, and situated to keep an eye on both doors to the bar, front and back. He didn't even have a drink in front of him.

How can you trust a man who doesn't drink? Wally wondered. Then again, how can you trust a slime bucket like Gillette?

Gillette took a drink, then cleared his throat and leaned close to Wally.

"I don't wanna ruin your night out, Capt'n, but I been hearin' things."

Wally sniffed.

"Things? Like what *things?*"

Gillette shifted his eyes from side to side, a perfect parody of a suspicious spy in an old-fashioned movie. Wally expected him to say: *The walls have ears.*

"I hear there's a new DEA guy around town. Guy named Lincoln something or other. Word is, he's gonna bust balls."

Wally snorted with laughter, shook his head, and then took another gulp of beer.

"I'd say you have more to worry about than I do," he said. "But now that you mention it, you got a couple of fuckwads working for you who are shit for brains."

"You mean French Fry and Chuckles?"

Wally tossed his head back and finished off what remained of his beer. Without turning around, he raised his hand, signaling for another.

"You see this guy put away the beer?" Gillette said, leaning close to Zimmerman and nudging his arm. "Drinks like a goddamned pirate, he does."

"'N you drink like a goddamned pussy," Wally said. "You sure that ain't white wine you're sipping?"

"Bud Lite."

Wally sniffed and said, "Fuck that shit. That's what I piss out. You should drink real beer." He couldn't stop himself and, reaching over the table to slap Zimmerman on the shoulder, he added, "And you should drink…something…anything to loosen up. Come on, man. Ease up."

Zimmerman shot him a thin half-smile that make it look like it hurt him to smile, but Wally ignored him when Shantelle came back to the table with his beer and slid it in front of him. She grabbed his empty and, once again, brushed her hips against his shoulder, harder than the last time. All Wally could think was—*Damn…looks like I'm gonna have to oblige her.*

Gillette was still bristling at the insult, but he didn't say or do anything. Wally noticed how the man's knuckles went bone-white as he squeezed his beer glass, but that was the extent of it. Gillette didn't really have the balls the start something. Not here and now, anyway. He was your typical small-town hood who, at the core, was as insecure as a four year old. When he needed something done, he'd have someone like Zimmerman handle it…outside…in the dark…no witnesses.

"Anyways," Gillette said, "Richie says you had some unkind words about French Fry and Chuckles."

"I said neither one of 'em could find his own bunghole without a GPS, and even then I wonder."

Wally sipped his fresh beer and then, lowering his glass to the table, stared silently at Gillette until the man began to squirm uncomfortably.

"You know damn well what's gonna happen eventually," Wally said. "Those two fuckups will do something bone-headed and get caught. And the feds will threaten to throw 'em in jail unless they give someone up. And that someone who's next in line is you."

He didn't need to add that, faced with prison, Gillette would fold like a fifty-cent lawn chair and give up his boss until it worked its way up to Richie.

"Why wouldn't the feds come down on you?" Gillette asked, beaming proudly, like he had thought of something no one else ever had.

"They already have," Wally said simply. He let it hang out there, enjoying the confused expression on Gillette's face while he drank some more of his beer.

"The fuck," Gillette said after a moment.

Zimmerman still hadn't said a word. He barely blinked his eyes. Wally chuckled to himself, thinking he might have to hold a mirror under the man's nose to see if he was breathing, but he was beginning to think this guy was a hard-ass who might have some chops.

"Coast Guard hauled me over t'other night when I was headin' out to The Nephews for a pickup."

"Oh, yeah. I heard about that," Gillette said, "But that's just the goddamned Coast Guard. I'm talking about a serious motherfucking DEA…the feds."

"What, you think the Coast Guard is a bunch of fuckin' Boy Scouts?"

"Yeah…well, what's more—" Gillette folded his hands in front of him, embracing his beer glass as he leaned across the table toward Wally, lowering his voice. "Word is they got a guy on the inside… someone local."

"And who might that be?" Wally asked.

The truth was, he could just about give a flying fuck. The feds had been trying for years to stop or at least make a dent in the drugs coming into The Cove. Even when they made a bust or two, even when a couple of fall guys went off to Warren, it didn't stop diddle.

"I ain't sure yet. I'm just saying…things ain't looking good."

"Look," Wally said, trying without much luck to suppress the sarcasm in his voice. "You wanna get your undies in a bunch, go ahead. 'S no sweat off my ass. I do what I do. I get caught? Which ain't too fuckin' likely. I take my rap."

"I hear it might be your son-in-law, Tom," Gillette said, his voice so low Wally strained to hear him. He was in the process of raising his beer glass, but he stopped and, lowering his glass to the table, stared at Gillette.

"That wet end?" He caught himself before he spat on the floor. "Christ, if I'd a' known the bar was bringing in comedy acts these days, I'd a' brung a date." He paused, but only for a second. "You actually are gonna worry about Tommy Marshall posing some kinda threat? Jesus, I'd worry more about getting crabs from the crapper seat here."

Gillette regarded him with a cool, steady stare. Zimmerman still hadn't even blinked.

"That ain't too fuckin' likely," Wally said. "Marshall wouldn't know what to do if a bale of weed sat on his face and did the Hoochie-Coochie."

Gillette frowned and shook his head.

"I'm not sure I get what you mean there, Capt'n."

"The Hoochie-Coochie. It's an old stripper routine."

Gillette looked confused, like he knew Wally was making fun of him personally, but he couldn't figure out how.

"Look...all's I'm saying is, he's married to your daughter, so he may know what you're up to. My advice is—keep an eye on him. Make sure he doesn't end up fucking over anyone close to him. No one likes a snitch."

Wally would have been an idiot not to catch the implied threat to Tom—and himself—but he dismissed it. As far as he was concerned—especially after the way Tom had treated his daughter—he didn't give a rat's fart what might or might not happen to Tom Marshall. If he was squealing on locals to the feds, then fuck him. He deserved whatever happened to him.

"Your problem ain't Tom Marshall," Wally said. "It's those *morons* you got working for you. That's who I'd worry about if I was you. I guarantee, by the end of the summer, both a' them fools will be in jail and singing to the prosecutor."

"You ain't telling me how to run my business, are you?" Gillette asked, glowering.

"Wouldn't dream of it."

"Good. 'Cause if you think you can tell me how to run my fucking business, you better think again."

Wally said nothing as he sipped his beer.

"I'm giving you a heads up, is all," Gillette said. "Keep an eye on that cocksucker."

Wally slammed his empty down on the table hard enough to put a half-moon dent in the wood. Casting a glance over his shoulder, he saw his buddies, Horse Lips along with Travis "Beaver" McCutcheon and Danny "Preacher" Clayborn slumped over the bar.

"I gotta go see some friends," he said belching as he stood up, pushing the chair back with his legs. "Thanks for the brewski."

"No problem," Gillette said touching his forehead with the tip of his forefinger.

"Nice talkin' to you, too," Wally said as he clapped Zimmerman hard enough on the shoulder to knock him forward. Zimmerman still didn't blink. Wally was beginning to think the man had a medical condition.

With that, he sauntered over to the bar. Shantelle already had another one poured and placed it in front of him. He couldn't ignore how she brushed the back of his hand with the tips of her fingernails as she pulled her hand away. When they made eye contact, Wally knew what he'd be doing after last call.

It was late. Past midnight. As usual, Pete had been down at The Local, but for some reason—it didn't take much brainpower to figure out why—the last thing he felt like doing was tying one on with his buddies, so he had come home long before last call, feeling barely buzzed.

He clumped up the stairs and walked down the hall, past the closed door to Louise's bedroom to the narrow room under the eaves that, once again, he was sharing with Ben. When he flipped the switch for the overhead light, a warm glow flooded the room like a coating of yellow paint. He grimaced as he looked around, taking it all in.

Just like fuckin' old times, he thought as a bitter taste filled the back of his mouth.

That afternoon, Ben had moved all of his stuff into the room to give Louise back her room. It wasn't much, but it was stacked up on the left side of the room by the window…the side that used to be—that *always* had been—Ben's. He had dragged his old bed and mattress down from the attic and set it up where it had always been. Two desert-tan duffel bags stuck out from underneath the edge of the bed, which was neatly made, the corners tucked in with military precision, the pillow smooth and centered at the head. A handful of books—suspense thrillers by Preston and Childs, James Rollins, Clive Cussler and one by Dean Koontz—were stacked on the bedside table beside the old reading lamp with the red metal shade. All of Ben's other possessions were carefully arranged on the bureau and the floor at the foot of the bed. Without even looking, Pete knew Ben's clothes would be hanging in the closet or folded neatly away in the dresser.

At least his years in the military had cured Ben of his youthful sloppiness.

But not Pete.

Like when they were kids, his side of the room was a jumble of dirty clothes, CDs—mostly Heavy Metal groups like *AC/DC* and *Metallica*—"stroke" magazines, dirty plates and glasses, beer bottles, crumpled food wrappers, and an unmade bed. The sheets and blanket were knotted together and hanging off the edge of the bed onto the floor. He couldn't remember the last time he'd changed the bedding, but what did it matter? Dirty sheets didn't bother him, and with Ben in the room now, it wasn't like he'd be getting any pussy up here for a while.

Pete kicked off his boots, banging them against the wall, and flopped down onto his bed. He sighed as he flung his arm across his face and covered his eyes.

"I can't get away from you, can I, you son-of-a-bitch," he whispered to the empty room. "No matter what I do, I'm always gonna be your goddamned little brother."

Squeezing his eyes shut so tightly faint explosions of light streaked across his vision, he started to ruminate on his all too familiar list of resentments.

When they were kids growing up, Ben had *always* gotten the first and the best. His parents made a show and talked a good game about being fair, but in everything, Pete felt as though he'd been cheated.

And even if his folks had been fair, there was always school. Every goddamned one of his teachers from grammar school through high school had reacted to his low-level work the same way...by shaking their heads and saying, *"Well, Peter, you certainly aren't half the scholar your brother is, now, are you?"*

Ben was "The Man"...Gunner...high school basketball and track star...good, not great, student...lady's man...Boy Scout...and one of the most popular kids in school and around town...Good old ball-bustin' Ben, who all through high school spent most of his time getting stoned or trying to feel up as many cheerleaders as he could in the woods out behind Moulton's Store or underneath the grandstand. All things considered, Ben was lucky he hadn't knocked up at least half a dozen girls before graduation. Meanwhile, the best Pete could ever do was play second string on the football team, struggle along academically, and do the best he could with girls. His only good grades were in shop and metalworking, and he didn't have anywhere near as many friends as Ben did. While he did all right with the girls, he had hooked up with Mona in his sophomore year and stayed with her all through high school and beyond—until about two weeks ago, when even she got tired of him. Mona was pretty enough, if you liked redheaded, corn-fed girls, but—*goddamnit!*—he was sick and fucking tired of living in Ben's shadow.

It was the little things that irked him the most...things like when Ben got that goddamned high school class ring. Mom had said she bought it for him with money she'd scrimped and saved, but what that meant was she swiped money from Pops' wallet when he was sleeping off another bender. For some reason—pure spite, no doubt—Ben thought it was great fun to walk up behind Pete and crack him a good one on the back of the head with the heavy stone of that ring. It got to the point where Pete instinctively flinched whenever Ben came anywhere near him, which only made Ben laugh the harder.

Ben ended up losing the ring a month or so after graduation, or so he thought. He never knew that Pete had stolen it and taken it out on their father's lobster boat one day and dropped it over the side out past Hatlen's Point. He laughed whenever he wondered if a fish might eat it, and someone would eventually catch the fish, cut it open, and find the ring. He'd heard about something like that happening a few years ago but always wondered if the stories were true.

Of course, a few years later, when it was Pete's turn to get a class ring, which he had been looking forward to, his Mom didn't buy him one because, she said, she had paid damned good money for Ben's ring, and look how irresponsible he had been, losing it like that. Pete was sure this was what Mrs. Miller, one of his English teachers, would have called "dramatic irony." Instead, his Mom told him she would help him buy a car when he graduated; but before long, she started getting dementia, and soon enough she forgot all about that promise. *More dramatic irony,* Pete thought, because he got her car after she was diagnosed with early onset Alzheimer's and sent off to the old folks' home.

But that was another thing that bugged the ever-loving shit out of Pete. Ben had lived at home for a year or so after high school, going to college at Central Maine Community College and helping out—minimally—on the lobster boat. He was dating Kathy Brackett and looking like he was going to settle down into his rut like everyone else in The Cove.

And then Ben went and changed the goddamned rules, which galled Pete something fierce.

Ben joined the Army and then got stop-lossed when his terms of enlistment expired. He came home on leave between tours of duty. When he did, he stayed with Kathy as much if not more than he stayed at home. Pete was pissed that his brother had gotten out of The Cove, even if it was only temporarily, and then he and Kathy started talking about moving away once he got out…until, that is, they had a major falling out before Ben went back for his last stint in Iraq.

But with or without a woman like Kathy, Pete was stuck here with his Mom and Pops. Louise tried to help some, but she was all goo-goo over that douche bag Tommy Marshall. Then they had to get married in a big fucking hurry when she got knocked up. So good old Pete—like the son in that Bible story the Prodigal Son—was the one left holding the bag, helping the old man run the family business and—eventually—slated to take it over, no questions asked. And Pete was left watching his mother deteriorate before his eyes, his father too self-involved and unloving even to visit her more than once or twice a week.

It wasn't like anyone ever asked me *what* I *wanted to do,* Pete thought, rolling his head from side to side and seething with anger. He started grinding his teeth so loud the sound filled his head like he was munching popcorn.

That's what caused him the most resentment.

Everyone—family and friends and neighbors alike—naturally assumed he wanted nothing more in life than to be a lobsterman like his goddamned father, like Capt'n Wally was any kind of role model.

But had anyone—had one single person ever asked him if he wanted to spend the rest of his life as a Cove-ah, fucking around with lobster boats and fish guts and bloodworms and drunken fools like the men down at The Local or any other of that shit?

Then Julia Meadows came to town.

Now *there* was a woman. Beautiful, classy—the fact that she wasn't a Cove-ah was one of her biggest attractions to Pete. He had spent months watching her, thinking about her, fantasizing about her. Even when she took up with his brother-in-law Tom, it didn't faze him. He knew how those things worked in The Cove. It wouldn't last. What he needed was a way to figure out how to catch her eye.

And then Ben came home a Christless war hero with an honorable discharge and a fucking medal. Everyone started acting like he was goddamned Superman. All the guys, including Pete's best friends, wanted to buy his brother drinks. Even worse, as far as Pete could tell, plenty of women around town—married and not married—wanted to fuck him silly. If he wanted to, he could get more ass than a toilet seat. And who did Ben pick?

Julia Meadows, of course.

Pete raised his arm from his eyes, rotated his head slowly, and glared over at Ben's empty bed. He hissed through gritted teeth and, raising his hand, pointed his forefinger with his thumb up like his hand was a gun.

"Pow!" he said, smiling as he snapped his thumb down like the hammer of a gun. A smile spread across his face, tightening the skin.

He tensed when he heard someone moving around downstairs. Not wanting to face anyone—his father, his sister, and especially his brother—he slid off his bed, tiptoed over to the door, switched off the light, and lay back down on the bed, pretending to be asleep.

Overnight, rain moved in, and it was still pouring hard by morning. After spending the night at his house, Wally had to give Shantelle a ride home. He dropped her off at her place and drove down to the harbor. Even if the sea was too rough for him to go out and haul traps, he could spend the day working around on the boat and knocking back shots of rum. Maybe he'd even figure out what was wrong with the electronics. Tonight, he and all his cronies would gather at The Local and spend a considerable amount of time bitching about how many traps they lost in the storm.

Before he got out of bed, Ben thought he heard a high-pitched giggle or two coming through the wall from his parents' bedroom, but he wasn't about to check out what was going on. He assumed Bunny was with his dad again, and he didn't want to see her again, so he waited until they left. Once the house was quiet, he got out of bed, took a quick shower, and went out into the hallway.

He tiptoed to Louise's bedroom and, opening the door quietly, peeked in on her. He had moved his stuff out last night, but she was sleeping in the sheets he'd been using. They hadn't had time to launder them.

He watched her sleeping for a moment or two, her left arm across her face, covering her eyes. Once again, he was struck by how much she resembled their mother. He felt a sudden, deep longing for the good old days when he was a kid, growing up here. He knew, of course, there was no such thing as the "good old days." In fact, some of them had been downright horrible. Still, his memories of growing up in this house had acquired a golden luster. Maybe surviving in a war zone for four years had something to do with it. That suddenly reminded him of last night at Julia's house when the strange, frightening feeling of—

Of what?

He wasn't even sure.

Was it rage? Terror? Panic?

Something had swept over him like a sudden squall.

Whatever it was, he sure as hell didn't want to think about it now.

Louise stirred and then opened her eyes with a start. Sitting up in bed, she looked around not quite remembering where she was until she saw Ben in the doorway. She yawned and smiled.

"Sorry," he said. "I didn't mean to wake you."

"'S okay." She stifled a yawn behind her hand. "I should get up, anyway."

"It's a shitty day. You might 's well sleep in." Ben indicated the bedroom window with a flick of his head. Windblown streams of rainwater trickled down the panes in squiggling, quicksilver lines.

"You can say that again." Louise sighed. "What was all that commotion last night?" She shifted her legs around so she was sitting on the edge of the bed, but she made no move to get up.

"I think the old man had some—ahh, company last night."

Louise lowered her gaze and, biting her lower lip, shook her head sadly.

"He is such a pig," she said as much to herself as to Ben. Then she looked up at her older brother and added, "It's not right. It's not like Mom's dead or something."

Ben shrugged and said, "Never stopped him before, did it?"

"I guess not." There was resignation in her voice. "Want me to get breakfast for yah?"

"How 'bout I cook for you for a change?"

Ben turned and left her, going downstairs to the kitchen where he set to work.

"Pete up yet?" Louise called out from upstairs.

"Nah," Ben replied. The mere mention of his brother's name reminded him of their squabble last night, and he felt guilty about it. Maybe getting so pissed at Pete is what made him have that freak-out at Julia's.

The view out the kitchen window was amazing, especially for someone who had spent the last two years in a desert. Fast-moving clouds looking like ink-stained quilted cotton scuttled across the sky, blowing out to sea. Rain lashed against the house, hissing on the windows. It was heavy enough to obscure Ben's view, but close to shore, white-capped breakers were slamming against the rocky shore, sending towering plumes of water into the sky to be blown back into the ocean in a white spray.

As he set to work, scrambling eggs, frying bacon, making toast, and—most importantly—getting the coffee brewing, he wondered if his father was already down at the boat. He figured only an idiot would go out to sea on a day like this. The smell of breakfast cooking filled him with contentment, and he felt cozy and warm in the cocoon of light in the kitchen. He turned and looked at the kitchen doorway when he heard Louise's footsteps on the stairs.

"I changed my mind," she said.

"'Bout what?"

"About you coming out to the house with me so I can get some of my things. Will you?"

Her question was almost lost beneath the sound of sizzling bacon as Ben flipped it over, but he looked at her and nodded earnestly.

"Bet your ass I will," he said.

"Maybe we can stop by 'n see Mom, too."

"Yeah…maybe," he said. He had enough to think about without trying to deal with his mother's situation. Between the cracks widening in his psyche, the fraught possibility of a confrontation with Tom, and Pete getting weirder and weirder lately, the last goddamned thing he needed was to see the shell of a person his mother had become. After last night, he didn't need that kind of stress on top of everything else.

Like a good soldier, he resolutely pushed those thoughts far away as Louise sat down at the table, and he served her breakfast. She made a motion to get up to pour coffee, but he wouldn't allow it. Once everything was served, he sat down with her, and they began to eat.

Throughout the meal, they didn't talk much. Ben made small talk that he knew was really his way of avoiding having to deal with the things that were really bothering him. A few times he almost mentioned that he'd stopped by Kathy's house last night, but he let that go, too, concerned that he might let slip the truth about being Amanda's biological father. When they were done with the meal, Louise went upstairs to shower while Ben cleaned up the kitchen.

The rain was coming down hard by the time they were ready to leave. As they stood in the doorway, preparing for the dash out to the car, Ben clutched the car keys in his hand so hard the metal pressed into his flesh. On a count of three, they ran out into the storm to the car.

They were both soaked by the time Ben got the car unlocked, and they threw themselves onto the seat. Instantly, the cars windows began to steam up from their body heat. Ben cranked the ignition and put the defroster on full blast.

"Your place first?" Ben asked, figuring it was the errand he dreaded least.

Louise's face was pinched and pale as she stared straight ahead and nodded. The wipers slapped back and forth, spraying water to both sides of the windshield.

"Yeah," she said. "Best get this done quick."

Ben shifted into reverse, backed around, and headed down the driveway to the street. Heavy rain pelted the car, sounding like bullets dinging off the roof and hood. Ben snapped on the headlights. They illuminated the shifting gray mist that rose like ghosts from the asphalt.

"Not exactly looking forward to this, are yah?" Ben said, casting a quick glance at Louise and then looking back at the road. She was twisting her hands in her lap and gnawing on her lower lip.

"When'd you get your first clue," she said in a strained voice without looking at him.

Louise's fear and tension must be contagious, Ben thought, when he realized he was gripping the steering wheel so tightly his knuckles stood up like the white ridges of a distant snow-covered mountain range. The close, warm air inside the car made it difficult to breathe. He began to worry that he might have another incident of…whatever had hit him last night at Julia's.

Keep it together, he kept telling himself. Don't lose it now… you're here to help Lou-Lou…that's all…

But the closer they got to Louise's house, the more the tension wound up inside him until he felt like he was going to start screaming and pounding the dashboard in order to release it. He wasn't in a good place…especially if Tom was home when they got there.

And he was.

As they slowed for the turn into the driveway, Ben looked up to see Tom's truck and police cruiser parked in the driveway.

"Shit," Louise said, and she took a quick sip of air between her teeth. As they went up the driveway, Ben realized something was wrong with the house. The upstairs window was hanging open, and piles of clothes were strewn about the side yard and hanging in wet, heavy clumps from the shrubbery beside the house.

"Jesus H.," Ben said.

"That no good son-of-a-bitch," Louise whispered between clenched teeth.

She cast a quick look at Ben and then leaned forward, her hands pressed against the dashboard, her fingers splayed.

"Is that—?"

"Yeah. The son-of-a-bitch threw my clothes out the bedroom window."

Ben clenched his teeth and shook his head.

This is going to get nasty, he thought as an electric charge tingled through the palms of his hands.

"Lou-Lou. You know, now might not be such a good time," he said as he pulled to a stop halfway up the driveway.

Louise didn't answer right away. Her fingers hooked into claws, and she dug her fingernails into the padded dashboard. She exhaled through her nose, reminding him of an enraged bull about to charge.

"I'm serious, Lou. He's home, and it's only gonna get worse if we go up there now."

"The fucker!" she said with a snarl.

"We can come back later."

"The hell we can. My clothes are getting ruined." She looked at him, her jaw set. Rosy splotches had appeared on her cheeks. "Don't tell me you're afraid of him."

"I'm not afraid of him," Ben said, "but there's no need to—"

"'Cause I'm not leaving without my stuff, and I ain't afraid of that limp-dicked mother-fucking loser! I can't believe I ever—"

She went silent when Ben put his hand on her shoulder, restraining her. After taking a calming breath, she reached for the door handle and pulled the door open. The instant there was a crack, a gust of wind whistled into the car and all but tore the door from her hand. Rain slashed her, but she barely noticed as she stepped out of the car and slammed the door shut behind her. She started walking up the driveway, her hands clenched rigidly at her sides. She appeared to be oblivious to the rain.

Knowing this was going to get ugly, Ben watched for a count of ten before shifting into gear and trailing alongside her in the car. When she was almost to the house, he pulled up beside her and rolled down the passenger's window.

"Come on, Lou. This is insane. *He's* insane." He had to shout to be heard above the downpour that had already soaked her to the bone. Her hair was plastered against her pale forehead, and her shoulders dropped down with the weight of her saturated blouse.

Louise looked at him but didn't say a word. After staring at him for a second or two, she turned and marched across the lawn to the side yard. She looked pathetic as she stood there, surveying the heaps of sodden clothes. Ben parked close to the edge of the lawn and got out. Shielding his face from the rain, he walked over to her.

"We'll go to Reny's and get you some new clothes," he said, trying to keep his voice as reasonable as possible. "You don't need this."

He took hold of her arm and tried to guide her back to the car, but she broke his grip. Clenching her fists, she fairly vibrated with rage.

"The *fuck* I *don't!*" she wailed. She glared at him like a cornered animal—desperate and dangerous. "I'm not gonna let that son-of-a-bitch get away with this shit!"

Then she let out a warbling animal-like sound that was half scream, half moan as she strode over to the clothes and began picking them up, shaking them out and then draping them over her left arm. Ben watched for a while, not sure what to do next, but then he went over and started helping. He picked up a few items and shook them, snapping the water and muck off as best he could.

"This is absolutely crazy, you know?" he said.

"I know. It's nuts."

Louise looked at him, and then a wide smile spread across her face. It looked like dawn spreading across the land. "It's absolutely fucking out-of-our-skull insane!"

"We've lost it," Ben shouted, and he started laughing, too, at the utter absurdity of it all.

"Out of our ever-loving minds!" Louise wailed.

Ben realized this was the only way to relieve the tension…to see the absurdity of it all and embrace it. So he and his sister made it a game, scooping up clothes that were so saturated with water they were twice their weight, wringing them out and waving them around their heads as they carried them back to the car and threw them onto the backseat. They whooped and hollered and laughed like little kids. All Ben could think was: *This is exactly what she needs… This is what we both need.*

It took about ten or fifteen minutes to get everything off the lawn and into the car. The last thing Louise did was pick up the screen that had fallen from the upstairs window and set it up at an angle against the house. With a savage giggle, she brought her foot down on it, ripping out the screen and bending the frame beyond repair. To be sure, she kicked it again and snapped it in two places.

"There!" she shouted. "See if the dickhead can fix *that!"*

Ben was roaring so hard with laughter that his belly began to ache, but the sound of a door slamming open brought both of them up short. The sudden crack of a pistol shot split the air. Louise let out a piercing scream when a clump of damp earth less than five feet from where she stood jumped into the air and then landed with a soft plop at her feet. The sound of the shot was still ringing in Ben's ears as he turned and looked to the house. Tom was standing in the doorway, but Ben saw a memory from the other side of the world.

A sudden rush of adrenalin surged through him, and he reacted with years of training honed by raw experience in the field.

"Sniper! Get down! Get down!" he shouted as he dashed over to Louise and, grabbing her by the waist, threw her to the ground. He covered her with his body, pressing her flat against the grass.

"What the hell?" she shouted, her voice distorted because he was mashing her face into the grass. She wriggled under him, trying to see under his arm.

Panting heavily, Ben scanned the area, looking up at the rooftop, expecting to see a sniper up there, zeroing in on them with his rifle and scope.

"Jesus! Get off me!" Louise wailed. "I can't breathe!"

"There's sniper fire," Ben shouted as he shifted his full weight off her, but he didn't let her up. The rain pelted his face, stinging like blown sand. He wanted to make sure they weren't surrounded by enemy enfilade fire. He eyed the distance to the house, calculating the time it would take to reach it if they ran in a crouch, in a zig-zag pattern...

"I could have you both arrested for trespassing and vandalism," Tom said. He was standing on the front steps, wearing a thick, black rubber raincoat with the hood pulled down low over his eyes. His service revolver was aimed squarely at them.

Neither Louise nor Ben said a word as they stared at him. The initial rush of adrenaline was slowly seeping away, and Ben began to realize what had happened. He'd had a flashback to combat back in Iraq. He blinked stupidly as reality crept back in. For one thing, it never rained like this in Iraq. His body began to tremble uncontrollably.

"Both of you," Tom shouted, "get the fuck off my property. *Now!*"

"This is as much my property as it is yours," Louise said. She cast a worried glance at Ben as if still unsure what had just happened to him. Her face was smeared with mud from being pushed into the dirt.

As his pulse slowed, Ben was aware of the quaver under his sister's belligerent tone. He hadn't been wrong, shielding her with his body. He'd rather take a bullet than let her get shot. He looked from her to Tom, convinced Tom was crazy enough to shoot both of them if they weren't careful what they said and did next.

"Get back into your fuckin' car *now* and get the hell out of here." Tom's voice was low and rigid with command. The look on his face convinced Ben he meant business. He raised his hands and slowly got to his feet, then helped Louise get up. She was scowling as she sluiced water and dirt from her arms and chest.

"C'mon, Lou-Lou," Ben said, moving so he was between Tom and his sister. "He means it. We gotta go."

But Louise didn't move. She stood there, glaring past Ben at her husband. She folded her arms across her chest as if that would protect her from any bullets.

"We got what we came for," Ben said, turning to her and speaking harshly. "Let's go before this gets any uglier."

"Oh, it's gonna get ugly, all right. You wait and see." Louise spoke in a low, controlled voice that had real iron in it. Then, shaking her fist, she shouted past Ben at Tom. *"You wait and see!"*

Tom didn't flinch. A cold gleam lit his bloodshot eyes as he raised the revolver and sighted down the barrel at them. Then he pulled the trigger. The bullet whizzed past them, whining like a bee above the steady downpour of rain.

"You can't shoot us in cold blood," Ben said.

"You think I care? I'm protecting my property. I have a constitutional right to defend my—"

"Shut the fuck up!" Ben shouted.

He was seething with rage and frustration because he knew if Tom didn't have a gun—or if Ben had one himself—things would be playing out much differently.

"Lou," Ben said, dropping his voice low. "Go down and get into the car. The keys are in the ignition."

"Do what your asshole of a brother says," Tom shouted. "For once, the dipshit is making sense."

"You are such a jerk," Louise said, her upper lip curling into a sneer. "You know that? A total limp dick."

"Get off my property," Tom said, his voice low and steady.

When Louise still didn't move, he fired a third shot. This one ricocheted off the side of Ben's car with a loud whine that left an angled crease in the rear wheel panel above the back tire.

"You gonna flatten my tires again? Is that it?" Ben said.

Louise turned and walked over to the car as slowly and easily as if she were out for a morning stroll.

"That's the second time you've mentioned your goddamned tires. I don't have the faintest fuckin' clue what you're talking about, but if you don't get out of here now..." He waved the gun around, inscribing small circles in the air as if to encourage Ben to move along.

Behind him, Ben heard the car door open and slam shut. Once he knew Louise was safely inside the car, he started backing up, his hands raised, all the while keeping a wary eye on Tom.

"Get the fuck out of here and don't ever come back," Tom said.

"I'm gonna file a complaint with the department about this," Ben said. "You wait and see."

Tom snorted with laughter and spat onto the rain-soaked ground.

"Look at me shaking. I'm so scared."

Ben's body was coiled with tension, and a chill reached deep inside him. He was shivering by the time he got to the driver's side of the car, opened the door, and sat down on the front seat. Rainwater ran down his face, blurring his vision. He was so tense he thought he was going to vomit, but as he gripped the keys and started the car, the feeling soon passed.

"Let's get the hell out of here," Louise said.

He didn't need to be told twice.

Ben was glad when Louise agreed that they couldn't very well show up at Harbor's Edge soaking wet and covered with grass stains and mud, so they went home, started a load of laundry with their muddy clothes, and took showers.

"You still might want to go buy some new stuff," Ben suggested once they were dressed in clean, dry clothes and sitting in the living room. He was sprawled on the couch. Louise sat in the armchair that used to be their mother's, one leg slung over the padded arm. Fitful gusts of wind drove rain hard against the windows, making the living room feel warm and cozy with a single table light on casting soft shadows across the floor.

She heaved a deep sigh as she gazed off into the distance, her eyes fixed on the large picture window as she watched the trees across the way bend and sway in the wind. Gray clouds shifted rapidly across the sky.

"It can't keep up like this for long," Ben said.

"You mean the rain?"

Ben nodded but realized that wasn't all he meant. After a lengthening moment of silence, he said, "So…I guess you and Tom'll be heading for a divorce."

"You think?"

Louise kept staring out the window, her jaw muscles clenching and unclenching as though she was chewing a wad of gum. The patter of rain hitting the picture window sounded like tiny pellets hitting the house. Ben exhaled as he eased back on the couch and closed his eyes. He wanted to relax and absorb everything that had happened this morning. He was particularly concerned about the flashback—there was no other word for it—he'd experienced when Tom shot at them.

He was still angry enough about being shot at that he considered reporting the incident to the police. If it hadn't been raining so hard, he might have gone down to the station right then, but he convinced himself that it wouldn't do any good. In a small town like The Cove, the police department wouldn't do a damned thing. They'd take his complaint, file it away, and then forget about it. Ultimately, nothing would come of it. That's how things worked.

If Ben was going to get even with Tom—and he had every intention of doing so—he was going to have to do it on his own terms.

The only question was how and when?

He thought to call Julia and see how she was doing. He wanted to understand what had happened last night at her place, but the way he had reacted out at Tom and Lou's house only made matters worse. He wished there was someone to talk to about it all—his sister, his brother, his father, Julia, or a friend—anyone, but he was absolutely alone with this. The anxiety and stress churned and twisted in his gut as if he'd gulped down a gallon of spoiled milk.

As if she was reading his mind, Louise spoke.

"So you gonna talk to someone about this war stuff? The dreams and whatever the fuck happened today?"

"What dreams?"

Fucking Pete and his big mouth, thought Ben

"Pops told me last night, after you left. He hears you at night. And then the other night you thought everyone was under attack or something and you were sleepwalking—'sleepcrawling,' he said—all around the room looking for your rifle and screaming to wake the dead."

"Lou-Lou, I'm readjusting to being back in civvies after four years."

"The hell! You never talk about what you did over there. I watch the news. I read the newspaper. I know about guys who lose it and go crazy over there and rape and kill people or off themselves. I'm not stupid. I'm worried about you, Ben. I really am."

They sat in silence, listening to the storm. Sometime later, a car pulled into the driveway, the tires crunching on the gravel.

"Goddamn! If that's him…I swear to Christ," Louise said.

In a flash, she was out of the armchair and running to the front door. She was trembling as she looked out one of the sidelights. Ben got up from the couch, but before he reached the door, he heard Louise call out, "It's only Pete."

Moments later, their brother clomped up the steps to the kitchen door. Relieved, Ben and Louise went back into the living room and sat down.

"Christ on a crutch," Pete muttered. He slammed the kitchen door shut behind him hard enough to make the pictures on the living room wall vibrate. He stomped his feet a few times and then he scuffed them on the throw rug; but Ben knew from a lifetime of experience that Pete wouldn't remove his shoes—no matter how wet and muddy they were—before he walked into the living room.

Sure enough, Pete walked in, leaving wet, dirty streaks in the entryway and on the carpet.

"You raised in a barn or something?" Ben said, indicating the mud on the rug.

"Screw you. This ain't your house."

Obviously Pete hadn't forgotten or forgiven that punch in the gut last night. The way Ben was feeling right now, he'd be damned if he was going to apologize.

"What you two been up to?" Pete asked as he dropped down onto the other end of the couch, bouncing it hard enough to irritate Ben.

"Nothing. You?" Ben said.

Pete shrugged but didn't say a word.

"Still on the outs with Mona?" Louise asked.

Pete frowned and shook his head. He looked like he was about to say something, but then he got up off the couch and, without another word, clomped into the kitchen. Ben and Louise listened as he knocked around, getting himself something to eat.

"We out of mayo?" he shouted from the kitchen.

"There's some in the cupboard, I think," Louise said with a tone in her voice that asked: *Why is it always the woman who knows these things?*

They heard Pete walk over to the cupboard and open the door, but then he called out, "Christ. There's just this mother-fucking industrial-sized jar. Why does Pops buy these big fucking things?"

"Saves money, I guess," Ben shouted back, thinking it was just like Pete not to offer to make a sandwich or something for them.

"Not if half of it spoils before you use it." They heard the clink of a dish and glass as he set them out on the counter. "So what happened to your car?" Pete called out.

Louise started to say something, but Ben caught her attention and hushed her with a quick wave of the hand.

"What d'yah mean?" he said.

"You got one helluva dent on your rear panel. Looks like you might've been hit by a bullet."

With that, Pete leaned around the edge of the doorway and

looked at Ben as though trying to gauge his reaction. Ben shrugged as if he had no idea what he was talking about.

"Someone takin' pot shots at you now?" Pete said.

Ben caught the malicious glee in Pete's eyes, but he still played the innocent.

"I'll have to check it out once it stops raining," he said.

Before Pete said anything more, the telephone rang. He shouted, "I got it," and disappeared from sight. Ben, who was sitting on the edge of the couch, eased back against the cushions while exchanging meaningful glances with Louise.

"Why not tell him?" she asked.

They heard Pete say into the phone, "What? Right now, you mean?"

Ben frowned and shook his head.

"'S none of his business," he said. "That's why."

"You afraid he'll say something to Tom?"

Ben pursed his lips and shook his head.

"Jesus *Christ!*" Pete said, and then they heard a heavy *clang* as he slammed the phone back onto the hook. After some muffled sputtering and other noise as Pete slammed around, knocking things over and throwing things around, Ben called out, "What's the problem?"

At first, Pete didn't reply. He kept banging things around, making one hell of a racket. Then he stormed into the living room, his face pinched with anger.

"Fuckin' Pops."

"What about him?" Louise asked, looking suddenly fearful.

Pete glanced at her, then at Ben, and then he looked out the window. He clenched and unclenched his fists at his sides, looking like he was about to punch a hole in the wall.

"He wants me to come down to the wharf."

"Now?" Ben asked.

Pete nodded, too angry to say anything more.

"He can't be heading out." Ben looked at Louise as if for affirmation. "It's stormin' a bitch. Did he say what he wants?"

"Fuck, no. This is Pops we're talking about."

Ben cast another quick glance at Louise and then said to Pete, "How 'bout we all grab a quick lunch, and we'll go with you?"

Pete didn't say a word as he turned and strode back into the kitchen. They heard him kick the cupboard door shut hard enough almost to split the wood.

"It's always something, isn't it?" Ben said, smiling thinly as he looked at his sister.

FOURTEEN

Undertow

Louise decided to stay at the house and keep the laundry moving while Ben and Pete went down to the wharf to see what their father wanted. As soon as they were out the door, though, fearing the worst from Tom, she went up to her father's bedroom and got the shotgun from his closet. She and her brothers had known it was there since they were kids. A few times—when they were sure their father would be out lobstering all day and their mother was off running errands—Ben and Pete had taken the gun and gone out to the dump to shoot cans and bottles and—if they were lucky—some rats.

After loading it with shells from a box on the top shelf, she went back downstairs, confident now that she could protect herself if Tom was stupid enough to show up at the house. She hoped he wasn't that far gone, but she kept the shotgun close by her side, carrying it from room to room as she set about dusting and tidying up just to keep herself busy. When she went down to the basement to get the first load of laundry from the dryer, she brought the gun with her. She filled the laundry basket and was bending over to shift a load from the washer to the dryer when the telephone started ringing upstairs. She ran over to the foot of the cellar stairs but stopped before going upstairs to answer it.

"Go fuck yourself," she whispered, positive it was Tom calling to harass her.

She held her breath and stood there, damp clothes in hand, and listened to the phone as it rang three more times. She craned her head to hear the answering machine click on, but when it did and the greeting started playing, the caller hung up without saying anything.

All the more convinced it had been Tom, she was scowling as she finished shifting the load from the washer to the dryer and was about to put a third load into the washer when the phone started ringing again.

Once again, after four rings, the answering machine kicked on, and the caller killed the call without leaving a message.

Balancing the shotgun on top of the load in the laundry basket, Louise carried everything upstairs. She considered calling Tom and telling him to stop harassing her, but she decided not to.

Carrying the laundry basket, she bumped the cellar door closed with her hip and was about to go upstairs to fold the clothes when the phone started ringing for a third time. Unable to take it any longer, she dropped the basket and grabbed the receiver of the wall phone. Pressing it to her ear, she shouted, "Will you *please* leave me *alone?"*

There was a long silence at the other end of the line. Louise suspected Tom was playing some bullshit mind games with her when she heard a sharp inhalation in her ear.

"I…I'm sorry," a woman's voice said. "Is this…. Do I have the Browns' residence?"

Louise flushed, her eyes widening as she stared at the wall in front of her.

"I'm sorry. I thought you were—Ah, geez. Yeah. Yes. This is the Browns'."

"Is—umm—Ben home?"

"No, he's…he had to run a quick errand. Can I take a message?" she asked.

"Do you know if he has his cell with him? This is his…Julia. I tried calling his cell, but it goes straight to message."

Louise finally calmed down enough to realize that the caller was upset. Her voice was high-pitched and wavering. It almost broke at the end of each sentence, like she was having a difficult time getting the words out.

"When he gets back, I'll tell him you called. I can give him a message if you want."

"I—umm, no…. Just tell him I…tell him Julia called, and I can't see him tonight. I—I'll explain later."

"Yeah…sure thing," Louise said, trying to sound nonchalant.

She had no reason to care, but she felt a sudden twinge of sympathy for the woman and, after a brief pause, she added, "Are you sure you're all right?"

For the space of a few heartbeats, she got no answer. Then she heard the woman's breath hitch as if she couldn't quite catch her breath.

"Tell him I've been trying to get in touch with him, and I…I don't know when I can see him. Thank you."

With that, she ended the call, leaving Louise with the buzzing phone pressed against her ear. Wondering what this was all about, she replaced the phone gently in its cradle and stared at it for a long time. She jumped when the phone rang again. Convinced it was Tom this time, she controlled herself as she picked up the phone and calmly said, "Hello?"

"Louise? Hi. This is Kathy."

For a split second, Louise didn't quite believe it was the Kathy she thought it was—not Kathy Brackett—but she was at a loss to think of anyone else it might be.

"Oh…ah, hi," she said.

"Hi, Lou. I was wondering if Ben's around," Kathy said. Now that she had spoken again, Louise realized it was Kathy Brackett, but that raised the immediate question—*Why the hell is she calling Ben?*

"No, he—umm, he's out. Can I take a message?" She was beginning to feel like her brother's social secretary.

After a pause that was long enough for Louise to suspect that maybe it wasn't as over between Ben and Kathy as Ben had indicated, Kathy said, "He asked—I wanted to talk to him about going over to Harbor's Edge and visiting your mom."

"Really?" Louise said, unable to mask her surprise.

"I…umm, I just thought it'd be a nice thing to do, you know? I…I'll never forget how nice your mum was to me when Ben and I were…you know, seeing each other."

And making babies, Louise thought.

"I don't think he's gonna be around for a while, but I'll tell him you called."

"I'd appreciate that," Kathy said. She paused, and Louise sensed that Kathy had more to say, so she waited until she added, "You think it would be okay if I went over there by myself?"

"I don't see why not." A sudden chill wound around Louise's heart. "I mean—the truth is, she probably won't even recognize you, but—yeah, I think that'd be nice if you did that."

Kathy grunted and then said, "Thanks...ah, you don't have to tell Ben I called. I—he doesn't need to know."

"Sure thing. Catch yah later," Louise said, and then she hung up the phone.

For a few moments, she stood there, her arms folded as she leaned against the kitchen wall and stared at the shotgun on top of the pile of clean laundry. Then she looked up and saw her reflection in the mirror her mother had put next to the kitchen door.

"So I can make sure I don't look a fright before I leave," her mother used to say.

Well, I look a fright now, Louise thought. Her hair was lank and untrimmed, her face pale and still splotched purple and green where Tom had hit her. Her lips were cracked and raw. She was twenty-four and looked forty.

"God damn it!" Louise shouted to the empty house. "That bastard isn't sucking the life out of me anymore!"

Muttering that the laundry could go fuck itself, she grabbed her purse and car keys, and drove down to *Monica's Hair By The Sea.* She parked her car and got out. Rain beat on her back and shoulders as she pushed the door open. Bells tinkled as she entered and slammed the door shut against the wind.

"Well, if it ain't Louise Marshall. How you doin' there?"

Monica was a big woman with a big smile. She was wrapping Edna Chadbourne's hair in pencil-width perm rollers. Before she sat down in one of the white wicker chairs, Louise inhaled the warm, uniquely feminine smell of the salon—fragrant floral shampoos, acrid perm solution, the chemical tang of nail polish. The salon was airy and relaxing, painted in tones of green and blue with dozens of hanging plants. After the male-dominated nightmare of the past few days, Louise felt as if she had found a haven.

"You lookin' for a trim today? If you can wait a few, I'll be right wit'cha," Monica said, squirting perm solution on Edna's rollers. "Weather like this, everyone's got a bad hair day."

"I need a haircut. A real haircut. And maybe a makeover, too,"

Louise said, scowling at her reflection in the mirror.

"Oh, you're gonna surprise Tom tonight?"

"You might say that," Louise replied. Then her shoulders dropped, and she added, "You haven't heard? Tom and I are—I left Tom."

Monica looked at her sympathetically. Edna peered at her over her coral-shaded glasses. Louise felt exposed...vulnerable, like she was onstage in her underwear.

"Okay, dear. So what's his name?"

"His name?" Louise let that sink in. Then she smiled and said, "I don't know yet, but he's gonna be either a lawyer or a hit man."

Monica laughed and winked, and then bellowed, "Lina!"

An Asian woman, as small and petite as Monica was tall and large, came out of the back room. She had inky black hair spiked high in a punked-out short cut with bright blue sideswept bangs. Louise smiled at the thought of blue bangs on herself.

"Lina is my makeover expert," Monica said. "Hair, face, nails—she can do it all."

Lina smiled at Louise. "So, what are you looking for?" She had a lilting Asian accent.

"Not quite what you have," Louise said, "but close."

Lina laughed, a sound almost as tinkly as the bells on the door.

"Have a seat, then." She motioned to a chair in front of a mirror. "Let's have some fun."

"Got no choice, boys" Wally said as he looked back and forth between Ben and Pete. He cocked one eyebrow up high so it looked like a furry white caterpillar crawling up to his hairline. "Soon's the weather lets up, we're goin' out. Gotta go."

He was standing in the wheelhouse of the *Abby-Rose,* leaning to one side with his elbow propped on the helm. Rain slashed the windows and washed the deck as the boat heaved with the swells. It was obvious he'd been drinking for a while now. A hazy, distant glaze frosted his eyes, like he was focused on the far horizon. In his right hand was a bottle of Myers' dark rum that looked about half-empty. It was hard to tell, looking through the dark glass.

Ben narrowed his eyes and shook his head, looking from his father to his brother and then back to his father. The rain was making a thunderous racket on the roof of the wheelhouse. The surface of the ocean was dented like a sheet of metal that had been hammered repeatedly. To the west, past Martin's Hill, the sky was clearing. Thin lines of a deep, rich peacock blue showed through swift-moving rafts of charcoal-colored clouds.

"No, we don't. What you have to do is grow some onions and tell Sullivan to go fuck himself." Ben was trying hard but was unable to keep his anger in check. "He thinks he's got you by the *cojones,* and he's gonna keep squeezing."

"He doesn't think he's got me by the balls…he *knows* it."

Wally sneered before taking a swig of rum. Then he smiled and wiped his chin with the back of his hand.

For the first time in his life, Ben saw vulnerability in his father. It was lurking below the surface, almost hidden, but it was definitely there. This both surprised and bothered him. His father had always been so strong, so savvy, so confident. Maybe he wasn't book-smart, but he was smart enough and clever enough to make a damned decent living doing what he loved…going to sea. It didn't matter if it was fishing or lobstering or taking a gaggle of tourists for a cruise of the bay. He did things his way, and the whole town knew it.

"How much do you owe him?" Ben asked. He began pacing back and forth in the narrow confines of the wheelhouse. His sneakers squeaked on the wet deck every time he turned around.

"The Crowbar?" Wally said and then sighed, casting his eyes downward as he took another drink. "More'n you can imagine, my boy. More'n you can imagine."

"You think if we scrape together all the money we can—my savings included—we could pay him off?"

Wally looked at Ben, his eyes vague and unfocused, as if his memory was a book, and he was idly flipping the pages.

"I don't like the idea of you being under his thumb like this, Pops," Ben said. He knew his father didn't like him seeing him up against the wall like this, either. It wounded his pride, and if there was one thing Capt'n Wally had in spades, it was pride.

"I ain't the only one," Wally said. "There's plenty of fellas working the docks carryin' water for Sullivan."

"That don't make it any better," Ben said, "and that sure as shit don't make it right."

"Aww—hell!" Wally curled his upper lip in disgust and bit his inner cheek. "I got other debts that're killin' me just as much. You know I ain't got any insurance for your mother, being in that nursing home. The bills from that fuckin' place are enough to...to... Aww, *fuck* it. You don't want to know."

"How 'bout I take out a loan, then?" Ben said, "enough to pay off the boat and throw some against the nursing home bills."

Wally didn't consider the suggestion for even a second before he started shaking his head.

"It ain't your goddamned responsibility." His voice was a low growl. It was obvious he was getting drunker by the minute, and the drunker he got, the nastier he got. "I don't want you getting involved. It's bad enough that I am."

Ben chuckled darkly and, staring his father straight in the eyes, said, "This is *family* we're talking here. I'm involved whether you like it or not, and if someone's putting the screws to you, I'm *definitely* involved. We're *all* involved. Right, Pete?"

Ben glanced at his brother who, throughout the conversation, had been hanging back, barely watching or listening to them. He was staring out over the water at the far side of The Cove, looking like he had something else entirely on his mind. When Ben addressed him directly, Pete shook his head as though he was just waking up and said, "Huh? Oh, yeah. Sure."

"For fuck's sake, Pete!" Ben said, and then he turned his attention back to his father. "You want me to talk to Richie?"

Wally snorted with laughter and then took a bigger slug of rum. His Adam's apple bobbed up and down as he swallowed with loud gulping sounds.

"What good'll that do?" he said, his words slurred now.

"I dunno." Ben took a step forward and was going to put his hand reassuringly on his father's shoulder, but he held back. "What d'yah say we find out."

Wally exhaled with a blubbering sigh and shook his head. His gaze was cast down at the deck like he had lost something and was looking for it. His eyes kept darting from side to side as he kept shaking his head, his shoulders hunched. Ben had never seen his father look so defeated, so hopeless, and it pained him deeply.

"So Pops.... How 'bout you forget about drinkin'...least for the time being?" Ben said. "Lou and I were planning on going out to Grave's Edge to visit Mom. Why don't you come along, too? She'd love to see you."

Wally winced as though his rum had left a bad aftertaste in his mouth. He shook his head in firm denial.

"She won't be *happy* to see shit," he said, as much to himself as to Ben. As his gaze drifted out over the water, he took another long gulp of rum. "In case you hadn't noticed, she ain't there no more. The lights are on, but no one's home."

Ben wasn't sure, but he thought he saw tears welling up in his father's eyes. Whatever they were—tears or raindrops or spray from the ocean—Wally quickly wiped them away on his sleeve.

"I gotta meet up with the trawler as soon as it clears," he said. "So when the rain lets up, I'm going."

"Where are you meeting the trawler?" Ben asked. He cast another quick glance at Pete and could tell that he was still not really paying attention to what was going on.

"The Nephews...as usual," Wally said. "'Spozed to be there 'round midnight."

"For one thing, you're in no condition to pilot a goddamned boat...especially in rough seas. It's gonna be heavy seas, especially out beyond the headlands."

"You think I don't know how to skipper a goddamned boat?" Wally shook his head in disgust and spat over the rail. "I can take this boat to Boston and back again in a Christless hurricane. Blindfolded."

But even as he said that, he lost his balance and had to grab onto the wheel to keep from falling down. Ben lunged forward and grabbed him by the arm to support him, but his father quickly shook him off with a snarl.

"Don't fuck with the capt'n on his own goddamned boat." Wally slurred the words so badly Ben almost couldn't make them out above the heavy patter of rain on the wheelhouse roof. His father's breath was nearly toxic with alcohol fumes.

"You're in no shape to do anything but go home and sleep it off," Ben said as he grabbed the bottle of rum and all but tore it from his father's grip.

Wally lunged at him to retrieve it, but Ben backed out from

underneath the roof and stood in the pouring rain, dangling the bottle over the side of the boat.

"I'll drop it overboard if you come any closer," he said, staring at Wally.

"'N I'll toss you overboard with it 'n make you fetch it back," Wally said.

He looked angry enough to rip Ben's head off, but Ben noticed that his father never let go of his grip on the wheel. It was the only thing keeping Wally on his feet.

"Pete and I'll take you home so's you can sleep it off."

"Sleep what off? Christ on a crutch!" Wally bellowed, but the unfocused look in his eyes told the true tale.

"If this run's so goddamned important to you—then let Pete and me go meet the trawler. Can you live with that?"

Pete snapped to and said, "No goddamned way. I ain't taking this boat out…not at night and with the electronics all frigged up."

"Well I sure as hell can't go alone," Ben said.

Wally's face flushed with rising anger. His cheeks blossomed with red splotches, and his eyes bulged. When he started to sputter, no intelligible words came out. Ben jumped when a woman's voice called his name out behind him. He turned and looked up at the wharf, expecting to see Julia, but Louise was walking quickly down the gangplank to the dock. She was almost lost inside an old, black rubber raincoat with the hood pulled down all but covering her eyes. The rain popped as it hit the rubber.

"What the hell are you doing here?" Ben asked.

Louise climbed over the gunwales and, once under the shelter of the wheelhouse roof, slid the hood back.

"Whoa," Ben said.

Louise's hair was now chin length and hung in coppery, bouncy waves around her face. Long bangs brought out the green flecks in her hazel eyes, which were artfully made up. Ben couldn't see a trace of the bruise on her cheeks, which were softly flushed. She wore a reddish lip-gloss that made her lips look full and plump.

Even Pete was moved to say, "Wow, Sis."

Louise grinned, satisfied with the effect, but then she was all business.

"You had a couple of calls," she said to Ben, and he knew instantly who at least one of them was from. A cold feeling twisted in his gut.

"Julia's been trying to get you all day, but your phone's not working."

Ben fished his cell phone from his pocket, opened it, and looked at the display. The battery strength was at zero.

"Fuckin' thing," he muttered. He pressed several buttons, but nothing worked. Without thinking, he cocked back his arm and threw the cell phone far out over the water. It hit with a dull plunk and sank out of sight, leaving behind a widening ripple that was quickly erased by the falling rain.

"Can you hear me now?" Ben shouted, and then he slammed his clenched fist against the pile of traps leaning against the gunwales.

Pete stared at Ben, incredulous. Then he started laughing.

"Oh, that's good," he said. "That'll help."

"Shut up and gimme your goddamned phone," Ben said as he held his hand out to his brother, shaking it with impatience.

Pete hesitated, but only for a moment. Then he reached into his jeans pocket, pulled out his cell phone, and handed it to his brother. Ben flipped it open and, without thinking, hit the button to go to the directory. He was startled when the menu came up, and he saw the third listing on the screen.

It read "Julia M" and was followed by her home phone number.

"What the fuck?" he said, turning slowly and glaring at Pete.

"What?" Pete looked bemused as he glanced back and forth between Ben, his sister, and his father.

"Why do you have Julia's number on your speed dial?"

Pete's face turned as pale as chalk.

"Mrs. Brown?" Kathy said, her voice hushed as she opened the door and stuck her head inside the room.

The air was thick with the smell of disinfectant, but that didn't mask another, worse smell lingering below it. Kathy wrinkled her nose and on reflex leaned down and covered Amanda's nose with her hand as she wheeled the stroller into the room. Amanda was dozing and faintly stirred.

"I'll leave you alone," Mrs. Appleby said, taking a few steps back.

Lilly Brown, wearing a tattered pink nightgown and brown slippers, was sitting by the window. Her hair was unwashed and hanging down to her shoulders in thin, greasy strands. Kathy barely recognized the woman who had been so warm and welcoming to her back when she had dated Ben.

The window blinds were open, and Lilly was staring out at the falling rain. A short distance across the parking lot was a gentle slope, covered with short pine trees. Tangles of mist flowed and twisted between them, low to the ground.

"Hello, Mrs. Brown."

Feeling a little braver, Kathy pushed the stroller into the room and approached the woman. She jumped, feeling trapped when Mrs. Appleby closed the door behind her, shutting her inside.

"I thought I'd stop by and see how you were doing," Kathy said smiling.

Still no response from the woman. She sat there, her eyes glazed as she stared outside. Kathy might have thought Lilly was dead except, every now and then, she blinked. When she did, her eyelids made faint clicking sounds.

"How are you doing?" Kathy asked.

She was getting used to getting no response, so she jumped again and pulled back when Lilly rotated her head slowly and looked at her. As soon as she saw the baby in the stroller, a thin smile spread across her face, and her eyes lit up. Then she lifted her eyes to Kathy's face, and a cold anger spread across her features.

"What the devil are you doing here?" she said, her voice cracked as if from disuse.

"I was—umm..." She considered telling the truth, that Ben had asked her to visit, but she decided not to confuse things and finished, "I wanted to stop in and say 'Hi.'"

"Why do you have Louise out on a day like this?" Lilly raised her right hand and hooked her thumb in the direction of the window.

"Louise?" Kathy said, confused. She wondered what Lilly was talking about. Had Louise been by earlier, and she was mixed up? Did Lilly even know what day it was? Perhaps she was remembering another time Louise when had visited.

"I—umm.... We were out doing errands, and I thought I'd stop in and...and—"

"I want you to take her home. Take her home this minute, and get her into some dry clothes," Lilly said.

The edge in her voice genuinely frightened Kathy, and she suddenly feared for her daughter's safety as Lilly stared at her. The old woman looked like she was about to get up out of her chair and rush them, so Kathy backed the stroller up, thankful that Amanda was still sleeping.

"She'll catch her death, being out on a day like this," Lilly said.

"Do you mean Amanda?"

No matter what she had heard before about Alzheimer's, Kathy wasn't at all prepared for this. She was annoyed at Ben for even suggesting she come and visit, and now, all she wanted to do was make a graceful exit.

"I—ah—I'm sorry," Kathy said. "Maybe…maybe we'll come back some other time."

"That's right," Lilly said, her voice barely above a whisper. "I'm paying you damned good money to baby-sit my little girl, and if you think…if you think…"

Her voice trailed away, leaving the emptiness in the room broken only by the faint sound of wind-blown rain hitting against the window.

"I…I'll do better," Kathy said. "I'm sorry I upset you."

She wheeled the stroller around so fast Amanda's head lolled to one side, and her eyes snapped open.

"It's okay, baby," Kathy whispered as she pushed the door open, blinking as she stepped out into the harsh, glaring light of the hallway.

"Done already?" Mrs. Appleby said from behind the front desk as Kathy wheeled the stroller toward the front entrance.

"Yes," Kathy said, her voice pitched high like it was trapped in her throat. "I—she wasn't in the mood for a visit, I guess."

"Thanks for stopping by," Mrs. Appleby said with a friendly wave. "I'm sure she appreciated it."

But Kathy barely acknowledged her. She was out the door and heading to the car, unmindful of the downpour as she belted Amanda into her car seat as quickly as possible. She was drenched to the skin and shivering by the time she got the driver's door open and dropped onto the seat behind the steering wheel. She was panting hard.

Her tires chirped on the wet pavement as she stepped a little too hard on the accelerator. She couldn't stop thinking about Lilly Brown, imagining her staring out the window of her dark room and watching with a cold, empty stare as she drove away. It was only after she got home, carried Amanda inside, and got her settled with a bottle that Kathy finally realized why Lilly had gotten so agitated.

Kathy had always thought Amanda favored Ben more than her side of the family. Lilly must have seen the family resemblance.

Lilly had mistaken Amanda for her own daughter, the baby Louise she remembered from so many years ago.

Julia was unable to sit still in the hospital waiting room. She'd sit down on one of the chairs in the waiting room, but after less than a minute fidgeting, she would get up and start pacing again, all the while slapping her clenched fist repeatedly into the palm of her hand. It made a wet smacking sound that kept time with her pacing. She knew she should sit down…take some deep breaths…and relax…but she simply couldn't.

The emergency room had five other occupants. Closest to the door, a mother sat, hugging her three or four year old son whose right hand was wrapped in a small, white hand towel. A red blossom of blood was slowly spreading across the fabric. The mother's face was pale and pinched with worry. The kid's shoulders shook with dry sobs as he buried his face against his mother's neck, exhausted from all the crying he had already done.

Across from them, at the far end of the room, a thin man who looked to be in his early thirties was sprawled in a chair, his legs thrust out in front of him, his head thrown back against the wall. His eyes were closed, and he kept rolling his head from side to side while moaning softly and muttering to himself. Julia could only make out fragments of what he was saying.

In the chairs lining the wall opposite the front desk, underneath an oil painting of a farm in autumn, a very pregnant girl who couldn't have been more than seventeen or eighteen was sitting next to an equally young-looking boy who was holding a baggie filled with ice against his jaw. His eyes were bloodshot and watery. He looked dazed with pain, and he winced whenever he shifted his position in the chair.

As Julia contemplated the private tragedies befalling her

theoretical neighbors, she felt lonelier than ever. Since moving to The Cove, she had tried to engage in the rhythm and flow of life in a small town, but she had felt...if not rejected, exactly, certainly not welcome or accepted by anyone...none, that is, except for some of the men, who had made it all too obvious what *they* wanted.

And then there was Ben...

What about Ben?

He had finally returned her call and said he was on his way to the hospital, but she was thinking it was already too late. The anticipation of seeing him mixed with a rush of conflicting emotions. As much as she cared about him and as much as she wanted to see if they could make a go of their relationship, she was worried about the panic attack he'd had last night and that he'd been so unnerved by it he left rather than stay with her. He kept so much locked away from her.

But the ultimate truth dawning on her was that she was going to have to create her own destiny rather than depend on a man—*any* man—to "save" her.

"Hey, there."

She jumped when Ben spoke suddenly behind her. She hadn't heard or seen him enter the emergency room. Spinning around, she forced a smile as he came toward her, his arms upraised to embrace her. The look of intense sympathy in his eyes touched her heart. Any doubts she might have entertained about him—at least at that moment—evaporated in an instant. They hugged in the middle of the room and then kissed, long and passionately, clinging to each other. Julia couldn't help but feel self-conscious, knowing that everyone in the room was probably watching them and wondering what *their* personal little drama was.

"How you holding up?" Ben asked as he broke off the hug and looked down at her up-turned face. His eyes sparkled like chips of blue diamond, but his mouth was set in a grim, straight line.

"Okay, I guess...I'm okay," she said. She eased out of his embrace and then, hand-in-hand, they walked over to two empty chairs and sat down.

"So tell me.... What happened?"

Julia shuddered and blinked her eyes rapidly to hold back the tears.

"I had...I had fixed him lunch, like I always do, and we were eating in the living room...with the TV on. He likes to watch the noontime news, and then he...he.... Oh, Ben. It was *really* scary. He started acting so weird."

"Weird? Like how?"

"I asked him a question. I don't even remember what it was now, and he started to stutter and then...then, when he tried to pick up his sandwich, he couldn't get his left arm to move."

"Good God," Ben said as he cupped her hands and gave them a strong, reassuring squeeze. "Sounds like—"

"—Like a stroke. I know. They're checking him out now, but I have no idea what's going on. Nobody's told me anything."

Ben glanced at the person—an elderly woman with short, gray hair—who was sitting at the desk behind a glass partition. The overhead lights reflecting off the glass made it difficult to see, but he thought it was Edna Anderson, who lived on Bay View Road.

"You want me to ask?" he said as he made a move to go to the front desk.

"No...no." Julia grimaced and shook her head. "I—" She faced Ben and, freeing one hand from his grip, slid it up his arm and around his neck. "I'm glad you came. I was feeling so alone."

Ben smiled and nodded.

"You're not alone anymore," he said, but even as he pulled her close and hugged her again, she sensed that something was different. His body was wire-tight with tension, and he didn't yield to her the way he usually did.

They held each other in silence for a long time, breathing into each other's ear. Julia fought hard to control the sobs and tremors that kept rippling through her. They both jumped when the doors to the examination rooms slammed open, and a young man dressed in hospital "greens" stepped into the corridor. His thick, dark hair looked like it needed a good washing. He had small, dark eyes and a sallow complexion, and looked entirely too young to be a doctor. He couldn't be more than a year or two out of med school.

He looked around the waiting room, his gaze quickly landing on Julia.

"Miss Meadows?" he said, raising his eyebrows as he started toward her.

Julia's legs felt too weak to support her as she stood up and nodded. She tried to speak but couldn't. Ben stood up slowly beside her and slipped an arm around her waist. The support was amazing, and she thought to herself that she could never have faced this without Ben here.

"Would you come with me please?"

The doctor had a small plastic badge that read: *DR. ROBBINS* pinned above the pocket of his hospital shirt. He looked at Ben and, frowning, said, "Are you family?"

Before Ben replied, Julia said, "Yes. He is," and tugged him along with her as she moved forward.

They followed Doctor Robbins down the brightly lit hallway to a closed door. He opened the door for them, stepping to one side so they could enter first. Inside the small room was a desk. It was covered with multi-colored folders and reams of computer printouts. Next to the desk were two metal chairs with padded seats, seatbacks, and arm rests. The green vinyl was worn and cracked with use. Julia wondered how many people had sat in these very chairs and heard the bad news that a loved one had died.

"Please," Dr. Robbins said, indicating the chairs with a quick sweep of his hand like he was brushing away cobwebs. "Have a seat."

Julia sat down, poised on the edge of her chair with her knees pressed tightly together. The cold, winding apprehension in the pit of her stomach was almost unbearable. She shot a quick glance at Ben but then looked back at the doctor, not wanting Ben to see how scared she was.

"Well, as we suspected when he first arrived, your father has suffered a stroke," Dr. Robbins said without preamble.

Before he said anything more, Julia blurted out, "How bad was it?" Horrible images filled her head of her father as a pale, drooling invalid.

The expression on Dr. Robbins's face froze, and a heavy curtain dropped behind his eyes as though he was cutting himself off from what was really happening here.

"A bad one, I'm afraid," he said.

"How..." She gulped. "How bad?" She heard her voice as if someone else was speaking in another room.

"He's..."

Dr. Robbins blinked his eyes rapidly a few times as he glanced up at the ceiling. He looked as though he was wishing he was doing something—anything else besides having this conversation.

Julia wondered if it was his youth and lack of experience or the severity of her father's conditions, but something was making it difficult for him to tell her exactly what was going on. Anger flashed inside her like the glint off a honed knife blade. All she wanted—*right now, damnit!*—was the truth, no matter how bad.

"He's in a coma, and while it's impossible to predict what will happen next, I would say the prognosis is not very encouraging."

"Not very encouraging," Ben muttered, as if he were the doctor's echo. Julia winced as his grip on her hand tightened painfully. She shot him a quick look that said: *Leave this to me.*

"When will you know?" she asked.

"We'll have to conduct a battery of tests to determine the extent and exact nature of the damage and the possible outcome, but for now I...I'm sorry to have to tell you this, Miss Meadows, but I don't hold out much hope for a full recovery."

"Aren't you being a little too pessimistic here?" Ben said. His voice snapped in the air like a bullwhip. Julia was taken aback by his reaction, and she looked at him, puzzled.

"Beg pardon?" Dr. Robbins said, leaning forward, his hands folded on a stack of papers on the desk in front of him.

"I mean—if it's too early to tell, like you say, and you need to do more tests, I'm not sure it helps the situation here to be telling us you have no idea what happened and that you don't hold out much hope that he—her father—that Mr. Capozza will recover."

Ben's tone was stinging, and for a heartbeat or two, Dr. Robbins looked flustered, unable to speak. He raised his right hand to his mouth and pinched his lower lip while staring blankly straight ahead.

"At this point, there's no way of knowing. I simply wish to prepare Miss Meadows for what might prove to be a negative patient outcome," Dr. Robbins said.

"'Negative patient outcome?'" Ben almost barked the words, and Julia looked at him, wide-eyed. "Jesus Fucking Christ! Is *that* what you call it now? A 'negative patient outcome?' What happened to good old-fashioned words like 'death' and 'dying'? Cut to the chase, will yah Doc?"

Dr. Robbins let his shoulders drop as he took a breath, held it for a few seconds, and then exhaled slowly between his teeth. His eyes had a distant glaze as he focused on—or past—Ben.

"As I said—it's entirely too early to tell, but I can assure you that the stroke your father—Is he your father?" He nailed Ben with a steady stare.

Neither Ben nor Julia replied, and after a brief silence, Dr. Robbins continued as if he hadn't asked the question.

"I can assure you that your father has had a serious stroke and that you have to prepare yourself for a very long and difficult recovery."

"I…I understand that," Julia said. "Is there…. Did he suffer any brain damage?"

"We need to do more tests to determine that, but I'd say—yes. The stroke appears to have been massive."

Julia moaned as she cast a quick glance at Ben. Ben looked like he was coiled and ready to spring out of the chair and throttle Dr. Robbins. Still, she had to appreciate the way Ben was trying to get Dr. Robbins to cut the legalistic medical mumbo-jumbo and tell them in plain English what was going on.

Say what you will about people from small Maine coastal towns, she thought. They sure don't tolerate bullshit of any flavor, color, or aroma.

"For the time being," Dr. Robbins said, "I'd suggest you both go home and try to relax. Your father's in intensive care, and you won't be able to see him for some time yet. We're doing everything medically possible."

"When will you know?" Ben said, still sounding snappy. At least he was no longer threatening violence.

"We have your cell phone number. We'll call you at home," Dr. Robbins said. He pushed away from the desk as if he was going to stand, but he remained seated.

Julia noticed how the doctor still had a difficult time making direct eye contact with her. Her only hope was that his medical skills were much better than his social skills.

"Thank you," she said, although the words rang hollow in her ears. She didn't know anything more than she had when she first came in, and the single, clearest thought in her mind was that her father was going to die.

There was no way around it.

And as this horrible thought echoed, another, even more disturbing thought began to gnaw at the back of her mind. She tried to deny it, but she experienced a disquieting sense of relief…of liberation at the prospect of her father's imminent death would give her. As much as she loved him, once he was gone, only then would she…finally…be able to start living her own life.

And then another thought occurred to her.

Would Ben be a part of that new life?

FIFTEEN

Goin' Down

It was late in the afternoon. The storm had passed, and the sun was setting, lighting the thin, bright band of clouds on the western horizon. The air was warm and moist, more like summer than spring. The wind coming off the ocean carried a bracing, salty tang. Puddles on the street and sidewalk glistened from the recent downpour.

Tom Marshall was nervous as he sat behind the steering wheel of his car, which was parked across the street about fifty feet from the front door of The Local. His window was rolled down, and he was taking deep breaths, filling his lungs to capacity and exhaling slowly to relieve his tension.

He told himself he didn't have to be this nervous.

He could always try to fly the excuse that he had simply been doing his job. Jerry Lincoln, the new DEA guy, had asked him to investigate anything and everything about the local drug traffic. If worse came to worst and he had to kill Gillette, he had a throwdown in his glove compartment he could drop beside the body and claim that the dipshit had drawn on him first. He had every right to shoot him in self-defense.

But the truth was, Tom had never killed a man in the line of duty or otherwise.

Sure, he had seen enough dead people. Murder victims and suicides…car accidents…medical emergencies. But he had never sighted down the barrel of a gun and pulled the trigger to end a man's life.

He wondered if he really had the balls to do it.

If anyone deserved to die, though, it was Tony Gillette. The bastard should never have shorted him on that deal. If he'd been honest, Tom would have been long gone by now, and Gillette wouldn't be a walking dead man.

The problem was, getting Tony Gillette in a situation where he could bring him down without any witnesses would be difficult if not impossible. It was no use demanding the rest of the money. Gillette would never give it up. He had Tom by the short hairs, and both of them knew it. Tom couldn't very well go to the department and complain, now, could he?

Tom tensed when the front door of The Local opened, and Danny "Puppy" Lawrence stepped out into the gathering evening gloom. His face looked pasty white in the dimming light. His eyes were twitching back and forth as he looked up and down the street until he saw Tom's car.

Tom gripped the steering wheel with both hands. Then he raised his forefinger in greeting, a gesture he doubted Puppy even saw, but the man started walking toward the car. He looked unsteady on his feet, weaving from side to side until he got to the car. He stopped on the driver's side.

"Get the fuck in the car," Tom said, glancing around to see if anyone was watching. He didn't see anyone, but that didn't mean someone wasn't watching.

"Oh…yeah…sure," Puppy said. He belched as he staggered to the passenger's side, opened the door, and got in.

"Are you fuckin' coherent?" Tom asked, wrinkling his nose in disgust as he studied the man for a moment. Puppy's dirty blond hair was disheveled, and his eyes were red-rimmed and bloodshot. The corners of his mouth were edged with a thin coating of yellow mucous.

"'Course I am…I'm sharp as a tack." Puppy punctuated his statement with another belch that filled the car with a sour stench. Tom waved his hand in front of his face to drive away the smell.

"Christ, man! You ever hear of Listerine?"

Puppy stared at him like he'd spoken Swahili.

"So…" Tom said, "you talk to him?"

"Him…who's 'him?'"

Tom shook his head, thoroughly disgusted. It took great restraint not to open the door and shove Puppy out onto the street.

"Gillette, you moron. You talk to him for me?"

"Oh, yeah...yeah, I tole 'im what you was thinking."

"And?"

"Whadda yah mean, *'and?'*"

"For Christ sakes. What did he say?"

When Puppy didn't answer him immediately, Tom lowered his gaze, puffed out his cheeks, and shook his head sadly.

"Jesus Christ," he said. "How the hell do you get by?"

"I dunno...lucky, I guess."

"I should bust your sorry ass right here 'n now, and drag you down to the station. You gotta be holding."

Puppy jerked his head back and belched again.

"Aww...you wouldn't do that, Tommy," he said with a casual wave of his hand. "'Sides, you wouldn't know where you're 'spozed to meet 'im if you did."

"Are you gonna tell me, or do I have to beat it out of you?"

Puppy's eyes lit up and he said, "How 'bout you buy me a drink first?"

"How 'bout you suck my dick?" Tom said.

Puppy belched again and shook his head.

"And stop it with the fucking burping. Christ!" Tom said. "I don't want you hurling in my car. Damn!" He wrinkled his nose and had to stick his face out the side window to catch a breath. "You sure you're not fuckin' dying inside."

"'F I am, it's prob'bly the cancer," Puppy said as he stared straight ahead with a glazed look in his eyes. He had one hand on the dashboard, as if that would steady his spinning world.

"I sincerely hope it is," Tom said. He heaved a sigh. "So is Gillette gonna meet me or what?"

Tom's rising anticipation was almost too much to handle. All he wanted was to get Puppy out of his car and get down to business.

Puppy nodded and said, "He says you know where to meet s'long as you got the stuff."

"When?"

"Said at nine."

"Tonight?"

Tom glanced at his watch. It wasn't eight o'clock yet. He had plenty of time to prepare.

"No. Last night." Puppy belched but tried to hide it behind his fist. "A' course tonight."

"And he's not gonna cheat me like he did last time?"

"I don't know nothin' 'bout any a' that," Puppy said, but there was a sudden shift in his tone of voice that made Tom think he knew all about it. Gillette would never have said a word to him about it, and neither would Zimmerman, but that's how small towns are. Somehow—even when there's a secret between two or three people and no one says a damned thing—word gets around.

The truth was, it didn't matter anymore because Tom didn't have a goddamned gram of coke on him.

"Okay," Tom said. "Now get the fuck outta here." He would have reached across in front of Puppy to open the door for him, but he didn't want to get that close.

Puppy needed a few seconds to focus before he caught hold of the door handle, pulled it, and pushed the door open. He almost fell onto the sidewalk, but somehow he caught his balance and started walking away in a zigzag path. By now, the streetlights had come on, their harsh sodium glare illuminating Puppy as he made his way home or, more likely, back to The Local or over to a friend's house to keep the buzz going.

Tom was satisfied, though.

He knew where and when he'd meet up with Gillette.

He glanced at his watch again, reassuring himself that he had plenty of time to drive out to the dirt road out of town and case the area. He wanted to be absolutely ready for anything by the time Gillette got there.

And then…?

Well, he thought, let's wait and see how this all plays out.

If he had to kill the son-of-a-bitch, that would teach Gillette once and for all not to fuck with him.

"You still haven't explained what that was all about," Julia said.

He and Julia had stopped at Judy's Clam Shack, a little place out on Route One a mile or so outside of Bath. They were the only customers. Night had fallen, and they were sitting side by side at a picnic table under a striped green and white canvas awning. A string of overhead lights caught them in a warm, yellow glow that pushed the darkness back. Moths flapped around it and bumped into it, making faint ticking sounds. In the marsh behind the shack, frogs and crickets sang. Occasional gusts of wind made the canvas awning snap like a flag in a stiff breeze.

They were sipping Coke from paper cups that were beaded with moisture. They had ordered a half-pint of clams and some fries, but Judy, the cook, was taking her sweet old time getting the food to them.

"Explained what…when?" he finally said.

"At the hospital."

Ben shrugged innocently and said, "I was trying to get some straight answers from the guy if that's what you mean."

"And you thought yelling at the doctor who's taking care of my father…that trying to intimidate him was going to accomplish… what exactly?"

"He wasn't being straight with you, is all," Ben said. He realized he was clenching his fists in his lap under the table and consciously relaxed them, resting them on the table on either side of his drink. "I wanted him to talk to you honestly and acknowledge we were real people, with emotions and…and friggin' brains. I didn't want to hear a bunch of medical and legalistic jive. I'm *sick* to death of it!"

He clenched his right hand into a fist and pounded the tabletop hard enough to make their cups and the plastic-ware rolled up into napkins jump.

Julia pulled back and looked at him, surprise and fear lighting her eyes. Ben realized she was afraid of his anger, but if they were going to make a go of this relationship, then she was going to have to accept that sometimes he got angry. The problem was, and he wasn't sure why, lately—especially the last few days—he was feeling like he was on a short fuse. Pretty much anything would get on his nerves and set him off…and it was getting worse.

"I'm just saying…. You know, my ex-husband was—*is* a recovering alcoholic."

"And?"

"And…and he was always talking about how if you're pissed about something and you won't admit it, your anger can come out sideways."

Ben couldn't help but sneer at that and think, *Oh, great…here it comes...more Dr. Phil crap...more touchy-feely bullshit instead of talking honestly about shit.*

"I really don't give a damn about your ex or any bull he may have spouted."

Julia looked genuinely hurt by his reaction, and it bothered him, but he couldn't unsay it now. He wiped his face with the flat of his hand and then took a sip of Coke. Before either of them said anything else, Judy dinged the bell at the counter to let them know their food was ready.

They both got up and walked to the window. Judy, whose long, gray hair was tied up in a knot at the back of her head and covered with a net, slid the red and white striped boxes of clams and fries onto a tray and handed it to them. She had the bored expression of someone who had been doing this job or one exactly like it her entire life and knew nothing better was ever going to come along.

"There's ketchup and tartar sauce in the cooler," she said, nodding to her left. "Refills on the soda are free."

"Thank you," Julia said in a pleasant voice as she took the tray. Without a word, Ben opened the small cooler and took a handful of condiments.

"It wasn't bull," Julia said once they had sat back down under the awning. This time, they sat on opposite sides of the table, facing each other.

"What isn't?"

"The whole 'anger coming out sideways' thing."

"Bullshit," Ben muttered.

Julia raised her hands in exasperation and gripped the edge of the table.

"You're doing it right now."

"I am not."

"You are too. You know what your problem is? You—"

"I don't need *you* to tell *me* what *my* problem is. That's what the AAs in the Army call 'taking someone else's inventory.'"

"You're not dealing with what's really bothering you. You get upset about other things—things that have nothing to do with the real issue."

"So it comes out sideways," Ben said. He took a sip of Coke, thinking how good the carbonation felt on the back of his throat. It gave him a moment to let what she had said sink in.

"Exactly," Julia said, her expression softening. "You're acting like you're mad at me, and you know you're not. What did I do?"

"Okay. I get it."

"So why'd you get so angry at the doctor?"

"Because he wasn't being straight with us."

"Maybe, but you didn't have to lash out at him."

Julia leaned forward, her breasts pushing the tray forward as she slid her hands across the table and clasped his. Their eyes met, and a sudden wave of inexpressible sadness swept through Ben.

He knew she was right, but he didn't want to get into it.

Not now. Not when they were trying to have a nice evening out to forget their worries if possible. His day had been stressful enough, and she was worried sick about what was going to happen to her father.

"You're right," he said at last. "There's some…some crap going on with my family, is all, and I—"

He stopped speaking suddenly when it felt as though someone behind him had wrapped powerful hands around his throat and was strangling him. He hunched his shoulders forward and, shaking his head, gasped for breath. The alarm in Julia's eyes was obvious, and as an oily tension coiled up inside him, his first thought was that what had happened to him the other night at her house was happening again.

"Just relax," Julia said, but her voice seemed to be coming to him from miles away.

Ben looked at her, his vision telescoping crazily. He was terrified to see how far away she appeared even though she was still reaching across the table, holding his hands and squeezing them reassuringly. Her arms were impossibly long, stretching out and sagging like long tubes of rubber.

"You're safe with me," she said in an airy whisper. "Right now… it's just you and me, and everything's fine. There's no need to—"

"Can I see your cell phone?" Ben spoke so suddenly Julia let go of his hands and pulled back.

"My cell phone?" she said, her voice twisting into a high note.

"Yeah. Your cell phone."

He held his right hand out, palm up, and shook it demandingly.

Obviously confused by his sudden shift in attitude, Julia slowly reached into her purse and pulled out her phone. She looked curious as she handed it to him.

Ben took the phone from her and sat back. He frowned with concentration as he snapped it open and glanced at the buttons as he tried to figure out how to use it. He pressed the round black button in the middle of the dial, and a menu popped up. After a few clicks, he found the "Calls Received" file and opened it. As he ran down the list of displayed numbers, his frown deepened.

"What the hell are you doing? What's this all about?" Julia asked, her voice tight with worry.

"I'm making sure nothing's coming out sideways," he said.

What's she sounding so worried about? Ben wondered. Is she afraid she's been found out?

"Who do you think you are?" she asked, her voice high-pitched and full of irritation. "Give me my phone back right *now!* That's my private property."

She made a grab for the phone across the table and knocked into the tray, spilling fries and clams all over the table. Ben twisted to one side, fending her off as he scrolled through the list he had brought up.

"Ben…I mean it." Her face was beet-red now. She cast a quick glance around to see if Judy was watching them from the order window. "You're really starting to piss me off."

"Am I?"

But as he scrolled through the list, he saw nothing. Certainly no calls from Pete.

He loosened his posture and looked at her as a feeling of satisfaction ran through him.

He handed her cell phone out to her. Glaring at him, Julia snapped it from his hand it and stuffed it back into her purse.

"Do you mind explaining what that was all about?"

"I found your number on my brother's speed dial today," he replied.

"Wha..." Julia's voice trailed off.

"So I had to see if you've been talking to Pete."

"You could have asked me, you know. That might have been less dramatic than grabbing my phone and snooping." Julia's eyes were dark with anger.

"I don't know what to think anymore," Ben said, lowering his gaze. He took a long gulp of Coke, letting the sugary carbonation burn against the back of his throat. "I feel like the whole world has gone crazy ever since I came home."

"You really are a jerk sometimes, you know that?" She huffed her breath, trying hard not to yell. Ben sat there and watched her. Finally the pain he was causing her registered, and it cut deeply.

"You have absolutely no consideration…no concern for what I… what I'm going through, do you?" Julia said.

"Yes, I do." Even to his own ears, Ben's words sounded false.

"You have a hell of a way of showing it, then," Julia said. "But as for your brother…I think he's been interested in me since I moved here. He's never called or anything, but he always seems to turn up wherever I am. And he's watching me."

"You mean stalking?"

"No. Not really."

"If he's stalking you…giving you a hard time, you should call the police."

Julia shook her head and said, "I can handle it on my own, Ben. But honest…I have never had any interest in Pete. Never."

Ben suddenly felt like a colossal fool.

"And after all the trouble you've been having…" she said.

At first, Ben thought she was talking about his father's dealings with Richie Sullivan, but then it flashed on him.

"You mean the slashed tires?"

"Uh-huh. That…and when you got jumped outside The Local. At first, I thought it must have been Tom, but I didn't want to say anything if it was Pete. I didn't say anything because I didn't want to cause any more problems for you and your family."

Her voice choked off, and her shoulders wrenched and collapsed inward as she heaved a deep sob and had to look away.

Ben was speechless. He began to put the pieces together and realized that Julia was telling the truth. Pete had been acting so hostile because he was pissed Julia had chosen his brother, not him.

"Son-of-a-bitch," he whispered. "I don't know what to say. I…I had no idea. I'm really sorry." He wished he didn't sound so weak.

Tears were spilling from her eyes, carving glistening tracks down her cheeks. She sniffed loudly and, grabbing a napkin, dabbed her eyes and then blew her nose.

"You should have said something before now," he said.

"I know." Her eyes brightened as she looked at him and nodded. "You're absolutely right. I should have, but I honestly didn't want to cause you any more grief."

She grabbed another napkin and wiped her eyes, harder this time. When she looked at him again, her lips were thin and bloodless. One corner of her mouth was twitching.

"I'm such an idiot," Ben said, smiling weakly and hoping to relieve or reduce the tension between them. He wouldn't blame her if she got up and walked away right then, but he prayed she wouldn't.

"I guess we both have some personal issues to work on, huh?" she said.

It gladdened his heart to see a ghost of a smile light her face.

"Amen to that," Ben said, his smile widening.

Both of his hands were clammy and trembling as he slid them across the table and took hold of her hands. He squeezed them tightly.

"Forgive me?" he asked, but Julia didn't answer him, and he couldn't blame her. She kept staring past him, looking over his shoulder into the darkness beyond their cone of light.

Tom turned off onto the dirt road twenty minutes before nine o'clock. The sun had set, but a cobalt blue glow lingered in the western sky. A chorus of frogs was singing in a nearby pond, and far off in the distance, a whippoorwill whistled its mournful song.

Using his training as a police officer, Tom parked so his car was facing toward the main road and angled so he could pull out quickly and drive away without having to back up.

He got out of the car and, leaving his headlights on, surveyed the surrounding area. He wanted to scope out every place Gillette might be able to park. Tom had no doubt Zimmerman would be with him, but Gillette always drove. It was one of his ways of staying in control. Tom was counting on Gillette being a creature of habit and parking in the same spot he had parked before with his car positioned so it was facing the woods. That would be perfect because he would have to back up and turn around before he could get out of there.

He paced off the distance, trying to guess exactly where Gillette's car would be and what would be the quickest way for him to get the drop on them. If it came down to it, he wanted to get a few shots off before they knew what hit them. Once Zimmerman started shooting, Tom was pretty sure all bets would be off. He was positive the man would prove to be a dead-eye shot, so he would have to go for him first and then finish off Gillette, who had a reputation for never going armed. It would have violated the parole conditions from a previous arrest, but Tom was also sure Gillette wasn't very good handling a gun. In fact, Tom was counting on that.

Once he was satisfied that Gillette would have no choice but to pull into the same spot, Tom got back into his car and waited. He kept fidgeting, checking the ammo in his revolver, which he kept tucked under his waistband in the small of his back. He hoped Gillette wouldn't notice the bulge under his loose-fitting shirt. In the darkness, he probably wouldn't, but after what had happened last time, both Gillette and Zimmerman would be fools to think he hadn't come to this meeting armed.

Time moved slowly as he waited, listening to the night sounds of insects, birds, and frogs. The sky to the east was pitch black with not a cloud in sight. No breath of wind stirred. Tom jumped when an owl suddenly hooted in the nearby woods. When he leaned across the steering wheel and scanned the night, the bird launched itself from a nearby tree and drifted as silent as a phantom out across the nearby marsh.

"Happy hunting, *compadre*," he muttered as he tracked the bird until it dissolved into the darkness.

He willed his racing heart to slow down as he looked at his wristwatch for what seemed like the hundredth time, took a few deep breaths, and stared at nothing. After an unaccountably long time, far down the road, the glow of approaching headlights lit up the surrounding trees. After touching his revolver one last time for reassurance, he sat with both hands on the steering wheel and looking straight ahead.

Happy hunting, indeed, he thought, smiling grimly as the yellow glow of headlights grew steadily brighter.

Julia hung her jacket in the hall closet. She asked Ben to stay the night with her, but he had said he couldn't—Louise had moved out of Tom's house, he said, and there was family crap to attend to. Julia told him about the phone exchange she'd had with Louise earlier, and they laughed. That—*finally*—broke the tension over the cell phone snooping.

"Tell Louise…tell her I…" Julia's voice trailed off, remembering that Louise might not think too kindly of her.

"I'll tell her you said 'hi.'" Ben said. "Don't worry about Lou-Lou. And call the house if you need anything, any time. 'Kay?"

"I will," Julia replied, and they had clung tightly to each other for a long time on her porch. Then she watched Ben walk over to his car, get in, and drive away.

Now the house was empty for the first time since Julia had come to live here. She thought of her father, alone in the hospital. Tears welled in her eyes.

Maybe a shower and a nap, and then I'll go back to the hospital and keep him company. I can't stand to think of him being there alone, and I sure don't want to be here alone.

The front door flew open with a crash. Startled, Julia whirled around, thinking…hoping for a split second that it was Ben.

But it wasn't Ben.

"Pete? What are you doing here?" Her voice was pitched high with astonishment and a sudden jolt of fear. "Ben just left."

Pete nodded, and she knew he must have been watching and waiting. He stared at her mutely for a long time. His jaw and throat muscles knotted, looking like he was trying to swallow a handful of walnuts. Then his face flushed.

"Then you prob'ly know that my brother found your phone number on my cell." He was visibly shaking. "And you prob'ly had yourselves a good laugh at my expense, right? Stupid old Pete! What was he thinkin'? Huh? You wanna know?"

Julia was incapable of reacting.

"Well," he said, "I'll tell yah what I was thinkin'!

"Hold on, Pete," Julia began. "You can't just burst in here—"

He cut her off by taking a step closer and raising a fist.

"Shut up!" he shouted. "Just *shut* the *fuck* up!"

Trembling, Julia nodded and took a step back. She eyed the

doorway leading into the kitchen and the wall phone, but she calculated that she'd never make it if she made a dash for it.

"I'm finally gonna say what I've been wantin' to say."

"Okay," Julia managed.

Pete took a deep breath, but his posture was still wire-tight.

"You see, I was thinkin'...when you came to The Cove...that I'd never seen a finer woman in my life, and I've been waitin' for a chance to...to talk to you, maybe even take you out and...and treat you good. I was willing to wait 'til you got tired of my dipshit brother-in-law, 'cause I knew you would. He's always been an idiot and not much good in the sack."

How'd he know that? Julia thought irrelevantly.

Pete's voice was steadily rising. "'N then Big Ben the war hero breezes back to town. And just like he's always done all his fuckin' life, he just takes what *I* want."

"No, he didn't. Listen to me..."

"I told you to shut the fuck up, goddamn it! Listen!" His eyes rolled ceiling-ward when he took a deep breath. His tanned cheeks were splotched with red. "I never got *anything* new in my life. Always handed down from *him*. Always shared with *him*. I stay here, help my old man, keep the family business goin'. I'm just good old Pete nobody gives a shit about, but he...he goes off to Iraq, shoots a couple desert rats, 'n he's a Christless hero! Everyone wants to kiss his ass. And he goes and picks you up like you're a fuckin' nickel he found on the sidewalk." He took another shuddering breath. "After I waited so goddamned long for you just to *notice* me...to fuckin' *look* at me!"

The cords in his neck were strained, and his eyes were bulging. The corners of his mouth were flecked with spittle.

Julia could only shake her head *no*. She was trembling with fear and exhaustion.

"I tried to stop him, y'know," Pete went on. "I was tryin' to make him think twice...especially since he could have any girl he wanted. But no, the Gunner, he always gets the girl. And now it looks like you two are crazy in love."

He snatched a heavy glass lamp from the end table next to her father's easy chair and tore the beige shade from it. Ripping the plug from the wall, he brandished it at her like it was a club.

"I can't *stand* it, goddamnit! No more of this shit! I'm not losing out to my fucking brother anymore! So you know what I'm gonna do?"

Julia stared at him, wide-eyed, and shook her head. She couldn't speak.

"I'm gonna mess you up so fuckin' bad that Ben and nobody else will ever wanna look at you ever again!"

Julia's face contorted with fear, and tears began to stream down her cheeks. It was foolish to run and try to get to a phone to call 911. She certainly couldn't defend herself. Pete was too big and strong. And she was dreaming if she thought Ben would come charging in like the US Cavalry and save her.

But—somehow—she found the courage to stand there and stare into Pete's eyes, willing him to look at her…really *look* at her.

"I'm a person too, Pete…I'm just like you…I'm hurting…. Look at me, Pete…. Look at me…I'm sorry, Pete," she sobbed softly. "I'm so sorry."

Trembling and breathing hard, Pete looked back at her for what seemed an eternity. Then the red slowly drained from his face. His hand was shaking as he placed the lamp back on the end table and stood there, looking guilty and confused. Without making a sound, he went to Julia and put his arms around her. She leaned forward, sobbing like a child into his shoulder while he awkwardly patted her back.

After a time, he kissed her forehead and lifted her blotchy, tear-stained face to his.

"Goodbye, Julia," he said.

Without another word, he walked away, closing the front door behind him.

Julia jumped when she heard the door latch click. It sounded like a gunshot. Then she ran to the door, locked it, and pressed her back hard against it. She stayed like that until she heard his car start up and drive away.

Then and only then did she let the tears fall.

SIXTEEN

Night Cruise

The car's taillights flickered and glowed like flame through a swirl of dust as Gillette pulled to a stop in the turnoff. He stopped the car right where Tom expected he would and killed the engine, but he didn't get out. Apparently he was waiting for Tom to make the first move. Leaving his keys in the ignition, Tom opened his door and stepped out. The dust was still suspended in the motionless air as he started walking slowly over to the car.

Keeping his gaze fixed on the rear window, he resisted the urge to reassure himself by patting the revolver under his belt in the small of his back. Only now did he realize he should have gotten a suitcase or a gym bag or something to make his ploy look more convincing.

As he approached the car, his feet crunching on the gravel, he discerned by the dim dashboard lights two silhouettes in the front seat. Tom was sure the passenger was Zimmerman, riding shotgun for security. He smiled as he approached the driver's side of the car. Bracing both hands on the roof, he leaned down. The tinted automatic window slid down like a polished piece of marble that reflected the night.

"Evenin' to yah," Tom said, touching his forefinger to his forehead as if saluting. Gillette was wearing a pair of Wayfarers that caught and held a dark, distorted reflection of the dashboard lights.

Sunglasses at night, he thought. He really does work hard to maintain his image.

"We can dispense with the pleasantries," Gillette said, sounding more irritable than usual, which was saying a lot. He raised the shades, perching them on his forehead, and squinted up at

Tom. "You got the shit?"

"We gotta talk price first," Tom said in a low, measured voice. "Meaning no disrespect, Tony, but after last time, I can't say's I entirely trust you."

"You got paid a fair chunk of change for something that wasn't yours in the first place," Gillette sounded peeved. Tom wondered if he and Zimmerman had had an argument about something. "You wanna report me to the cops? Go right ahead."

Tom leaned down and, placing one hand on the side panel of the car door, twisted to the right so he presented a narrower target if ole Zim started shooting. In the darkness, though, it didn't look like Zimmerman. Tom bent down to try to see who it was.

"Who's your new girlfriend?" Tom asked, nodding at the man, who sat there silently. His face was turned away slightly, and his features were indistinct in the darkness. His head was a black silhouette against the view out the side window.

"None of your goddamned business," the man said with a gravely snarl that sounded put on to disguise his voice.

"Where's your buddy Zimmerman...the Zimster...Zimmerrama?" Tom said, laughing foolishly at his attempt at humor.

Gillette glanced at his partner and then rolled his head around so he was looking straight at Tom.

"You can cut the comedy routine any time you want," he said. "You got some shit to sell me or not?"

"'Course I do," Tom said, but even as the words left his mouth, a tingling cold tightness filled his gut.

This is it...showtime, he thought, shivering as a rush of adrenalin filled his chest. He wondered if he really had the *cojones* to draw a gun on these guys and shoot both of them in cold blood. His beef was with Gillette, so this other guy—whoever the fuck he was—was nothing more than collateral damage.

It was unavoidable.

"It's in my car," he said. "You wanna come have a look-see?"

"Get it and bring it here," Gillette said without moving a muscle to get out of the car.

Something set off an alarm in Tom's head. At that exact instant, he was sure *he* was the one being set up. He glanced over his shoulder quickly to see if anyone was watching them. He was suddenly positive that Zimmerman was lurking somewhere in the dark woods with a rifle and scope, waiting to take his shot.

Tom reacted without thinking.

Reaching behind his back, he grabbed for the revolver. His right hand clasped the curved handle, and he yanked it free with a snap. Sucking in his breath, he swung the gun around and pointed it at Gillette. Without even thinking, he squeezed the trigger three times. The gun kicked in his hand as the barrel flared with yellow flame, but he never heard or registered the sound of any of the shots.

The first slug caught Gillette in the side of the head, an inch or two in front of his left ear. His head snapped back and to the side. The other two shots missed entirely. One of the bullets ricocheted off the dashboard and punched through the windshield, leaving behind a fist-sized hole with white spider-web cracks. The other took out the CD player.

Tom dropped to one knee so he'd have a clear shot at Gillette's passenger, but in the sudden confusion, the mystery man snapped the car door open and was on the ground on the other side of the car. Tom got off one more shot, but he knew he missed when it ricocheted off something metal. Realizing he had to save his ammo, he dropped to the ground and pressed his back against the side of the car.

His heart was pounding, fast and hard as he considered what to do next. Panting heavily, he stared at his car parked by the side of the road less than fifty feet away. It might as well have been on the moon. That mystery man would gun him down the instant he made a dash for it.

"Yo! Can we call a truce here?" Tom shouted. His breath was burning his throat like he'd swallowed jet fuel.

There was no reply...only the steady chirring of insects in the grass and the croaking of frogs in the nearby swamp. No wind stirred the leaves overhead.

Tom's shoulders throbbed with tension as he crouched beside the car with no idea from which direction the danger would come.

Gillette's gotta be dead, he thought with equal measures of joy and amazement.

He knew at least one bullet had hit him.

And that's all he'd been looking for. He had wanted Gillette to pay for cheating him out of that hundred thousand dollars, so as far as he was concerned, he was good.

"Hey!" he called out. "I mean it. I got no beef with you." His voice echoed oddly in the night, sounding flat and empty.

Still no answer.

His best option, he knew, was to make a dash for his car and count on darkness and confusion to give him the break he needed. He'd been smart to position the car where it was. All he had to do now was get to it.

He licked his lips, tasting the tang of salt and wondering if it was sweat or tears. The palm of the hand holding the gun ached with a bone-deep throb. By his count, he'd shot four times. That meant he had only two shots left. He wasn't about to jump up and, in a blaze of glory, make a brave dash to the car, running zigzags to avoid the return fire he was sure would come his way.

"I mean it, buddy!" Tom shouted, cupping one hand to his mouth like a megaphone. "We can both walk out of here intact. It's your choice."

The only reply was the sound of a gun going off and an instantaneous dull *thunk* sound as a bullet hit the car door inches from his head. Tom dropped to the ground and then, not really thinking it through, leaped to his feet and started to run.

Wind whistled shrilly in his ears, and his heart was thudding so loudly it blocked out every other sound except for a distant, muffled *thump…thump…thump*.

And then something smacked him on the right shoulder, throwing him off balance as if the mystery man had reached out of the darkness, grabbed him by the arm, and viciously tugged him around.

For a few more steps, there was no pain, but then his skin felt as though the biggest damned hornet in the world had stung his right arm. His hand went numb, and by the time he slammed into the side of his car, he had forgotten that he was still holding onto his gun.

He remembered he'd left the car keys in the ignition. That was good. His only thought now was to get into the car and drive the hell away. The wound couldn't be all that bad. Before he had a chance to run around to the other side of the car, placing the bulk of it between him and the shooter, there was a loud pop, and searing pain ripped into his left leg just above the knee. Tom's first thought was that he'd banged his leg against the bumper, but with the next step, when he put his full weight onto his leg, his knee folded on him, and he went down.

He hit the ground hard enough to knock the wind out of him. He thought crazily how he hadn't heard the gun go off, and that was supposed to mean it was the shot that killed him, but then another shot exploded in the night. A split-second later, a bullet whizzed through the air. It sounded like an enraged hornet, buzzing overhead as it clipped leaves from the trees behind him.

The side of Tom's face was pressed into the dirt. Sweat and tears streaked his skin. Blood was leaking out of him, soaking into the dirt. He was breathing so heavily his lungs felt like they were ripping into shreds.

Had he been shot in the chest, too, and he simply didn't realize it yet?

Am I dying?

He prayed that the shooter would see he was down and come forward to finish him off quickly...before any more pain set in. He was more afraid of suffering than dying.

Christ, I fucked up, he thought as his eyelids fluttered. With every breath he took, the night hissed as it rose and fell around him like a surging tide. His vision was getting hazier by the second, but he could see, far across the dirt road, a dark figure moving toward him in a slow, watery blur.

It grew steadily larger until it took up more than half of his sight.

Tom was lying on his right hand, and now he dimly realized that something hard and cold was pressing into his side. When his hand twitched, he finally realized he was still clinging to his gun.

From my cold, dead hand, he thought.

He rolled over and dragged his arm forward. Raising the gun, he wasn't conscious of aiming it at the black figure that swelled in front of him. It was so big, how could he miss? He narrowed his eyes in pain the instant before he pulled the trigger.

The gunshot was deafening. The night lit up with a blaze of light that looked like the gates of Heaven—*or the fires of Hell*—opening to receive him.

Somehow, the dark shape miraculously vanished. Gone. Like an illusion.

Tom stared at the indistinct line of trees on the horizon. They rose up against the night sky like a doily edge. Above them was a glittering array of stars that looked like flecks of powdered crystal.

Tom heaved a sigh that blended into a moan as he dropped his head to the ground again. The hard-packed dirt felt much softer now. It was as if he were lying on an air cushion that was floating on the ocean, bobbing gently on the swells…up and down…up and down. His strength was swiftly ebbing away…seeping from him as the rapid, thunderous pulse in his head got steadily louder.

And louder until…

There was another sound…a sound that blended into his awareness so gradually he had no idea when it had started or where it was coming from or even when he had first noticed it. It rose and fell… rose and fell in a wild, warbling wail, and then flashing blue and red lights that, at first, Tom thought were strokes of lightning, filled the night.

But the lights were too regular to be lightning, and as they grew steadily brighter with each passing second, the warbling sound came closer and closer until it split the night like a silver wedge.

Tom heard what sounded like a fleet of vehicles pulling to a stop close by. Engines roared. Sirens wailed. The harsh glare of headlights focused on him, pinning him to the dirt.

The sirens gradually cut off, fading with a whoop, and then car doors opened and slammed shut and rapid footsteps approached. A swirling mass of dark figures converged on Tom, surrounding him like demons, come to drag him to Hell. He was so far gone he allowed them to manhandle him as several people leaned over him and checked his wounds. The cacophony of voices was like a whirlwind all around him. It was all but impossible to make out what anyone was saying, but by concentrating, he made some sense of them.

"…doesn't look life-threatening…"

"…lost a lot of blood…"

"…knee is blown to shit…"

Then someone—Tom had no idea who—mentioned the name "Lincoln."

Lost in pain and confusion, and unable to resist as his body was dragged like a slab of beef onto a stretcher, his first crazy thought was that for some reason someone was talking about Abraham Lincoln and making a connection between him shooting Gillette and Lincoln's assassination.

But then he remembered…Jerry Lincoln, the new DEA agent who had asked him to inform on local drug dealers. As he drifted down into darkness, he heard more voices, sounding further and further away as they carried him toward what he thought—what he *hoped*—was an ambulance.

"…told him this was a bad idea…"

"…not to do it without better backup…"

"…helluva shot…"

"…took half his fucking head off…"

"Hello, Dad? Are you there? Is anyone home?"

Julia was trying without much success to hold back a flood of tears as she sat by her father's bedside in the ICU and looked at the all but empty husk of the man lying beneath the thin, white sheet and blanket. The monitors and medical equipment that surrounded him clicked and beeped steadily. In a setting like this, it was all but impossible to accept that it really was her father lying there.

He looked so diminished…impossibly small.

How could *this* be the big, strong man who had bounced her on his knee and given her piggyback rides when she was a baby… the man who had taught her how to drive a stick shift…the father who had taken her to Red Sox games and went to all her soccer games…the proud father who had been the first to applaud at her high school and college graduations and who had given her away at her wedding?

How could *this* be the man who had been so rock-solid all through her life... the one person she knew she could count on for anything…the man who had fought so hard after his heart attack and open heart surgery…the husband who had broken down and cried and the father she had comforted when his wife—her mother—died?

And now, here they were.

She was sitting at his bedside the same way he had kept vigil at his wife's bedside through all those horrible, horrible months.

She wondered if, as her father watched his cancer-ridden wife die by inches, he had ever entertained some of the same thoughts she was having now. She wished she dared to ask him, but she was afraid of what he might say.

Had he wished…had he *prayed* as she did now that Death would come swiftly and mercifully to end his suffering?

Did he have similarly conflicted thoughts, wondering and impatiently waiting to begin living a new life without the crushing responsibilities of being an around-the-clock caregiver?

Her circumstances were completely different from his, of course. Her father had chosen to live in The Cove, and even though he—like anyone else who hadn't been born here—had never been and would never be fully accepted by the locals, he had chosen to stay here. He had liked it here. Acceptance hadn't mattered to him like it did to her. He'd had his wife…for a while.

"And all I want to do is get the hell out," Julia whispered as she stared down at her father's pale, expressionless face. She slid her hand across the sheets and clasped his hand in hers. It felt boneless…as light as a bird. She was sickened by how cool and lifeless it felt.

She twisted with guilt.

Now that she was face to face with her father's mortality and, by extension, her own, all she could think about was her own liberation, how frightening it was, now that it was apparently so imminent. The *only* thing holding her back was Ben.

She had never admitted it to anyone, Ben most of all, but as little or as much as she knew what love was, she was positive she loved Ben. She hoped he loved her. And as much as she wanted to make a new life with him, she wanted more than anything to do it someplace other than The Cove. With whatever money she would inherit from her father, she and Ben would be free to go anywhere he wanted and start over.

Anywhere but here.

But she couldn't deny how tightly Ben was tied to this town. No matter what he said about wanting to get out, a big part of him belonged to The Cove. The ocean and the town were in his marrow. He was as much a part of this town as she wasn't. Even if they got married and stayed, she would never be accepted as a *Cove-ah*. And worse than all of that, his erratic behavior…his drinking binges and rapid mood swings were all indications of PTSD. She'd researched it a bit on the Internet and learned that people who had it tended to be in denial about it, and that recovery was long and slow, and there was never a guarantee.

Did she love him enough to trade taking care of her father to become a caregiver for Ben?

Staring blankly at her father, she thought about how she never would have met Ben and fallen in love with him if she hadn't moved to town to help him out after his first heart attack.

And now, here he was…dying.

The prognosis was worse than bad. If her father ever regained consciousness—and that was increasingly unlikely—the doctors at the hospital would have to perform batteries of tests to determine the full extent of the damage. At this point, it was obvious the damage was severe and extensive. Her father would be lucky if he ever spoke or moved again.

"What do you want me to do, Dad?" she asked, leaning forward and bringing her mouth close to his ear. The heat of her breath rebounded from his face. Tears gathered in her eyes as she squeezed his hand more tightly. The bones beneath the skin felt as fragile as glass tubes.

She got no response…of any kind. As far as she could tell, nothing even changed on any of the monitors. Everything kept on beeping and clicking with monotonous, infuriating regularity.

She sniffed and wiped her eyes with her free hand, all the while staring at her father. Her mind filled with exhortations about fighting back hard because she loved him and needed him in her life… about how he had to hang in there because life—in spite of all of its pain and suffering—is always worth clinging to. But she was afraid if she opened her mouth now, she would scream at him that he had to accept that his time had come.

"It…it's all right to let go now, Dad," she said in a forced whisper into the cup of his ear. Strands of white hair like wire protruded from the inside of his ear. "You've lived a good, long life. You've been a loving, caring husband and father. You worked hard your whole life, and you provided well for you family. You done good."

Wracked by a wave of guilt and grief, Julia let go of his hand and leaned back in her chair. Her throat filled with a sour taste that almost made her gag as she cried.

"Please, Dad…please…let go. It's all right to let go."

She wanted to say more. She wanted to tell him that as painful as it was for him to lose his life and for her to lose him, it would be much worse if he clung to it too hard now. If he let go, he would be freed from a life that honestly might not be worth living…and it would most certainly deliver her from weeks or months or years of taking care of him while she put the remainder of *her* life on hold.

It was a selfish thought, she knew, but it was there nonetheless.

Filled with misery, she let her gaze shift around the hospital room, but her eyes kept coming back to rest on the array of plugs in the wall outlets and the surge protector that rested on the floor next to the bed.

She shivered when a terrible thought occurred to her.

The doctors hadn't discussed with her whether or not she wanted to take him off life support. She assumed it wasn't time yet. They had to observe and test his reactions—or lack thereof—before they made a final determination.

But what if she did it?

What if she pulled the plug?

"No! God Almighty! *Stop* it!"

She covered her face with both hands and sobbed, ashamed and horrified that she would ever think such thoughts.

"You all right there?"

The voice, speaking suddenly behind her, startled her, and she jumped and looked around to see a nurse, standing in the doorway.

"I'm sorry…I didn't hear you come in," Julia said, flustered and concerned that the woman might have heard her speaking and divined what she had been considering.

The nurse—the nametag above the pocket on her floral hospital smock read *JOYCE BARNES*—moved closer to the bed. She was young—probably in her late twenties or early thirties. Her face and lips were thin and pale, but her smile was genuine. Julia thought the woman could use a little makeup. She looked as though she didn't get to see much sunlight, maybe because of working such long hours.

"Do you think.... Can they hear us?" Julia asked, indicating her father with a solemn nod of her head.

Joyce shrugged.

"I dunno," she said. "Different people have different ideas, but I'm pretty sure they can."

"Really?"

Joyce nodded.

"But when I talk to him...when I say things that I *know* would get a reaction from him, there's...nothing. His breathing doesn't change, and none of the monitors flicker or anything."

Joyce came over to the side of the bed opposite Julia and, folding her arms across her ample chest, looked down at Frank Capozza. Her face was lit with a beatific smile. Julia thought if her father opened his eyes right now, he might think she was an angel come to take him to Heaven.

And that wouldn't be such a bad thing, would it?

"Whether or not they can hear us," Joyce said, "I think it's nice to say positive things so they maybe can hear our voices and know someone who loves 'em is right here with 'em. I think it helps get them through."

A blade of guilt slid between Julia's ribs when she thought that here she was thinking—*and telling*—her father that it was time for him to leave...time for him to *die.*

Why can't I think only positive, loving thoughts? she wondered, but she knew the answer—Because she was only human.

Joyce did what she had to do, recording the vitals and making sure her patient was comfortable. Then she turned to leave. Before she went out the door, though, she looked back at Julia with concern and compassion in her eyes.

"You've been here quite a while," she said. "If you need a break or something...I'm sure nothing's gonna happen if you take a little time for yourself."

"I'm all right," Julia said without even considering the suggestion. She felt duty-bound to stay right where she was...maybe not until the dire end, if that was coming sooner rather than later, but certainly until she got some more answers and a better understanding of what might happen.

"Can I get you some coffee or tea, then...maybe some water?"

"Water would be nice," Julia replied, realizing how dry her throat was, probably from the air-conditioning.

Joyce nodded and left the room, closing the door quietly behind her. Once again, Julia was left alone with her thoughts and her fears. She took a deep breath and closed her eyes so tightly they squeezed out thin trickles of tears as she leaned close to him and whispered, "Let go or stay, Dad. It's okay…I love you no matter what."

"This is complete and total *bullshit,*" Ben said. "There's no goddamned reason why we have to do this."

"Yeah there is," Pete said. "Pops puked all over the living room and passed out on the sofa, and if we don't do this, The Crowbar will have his ass in a fuckin' sling. 'Sides, it was *your* idea, as I recall."

In the wheelhouse, Pete was busily preparing to start up the *Abby-Rose.* He all but ignored Ben, who was sure Pete could hear him even above all of his slamming and banging around. His brother's silence only served to make him all the angrier. He was tempted to haul off and punch him if only to get his attention.

Pete busied himself fiddling with the boat's electronics, but all he was getting was a wash of static. The GPS screen was still dead.

"Fuckin' piece of shit," Pete kept muttering to himself as he twisted more dials but got no better results. Finally, he shut the system off and said, "We'll have to wing it…do it old school."

Ben tried not to react, but he couldn't help himself. It was one thing to leave Julia alone after such a bitch of a day, but there was no way he was heading out to sea at night without the navigation equipment in working order.

He stared at the dock and the ramp leading up to the wharf, imagining striding up there and leaving his brother alone to do their father's dirty work. But he couldn't do it. He couldn't leave his brother stranded like that. The sense of family obligation was too strong.

"A fucked GPS and radio'll give us a good excuse if we bump into the Coast Guard again," Pete said.

"I thought you already tried that with them."

Pete said nothing, but he turned the ignition. The boat's engine started up with a low, steady grumble. Water boiled up from the stern as threads of exhaust rose into the air.

"Cast off," Pete called out to Ben over his shoulder.

For the longest time, Ben didn't move. He simply stood there, his arms folded across his chest as he glared at Pete, wondering who the hell he thought he was, trying to take over Capt'n Wally's role. It was galling that his little brother would try to boss him around like that, shouting out commands like he was a damned rookie deckhand. If anything, he—Ben—should be piloting the boat tonight, but he had to acknowledge that Pete probably was better at it than he was. It had been too long a time since Ben had piloted a boat. For the longest time, he hoped he would never have to get onto a boat again.

"Fuckin' bullshit, is what it is" Ben grumbled as he finally relented and walked over to the thwarts. He quickly undid the knotted ropes from the cleats and dropped the coils onto the deck. He pulled the buffers in and, reaching across the gunwales, pushed off. The motion was wasted, though, because Pete engaged the engine and started slowly backing away from the floating dock. The boat heaved up and down on the gentle swells, and the rumbling engine echoed like rolling thunder from the granite block walls that lined the inner harbor.

As Pete brought the boat around, moving forward, Ben took a moment to look around. The town was Maine postcard beautiful, with lights on in many houses, and the dark hump of the mainland rising against the starry sky, topped by the Congregational Church steeple. Starlight and the streetlights lining the road shimmered like orange snakes on the oily, black water. The seas were calm, and a warm breeze redolent of salt and seaweed wafted inland.

It was a gorgeous night for a cruise. At least they had that going for them. If the Coast Guard spotted them and approached, they could always say they were out for a late-night cruise...a little male bonding between brothers who hadn't seen each other in a long time.

Ben snorted at that thought and watched the shore slide quietly by as Pete skillfully guided the boat through the maze of anchored boats and buoys that bobbed in their wake. Before long, they rounded the headlands and were heading out to sea. Pete gave the engine a goose, and soon they were skimming across the water, the waves choppier now, slapping against the hull. In case someone was watching from the shore and got suspicious of what they were up to, Pete took an easterly bearing. Once they were well out of sight, he would turn southeast and head out to The Nephews for the pickup.

Ben had to admit that he'd never liked being out on the ocean—especially at night. The sea simply wasn't in his blood the way it was with his father and Pete. He had always assumed that a large part of his distaste for the ocean was his way of rejecting his father and his father's way of life. Since high school, he'd been determined not to end up doing the same things his father did. After being overseas for four years, he had come back to The Cove, but he still wanted to get out...somehow. He kept telling himself he was simply taking his time trying to figure out what to do next; but with each passing day, he felt more and more like The Cove was doing its damndest to keep him here. And on a night like this, looking at the town as it rapidly receded, he had to admit that it wasn't such a bad place to end up.

The brothers barely spoke. They couldn't hear each other, anyway, above the sound of the engine. Pete piloted the boat further out to sea, picking up speed. For his part, Ben had nothing to say. He was still thinking about what Julia had told him...about how Pete had been after her. He wanted to ask Pete about it if only to tell him that he never meant to hurt him, but Pete was more sullen than usual, if that were possible. Ben decided not to bring it up now. They had a job to do.

Without any illumination from the dead navigational equipment, his brother was no more than a silhouette etched sharply against the night. He was motionless as he stared straight ahead out the wheelhouse's front window. He could have been a statue. It was impossible to know without asking, but Ben was sure Pete was nervous and not admitting it. He might be worried about getting stopped by the Coast Guard after making the pick-up, but Ben suspected that something else was bugging his brother. He wished he didn't feel so closed out.

"So," he said, moving into the wheelhouse and standing next to Pete.

Pete didn't reply. He didn't even bother to glance at him.

Ben told himself to keep what he was thinking to himself, but he knew himself well enough to know he wasn't going to be able to. He found it difficult to admit—even to himself—that he was in love with Julia. The power of such emotions confused and frightened him. He wondered if or how much he could trust her. A woman who would screw around with a married man, especially a shit-for-brains loser like Tom Marshall, might not be as honest and open as he wanted or needed. It was obvious she'd put all that behind her. It was also obvious that she loved him. He wished he knew what he was so afraid of.

Ben started pacing back and forth as the boat rocked beneath his feet. The motion kept throwing him off-balance. When they were a couple of miles from land, Pete heaved to and headed south toward The Nephews. The wind was blowing across the bow, and the waves slapped against the hull with an irritating, steady rhythm that gradually gathered strength.

Is this how it's going to be all night? Ben wondered. *Neither one of us saying a goddamned word?*

That might be the best thing, Ben decided, because he didn't like what he was thinking about his brother *or* Julia. He replaced the gaff on its holder and was about to sit down when the boat hit something so hard it threw Ben forward onto the deck. He landed hard, his knees banging the decking, sending an electric shock up his hips.

The boat's engine kicked and started whining with a high-pitched wail, but the sound was all but lost beneath the explosive sounds of wooden beams snapping and the hull ripping apart. The night suddenly collapsed on top of them. The world began to spin madly out of control.

"What the—" Ben shouted, scrambling to get back onto his feet.

His brother was sagging as he held onto the wheel. His feet kept slipping out from under him like he was trying to stand on a tilting sheet of ice.

"Son of a *bitch!"* Pete shouted, but his voice was lost beneath the sound of fiberglass snapping like a string of firecrackers going off inside Ben's head.

Before Ben could react, the *Abby-Rose* heaved hard to port. Lobster traps and other gear clattered across the deck and banged against Ben. Something pinned his leg down as most of the equipment spilled over the side, hitting the water with loud splashing sounds.

The world didn't right itself. It kept tilting crazily to one side until the sky was where the ocean should be. In a terrifying instant, a deafeningly loud *whooshing* sound filled the night as a huge wave swept Ben overboard.

He hit the water hard on his left side. The cold slap of the wave stung his face. Then, before he could react, he was sinking like a stone into the pitch-black ocean.

SEVENTEEN

All the King's Men

The house was dark as Louise pulled into the driveway. Tom's car wasn't there, so she was confident he wasn't home, but she had waited until dark just to be certain. There was a slim chance he'd left his car off at the garage for some repairs or something, and she wanted to make sure there were no lights on in the house before she went in.

Holding her breath, she counted to ten. Her hands clenched the steering wheel as she studied the darkened house. It felt weird to think that she used to live here. It already seemed so long ago, a distant part of her life even though she'd been married to Tom less than a year. Looking up, she wouldn't have been surprised to see herself staring out from the upstairs window of her old bedroom… a ghost, trapped there forever.

But that was exactly what she was trying to prevent.

She wasn't about to let Tom or anyone else run her life. This was still her house, too, damnit! Unless or until they got divorced, she had as much legal right to be here as Tom did. It might have been smarter to wait until one or both of her brothers were available to come with her to get the rest of her things, but she was determined to face this alone. She had to prove how tough she was, if only to herself.

Finally, she killed the engine, pulled the key from the ignition, opened the car door, and stepped out. The night was quiet and warm. A faint breeze was blowing in off the ocean. She took a quick breath, smelling the distant salt marsh. The tide was definitely out. Her feet crunched on the gravel as she started up the driveway to the kitchen door. She hoped Tom hadn't changed the locks, but if he had, she was prepared to break a window to let herself in.

The bastard deserves everything bad that ever happens to him, she thought as she stood on the doorstep and fiddled with her key ring until she found the right key. When she did, she held her breath again for a count of ten before slipping it into the lock and turning it.

After a moment of resistance, a faint *click* sounded as the bolt turned.

She let her breath out in a long, slow whistle and wiped the sheen of sweat from her forehead.

"I hope your dick dries up and falls off, you fuckin' warthog," she whispered as she pushed the door open and entered the kitchen.

The place was a mess. Teetering stacks of dirty dishes and pans were piled high in and around the sink. The smell of rotting food and trash was almost enough to make her gag. She resisted the urge to turn on the overhead light. There was no telling when Tom might show up, and if he caught her snooping around like this, he very well might follow through on his threat to shoot her.

Besides, she knew her way around the house well enough without lights. She wouldn't need them until she got upstairs and started collecting the few things of hers she wanted to bring home.

The stairs creaked with every step, setting her teeth on edge. Her eyes darted from side to side. She felt like an intruder in her own home. Moving about in the darkness, once again she found it all too easy to imagine that she was a ghost come back to haunt the place where she had once lived. The sense of unreality was so powerful it almost overwhelmed her until she got to their bedroom. Once there, after drawing the shades, she turned on a single bedside light.

Like the kitchen, the bedroom was a shambles. The bed hadn't been made in days, and dirty laundry was strewn all around. She found a pair of her panties on the floor by the window and guessed they must have fallen there when Tom had been throwing her stuff through the screen. She put the rest of her clothes and some family photos and mementos into a couple of shopping bags she'd brought along, and slipped her jewelry into her pockets.

Get what you came for and get the hell out, she cautioned herself, but she couldn't stop from snooping around a little. She opened the top drawer on Tom's bureau and started rifling around, pawing through his socks and underwear. She considered throwing everything onto the floor along with the dirty clothes but decided not to.

He probably wouldn't notice, anyway.

When she tried to open the second bureau drawer, it was stuck. She wiggled it back and forth, and tugged on it until, finally, she pulled back so hard it came flying out of the bureau. The drawer landed on the floor, clipping her left ankle hard enough to make her cry out. Trying to shake off the pain, she looked down. That's when she noticed a thick manila envelope that had dropped onto the floor. It was held shut by a thick rubber band. Curious, she reached down and picked it up, not knowing or even suspecting what it was until she removed the elastic, undid the metal clasp, and opened it.

"Holy fuckin' shit," she whispered.

Her eyes bulged from their sockets when she saw the contents of the envelope. She looked around as if suspecting someone was watching her.

"You son-of-a-bitch," she said, smiling as she hefted the thick stack of money. The top bill was a hundred dollar bill. She rifled the stack quickly, making sure they were all hundreds. Her smile widened, and her breath caught in her chest. Then, moving fast, she closed the envelope and wrapped the rubber band around it. She looked around again, keenly aware of her heart hammering hard in her chest.

"Sweet Mother of Jesus," she whispered.

Her head snapped around, and she fully expected to see Tom standing in the doorway, glowering at her with his revolver aimed right at her head. She folded the envelope up and stuck it into the waistband of her jeans, un-tucking her blouse to cover it.

She hadn't counted how much there was, but it was a lot, no doubt. She wondered why Tom had hidden it in his bureau, but it didn't take her long to figure it out.

He wasn't just leaving *her.*

He was planning on leaving town.

He must have come by this money illegally, and she'd be damned if she was going to let him keep it.

She set about picking up the clothes she had scattered around the room and put the drawer back, reassuring herself that everything looked like it had when she'd first come in. Ultimately, it didn't matter because Tom wasn't the most observant guy on the planet. Her breath came in thin gulps. A metallic taste filled her throat, making her wince as she gripped the shopping bags she had filled and snapped off the bedroom light. She closed the door—*It had been closed when she came upstairs, right?*—and carried her booty downstairs.

When she reached the foot of the stairs, she resisted the urge to run out the door and get the hell gone. She slowly, carefully locked the kitchen door behind her and then walked across the lawn to her car. She was fearful that—*any second now*—headlights would appear on the road and—*just her luck*—turn into the driveway, blocking her, but she made it.

She was panting heavily, her armpits damp with sweat as she opened the passenger's door, threw the bags of clothes onto the front seat, and then walked around the car to get in the driver's side. She was hyperventilating. Her hands were tingling as she shoved the key into the ignition, convinced her car wasn't going to start, and she'd be stranded here.

But the engine turned over easily and ran with a low, reassuring rumble. She hardly breathed as she shifted into gear and did a three-point turn to back around. Just as she shifted into *drive,* her cell phone chirped. Wound as tight as she was, she jumped and let out a piercing scream.

Her hands shook out of control as she twisted to one side and fished the cell phone from her jeans pocket. Some of the jewelry she had taken spilled onto the car seat, but she didn't care as she flipped open her phone and looked at the caller ID. The phone rang a second time.

"Fuck!"

It was Tom.

Cold sweat broke out across her forehead as she wondered whether or not to answer.

Was he close by?

Was he watching her now?

Did he have his gun aimed at her head, ready to blow her the fuck away?

Louise craned around and looked, but she didn't see anything.

The phone rang a third time. She shifted the car into *park* and, sucking in a breath, pressed the green *answer* button on her phone.

"Hu'lo?" she said, trying hard to sound perfectly normal.

"Hey, Lou."

It was Tom, all right.

"I wasn't sure you'd answer if you knew I was calling."

Immense relief flooded her. If he was out there in the darkness, watching her, he wouldn't have responded like that.

"What d'yah want?" she asked, feeling braver and beginning to think she actually might get away with this.

"I…umm, I kinda need your help," Tom said. For the first time, she noticed the note of contrition in his voice.

Louise stuffed back a burst of laughter and shook her head, wishing he *was* standing right in front of her so she could spit into his face.

"Really?" she said, not believing what she was hearing.

"Yeah, uhh, this is serious, Lou. I…I'm in a bit of a jam."

Louise was tempted to say: *Good…now go blow it out your ass,* but she held back. She had just stolen a pile of money from him. The least she could do was hear him out.

"What's the problem?" she asked, forcing herself to sound patient and understanding even though she wanted to laugh out loud at him.

"I—I've been shot," Tom said.

"What?"

Not that she cared all that much, but she couldn't help but react. Now her curiosity was piqued.

"Wha—what happened?"

"Long story," Tom said. "I was in a…in a shootout with some drug dealers."

"You've got to be kidding," she said.

Her free hand drifted to the envelope of money stuffed into her waistband. If she played along with him now, she realized, he'd be less likely to suspect her when he found out the envelope of money was missing.

"Yeah…I took a slug in the shoulder and one in the leg. Nothing life-threatening, I don't think. At least that's what the doctors tell me, but I—" He heaved a shuddering sigh after his voice choked off.

"You *what?*" Louise asked, forcing herself to sound concerned.

"It looks like I...I might have shot and killed a DEA agent."

"Jesus, Tom."

"I'm gonna need a lawyer."

His words stunned her. This was so surreal it couldn't really be happening.

"Look," Tom said, his voice wavering. He sounded like he was trying not to cry. "I...I know you have every reason to tell me to go fuck myself."

Louise bit her tongue, thinking, *You got that right.*

"But...I'm askin' you...I'm *beggin'* you to *please* come to the hospital and help me out? I don't know what else to do. There—there's something I have to talk to you about, and I...I don't want to talk about it over the phone."

I'm sure you don't, she thought, barely repressing a grin because she knew exactly what he was talking about.

"Umm—ahh...yeah," she finally said, hoping she sounded reasonably sympathetic. "All right. Sure. Be right there."

"Thanks, Lou. I can't tell you how much I appreciate this. 'Stand by Your Man,' right?"

"Yeah...right. I—umm, I have to run a quick errand first, and then I'll be over. Be 'bout half an hour?"

"Sure," Tom said. "I ain't goin' anywhere."

Before he could say anything else, Louise clicked her phone shut, ending the call.

For a long time, she sat there with the car running as she stared straight ahead. Her vision kept shifting in and out of focus as she stared up the rise toward the darkened house. Her pulse was racing fast in her throat, making her vision bounce with every beat. When she took a breath, the air burned her lungs like she had sipped fire.

Finally, she shifted into gear and drove away. She was thinking once she found a safe place to hide the money—someplace Tom and the cops would ever find—if Tom was in so much trouble, she had to fake it and be the dutiful, supportive wife to cover herself.

"CYA, Dad always said," she whispered. "Cover your ass."

It didn't bother her in the least that her clearest, strongest thought was that if Tom had really been in a shootout, it was too damned bad one of those bullets hadn't blown his stupid ass to Kingdom Come.

Ben was sinking down…down.

His clothes were instantly soaked through. They pulled him down like an anchor. The darkness below and around him was so dense he soon lost any sense of direction. He was suspended in a dimensionless, timeless void that was squeezing in on him.

Am I already dead? he wondered when he realized he should be panicking more than he was.

He had swallowed a mouthful of water when he'd gone overboard. Now his lungs were aching…burning for oxygen. They felt like they were ready to burst as a heavy pounding filled his head, keeping time to the thundering of his heart. His chest ached, but the pain was distant…almost like it was happening to someone else.

But a small part of him told himself he *wasn't* dead…not yet… and where there's life, there's hope. He wouldn't surrender willingly to the abyss that wanted to swallow him whole.

Not without a fight.

Struggling mightily, he kicked off his sneakers and then undid his belt and zipper. He peeled his pants down over his knees and kicked them free. They drifted away from him, fluttering like dark wings under the water. It was only after he'd let them go that he remembered his wallet and car keys were in the pockets. There was some cash in the wallet, but his first thought was what a bitch it was going to be replacing his license, other Ids, and credit cards…and his car keys…

How was he gonna drive home from the wharf…or pick up Julia…or go anywhere without his car keys?

If I survive this, he thought. He was surprised by his mental clarity in such a terrible situation, but the idea that he actually might die spurred him to action.

First, he had to get back to the surface and then…

Then what?

He was wearing a long-sleeved shirt over a t-shirt. He tore off the top shirt and let it drift away from him. For a moment before it disappeared into the dark water below, it looked and felt like a huge billowing jellyfish brushing up against him.

Trying to calm himself and knowing he would never survive if he panicked, he stopped thrashing about for a moment and just let go. All things being equal, if he didn't fight too hard, he should start rising to the surface like a cork. Craning his head back and forth, he looked for some slight glimmer of light, but the darkness was solid…all but impenetrable.

Finally, though, when he let a small amount of air escape from his mouth, the stream of silvery bubbles trailed upward. Extending both arms above his head like a diver in reverse, he gave a powerful kick with his legs while scooping his cupped hands to either side.

He shot upward, satisfied when the crushing pressure lessened.

I'm gonna make it…I'm not gonna die…not yet…I'm gonna make it, he kept telling himself until it became his mantra.

He gave several strong, deliberate kicks and powerful strokes, but he was still surprised when his face burst above the surface into the night air. He threw his head back and took in a roaring lungful of air. When he exhaled, he coughed and sputtered, choking on the seawater that splashed into his mouth and nose.

The water was freezing cold, and he was shivering wildly as he tread water to keep his head above the surface while he looked around.

The ocean was still rough, and strewn all about was the wreckage of what had once been the *Abby-Rose.* Dark tangles of flotsam bobbed in the water near him, spreading out and around him in a widening arc. To his horror, there was no sign of his brother.

"Pete!" he called out, his voice ragged and strained, barely audible above the sloshing waves.

He splashed around frantically, trying to see in all directions at once, but the night was dark and close. With his head at water level, he couldn't see very far. To his left was the dark hulk of his father's lobster boat, at least what was left of it. The boat was lying keel up, its bottom glistening with a silver patina in the starlight.

"Jesus, Pete! Where the hell are you?"

His voice sounded flat and pitifully weak in the vast, swelling expanse of the ocean.

Ben realized the boat must have hit a submerged rock or reef that his brother either hadn't seen or didn't know about. He clenched his teeth in frustration to keep them from chattering. He recalled how his father bragged about how he knew the ocean so well he didn't need any damned electronics to navigate. Obviously Pete didn't have Pops' instincts or knowledge because here they were, in deep shit.

"Where the hell are you?" he shouted as he kept treading water, trying to distinguish if any of the dark objects floating in the water around him were his brother's corpse. A seat cushion was nearby, so he swam over to it and grabbed it. This provided enough buoyancy to give him his first ray of genuine hope that he might actually survive the night.

But where was Pete?

Had he already gone under?

He might have been knocked unconscious by the impact and plummeted straight to the bottom.

Or he might be clinging to some piece of wreckage out of sight, too dazed to answer Ben.

"For Christ's sake! Answer me!"

His only reply was the sound of seawater slapping against his face and the debris. Finally, convinced that his brother had gone down and—unlike him—had not made it up to the surface, he decided he had to do what was necessary so he, at least, would survive. Grief swelled inside him as he leaned forward on the seat cushion and started kicking toward the remains of his father's lobster boat.

The chill of the water bit bone deep, and no matter how much he tried to stop them, his teeth kept chattering wildly. His only thought was, *Goddamn it…this ain't over yet,* but a hollow feeling deep in his chest told him that for Pete, at least, it probably *was* all over.

"I understand completely this is a very difficult decision to make," Dr. Robbins said. His voice was mild; his expression, understanding.

Julia sniffed and wiped her eyes with the palms of her hands. Dr. Robbins snapped a few tissues from the dispenser on his desk and handed them to her. She took them and wondered how many times he had sat there like this at that desk and told family members and relatives of patients what he had just told her. He was so young, probably not many.

"I…" Her voice was as ragged as tearing old cloth. "It's so…so hard to…I don't know if I can do it."

"I understand completely," Dr. Robbins said, and Julia began to suspect this was his safety phrase.

I understand completely.

It was something he had to keep repeating perhaps to distance himself from the raw emotions involved in such life and death decisions.

She leaned her head back and stared blankly up at the ceiling as thoughts and memories flashed through her mind. Every image… every memory, both good and bad, of her father unspooled across her mind's eye. Bitter arguments, slammed doors, warm hugs, goodnight kisses, shared laughter...

But now her father was as good as dead. Dr. Robbins had presented her with the situation as he saw it, and he had told her there was little to no hope her father would ever recover even minimal brain functions.

He's already gone, she kept thinking as if repetition would make it any less true or any less painful.

"You don't have to decide this instant," Dr. Robbins said. "If there are other family members or close friends you wish to consult, perhaps a minister or priest, I understand completely."

There it is again. "I understand completely!" Julia thought, but she tried to squash down any bitterness. He was simply doing his job, and that was to advise her on all the medical options her father had.

No…my father doesn't have any options…. He's gone…as good as dead already…I have to choose for him.

She was awed by the terrible responsibility of holding someone else's life in her hands…someone she loved and cherished. She twisted with guilt, knowing that only an hour ago, she had been sitting in her father's hospital room, fantasizing about pulling the plug on his life support. How many people had gone through what she was going through now? Was it normal?

She found that she was shaking her head from side to side, and she didn't even care whether or not Dr. Robbins knew what she was indicating. She was lost inside her own head, feeling sorry for herself and being pulled steadily deeper and deeper into a dark, bottomless abyss.

Dr. Robbins remained perfectly silent. She noticed that he didn't fiddle with pens or paperclips on his desk or make a move to get up and leave the office in order to give her some time alone to decide.

Thank *God* he didn't say *I understand completely* again, she thought.

If he did, Julia was sure she would start screaming at him that *No!* He *didn't* understand completely...he could *never* understand completely. Unless or until he went through something like this for himself, he didn't even understand *partially*.

"I—I'm not sure I can do it...sign the papers, I mean." Her voice was so low it vibrated wetly, like she was clearing her throat.

Dr. Robbins looked at her with the deepest sympathy in his dark eyes, and she couldn't help but feel guilty. She began to reevaluate her earlier judgment of him. Maybe he *did* know a little more about human suffering than he was letting on.

"Beg pardon?" he said as he leaned forward and steepled his hands in front of his face, his elbows resting on the desk in front of him.

Julia wiped her eyes with the tissues he had given her. Already they were sodden and couldn't soak up all of her tears.

"I said I'm not sure I can sign the papers just yet...but that I...I'm afraid I'll have to."

She stared at the doctor, earnestly wishing he would say or do something—*anything*—that would relieve her of this horrible decision. She felt overwhelmed by the awful responsibility, but the neutral expression on the doctor's face told her this was all her decision.

"There really is no hope, is there?" she said huskily.

Dr. Robbins didn't hesitate for a moment. He lowered his eyes and shook his head from side to side.

"For all its benefits of medical science—like all the king's horses and all the king's men—we still can't put Humpty Dumpty back together again."

Oh, so now we're all Humpty Dumpty, she thought feeling a flash of anger that quickly subsided. It wasn't Dr. Robbins' fault she was sitting here now.

"I guess I have to do it then," she finally said. She sat up a little straighter in the chair and squared her shoulders. "Do you have the papers?"

Dr. Robbins nodded and reached for a file to one side of the desk. He opened it and took out a single sheet of paper.

"You should read this waiver before you sign," he said as he slid it across the desk toward her. Blinking back more tears, Julia looked around until she noticed the container holding a handful of pens. She took one, clicked it so the point came out, and scanned the paper, only looking for the line where she was to sign.

The legal technicalities didn't matter.

All she wanted was for it to be over and done with as quickly as possible so she could begin to grieve. She clasped the pen so tightly her hand went numb with pins 'n needles, but she shook it back to life as she made a pretense of reading. She knew there were all sorts of legal disclaimers, but she didn't care. Narrowing her eyes so she could barely see what she was doing, she signed her name and then dated it.

"Goodbye, Dad," she whispered, speaking so softly she hoped Dr. Robbins didn't hear her.

Louise found it difficult to keep a straight face when, after a quick search by the policeman stationed outside the hospital room door, she entered Tom's room. He was sitting up in bed, his face ashen. Dark circles ringed his eyes, giving him a raccoon look. All the cockiness and swagger was gone. It had been replaced by a tight, pinched look…as if he had a wedge of lemon in his mouth.

"You came," Tom said feebly, and Louise nodded. He looked like Hell had hit him and run.

"You thought I wouldn't?" she said.

Her tone of voice was pleasant enough, but she shot him a look that all but said: *If you were on fire, you'd be lucky if I crossed the street to piss on you.*

"I…uhh…like your haircut," Tom said. Louise had been careful to style her hair and reapply the makeup exactly the way Lina had showed her. She knew she looked good. She also knew Tom hated it.

"So what the hell happened?" she asked.

A police officer was sitting in an easy chair in the corner of the room by the window. Tom pursed his lips and nodded in the cop's direction, indicating that he wasn't able to talk freely in the man's presence.

Louise glanced at the cop, who appeared to be fully engaged reading an old copy of *People* magazine. She didn't know him from around town and wondered if he'd been brought in from out of town because of the seriousness of Tom's situation. She cleared her throat and said to him, "Excuse me."

The cop appeared a bit bewildered as he looked up. His eyebrows were raised in silent question. He was young—no older than twenty-five, tops—but he didn't have any of that earnest new cop *bravado* Tom had displayed when he first joined the force.

"Would you mind if I talked privately with my husband for a few minutes?"

The cop looked ceiling-ward and considered the request, but only for a moment. He shook his head *no* and said, "My orders are to stay with him until I'm relieved."

Louise smiled to herself, thinking she should ask him what he would do if he needed to relieve himself, but she knew she wouldn't get anywhere by being flip.

"It's only for a few seconds," she said with a hint of sultry undertone in her voice. "I mean—think about it. We're up on the third floor. He's been shot in the leg and is hooked up with IVs and whatever. I doubt he's gonna run. Where's he gonna go?"

The cop surveyed the room as if noticing it for the first time. Then he closed the magazine, dropped in onto the table next to the chair, and stood up. His leather gun belt creaked like an old saddle.

"I guess it'll be all right then," he said, and he walked slowly out the door, easing it shut behind him.

"Jesus Christ, Lou," Tom said, the instant he was gone.

Against her better judgment, Louise almost felt a spark of sympathy for Tom. He was, after all, still her husband; and she had loved him…at least once upon a time. But she had been through enough, and she knew the true content of his character.

"So tell me…" she said.

She made a point of not approaching the bed and getting too close to him or making any gestures that he might interpret as loving or even friendly. If she wanted to get away with what she intended to pull off, she had to keep up the façade and play the dutiful, concerned wife.

"I got shot…and it looks like I killed two people."

Louise's body went cold at his words. She had no idea how to respond.

"I took a bullet in the shoulder—" He raised his bandaged right arm as if performing a "Show and Tell" in grade school. "And in the left leg…in the thigh just above the knee. A fragment blew out my kneecap."

"Jesus, you *killed* someone?" Louise was still trying to absorb that simple fact while also thinking it was too bad he hadn't died, too. If he had, she'd be free and clear to do whatever she wanted with the money she'd found.

"Two guys," Tom said.

Apparently misreading her reaction and taking it as sympathy for his plight, he beckoned her closer to the bed. After almost a year of conditioning, though, she shied away from him, automatically expecting him, even in his present condition, to lash out at her.

"Come on," he said, seeing her hesitation. He patted the side of the bed. "I…since all of this went down, I've realized some things… lots of things"

I'll bet, Louise thought.

Tom kept patting the side of the bed, looking almost angry that she wasn't coming over to sit close to him. Taking a shallow breath, her body tense and ready to respond if he made the slightest move to hurt her, she lowered herself onto the edge of the bed, pressing her clasped hands tightly between her legs.

"One thing—I realized," Tom said, "is that I…that I haven't been treating you very good."

No shit, Louise wanted to say but didn't. Instead, she stared straight ahead at the blank beige wall. For a long time, the only sounds were the steady clicking on his IV feed and the soft, hissing sound coming from his oxygen tube.

"So who did you kill?" she asked, finally working up the nerve to speak.

"Tony Gillette. You know Tony?"

"Only by reputation."

"He was a small time punk-ass dealer from Darmiscotta who deserved it, s'far as I can see."

"You said two guys. Who else?"

Tom winced like he'd bitten the inside of his cheek. His face went a shade or two paler.

"Yeah, here's where it gets kinda fucked up…Gillette was with a DEA guy…guy named Jerry Lincoln. I went to meet them…I've been working on setting up this sting operation, and it went to shit."

"Jesus Christ, Tom," Louise said as the full impact of what he was telling her hit home. This wasn't a joke, and no matter how she looked at it, she knew Tom was in a world of trouble.

Tom winced and let out a small yelp of pain when he straightened up and leaned forward. His eyes were watery and bloodshot. His cheeks were lined with broken blood vessels.

"This is why you gotta help me, Lou," he said, his voice a desperate whisper.

Louise sat motionless, her hands cold, her gaze fixed on the floor. Then she started shaking her head from side to side, already denying what she knew he was about to say.

"There's some—"

He leaned forward and reached out with his left hand, trying to touch her, but Louise—braced for a slap—flinched and then quickly shifted out of reach.

"It's not like that," Tom said with a little boy pleading in his voice. "Not any more. I…I realized how shitty I've been treating you, but that's all gonna change from now on. I promise."

Louise looked at him, unable to keep her upper lip from curling into a sneer.

"I know I haven't treated you good. But I'm gonna change. I promise. I already have changed. And I…I'm gonna need you… your help because of all the shit that's gonna come down on me because of what happened."

Louise didn't say a word.

"I'm gonna be in a world of legal trouble, and it's gonna be expensive."

"I can't help you there," she said, but thinking about the money she had found in his bureau made her smile inwardly.

"Yes, you can." Tom tried again to reach out and touch her, but Louise was keeping her distance. She knew what he might do. She could see the monster, still lurking behind this thin mask of reconciliation and pretended love.

"In the bedroom…in my bureau." He looked around the room as though expecting to see someone lurking nearby, listening. "Taped to the back of the second drawer…There's a manila envelope."

"A manila envelope?"

Louise bit down on her lower lip to keep from smiling as she thought about what she had already done with that envelope. Earlier that evening, when she was at her father's house, she had fretted about what to do with the cash she had found. Any place she thought of to hide it was too obvious. When the cops came snooping around—which was inevitable—they'd be certain to find it if she stashed it anywhere in the house. The problem was, she didn't dare hide it anywhere outside the house, either. She was sure the police had equipment that would find it no matter where she hid it...or maybe they had money-sniffing dogs...or the house was already under surveillance.

So what to do? What to do?

And then it had hit her.

She wasn't sure if it was something she had seen on a cop show when she was a kid or if it was simply a stroke of genius on her part.

She had folded the envelope over into as small a package as she could make and then wrapped it in several layers of Saran Wrap. Then she had gotten the jar of mayonnaise from the refrigerator. It was one of those huge family-sized jars her father was always buying at Sam's Club to save money, even though he seldom if ever made himself a sandwich. She scooped out enough of the contents to make a cavity large enough to hold the envelope, and then she refilled the mayonnaise jar and smoothed it over. After making sure the edges of the envelope weren't visible, she washed the excess mayonnaise down the sink and washed her hands, making sure to clean under her fingernails.

She had put the jar back into the refrigerator, making sure it was way back on the bottom shelf where no one would notice it. She felt secure that it would be safe there for a while, at least until this shit-storm with Tom blew over.

"I've been—umm, saving up some money for us. You know—for a rainy day. And...well, this sure as shit constitutes a rainy fucking day."

"And you want me to do—what?" Louise prayed that what she was thinking didn't show on her face.

"You gotta get that money and hide it somewheres," Tom said, lowering his voice. "I'm gonna have legal bills up the ass if I'm gonna stay out of jail."

Louise was silent for a long moment. What galled her most was thinking how stump-stupid Tom must think she was.

After all the terrible things he had said and done to her, did he *really* think she'd come running to help him?

She wished to God she dared to tell him as much, but for now, she had to act the devoted, if not loving, wife.

She twisted her hands in her lap, her mind churning fast as she tried to think this through without giving herself away. Then a brilliant idea, as good as the mayonnaise jar, came to her.

"The cops already showed up at the house this morning."

"What?" Tom jerked forward and then winced with pain.

"Yeah. They were at the house this morning with a search warrant."

"You have got to be shitting me!"

Tom stared at her for a moment, and then his expression collapsed. Moaning, he sagged back on the bed. He looked like an inflatable toy that had a slow leak. His eyes went glassy; his face was sheet-white.

"I'm fucked," he said, sounding totally defeated.

Louise nodded and said, "Uh-huh. They came by the house. I didn't know what to do, like, if I should call a lawyer or whatever, but I let them in and then went back to my father's house. I…I had no idea what they were doing there."

"Whoa, wait…wait…wait." Tom's frown deepened as he raised his un-bandaged hand and shook his forefinger at her. "You were at the house? Our house?"

Louise realized she was on thin ice.

"Yeah, I—umm, I went over to…to get my jewelry," she said. "I knew you were out, and I thought it'd be safe."

Tom's face turned crimson with anger.

Louise said nothing, but she shied away from him, prepared for him to lunge out of the bed and throttle her right there and then. Even the cops outside the door wouldn't be able to help. She could yell for help all she wanted, but he'd get a few good licks in first.

But then, like a cloud passing from in front of the sun, Tom visibly relaxed. He smiled and shook his head and then sniffed with suppressed laughter.

"Yeah…sure. That's okay," he said. "Like I said—I knew I was an idiot for treating you the way I did. I was gonna ask…beg you to come back to me."

Louise didn't miss the note of insincerity in his voice. But she kept her expression neutral, her gaze fixed on her husband's face.

She had to play this all the way through. If she got lucky, this would be the last time in her life she would ever see Tom Marshall before he went to jail.

"I…" Louise began, but then she faked a wild shudder and put a hand over her mouth as though she was concerned beyond belief for his welfare. "There…there's no way of knowing what they found… if anything…I mean…how'll we know if the money's still there."

"It's *gotta* still be there! At least it was as of yesterday."

It pleased her no end to see how much Tom was panicking and trying so hard not to let it show. He started gnawing his lower lip, his eyes darting nervously from side to side.

"How will we even know if they found it?" she asked, struggling to keep the correct note of worry in her voice. "They might—Do you think they'd keep it and not even report it? And then use it for evidence against you?"

"Jesus H. Christ," Tom whispered. He was staring straight ahead at the wall behind her. It was obvious he knew he'd run out of options…and luck. She was practically bursting with demon glee.

Who was it who said, *Revenge is a dish best served cold?*

Man, did they ever get *that* wrong.

Revenge is a dish best served piping hot from the gates of Hell.

"You gotta go back there and get it," Tom said.

"I'm not sure I can even get back into the house," she said after a moment's thought. She stood up and started pacing back and forth at the foot of the bed. "You don't think the cops already have the house sealed up? They'll be watching me *and* the house, for sure."

Tom's face looked like it was etched in ivory.

"I suppose I can try…unless you don't want me to."

Tom's expression softened, but a worried tightness still pinched the skin around his eyes. She could all but smell his meanness lurking below the surface.

"It'll be wicked dangerous."

"I know," he said. "But I promise. You help me get out of this, and I'll be the husband you want me to be."

At that, Louise had had enough.

"You know what?" she said, snapping her fingers as she started backing slowly toward the door. She glanced over her shoulder and was prepared to call for help the instant he left the bed.

"What's that, Hon?"

Tom looked at her expectantly. He obviously was assuming she was going to say she'd find a way to get into the house and check if the money was still there. She could read the hope in his eyes that she was going to say that she still loved him and wanted to try to make it work between them.

"I think you're on your own here," Lou said. She was surprised by the calm, steady strength in her voice.

Tom stared at her, his mouth gaping in surprise as if he didn't believe he'd heard her correctly. He looked like she had slapped him across the face, and he visibly shriveled right there in front of her eyes. He looked like a heat-blasted plant, withering in the sun without water.

"You're not gonna fool me with your bullshit," she said in a low, controlled voice. "Never again. As soon as you get out of here, you're going straight to jail and then—" She clasped her hands in front of her chest and shook them. "And then—Oh, I pray to God that then you get convicted and sent to Warren for the rest of your miserable life. As far as I'm concerned, you can rot there."

Her stomach was knotted with tension when she turned her back on him. She expected him to pick up something close to hand and hurl it at her as she walked toward the door, but she made it to the door without incident.

As she flung the door open, she looked back at him one last time and almost laughed out loud when she saw him lying there in the hospital bed and staring at her in stunned silence. His eyes bugged from his head, and his mouth was hanging open. He was making a low sputtering sound like cold water hitting a hot stove. She thought he looked like a codfish that had been hooked and dragged up onto the deck, but he sure as shit wasn't a "keep-ah."

"Thank you," she said, nodding to the cop who was standing outside the door in the hallway. "I'm all done."

EIGHTEEN

Letting Go

The money…to hell with the money…but the IDs…that stuff is gonna be a royal pain in the ass to replace.

Ben was surprised how, with his life still very much in the balance, he could dwell on such mundane things like losing his wallet, which had sunk to the bottom of the ocean when he peeled off his pants.

He would die of exposure long before another fishing boat or the Coast Guard saw the wreck in the morning. He wasn't sure what time it was. It had to be well past midnight. No matter. It was going to be a hell of a long time before the first rays of light streaked the Eastern horizon.

Forget about the IDs and money…. His father's new boat—the *Abby-Rose*—was "a goner." It would eventually fill with seawater and sink, and—as far as he knew—his brother had already drowned. Treading water, Ben stared at the overturned hull some distance away. Either he had been thrown far on impact or else he had drifted while trying to find the surface. He thought he detected a current, pulling him away from the wreck. It took his stunned brain a long time to figure out that his best chance of survival was to stay with the boat. He sure as hell wasn't going to be able to tread water until someone showed up.

Moving stiffly, the cold penetrating his bones like nails, he started swimming toward the wreck. After a few seconds, filled with a surge to survive, he started taking strong, powerful strokes and kicking evenly. The current sweeping him away from the boat was also moving the boat toward him, so he closed the distance faster than he thought he would. Still, his muscles were burning with exhaustion by the time he got to the boat and, reaching up, slapped his hands against the stern and clung to it.

Okay…now what? he asked himself as he looked around at the debris floating around him.

Somewhere in the wreckage, there *had* to be a box of distress flares, but finding them or a life jacket would be next to impossible. Then he remembered that his father kept the flares in a closed cabinet in the wheelhouse—at least he had on all his other boats—but Ben decided that he wasn't about to dive under the boat and come up inside the overturned hull. It'd be pitch black in there, and he'd probably bang his head on something and go under again for the last time.

So what do I do now? he wondered. Hang on…and pray someone finds me…before I drown or die of hypothermia?

There didn't appear to be any other options. Even if he had a cell phone, if he hadn't already thrown it away, it would have sunk to the ocean floor with his pants. He hadn't been thinking. But he doubted he'd be able to pick up a signal this far out to sea, anyway, and the boat's radio was useless now.

A sudden loud thump from inside the boat made him jump. His first thought was that some piece of wreckage had come loose and banged against the inside of the hull. When the sound came again, though, a faint spark of hope stirred in his chest.

"Pete?" he called out, his voice a ragged croak.

Trembling and shivering deep inside from the cold, he made a fist and deliberately pounded on the hull three times. Then he paused and listened, hoping to hear his signal repeated above the steady slapping sounds of waves breaking against the boat.

His heart skipped a beat when, from underneath the boat, came three identical thumps that resonated in the night like a kettledrum.

"Pete!" he yelled, and he hit the bottom of the hull three more times.

He paused, waiting…

Then two times.

Again, the pattern repeated.

Three thumps and then two.

His brother was alive. He was in the air pocket beneath the overturned boat.

"Jesus Christ, Pete!" Ben shouted, bringing his face close to the hull and hoping his voice would transmit through the fiberglass.

In reply, his brother said something, but his voice was so

muffled Ben couldn't make out the words. It sounded like he was yelling from the bottom of a canyon. Warm tears of joy streamed down Ben's face. Without hesitation, he pushed away from the boat, tread water for a second or two until he got oriented, and then did a smooth surface dive and went under.

Darkness swallowed him immediately, but he felt and fumbled around until he found the gunwales and then pulled himself down and under and then inside the boat. He clunked his head hard on something when he broke the surface and took a breath of the air inside. The waves still slapped against the boat outside, but the sound was thin and distant.

"Mother *fucker,* Pete" he said, sputtering and panting, his arms flailing to keep him up. His voice echoed oddly in the dark, enclosed space. "Sure as shit, I thought you drowned."

"You're not that lucky," Pete replied.

Under the circumstances, Ben didn't stop to think what a strange comment that was.

"Are you stuck on something?"

Ben reached out, groping around in the darkness until his hand brushed against his brother's shoulder.

"Hell, no. I'm trying to find the goddamned flares, but damned if I can see for shit down here. My lighter don't work, 'n I figure the air won't last long, 'specially now that you're down here sucking it up."

"Get bent," Ben said. "I thought I was saving you."

Pete didn't say a word, so Ben was silent for a while until finally he made a decision.

"Forget about the flares," he said. "We gotta get our asses out of here. Someone'll see us if we can hang on 'til morning. You got any idea what time it is?"

Pete raised his arm and pressed a button on his watch. The dial glowed a faint phosphorescent blue that illuminated his features for a moment, and then the light winked out.

"A little past one," he said flatly.

"What d'yah say we get the fuck out of here?"

Pete didn't reply to that, either, but then Ben heard a loud splash as his brother dove under. A second later, Ben did the same. Swimming down perhaps deeper than was necessary so he wouldn't bump his head again, he swam until his breath burned in his lungs, and then rose to break the surface. A few feet to his left, his brother—little more than a black silhouette cut out from the night sky—was clinging to the boat as it rocked in the waves.

"Damn, that hurts!" Pete yelled.

"What?"

"I cut my hand on something." He held up his hand, but in the darkness, Ben couldn't see if there was any blood. "Salt water stings like a bastid."

"Probably good for it, though," Ben said. "It'll clean out the cut."

"Fuck you!"

"No...fuck *you*," Ben snapped back. "I'm not the *mo*-ron who ran us aground, you know."

"Goddamned nav system doesn't work for shit."

"I thought you said you knew the ocean like the back of your—"

"Shut the fuck up, 'kay? You're not helping."

"And you are?"

Both brothers were silent for a long while until Ben said, "Nice night for a swim, though, huh?" His attempt to inject a touch of humor into the situation fell flat. Pete had no response.

Why the hell hasn't Ben called?

Julia was sitting in the living room, periodically standing up and pacing back and forth in front of the fireplace before sitting back down again. When she sat, she bounced both legs up and down like a little girl who was desperate to go to the bathroom and was trying to hold it in.

He should have called by now.... Something's wrong...

She was utterly exhausted and knew she should go to bed. It had been an incredibly draining day—a day from Hell, emotionally and physically—but the house felt too quiet...too empty. Knowing that her father was no longer in it...and never would be again...filled her with a dull, aching sadness.

She had stayed at the hospital while Dr. Robbins ran through the paperwork with her, and then they removed the life support from her father. She had sat by his bedside, tears streaming from her eyes as she held her father's hand and kissed him repeatedly on the forehead and cheek as his vitals gradually slowed.

Finally, a little past one A.M., he was gone.

Shattered and shaken and riddled with guilt, she had driven home alone, thinking the whole time how desperately she needed someone to talk to.

She had called Ben's house and left a message, like he'd told her to do. She had been surprised when no one had answered.

By the time she got home, she was too exhausted to be angry. All she felt was hurt and loneliness. She couldn't stop wondering where he was. What was he doing that was so damned important he couldn't be there to comfort her?

Never in her life had she felt so utterly alone. Even in the midst of her divorce, she'd had plenty of support and advice—not always helpful, but advice nonetheless—from her parents and several close friends. Since moving to Catawamkeag Cove, she had never felt so isolated. E-mails and phones calls to and from friends back in Waterbury and around the country hadn't quite cut it. She thought she had found what she was looking for and needed in Ben Brown, but now...?

Now, she wasn't so sure.

She was on her own.

Tears gushed from her eyes, blurring her vision as she looked around the living room. It was all so empty...so devoid of life. Her father's presence lingered everywhere she looked, and she decided that, as soon as his affairs were settled, she was going to put the house up for sale and get the hell out of The Cove.

"With or without Ben Brown," she whispered as more hot tears flooded from her eyes.

She stared at her cell phone, which was lying on the coffee table where she had dropped it earlier. It irritated her that she was carrying it around like a goddamned ball and chain, waiting for Ben to call.

As if anything he said or did would help now.

She was alone in this town, and now—the aloneness was suddenly unbearable.

Galvanized by an irresistible urge to get the hell away from this place immediately, she got up from the couch and went upstairs. She knew she wasn't thinking straight, but what did it matter?

In a flurry of activity, she fetched two travel bags from the bedroom closet and began packing, moving quickly, flinging clothes and underwear into a heap that, she told herself, she would sort out later. Once she had the clothes she needed, she went to the bathroom, grabbed an armful of toiletries, and threw them in on top of one of the piles of clothes. As she worked, her grief shifted into anger. Trembling with rage, she closed the travel bags, jamming the clothes down, and zipping them shut. She didn't even care if some of the toiletries leaked out onto her clothes. She'd buy new ones once she was in Connecticut.

After she was finished packing, she dragged the travel bags downstairs, bouncing them on each step as she went down. She was exhausted by the time she got them into the entryway by the front door. Pausing to rest, leaning on the doorjamb, she knew what she was doing was foolish, but there was no turning back now. She considered leaving her cell phone where it was on the living room coffee table. If Ben finally decided to call, he'd get no answer.

Then she thought better of it and went and got her phone. After checking her purse to make sure she at least had enough cash for the turnpike and food along the way, she lugged her suitcases outside and heaved them into the trunk of her car. After a quick run back into the house to turn off all the lights and make sure the doors were locked and the appliances were turned off, she went back out to her car and got in.

The tangle of emotions inside her was intense. She spun from the grief of her father's death to her fear of being alone in the world to the guilt of all her sins of commission and omission while she lived with her father in Catawamkeag Cove. And Ben…Ben…. She tossed between anger at him for letting her down when she needed him most and her love for him. She knew now that she was never going to commit to him…at least not until he started to do some of the difficult work he needed to do on himself.

"Screw it," she screamed. She pounded the dashboard so hard something inside it rattled. Clasping her key ring tightly in her hand, she slipped the key into the ignition and turned it.

A thick sourness filled her throat and churned in her stomach. She was afraid she was going to throw up, but she steeled herself to do what she had to do.

She would call the hospital tomorrow morning and arrange to

have her father's body shipped down to Connecticut so he could be buried in the family plot in Waterbury with his wife. Once she found a place to stay in Connecticut, she would have her furniture and things shipped to her. That way, she would never…*never* have to see this godforsaken house in Catawamkeag Cove ever again.

She shifted into reverse and backed around and had shifted into *drive* when her cell phone chirped in her purse.

Gritting her teeth, she slammed on the brakes. The car skidded on the asphalt before she put the car into *park.* The phone rang a second time…and a third…and then she grabbed it from her purse and glanced at the Caller ID.

The number displayed was Ben's home phone.

The phone rang a fourth time.

Julia knew she had one more ring before the phone would go to voice mail. Her hand was slick with sweat. The phone was slippery in her grip as she sawed her teeth across her lower lip.

I'm a goddamned fool.

"Hello?" she said.

Louise listened to the tight tremor in her voice as she spoke into the phone. She kept her voice low because she didn't want to disturb her father, who was still passed out on the couch in the living room. She'd been through too much already today, and now she had something more to worry about.

"Hi—umm, Julia. This is—is Louise Marshall. Ben's sister. I was—ahh—wondering if Ben's with you now."

"No, he's not. I was hoping you knew where he was."

"He and my other brother went out on the boat tonight, and they're not back yet."

"Oh, God," Julia whispered, fearing the worst. "Oh, my God."

Louise stared at the phone in her hand for a few seconds and then hung it back up. The cord was twisted into a huge knot which she didn't bother to untangle. She looked around the kitchen, telling herself not to worry even after Julia had told her about her father dying and what she had told Ben about Pete.

Things are fine, she told herself.

Her brothers were fine.

There was nothing wrong.

She felt sorry she'd bothered Julia. How was she supposed to know Julia's father had died? Ben never told her anything.

Louise had promised to call Julia the minute she heard anything.

If they'd had any trouble, one of them…or the police…or the Coast Guard…or *someone* would have called.

She smiled when her gaze shifted over to the refrigerator, and she remembered the large jar of mayonnaise in there and what was hidden inside it.

"Yeah, everything's fine," she whispered to herself. Her shoulders shook with suppressed tears as she rubbed her hands together.

"Everything is *better* than fine."

"Okay. No radio. No flares. No cell phone. We're fucked," Ben said.

He was clinging to the boat, bobbing up and down in the gentle swells which were getting larger as the night went on.

How long can the boat stay afloat like this, he wondered.

The air bubble inside the wheelhouse had to be filling up with water.

How long before the boat went under?

Tangled debris floated like a tattered scarf around the wreckage…things they could use for floatation if they needed, but the current was carrying them further away, dispersing them across the surface of the ocean in an ever-widening fan. Ben wondered when someone would see the flotsam and realize someone was in trouble. Maybe the guys on the trawler they were supposed to meet would come to their rescue.

Wouldn't that be ironic?

But no matter where he looked, all he saw was the vast expanse of the heaving ocean and the thin, black line of land far to the west.

Pete was clinging to the bow of the boat, his silhouette a solid black stain against the starry night sky.

"I asked, how fucked are we, little brother?" Ben called out. His voice sounded curiously flat in the night.

Pete didn't answer. Ben knew his brother was still alive only because he hadn't slipped off the boat and gone under. He couldn't stop shivering. His chattering teeth sounded like he was rattling dice in his hand.

"Someone's gonna see us...sooner or later...right? All we have to do is hang on."

"It's cold as a witch's tit!" Pete shouted, his voice strained and shrill.

"Keep moving...keep your circulation going," Ben said.

He considered letting go of the boat and swimming closer to his brother, but he was so cold he was afraid his arms and legs might not obey his commands and move the way he wanted them to. It was hard enough keeping a grip on the slippery bottom of the boat. As new as it was, it already had a thin coating of slime that was as slick as oil. Even a few barnacles had attached themselves to the hull. They were cutting into his hands and arms.

"So...let's keep talking at least," Ben said. "It'll help pass the time...keep us awake and focused."

"I'd rather you kept your goddamned mouth shut, if you don't mind," Pete shouted.

Ben was taken aback. He shook his head and asked, "Why the fucking hostility? It's not like I—"

"We've got nothing to talk about, you and me," Pete said.

Even in the darkness, Ben knew that his brother had turned his face away from him like a child in the middle of a snit. This was followed by a long silence that was broken only by the huffing of their breath and the gentle slapping sound of water against the hull.

"What time's it now?" Ben shouted after a minute.

"What's it matter? We ain't gonna make it."

"Come on, now," Ben said. "I don't want to hear any talk like that. That's 'stinkin' thinkin'.'"

When Pete didn't laugh at the old *Saturday Night Live* joke, Ben started moving, hand over hand, closer to his brother. He told himself it was as much to keep moving to stay warm as it was to get closer to his brother in order to reassure him.

"Everything I've ever read about...you know, about survival situations like this, they say the people who survive are the ones who don't lose their cool."

"Really?" Pete said with a snarl. "So now you're gonna tell me how to behave so I'll live through this?"

He paused and must have gotten a mouthful of seawater because Ben heard him gag and then spit.

"No...I'm just saying..."

"You know what?" Pete said. "That's one of the shitload of things about you that pisses me the fuck off."

"What's that?"

"That you think you know *everything*...and you talk to me—you treat me like I...like I don't even have a goddamned brain."

"It's just...you're my little brother, and I...I gotta take care of you."

"Really?"

It was tough for Ben not to remind Pete that he was the one who got them into this situation. But Ben knew it had been his idea to do this tonight. He could have stayed home...or stayed with Julia at the hospital. He had done this to help the family out, but it was obvious Pete wasn't going to listen to *that*.

"This is about her, isn't it?" Ben asked after a long moment of silence.

"Who?"

"Julia."

Pete snapped his head around so Ben knew he was looking straight at him even though he couldn't see clearly in the darkness.

"It has nothing to do with that cunt," Pete said, his voice low and twisted.

Ben bristled at his brother's use of that word about Julia. He experienced a surge of anger like he'd never felt before. It took effort to tamp it down.

Now wasn't the time to confront Pete about this or that night behind The Local or his slashed tires. They had to depend on each other and hang on if they were going to survive the night.

"So...what time is it?" Ben asked again, hoping to move past the topic.

Pete raised his arm and then said, "Almost three o'clock."

"There, see? Night's passing fast. We'll make it. Only a couple of hours now 'til dawn."

As he spoke, he craned his head around and looked to the east hoping to see a hint of the approaching dawn. The sky shimmered with dusty starlight that turned the horizon a muted gray, but there wasn't even the faintest hint of the sun. The tangy smell of saltwater was cloying in his throat.

"And *then* what?" Pete asked. "I mean—seriously. You really think someone's gonna see us?"

"We have to hope so."

"I'm freezing my fuckin' ass off, and to tell you the God's honest truth, I don't see a whole lot to live for."

"Don't be talking like that, little bro," Ben said, panicking at the thought that his brother was giving up.

"Jesus, will you cut it with the little brother bullshit?" Pete clenched his fist and pounded the hull of the boat, making it resonate with a hollow thump.

"Fuck!" he snarled, and he shook his hand as though he'd hurt it bad.

"I'm trying to stay positive here, is all," Ben said.

"Well I sure as hell don't need any positive bullshit from *you,* all right?"

"Yeah…sure…fine."

"That's how it's been my whole goddamned life…and I'll tell yah—I'm sick to fuckin' death of it!"

"Jesus, relax. I didn't mean anything by it," Ben said. He was surprised by his brother's outburst, but he chalked it up to Pete's gathering panic and humiliation at getting them into this situation. He thought about moving further away from his brother. Forget about him. Let him roar all he wants, but before he could say or do anything, Pete dropped into the water and pushed off so he was treading water a few feet away from the boat. His head was a black sphere that bobbed up and down like a lobster buoy.

"What the *fuck* are you doing?" Ben called out as panic rose inside him.

He stared at Pete, terrified by what he was thinking while, at the same time, trying to grasp the dread seriousness of their situation. He had seen enough men panic in the heat of battle or crack under the constant, grinding strain of war.

He recognized it when he saw it now.

"Come back to the boat and let's talk about it," he called out. His brother made faint splashing sounds as he tread water.

"We're gonna be fine, Pete. We'll figure it out."

"No…fuck you," Pete said, his voice barely audible above the splashing of water against the hull. He was moving further away from the boat, but Ben wasn't sure if he was swimming away or drifting along with the current.

"Jesus Christ, Pete. Cut the bullshit and get back on the boat."

No answer.

"It's gonna be light soon. Someone's bound to see us."

"What's the point?" Pete said, his voice sounding weaker now… defeated. Ben knew exhaustion and hypothermia were setting in.

"No one cares if I live or die."

"What the hell are you talking about?"

"No one." His voice was strained, close to tears.

"Of course people care," Ben said. "I care…Pops cares…and Louise."

Pete's dismissive laughter sounded loud and clear, as if he were close beside Ben in the darkness.

"Am I gonna have to swim over there and kick your ass?" Ben said.

"You mean like you always did?"

"Jesus, what's gotten into you?"

"*You!* I'm sick and fucking tired of *you*, Ben!"

"Settle the fuck down, will yah? 'N get the Christ back here. I mean it. Look. The horizon's getting brighter. See?"

Pete didn't even bother to turn and look in the direction Ben was indicating, but an infinitely small streak of gray lighting was glowing on the distant edge of the sea. It flickered like a mirage.

"I'm tellin' you," Pete said. "I've had it. I'm sick to fuckin' death of always being second place…of always losing out to you. I'll never be anything but the loser brother of the big hero. Basketball star. Soldier. Friggin' war hero. So you know what? Go fuck yourself, Ben. You got that? Go *fuck* yourself."

"What the hell are you—" Ben started to say, but he paused when a thought struck him.

"If this is about losing Pops' boat, then screw it. We'll deal with that later. Pops'll get another one. All you have to do right now is calm down and get back to the boat."

"Will you stop telling me what to do all the time? Jesus *Christ!* You don't control me!"

Ben didn't know what to say, and he was in a quandary about what to do next. If he swam out to his brother and there was a struggle, they'd both end up going under. But it was obvious Pete was well past reasoning.

He had to do *something.*

But a dreadful sense of helplessness and hopelessness filled Ben, and he couldn't help but confuse what was happening now with what he had gone through in Iraq—especially one night in particular.

"You can't do this to me, Pete," he shouted, fighting back the panic that twisted inside him like a fouled rope. "You can't do this to me or to Pops or to Louise!"

"The fuck I can't," Pete said in a voice that had the vocal equivalent of the thousand-yard stare.

"This is because of Julia, isn't it?"

Pete stopped treading water and turned to look back at his brother. The tension crackled between them like a lightning charge leaping from sky to earth and back to the sky.

"Who?" he said sarcastically.

"You know goddamned right it is. You just won't admit it."

"I could give a shit about that bitch."

Ben strained, trying not to yell. If they had been on solid ground, they'd be at each other's throats by now. He stopped himself before he said what he was going to say and simply said, "Look, Pete. Get back to the boat. We can hang on…together."

Pete snorted and spat. After a long, tense silence, he started swimming back to the boat, moving slowly as though every motion took great effort. When he got to the boat, he clamped the flats of his hands against the overturned hull and rested his cheek against the slick, wet surface. He was panting like a racehorse.

In the gloom, Ben watched Pete staring at him, his eyes wide and as blank as marble. His hair was plastered in dark, wet ringlets against his pale forehead. Ben's immediate concern—for both of them—was that hypothermia would get them before the sun came up and warmed them.

"It's not about her," Pete said in a low, panting voice. "It has nothing to do with her."

"Then why was her number in your cell phone directory?"

Pete exhaled with a loud, blubbering sound.

"Because she was the finest thing I've ever seen, and I…I had to try."

"So you jumped me that night out behind The Local, and you slashed my tires at Sand Beach, hoping to scare me off."

No answer.

"Come on, Pete. I know it was you."

"I was hoping she…she'd give me a chance." Pete's voice was strained to the breaking point. "And then—*Bang!* You come home, and she falls all over you. Like I said…I'm always second place." Pete made a noise that sounded suspiciously like he was crying. "I went to her house tonight. I waited until after you left. I was so pissed off, you know what I was gonna do? I was gonna beat her face so ugly you wouldn't want her anymore. But I couldn't do it, man. I couldn't do it."

He let out a deep animal groan and then fell silent. For a long time, the sloshing of the waves was the only sound.

"'S ok, Pete," Ben said after a while. "I'm not pissed. Honest. We're brothers."

He felt sick to his stomach thinking about what Pete had almost done to Julia, but now was not the time to straighten him out. They had to get through this ordeal first. Then they could settle whatever needed to be settled about Julia and the rest of it.

Pete was quiet, his eyes closed.

"Pete…it's OK…really…"

He hoped Pete knew he meant it, but he didn't think he was getting through. The fear that he would lose his brother pierced his chest like a cold iron rod. After everything their family had suffered recently, he didn't think their father or any of them could handle another loss.

Pete remained silent as he turned away from Ben while clinging to the boat. His shoulders shuddered from the cold and wet, and whenever he exhaled, a high-pitched whistling sound filled the darkness.

The stars wheeled around overhead, and the tiny slip of a moon gradually set into the west, but Ben felt like they were frozen in time…like prehistoric insects, trapped in globs of amber. The cold cut through him and as the minutes and hours passed—if they were really passing at all—the lower half of Ben's body gradually went numb. He kept kicking his feet to restore the circulation, but he was increasingly convinced neither one of them was going to survive the night.

"What time's it now?" Ben asked, but Pete didn't reply. He didn't even move. Ben had the sudden panicky thought that his brother had already died and was still clinging to the boat.

"Hey!" he called out. His voice sounded infinitely small against the vast ocean and night sky.

Pete didn't move or speak.

Panic surged up inside Ben. He let go of the boat and started paddling over to his brother. His hand was numb and shaking out of control as he reached up and grabbed Pete by the waist. His wet clothes felt like they had been dipped in cement.

"You okay, man?" Ben asked, bringing his face close, searching for some sign of life.

Relief flooded him when Pete rolled his head around and stared at him. His eyes were glazed, and his mouth was split with a thin, cruel smile.

"Always the big hero," he said. When he laughed, it sounded hollow. "Always taking care of me as if I can't take care of myself."

"I want you to hang on, Pete. You *have* to! I'm not gonna lose you now!"

"Why the Christ is it so important to you?"

The exhaustion and resignation Ben heard in his brother's voice pained him. His first thought was that he didn't have to answer that. Wasn't it obvious? Pete knew the answer as well as he did. They were family, and family stuck together, no matter what.

Especially at times like this.

"You wanna know why? You *really* want to know why?" Ben said.

Pete didn't answer him. The only sound was the steady wash of waves against the side of the boat and their labored breathing.

"Because of what happened—because of something I did in Iraq."

"You honestly think I give a shit about *that?"*

Pete's words stung him, but if any time was a time for confession, it was now, when they were both facing imminent death.

"It was a day like any other." Ben grimaced at the memory of how boring his tours of duty had been. "We were on patrol on the outskirts of some godforsaken town in Anbar when we came under fire. Our orders were to drive right through, but the tail end of the convoy started taking fire."

"You know what?" Pete said. "I really don't give a rat's ass about any of this."

"I know you don't, but you're gonna listen because I'm telling you, and I've never told anyone else. Everyone—Pops, Lou, everyone in the whole friggin' town thinks I'm a goddamned war hero, but you know what I did?"

He paused. The silence that engulfed them was his only answer. At this point, though, it didn't matter if Pete was listening or not. It was imperative for Ben to say these words…to speak them out loud. By saying them for someone else to hear, maybe he would exorcise them…maybe they would lose their power over him…and maybe the guilt and shame he felt would at least begin to dissolve. Maybe then the nightmares and panic attacks would stop.

"I had my orders. My goddamn orders. I kept driving," he said, the words burning in his throat like he'd swallowed a huge gulp of seawater. "I didn't have the balls to defy my orders and turn back to help them."

Ben's memory flashed to the faces inside the Humvee—Rodriguez, Walters, Perry—their eyes burning into him…piercing through him and seeing him for what he really was—a coward.

"We have our orders," he had barked to his men as a mortar round thumped to the left, landing close enough to punch the side of the vehicle like an invisible fist. The Humvee behind them disappeared in the dust kicked up by the explosion.

Memories welled up inside him like molten lava, and shame bit so deeply into him he gasped.

"This…this was my fuckin' platoon! These were my buddies! We counted on each other for our lives, and I…I didn't go back for them. I couldn't. I deserted them because, I told myself, I was following orders. I kept driving like a fucking maniac to get the four of us out of there. And because of that…because I didn't go back to help, three men died. Three good men who didn't have to die." Ben's voice choked off in a sob.

Pete was silent for a heartbeat or two, and then in a low voice he said, "So now you have to—What? Be a *real* hero and save my ass?"

"Yeah…something like that," Ben said simply.

Pete snorted again and spat, but he didn't say another word. For a long time, he kept staring steadily at Ben. Before Ben realized it,

Pete was moving away from him, inching along the hull of the boat toward the bow. In the dim light, Pete's eyes held a glazed, distant stare that Ben tried to convince himself wasn't really there. After an even longer silence, Pete heaved a deep sigh that came from the center of his being. At first, Ben took this as a hopeful sign that his brother was still fighting, that he hadn't given up, but then Pete made a sudden move. Bringing his feet up underneath him, he planted them firmly against the side of the boat like a swimmer in starting position.

"You know what, big bro?" he said. Utter despondency filled his voice, leaving a terrible vacuum in the night. "Fuck it."

"Pete."

"Seriously…I mean it…just fuck it."

Before Ben could react, Pete kicked away. The boat started rocking wildly. Ben had all he could do to hang on as Pete shot out into the water, carving a wide, dark wake in the water.

He didn't flail…

He didn't even try to swim…

He floated on his back.

And as Ben watched in horror, helpless to react, Pete flipped over and made a smooth surface dive. His legs kicked the air, and then he disappeared with barely a splash beneath the slick, black water.

Ben's scream ripped the fabric of the night, but he didn't hear it. He stared in horror at the trail of silver bubbles that rose to the surface and popped, marking the spot where his brother had gone under.

Forever.

NINETEEN

Last Call

If anything, the next several weeks, months, and years proved the old adage, "The more things change, the more they stay the same." For some people, life in The Cove continued as it always had, with all its petty concerns, its ups and downs, its tragedies and comedies. For others, there were abrupt changes of fortune—both good and bad—and death...sometimes brutal, sometimes ironic, and sometimes damned hilarious.

As would be expected, Capt'n Wally took the death of his youngest son real hard, but some folks around town—especially down at the wharf and at The Local—thought he took it a little *too* hard and was trying to drink away his grief and guilt. It was as if he felt personally responsible for his son's death. Only Ben knew this was precisely the case because he thought—but never said to anyone—that if his father hadn't gotten roaring drunk that day, he and Pete would never have gone out at night to make the pick-up. If Wally had gone out and done the job, he might have run up on the rocks like Pete and Ben had, but, more likely, he would have known exactly which rocks were exposed and dangerous at low tide. Unlike Pete, Capt'n Wally really *did* know the ocean better than his own backyard.

After being rescued that morning by Henry "Dime's Worth" Martin, who was heading out at dawn to haul his lobster pots, Ben spent a few days in the hospital, being treated for hypothermia and dehydration. Although his physical condition improved rapidly, he spiraled into a dark depression because—even more so than his father—he felt directly responsible for Pete's death. He should have tried harder to find the right words. He should have grabbed onto Pete and never let go even if it meant they both went under together. The guilt of Pete's death, compounded with the PTSD, threw him into a tailspin that he tried to control by self-medicating with alcohol. He began drinking mornings, and was down at The Local every night until Julia and Louise staged an intervention. The following day he checked into the VA hospital in Togus and started getting the help he needed.

Julia returned to Connecticut when Ben was discharged from the hospital after the rescue. She buried her father and set about taking care of the legal matters, including putting the Steeple Road house up for sale. A long phone conversation with Louise brought her back to The Cove to help with Ben's intervention. While Ben was in rehab, Julia returned to Waterbury and bought what she called "a picket fence with a picket house" with money from her father's life insurance. It was a pretty little New England cottage with perennial gardens and shade trees, and it was landlocked.

It suits me, she thought, and if it suits Ben too, that's icing on the cake.

When Ben was discharged from Togus, she returned once more to The Cove to discuss their future. The house she had shared with her father out on Steeple Road sold, but she hadn't closed on it yet. She still had some furniture and personal things to move out. She drove from Connecticut in a U-Haul and met Ben at the house. He was thinner and paler than he was when she had first seen him at the launch of the *Abby-Rose*, but he flashed the old Gunner grin at her as she pulled into the driveway. The midsummer sun glinted off the river, flowing to the sea.

"Hello, handsome," she said, as she climbed out of the truck. Ben swept her into a bear hug, and they embraced silently for a few minutes, inhaling each other.

"God, I've missed you," Julia whispered, breaking the silence. He was trembling in her embrace.

"Me, too." Ben said. His grip tightened on her as if she were the only thing that could keep him afloat in the world.

Finally, they released each other. Julia unlocked the door, and they were barely inside the house before Ben kissed her hard on the mouth.

They left a trail of clothes leading to the bedroom.

Afterward, tired but exhilarated, Julia nestled close to Ben's sweat-slicked body.

"I never thought I'd be happy to come back to The Cove," she murmured.

Ben chuckled, then fell silent.

I have to know now, Julia thought.

"So…are you coming back to Waterbury with me?"

"Julia, I can't. Not now. My father's still half-crazy over Pete's death, and there's all the insurance mess with the boat, and Lou-Lou…

She lifted a finger to his lips.

"Shhh..."

He turned and looked at her. Her eyes were filled with tears.

"No need to explain. You're a Cove-ah. And I'm not." She propped herself up on her elbow so she could look directly into his face. The sheet was tucked tightly against her body, showing her curves. "But I love you, Ben, with all my heart."

Ben touched her face with his hand and said, "I love you too, Julia. I do."

She smiled, and tears leaked out the corners of her eyes. He wiped them away with his thumb. Then he grinned.

"Even if you *are* a flatlander," he added.

"You bastard."

She tickled him fiercely, and they wrestled across the bed until he pinned her underneath him, and they made love again. They shared four days of simple happiness, and then they packed Julia's U-Haul, and she was gone.

Late that autumn, while Capt'n Wally was working to repair the refrigerator at home, he suffered what, at first, was thought to be a mild stroke. While reaching for a screwdriver, he suddenly couldn't get his left arm to move. Louise rushed him to the emergency room where, following a brain scan, Dr. Robbins discovered a tumor growing on Wally's brain stem. He was given six months to a year to live, but after some aggressive chemotherapy, he showed remarkable recovery. Down at The Local, he liked to brag that he was being treated by the same neurosurgeon who treated Senator Ted Kennedy. At least once or twice a month, he came home at night with a woman half his age, but he maintained that screwing was the only thing that gave him the will to keep on living.

The next spring, Capt'n Wally was well enough to give tourists guided tours of the harbor and coast in his new boat, the *Lou-Lou Belle*. He hadn't needed Richie Sullivan's help to finance this one. The insurance money on the *Abby-Rose* and the life insurance policy he'd taken out on Pete paid off handsomely. Ben made up the difference with money from his savings. Wally liked to brag that he was debt-free…except for his tab down at The Local.

One curious fact: Wally never went lobstering again after Pete drowned. He also never ate another lobster. To his friends down at The Local, he maintained that he had to give up lobstering because the cancer treatments were "taking the piss" out of him, but he confessed privately to Louise and Ben that he would never eat another lobster because lobsters were bottom feeders…the carrion eaters of the ocean who lived on anything and everything that dies and rots on the ocean floor. He couldn't bear the thought that if he ever ate a lobster, it might be one that had feasted on the rotting flesh of his dead son.

Ben continued to live at home with his father and sister. His nightmares continued, but now they were about Pete instead of the war. The image was seared in his memory of watching his brother swim away from the boat, steadily receding into the darkness… fading…fading…until he was gone. He got a job at the local hardware store, working with Horse Lips. Along with Brian Hatcher, he got involved with the fight against the big box store on Five Corners. When the townspeople voted in November, they defeated the proposal handily. Ray and Jerry Hanson were pissed, but Ben's attitude was that they were always bitching about one thing or another, anyway, so fuck 'em both. He'd see them most every night when he went down to The Local, only now he was knocking back Diet Cokes instead of beer and whiskey chasers.

Louise didn't waste any time securing divorce papers. She served them to Tom while he was sitting in county jail after recovering from his gunshot wounds and awaiting trial for double homicide. His bail was set at fifty thousand dollars, a sum she could have paid easily with the money hidden in the mayonnaise jar, but she wasn't about to do that.

A week after Pete died, she took the envelope from the

mayonnaise jar and stashed it down in the cellar behind the boxes of Christmas decorations. She doubted the police would ever search Capt'n Wally's house. Why would they? After a few months, she started depositing the money into a savings account in small increments. If she ever had kids, she wanted them to go to college and—she earnestly hoped—get the hell out of The Cove and never come back except to visit on vacations and holidays.

For his part, Tom didn't take his situation very well. He didn't "man up," as the Red Sox Nation likes to say. He was charged with first-degree murder in the death of Tony Gillette and the third-degree murder of Jerry Lincoln. If he was convicted, he'd be spending the rest of his life in Warren, housed with convicts he helped put there. So he ratted out as many of the local drug dealers as possible, spewing fact and rumor in equal measure. That kept the investigators busy for the next few years. He even ratted out Dick Pilsbury, a local real estate agent and town selectman who was dealing cocaine and other high-end drugs to assorted area bigwigs—lawyers, doctors, and businessmen. Worst of all, Pilsbury kept a detailed account of all his customers and their purchases on his home computer, so after he was arrested, even more people found themselves under intense police scrutiny.

One of those people under scrutiny, of course, was Richie Sullivan. Everyone in town knew that Richie was behind most of the illicit drug traffic in the area. But Richie had distanced himself from the whole thing, covering his tracks so thoroughly the police and feds couldn't even make a parking ticket stick. Still, to take the heat off, Richie "retired" to Key West, claiming he'd had enough of New England winters. Word was some folks in Rhode Island weren't very happy with some of his other business dealings. So, all in all, it was probably a good time for Richie to take his retirement.

Late in September, Tom finally accepted that Louise was not going to change her mind and, Tammy Wynette be damned, "stand by her man." Convinced she had lied to him about the cops having the money he'd stashed away, and that she had it and was keeping it from him, he tore the bed sheet in his jail cell into several strips, tied a makeshift noose, and tried to hang himself from the top rung of bars.

Problem was, although he didn't die, the blood supply to his brain was cut off long enough so he suffered some minor brain damage that led to memory loss and problems with physical coordination. Days before his case went to trial, a fellow inmate—a guy named Eddie "Critter" Winston—decided on a little vigilante justice. A few years ago, Tom had beaten Eddie up badly while bringing him to the station for questioning and then brazenly lied about it in front of Critter, and had gotten away with it. Using a spoon with an edge sharpened in the prison workshop, Critter laid open Tom's throat. "Gave him a 'new smile' below his chin," as Critter so eloquently phrased it. Tom bled to death before the prison guards realized what had happened.

That winter proved to be one of the hardest in recent history with blizzard after blizzard piling up snow in record amounts. One night in February, Kathy Brackett was driving home from visiting her mother in Brunswick. Her daughter, Amanda, was in the baby car seat in the back when she hit a patch of black ice on Route One in Wiscasset. The car careened into a utility pole. Amanda survived, but Kathy died in the ambulance on the way to the hospital.

She was buried in Pine Grove Cemetery on the outskirts of town. Amanda lived with her father in the house on West Tower Road, but Dwight soon realized that he couldn't handle being a full-time parent. After a few months, Amanda went to live with his parents in Portland. Without any females there to domesticate him, Horse Lips soon slipped back into his old life. Seven nights a week, he was down at The Local, drinking with Wally until closing time. He seemed to forget he had a daughter, which made Ben feel sorry for Amanda. He briefly considered admitting paternity and bringing up Amanda himself, but he decided to let the child live her life without any more grief or complications.

Also buried in the same cemetery was Lilly Brown, Ben and Louise's mother. Lilly had continued to be a "wanderer" at the nursing home. One night in late November, a few days before Thanksgiving, she somehow escaped the notice of the person on watch at the front desk and walked out of the nursing home sometime after midnight. She wandered around town for hours. Apparently no one even saw her.

As she was making her way through the woods, heading in the general direction of the home she had once shared with Capt'n

Wally but no longer remembered, she crossed the old Miller property, which had been abandoned for years. The house was a tumbled-down ruin, populated by bats, mice, and a family of owls. The old wooden door someone had used to cover the old well had long since rotted away. When Lilly stumbled over it, she crashed through the wood and plummeted to the rocky bottom.

Of course, the nursing home was in an uproar as soon as it was discovered that she was really missing, and not lurking in the darkened corner of the TV room or hiding under her bed as she had taken to doing recently because she was convinced that her father—who had been dead more than forty years—was coming into her bedroom at night and molesting her.

The police mounted a massive search and rescue effort, which included dozens of volunteers, but her body wasn't discovered until three days later. By then, the rats and other vermin living in the well had done a good job of stripping her flesh from her bones. She was buried under a rose granite headstone Wally had carved for her which also included Pete's birth and death dates even though he was not buried there.

One warm spring day, Ben was sitting in his car in the parking lot at Sand Beach. It had been a year since he'd come back home. His mind flashed through the losses.

The memory of Pete still burned like a red-hot coal, but like all things, with time it was getting better…slowly.

As for his mom, dying the way she did was so goddamned awful it was tough to think about, but in the end, it was probably a mercy. She had stopped being his mom a long time before she died.

And as for Tom Marshall? Good riddance. A shank across the throat couldn't have happened to a nicer guy.

But there were the gains as well.

Capt'n Wally had the *Lou-Lou Belle,* which he owned outright and had no more pressure from Richie Sullivan or anyone else. Louise was seeing a decent guy from Durham, a high school English teacher named Nate Kenyon. He wasn't a Cove-ah, but he treated her as much like a queen as he could on his teacher's salary.

And, of course, Julia was never far from Ben's mind. They kept in periodic touch—not as much as he would like, but he didn't want to pressure her. His feelings for her hadn't changed, but he knew she would never come back to The Cove even to visit, much less stay. She had been hired to teach first grade in a small town outside of Waterbury. He often wondered about how long it would take her to find someone else in Connecticut.

Maybe she can find me *in Connecticut,* he thought…*maybe it's finally time for me to blow this taco stand…*

His cell phone chirped, making him jump. He fished it from his jeans pocket and glanced at the Caller ID. When he saw who it was, he smiled widely. With a quick flick of the thumb, he opened the phone.

"Speak of the devil. I was just thinking about you."

"Oh?"

"Yeah. I'm out at Sand Beach…just chillin'."

There was a long pause.

"So how you doin'?" he asked. "How's the teaching going?"

"It's good. One more week and it's summer vacation."

"So you finally got to use that college degree, huh?"

"Yeah."

He was trying to keep the eagerness out of his voice but was sure he wasn't succeeding.

"You know…I've, uhh, been thinking, too," Julia said.

"Uh-oh. That sounds dangerous."

He smiled, wishing she was there to see his smile.

"Oh, stop it. No, I was thinking how you must have some vacation time coming. Don't you? Well…I know a little place in southern Connecticut that would be great for a water rat like you to relax."

"Really?"

"Really."

"Are there trees and flowers and gardens?"

"Absolutely," Julia said, "and definitely no ocean."

"Hmm, sounds interesting. But is it *quaint?"*

"Oh, yes…very quaint. It's a lovely little private B 'n B with a charming hostess."

"Do I happen to know this hostess?"

His jaw was hurting now, he was grinning so hard.

"Quite intimately, in fact."

"And—umm…and how long, exactly, can I stay?"

"Totally up to you. How long are you thinking of staying?"

When Ben took a deep breath, he felt light-headed as the salt-tinged air and a gush of warmth filled his chest.

"I dunno. I 'spoze as long as you'll let me."

This was followed by a silence that went on a bit too long. He stared out over the ocean, his eyes unfocused.

"Julia? You there?"

He heard sniffling and knew that she was either laughing or crying…maybe both, but then there was such total silence.

"You there?"

"Yeah."

"I thought the call got dropped."

"I'm still here." She took a breath, hissing it between her teeth. *Is this a mistake?* she asked herself. But even before she could think about it, she added, "So how soon can you get your ass down here?"

"Give me an hour to get packed, and I'm on my way."

"Before our lives divide for ever,
While time is with us and hands are free,
(Time, swift to fasten and swift to sever
Hand from hand, as we stand by the sea)
I will say no word that a man might say
Whose whole life's love goes down in a day;
For this could never have been; and never,
Though the gods and the years relent, shall be."

—Algernon Charles Swinburne

ABOUT THE AUTHOR

RICK HAUTALA, 1949–2013

Under his own name, Rick Hautala wrote close to thirty novels, including the million-copy bestseller *Night Stone,* as well as *Winter Wake, The Mountain King,* and *Little Brothers.* He published three short story collections: *Bedbugs, Occasional Demons,* and *Glimpses: The Best Short Stories of Rick Hautala.* He had over sixty short stories published in a variety of national and international anthologies and magazines.

Writing as A. J. Matthews, his novels included the bestsellers *The White Room, Looking Glass, Follow,* and *Unbroken.*

His latest books include *Indian Summer,* a previously unreleased "Little Brothers" novella, as well as two novels, *Chills* and *Waiting.* Shortly before his death he sold *The Star Road,* a science fiction novel co-written with Matthew Costello, to Brendan Deneen at Thomas Dunne/St. Martin's.

With Mark Steensland, he wrote several short films, including the multiple award-winning *Peekers,* based on the short story by Kealan Patrick Burke; *The Ugly File,* based on the short story by Ed Gorman; and *Lovecraft's Pillow,* inspired by a suggestion from Stephen King.

Born and raised in Rockport, Massachusetts, Rick was a graduate of the University of Maine in Orono with a Master of Arts in English Literature. He lived in southern Maine and is survived by his wife, author Holly Newstein.

In 2012, he was awarded the Lifetime Achievement Award from the Horror Writers Association.

For more information, check out the author's website:

www.rickhautala.com.

BOOK LIST

Novels and Novellas

Beyond the Shroud
Cold River
Cold Whisper
Dark Silence
Dead Voices
Follow
Four Octobers
Ghost Light
Impulse
Little Brothers
Looking Glass
Moon Death
Moonbog
Moonwalker (The Siege)
Night Stone
Reunion
Shades of Night
The Cove
The Mountain King
The White Room
The Wildman
Twilight Time
Unbroken
Winter Wake
The Body of Evidence Series (co-written with Christopher Golden)
Brain Trust
Burning Bones
Last Breath
Skin Deep
Throat Culture

Story Collections

Bedbugs
Glimpses: The Best Short Stories of Rick Hautala
Occasional Demons
Untcigahunk: The Complete Little Brothers

CROSSROAD
PRESS

www.ingramcontent.com/pod-product-compliance
Lightning Source LLC
Chambersburg PA
CBHW060607310726
48982CB00008B/1263/J

* 9 7 8 1 9 4 1 4 0 8 0 7 0 *